DATE DUE			

AUG 1996

THE
SPRING

CLIFFORD
IRVING

SIMON & SCHUSTER

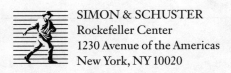 SIMON & SCHUSTER
Rockefeller Center
1230 Avenue of the Americas
New York, NY 10020

SIMON & SCHUSTER and colophon are registered trademarks
of Simon & Schuster Inc.

Manufactured in the United States of America

10 9 8 7 6 5 4 3 2 1

Library of Congress Cataloging-in-Publication Data
Irving, Clifford.
    The spring/Clifford Irving.
        p.   cm.
        1. City and town life—Colorado—Fiction. 2. Mountain life—Colorado—Fiction.
3. Immortalism—Fiction. I. Title.
PS3559.R79S65   1996   96-12357
813'.54—dc20   CIP
ISBN 0-684-81076-X

Author's Note

THE LANGUAGE USED at times by some of the characters in *The Spring* is not a fantasy. It is a variant of Boontling, an authentic American English jargon—a lingo, a synthetic slang—developed around 1890 by settlers in the Anderson Valley of California's Mendocino County and later transplanted to a remote area of Colorado's Elk Mountains, where it metamorphosed into what is called Springling. Although the language appears to be slowly dying out, some Boontling is spoken in Boonville, California (where there is a café called Horn of Zeese, which means cup of coffee). The Colorado variant, if you have a keen ear, can still be heard southwest of Aspen near Springhill and the ghost town of Crystal City.

For the curious or occasionally puzzled reader, on pages 286–87 I have appended a Glossary of Springling words used in the text, with their meanings.

I am grateful to many people in Colorado for help in my research. Among them: Pitkin County Sheriff Bob Braudis; Deputy Sheriff Ann Stephenson; Emergency Management Coordinator Steve Crockett; Aspen defense attorney Mac Myers, Steve Ayers, former coroner; Dr. Robert Christensen, forensic odontologist; Safety Officer Duchess

AUTHOR'S NOTE

McCay; Tom Dunlop of the Environmental Health Department; County Manager Reid Haughey; David Williams of the Tenth Mountain Division Hut System; Hank Charneskey of the Millers Building; Brooks Hollern; and Lila J. Lee, director of the Mendocino County Historical Society.

My particular thanks go to Robert Lewin, Maureen Earl, and Maurice Nessen for their passionate editing; to Frank Cooper for his unflagging enthusiasm; and to Julie Schall for her patience and devotion when I vanished into the high country.

C.I.
Bonnieux, France

This book, with my love, is for Margo

In memory of
Fred Schoneman

Prologue: Events at Pearl Pass

BASE CAMP FOR the searchers was at ninety-six hundred feet, near Lead King Basin in the Maroon Bells–Snowmass Wilderness. They were an older married couple, a young man and a young woman. At dawn the air was cool, sweet with the scent of pine, and the older man, the leader, slipped into his backpack and adjusted a Beretta semiautomatic shotgun into a safari sling. He was ninety-four years old, with white hair and a long face as powerful as if it had been carved in brown oak. Once six feet five inches tall, in the last decade he had shrunk a good two inches. He looked to be in his sixties, but he had the vitality and strength of a man much younger.

He led the way, and the two men and two women set out briskly along the North Fork of the Crystal River. They hiked eastward on a pack trail that curled like a thin worm through the dark green heart of Colorado's White River National Forest. Above them a turkey vulture turned slow circles in a sky that altered quickly from silver to a bright, rich blue.

The younger man was armed with a graphite bow, an electronic scope sight, and steel broadhead arrows. The women were unarmed. The foursome were looking for a couple they knew well, a man and a woman named Henry and Susan Lovell.

At noon they were close to eleven thousand feet, southwest of Pearl Pass. The leader checked his watch; it monitored altitude, barometric pressure, and temperature.

The August temperature had risen to eighty degrees Fahrenheit. "Let's get into the shade," the bowman suggested. "And it might be a good time to eat lunch."

The leader shook his head. "Chew on a protein bar, young fella. We have to keep moving."

In the shadowed parts of the mountain peaks, snowbanks lasted far into the summer. The searchers stuffed chunks of last spring's snow into their hats and pushed the crowns up to let air flow around their heads. They were at home in the high country; all four had been born less than thirty miles away in the mountain hamlet of Springhill. During the winter they skied cross-country or snowshoed over trails that Ute Indians had carved out of wilderness. In summer they hiked or mountain biked along the same trails. On either side of the trails the world was still wilderness.

The leader's wife would turn ninety-two the following day. She was a quiet woman, still attractive and shapely, with cool gray eyes and a sense of tranquillity that flowed with her like an aura. No one from outside the enclave of Springhill would have dreamed that she was older than her mid-sixties.

At 12,500 feet, in alpine tundra, the pack trail trickled out at a small saddle in a spur ridge descending from the peaks west of Pearl Pass. The hikers slowed the pace every twenty minutes in order to drink from their water bottles. The wind moaned in their faces, and at five o'clock the temperature dropped to sixty degrees. After sundown it would skid into the forties or lower.

The old leader had been noting signs along the trail that the others hadn't seen. "We're close," he said. "I think we can camp here."

"Are you hungry?" his wife asked.

"I could eat a mule raw and the tail off a dead skunk," he said, easing his long body down onto a fallen tree trunk.

Elk had browsed here among the few mountain maples, their musk still lingering faintly in pockets of brush. "This is the time of day I love most," his wife said. Sitting on the fallen spruce, she put on a woolen sweater. From her backpack she pried open a little silver pillbox that she had bought on the rue de Rennes in Paris more than thirty years ago. She selected an enteric aspirin and a calcium channel blocker, swallowing the pills with cold water from her bottle.

Her husband dropped a bony hand on her shoulder. "Tired, sweetheart?"

"My legs," she said. "Time catches up with you no matter what you do." She regarded him affectionately, but her gray eyes were less calm than usual.

"Could have been worse. They could have gone clear up to Wyoming." For a moment the old man sniffed the wind; he was working things out, measuring possibilities. "I think they'll listen to reason. We'll harp. Henry Lovell and I go a long way back. An old horse for a hard pike, that's what they say."

In the midst of unpacking his camping tools, he looked up and saw the expression of concern on his wife's face. "Sweetheart," he said, "it's something that has to be done."

"I know. It's just that I don't particularly want to do it. You and Henry are such old friends. Susie and I were close. Tomorrow's my borndy. It's not my idea of a good way to celebrate."

Susan Lovell had been the bookkeeper at the Springhill marble quarry until her eyesight worsened. In his heyday Henry Lovell had been a master carpenter. He had built cedar bookcases for the searchers when they married, and years later a pine cabinet for their television set. He and the man who now hunted for him had fought side by side in the fire of 1924 when the Black Queen coal mine had been put out of action for a year. Henry had been a hunter too; at the age of one hundred he was still a fair marksman.

When he looked into his wife's troubled eyes, the old searcher's brow furrowed. "You're not trying to tell me you won't do it?"

"You'll harp," she said, "and you'll work it out with Henry. I know you will. That's the codgy way to do things."

"We'll sand through the varnish, get down to the wood." He smiled; he was an educated man, but aside from the lingo that was peculiar to their town he liked to use the old colloquialisms of the semi-literate men who had settled these mountains. It made him feel anchored to the earth and connected to his forebears.

For supper they cooked lemon chicken and wild rice, using a flat boulder to support the gas stove. In an outback oven the older woman baked brownies. The leader had brought a bottle of '90 Château

Pommard from his wine cellar, hoping that it wouldn't be shaken up during the hike. They ate in cordial silence. The old couple and the two younger people had little to say to one another; they were merely united in their purpose, which was to track down Susan and Henry Lovell wherever they had vanished in this wilderness.

An hour before darkness the men set out to scout the trail ahead. In the slanting shadows every heel mark of their quarry could still be seen. So silent were they in their passage over the earth that a pair of cow elk ambled along the next ridge, drifting in and out of sight, not hearing or seeing them. The older man walked with his legs slightly bowed to prevent his pants legs swishing against each other. His grandparents had come West from Pennsylvania just after the Civil War. He had learned trail lore from his father, a man born in Springhill. Until the year he died at the age of one hundred, his father had never missed a hunting season. He had used a Winchester rifle manufactured in Missouri only a few years after the Confederacy surrendered.

A dog barked nearby, as hoarse as a chain saw cutting soft pine, and the searchers dropped immediately into a crouch. A horned lark flapped away in the darkness. The two cow elk vanished—a rustling of brush, then silence.

"That's Henry Lovell's haireem," the young man whispered. "You figure he smells us?"

"Does a ten-foot chicken lay a big egg?" the old man said. "But we're upwind. The dog is smart, but not smart enough to tell Henry who it is he smells. Could just as well be that pair of elk."

In twenty minutes, after the two men had zigzagged up some switchbacks and moved downwind through the forest behind a meadow of blue columbine, the dog stopped barking.

Soundless goshawks sped high above. The old man, a little tired now, took out his Warsaw Pact military binoculars, the kind that East German border guards had used a decade ago along the Berlin Wall. Peering through the brush, he spotted a bright blue nylon range tent on the edge of the meadow. White-haired Henry Lovell stood to one side of the tent, petting his dog. The air was so clear, crisp, and dry that the watchers sniffed the aroma of pipe tobacco lifted by the evening wind. A pastoral scene, one to cherish. An idle wish drifted into the old man's mind: to paint watercolors. He had never done it. But he had six years left to him. Time enough.

Five minutes later the watchers withdrew without even the cracking of a twig, and began the journey back to the women at their campsite.

In the cold starlit blackness at three o'clock in the morning, the leader woke ten minutes before his quartz alarm clock was due to beep. He woke the others. He wished his wife a happy birthday and in the candlelit darkness she offered him a wan smile and a light kiss on the cheek. The message was clear: in her life there had been happier birthdays than this one. But they were doing what had to be done. Wedging a couple of flashlights between rocks, he prepared coffee and hot buttery oatmeal.

In the starlight the younger woman came up to him and stood scuffing her boots in the dirt. "I've come with you," she said softly, "because I'm part of the community and you all made me feel I had to do it. I don't want to go any farther."

Sighing, the old man said, "I think you should come along. There's such a thing as moral force and persuasion, and it's reenforced by numbers."

"I know that, but I don't want to be part of *this* moral force and persuasion."

He mulled that over awhile, then smiled pleasantly. "You do whatever melts your butter." He turned away.

Leaving the younger woman behind to clean up the campsite, he and his wife and the bowman set out through the darkness along the trail leading to the wildflower meadow. This time they took the extra twenty minutes to work their way downwind. They reached the campsite at a quarter to five, half an hour before dawn. A breeze slipped through the long needles of the lodgepole pines, bringing the scent of unseen flowers.

A band of silver light appeared over the Continental Divide. The hunters were in place. At a few minutes past five there was enough light to see the outlines of the Lovells' blue nylon tent a hundred feet away. The old man frowned. From the spot they had chosen the previous evening he had thought the tent would be closer.

The bowman peered into the early gloom, distressed by their mistake. They were beyond his best range. The muscles bunched and rippled beneath his hunting jacket. "And where's the damned haireem?" he whispered.

The old man, bent to one knee with his shotgun upright, laid a gloved palm on the bowman's arm. Silently he tried to communicate a sense of calm and harmony. The dog might be somewhere out in the forest hunting, or in the tent with Henry and Susan Lovell, asleep at their feet.

When he felt his young companion relax, he picked a small rock out of the nearly frozen turf and lobbed it backhand into the meadow, ten yards this side of the tent. The rock struck softly in a patch of columbine.

The big brown dog came snuffling around from the other side of the tent and trotted to where the rock had landed. In the gathering light it pawed at the earth. Now it was about twenty-five yards away, its flank quartering away from the men in the forest. The old man nodded. The bowman nocked a broadhead arrow, lifted the black graphite bow and, quickly, with almost no apparent effort, came to full draw. There was no sound, just the movement of air. He delivered the arrow broadside in a flat trajectory at 250 feet per second, a double-lung-and-heart shot. The dog staggered, thudded to the turf, thrashed twice, twitched a few seconds—then was still. No cry came from him that the watchers could hear.

They moved at a quick and silent woodsman's trot through the meadow toward the tent. The old man's wife walked behind them. She was still unarmed, but in her backpack she carried syringes full of poison sufficient to kill a bull elk.

Stepping through the flap into the semidarkness of the tent, the old man made out two prone figures cocooned in sleeping bags. He snapped the switch on his flashlight, playing the beam first over Susie Lovell's gray hair, and then down to the fine wrinkles of her face. She was still asleep, gently snoring.

In his down sleeping bag Henry Lovell raised his head and began to blink in confusion. One hand clawed for the rifle he had placed by the side of the bag next to a box of Kleenex.

"Don't do that, Henry," the older visitor said—quietly, but loud enough to be heard.

Henry's hand instead plucked a Kleenex from the box, and he blew his nose. At that sound, Susie Lovell woke. She propped herself up on her elbows, immediately put on her metal-rimmed eyeglasses, and adjusted her eyes to the light and her mind to the situation. She said, in a sad, gravelly voice, "Well, hello. What a surprise. Why didn't Geron-imo bark?"

"I'm sorry," the bowman said. "He never knew what hit him." But there was more pride in his voice than sympathy. He couldn't control it, and the others heard it.

Susie Lovell said angrily, "You had to do that?"

"We thought it was necessary," the old man replied. "If we barged in on you at dawn or even daylight, and your haireem barked up a storm, you might figure this was the Alamo and you were Mr. and Mrs. Davy Crockett." His glance rested for a moment on Henry Lovell's Remington 30-30, which still lay next to the Kleenex box.

"That would serve no purpose," he added.

Reaching out to squeeze his wife's hand, Henry Lovell said, "Susie, it doesn't matter now."

The old hunter nodded agreement, although he realized the state-ment was said out of kindness and wasn't true. If the dog were alive they could have taken it back to Springhill. Someone in town would have been glad to see him through his canine golden years.

Susie Lovell began to cry almost noiselessly. Henry put an arm around her, trying to offer comfort. "They'll let us have some time," he said softly. Then he looked up with eyes that were grave and re-signed. "How did you find us?"

The hunter looked away. That was something he was not willing to discuss. He sat down cross-legged on the floor of the tent, still a sup-ple man, although at ninety-four the lotus position was beyond his ca-pability.

"Let's harp," he said. "It will help us all."

Before that could happen, he heard from outside the sound of foot-steps in crackling brush, a light cry of confusion, and then women's voices. From a distance his wife said something he couldn't under-stand, but she sounded relieved. He glanced up as the tent flaps parted. More light flowed in, and with it the scent of alpine clover and perfume. He saw a visitor who had appeared out of the wilderness.

His face broke apart into a warm, lined smile. "How about that. I didn't think you'd make it in time. Welcome, honey."

1 *February 1993*

The Woman on the Mountain

IN THE WINTER of 1993, Dennis Conway, a New York criminal trial lawyer, flew to Colorado for a week of skiing. But something else happened there to turn his life around.

He rented a small condo at the edge of the slopes of Aspen Mountain. In the early mornings, after he waxed and burred his skis, he worked on an opening statement for the bank fraud trial he was handling back in Manhattan. In the evenings he began to reread Conrad and Isaac Bashevis Singer. Now and then he drank a few beers at Little Annie's Eating House with a pair of old ski pals who lived nearby in the Roaring Fork Valley.

Dennis was a fairly tall, solidly built man with dark eyes and a gray-flecked beard that he often forgot to trim. Twenty-five years ago he had been on the Dartmouth ski team, but each year of city living took its toll: it was always a little bit harder to adjust to the altitude and get back into skiing shape. A Vietcong mortar fragment had given him a permanent ache in one knee. A calf muscle kept cramping when he dug in his edges for sharp turns. But the fourth day out he said to hell with it and tackled the double-black-diamond runs of the Dumps.

These runs, angling steeply between some aspen groves, were full of ungroomed moguls. Today they were almost empty of skiers: on

Short Snort, the run he chose, he noticed only one other, a woman. It had snowed heavily the night before, leaving six inches of fresh powder. The mountain was silent, and the dry cold air in Dennis's lungs felt rare and fine. Not a cloud in the sky, and on the whiteness below him as he shot down the bump run he heard his snow spray billowing behind and the sound of his edges carving through the turns. He let out a whoop of joy. This is *great*. This is the *best*. He flew down the steep hill, pumping his knees, placing his poles high on the crests of moguls, picking up speed, breathing hard. He passed the other skier, the woman, who had stopped to rest in the sun near some aspen trees.

A pain ripped his calf. His leg skidded out from under him—he felt himself falling. One boot, then the other, snapped loose from the bindings; the skis vanished from his sight. He was tumbling, sliding, trying not to tense up. Letting it happen: that was all he could do. Don't let me break a leg, he prayed—I have no time for that. He skidded, somersaulted once, then came to a jolting stop against the side of a mogul.

His sunglasses had been torn from his head and the snow in his eyes blinded him. The breath had been knocked from his lungs. He wiped his eyes with the wet edge of a glove. He sat up slowly—a few inches at a time—moved his legs, then his arms, then flexed his neck. No pain. Nothing broken. Lucky! He had been shocked by the fall, but the soft powder had saved him. Sitting upright, he spat cold snow from his mouth and peered uphill, searching for his skis. Gone. Invisible. Maybe buried in the powder. But he had to be thankful that the bindings had released, modern ski technology saving him from broken ankles or worse.

Feeling shaky, he raised himself up a bit more and scanned the slope. He saw the skis where he had first taken the fall, a good hundred feet uphill, jammed into a mogul. As soon as he could breathe properly he would get up and trek up there and haul them out.

Then he noticed the woman, the one who had been resting by the aspen grove, skiing across the slope and weaving gracefully through the valleys between the high moguls. She disappeared from view for a moment. Dennis blinked as a chunk of snow dropped from his hair into his eyes.

When he had cleared his vision and looked again, the woman was swinging down gently toward him. An angel now, even more than woman: she had his two skis slung over one shoulder. She carried her poles in her other hand.

She skied smoothly down to where he sat in the torn-up snow, and came to a quiet halt by turning a little uphill.

"You all right?"

"I think I am," Dennis said.

"Nothing broken?"

"Nothing I can feel."

"Rest awhile," the woman said. "Don't get up yet."

"Thank you. Thank you for everything."

He wiped more snow from his forehead. His hair and beard were still full of iced chunks of snow. The woman laid his skis between two moguls and then with a gloved hand scooped up more salvage: his prescription sunglasses. "Want me to clean these off for you?"

"That would be kind of you," Dennis said.

"Hit a rock under the powder?"

"Wish I had that excuse. Felt like a leg cramp. I'm out of shape."

The woman laughed warmly. "You looked pretty good up there until you wiped out."

"Not as good as you did coming down the bumps without poles."

She handed him his glasses, which she had cleaned with a handkerchief. Dennis slid them over his ears—the frames ice-cold on the bridge of his nose—got to his feet, and began slapping snow off his parka and ski pants.

He knew already by her voice and silhouette that she was more young than old. Her goggles shielded her eyes. Under them, he thought, she might be beautiful. Hard to tell. And it didn't matter. He'd come to Colorado to ski, not to hunt for the other kind of adventure. For several years now he had been divorced, and his ex-wife was dead. He was raising two children by himself. That was involvement enough.

"I'm okay now," he said. "I don't want to hold you up. Are you skiing alone?"

"This run. I'm meeting my friends up at the Sundeck at noon. They don't do the big moguls. You ready to try this again? I'll go down with you if you want company."

"I'd appreciate that. Let's do it." He knocked the snow off his boots and bindings and stepped into his skis.

She led the way, arms reaching out in easy rhythm with the poles. He could see she checked her speed now and then to accommodate him. By the time they had skied out of the Dumps and down Spar Gulch and had reached the groomed slope of Little Nell, which led to the base of Aspen Mountain, he felt fine again.

"You're good," he said, while they waited in line for the gondola.

"Well, I love it. I try to be good at what I love. Seems worth it."

He marked that down in his mind as something to remember, but made no comment. Despite his bluff appearance and despite being a silver-tongued courtroom advocate when such need arose, Dennis was not immediately at ease with strangers. But he wanted to be a friendly man, and it was a fifteen-minute ride to the summit at more than eleven thousand feet. Although each car of the gondola carried six persons, he and the woman who had saved his skis and glasses were alone, facing down-mountain. The red-roofed old mining town fell away from view as the whitecapped mountain range rose against the horizon.

The woman unzipped her black ski jacket, loosened her neck gaiter, and unsnapped the buckles on her ski boots. She took off her goggles and gloves. Her fingers were long and slender. She had clear, vibrant dark eyes, high cheekbones, a wide mouth. She wore hardly any makeup. What struck Dennis most was her sense of calm certainty.

"You're not a tourist," he said.

"That's right."

"Do you live here in town?"

"No. In Springhill."

"Springhill . . . I'm not sure where that is."

"On the back range. Gunnison County. Above the Crystal River Valley."

"Near Marble?" Marble, he knew, was a hamlet far away in the high country.

"About six hundred feet above Marble."

"That's seriously high. And have you lived there a long time?"

"I was born there."

Almost everyone who lived here had come from elsewhere; Aspen and the Roaring Fork Valley were a mecca not only for skiers and sybarites but for those in pursuit of the good life. At a party in Manhattan where a few people in a corner of the room were comparing ski destinations, Dennis had heard a social worker say, "Aspen? It's just not fucking *real* out there." Dennis, after a long year defending dope dealers and multimillionaire corporate thieves, had responded: "Three cheers for unreality."

"I'm Dennis Conway," he said to the woman in the gondola.

"Sophie Henderson."

Her hand when he shook it was cool, the fingers surprisingly delicate. He judged her to be in her middle thirties, but he was aware that women were always a few years older than his first guess.

"If you don't mind my prying, what do you do up there in nine-thousand-foot-high Springhill?"

"I teach science to the kids at school. And I'm the mayor." When she saw his expression she shrugged. "No big deal. There were only three hundred fifty people in town the last time anyone bothered to count."

"I'm still impressed. How far did you say Springhill is from here?"

"Fifteen miles from the back of Aspen Mountain and past the Maroon Bells, if you know a friendly eagle who'll give you a lift." Sophie Henderson's laugh was deep, vibrant, so that Dennis felt its echo in his chest. "By road, over an hour."

"You've come a long way to ski."

"You flew for five hours, Mr. Conway, didn't you?"

"If you include changing planes in Denver. How'd you know that?"

"I can hear New York. And probably Ivy League."

"New York, but not the city," he protested. "Not by birth, anyway." He wanted to tell her what he was, and hide his sins. "I'm from Watkins Glen—a small town on a lake in upstate New York you never heard of. And you're right, I went to Dartmouth, then Oxford for a year, a little detour in the military, and then Yale Law School. After that I decided to practice law in New York City for reasons that don't seem as valid as they did back then. I'm widowed. Or widowered. I'm not sure which is right. I live in Connecticut with my two kids. A nutshell biography. Tells you all and nothing."

"Well, we have widowhood in common," Sophie Henderson said. "And although I missed Oxford on my grand tour of Europe, it may surprise you that I've been to Watkins Glen."

"It doesn't surprise me—it amazes me. How did that happen?"

"I went to Cornell. Chemistry major. Ithaca is pretty close to Watkins Glen."

She tugged off her ski hat, and a torrent of reddish brown hair flowed over her parka. He sensed what it would feel like to clench that hair in his hand. His attitude toward her changed, increasing in tonal value. Something seized him: the effect of some scented cream holding memories of childhood, or the natural smell that rose from clean skin.

"My father's a lawyer," she said. "Retired, but I know the species firsthand. You remind me of him."

"I hope you get on with him."

Sophie Henderson said, "I adore him."

At the top of Aspen Mountain they stepped from the gondola and clicked into the bindings of their skis. "Do you see your friends around?" Dennis asked.

She scanned the flats in front of the Sundeck restaurant, then pointed to people near Lift Three who were waving at her. She poled over; Dennis followed. A minute later she introduced him to a blonde woman in her middle thirties and a man of about the same age; an older man with silver hair, gray beard and lively brown eyes; and a younger man, dark-haired and powerfully built. The latter offered Dennis only a surly nod. This might be Sophie's lover, Dennis thought.

He caught only the first names: Jane, Hank, Edward, Oliver. They talked among themselves for a minute—they were all from Springhill, he realized. Adjusting goggles and boot buckles, they faced down the mountain.

"Which run?"

"Dipsy Doodle?"

"Then Bonnie's for lunch."

Dennis asked, "Mind if I ski with you?"

The younger man scowled, but the three others looked immediately toward Sophie Henderson. Her eyes wavered.

Edward, the man with silver hair, turned to Dennis and spoke decisively. "By all means, do. Maybe you can keep up with Sophie."

"He can," Sophie said.

Dennis's parents, academics, were simple people living in a small town. Even in his late teens and early twenties their son's ambition had been to be like them: honorable, moral, and honest. Quite a few years later an opposing prosecutor said of him, "Dennis will whip your ass a hundred different ways in court, but he's a decent man." That prosecutor, Mickey Karp, at first had been Dennis's fellow apprentice at the U.S. Attorney's Office, when both young men had moved to the city from the provinces: Dennis from Watkins Glen, Mickey from North Carolina. Their common passion was skiing, and in four successive winters they traveled together, first north to Sugarbush and Killington, then west to Tahoe and Aspen. After the last trip Mickey said, "I've had enough of the city. Colorado's for me." He had found another lawyer recently moved West from Chicago, and together they opened a practice in Aspen.

Dennis's other Aspen pal was Josh Gamble, the six-foot-six-inch, 270-seventy-pound elected sheriff of Pitkin County, where Aspen was the county seat. Dennis had roomed with him at Dartmouth. Josh Gamble had slipped loose from a brokerage firm in Philadelphia eighteen years ago to be a ski bum, but even ski bums had to eat. He drove a bus for the Roaring Fork Transit Authority, then signed up to become a traffic control officer, chalking tires. It was an easy step to the raise in pay that went with the job of deputy sheriff. They gave him a gun; he put it on his night table and stared at it for a week before he ever opened the cylinder. He became patrol director and a year later ran successfully for sheriff. He didn't like to lock people up and never hired anyone as a deputy who he suspected really wanted to be a cop. "Anyone gets a wet spot in his jeans when he thinks of carrying a weapon and arresting somebody," Josh Gamble told Dennis, "I won't hire."

"Then who works for you?"

"People I like. Ain't that the point?"

Maybe it was, Dennis reflected. Most of the people he worked with, he realized unhappily, he didn't like.

On this most recent trip, over breakfast one morning at the Main Street Bakery, Josh said, "The way I see it, Denny boy, you're fed up with life back in the Big Rotten Apple. You got pollution, traffic, crowds, mayhem, designer drugs, fifteen-year-olds of all shades packing Saturday Night Specials. That's a hell of a world, and the burbs are part of it, man. Why don't you quit while you're young enough? Move out West, where kids are still kids, men are men, and women do the shopping."

Dennis squeezed his friend's beefy shoulder. "Because I'm a criminal lawyer. Who would I defend here? You don't have a criminal class. People have space, they're not hemmed in by a ghetto or high-rises, they're not pissed off at the world. Plenty of them are poor but they don't seem to give a rat's ass as long as they can ski in winter and hike in summer. It's close to being a crime-free valley. How could I make a living?"

"Got a rise in ski thefts this season," the sheriff said thoughtfully. "Fraud by check is known to happen. Cocaine's coming into the valley big-time. Mexican road workers get drunk on Saturday night. Domestic violence is also a solid growth industry. You could find work. I don't know about fees, but work, yes."

When Dennis paid the check the sheriff didn't protest. "I'll think about it," the lawyer said. "Meanwhile, I'm off for the mountain. You stay down here and defend the community against fraud by check."

That was the day he wiped out on the Dumps and Sophie Henderson dug his skis out of the snow.

They ate soup and salad together midmountain on the deck at Bonnie's Restaurant. It was a cloudless February day, warm enough for a few hardy skiers to strip down to T-shirts. Dennis discovered that Hank Lovell, among Sophie's companions, was the CEO of a marble quarry in Springhill. His wife, Jane, was a dental technician who worked for the older man, Edward Brophy, the town dentist. "If anyone develops a toothache today," Edward explained, "they'll have to find a bottle of brandy. I'm the only game in town."

The other man, Oliver Cone, was Edward's nephew. He was a shift foreman at the Springhill marble quarry. He still glowered at Dennis and had almost nothing to say.

By the end of the afternoon Dennis felt the first inchoate stirrings of that borderline psychotic state called falling-in-love. He forced himself to stay calm. *Do I need this?* he asked himself. *Do I want it?* More to the point: *Can I help it?* He was able to formulate the questions but unable to provide answers. When he and Sophie were leaning on their ski poles at Lift Three, waiting for the others to catch up, he said, "You're widowed, is that what you said?"

"He died in an avalanche five years ago."

"And Oliver?"

"Oliver is Edward's nephew, and Edward is a dear friend of mine. Oliver's not as unpleasant as he seems. And he's unusually bright—he's just a little shy about showing it."

"That's not really what I was asking," Dennis admitted. "Are you and Oliver—?" He let the sentence hang there; he knew she understood his meaning.

"No," Sophie said.

Dennis asked her to have dinner with him that evening.

"I can't. Town Council and Water Board meeting. Springhill is a corporation. We have a home rule charter—we vote a lot of our own taxes for roads, education, stuff like that. Nothing earth-shaking going on right now, but the mayor chairs the council. I have to be there."

"Tomorrow evening?"

Sophie bit her lip. She was thinking about it hard, and he wondered why. If not Oliver Cone, then another man in her life; it had to be. He felt gloomy for a moment.

But she said finally, in a strangely formal way, "Yes, if you'd like it, I'll have dinner with you tomorrow evening."

In the high-speed quad chair on the lift, after Dennis had said goodbye and skied off, Edward Brophy remarked to Sophie, "I like that lawyer fellow. He's no jeekus. He's intelligent and he's cheerful. Seems to me that he keeps something in reserve. Not out to charm you or bowl you over. And he's a ree bahl skier."

She nodded and tossed her dark red hair. "He asked me out to dinner tomorrow evening."

"I thought he would, if you gave him a chance."

"I must have done that."

"And what did you say?"

"I couldn't think of an excuse. I said yes. But I've decided to break the date."

"Just because he's a skibtail?"

A skibtail, in the Springling lingo, was a stranger. Frowning, Sophie said, "You don't think that's a good enough reason?"

The dentist smiled affectionately. "You seemed to be getting on so well." When Sophie frowned again, Edward raised his palm. "He asked you for a dinner date. It's not the rest of your life. Take a chance, Sophie. Enjoy your time on this earth. So he's a skibtail. I've looked around at home, and I'm sure you have too. You've turned down my bad-tempered nephew, for which I can't quite blame you. Who else that's decent is available?"

At the top of the lift she vaulted off the chair, planted her poles, kicked into a turn, and thrust herself alone down the mountain toward the long run of Copper Bowl.

Driving home later, she could not as easily thrust Dennis Conway from her mind. Craggy, a little rough-edged for a city fellow . . . doesn't trim his beard too well. My type, no doubt of it. A successful lawyer, she imagined, with that same confident air her father had always had. She liked the way he'd reacted to her helping him when he took the tumble on the mountain. He hadn't been embarrassed, hadn't done any macho things afterward. In the gondola he'd listened when she spoke, seeming to digest her words and thoughts rather than merely waiting for his chance to sound off.

Maybe it was an act. A good con job. A city slicker. A skibtail; not one of us. That hardly ever worked out.

But Sophie was moved by him, stirred at a level that she could deal with only in her heart, not her head, and she decided to take the risk.

2 *November 8, 1994*

Mystery of a Dead Dog

QUEENIE O'HARE WORE more than one hat. She was a Pitkin County deputy sheriff as well as one of five community safety officers working for the city of Aspen. And also at the moment, on this morning shift, she was supervising animal control officer.

She worked at a functional desk in a room with four other functional desks in the basement of the Pitkin County Courthouse. On the wall above the desk she had tacked two signs that said, "Wage peace" and "Be optimistic, even in the face of reality." Flanking them were photographs of her spayed tabby cat and her two dogs, a rottweiler and a black-and-white Jack Russell terrier. Queenie was thirty-five, unmarried and childless, but she had her little menagerie to keep her company and get her through the cold winter nights.

It was early November, elk-hunting season, and two burly men confronted her. The men smelled as if they hadn't washed in several days, so Queenie O'Hare kept her distance from them. They wore camouflage jackets, mud-stained trail boots and orange caps. They had called first from the Texaco station but had had the sense to leave their deer rifles in the Ford pickup parked on Main Street opposite the courthouse.

"Ma'am, I'm Fred Clark," the older of the two said. "And this is my brother Harold." He explained that he and Harold had been camped up near Pearl Pass. Yesterday morning they'd come across a dead dog.

"This coyote was chewin' at it," Fred said, "and we run him off. We figured he'd dug the dog up where it was buried, 'cause it was wrapped in a down sleeping bag."

"The dog, not the coyote."

"Yes, ma'am."

"Coffee?"

"Kind of you, ma'am."

In their early thirties, the brothers lived downvalley in a trailer park near El Jebel, where they worked on the construction of a new mall. They still had the broad drawl and country manners of rural Tennessee. Queenie didn't feel it would be appropriate to squeeze two big men into the little space between her desk and the desk of the duty sergeant. So she chose the conference room. The hunters doffed their caps and sat down at the conference table while Queenie poured from the Silex.

Queenie's father had been a longshoreman who had emigrated to the Roaring Fork Valley from Houston. She knew how to talk to Southerners and good ole boys. "You get your buck, Mr. Clark?"

Fred Clark smiled, revealing a missing front tooth in a jagged ocher row. "Yes, ma'am. A nine-point. Harold here got a ten. They're out there in the truck on Main Street."

"And the dead dog? He's in the truck too?"

Fred Clark lowered his eyes slightly. "No, ma'am, we didn't bring him in with us. He was pretty rotten."

And so are you after three days in the high country without a bathtub or a bar of soap, Queenie thought.

"This dog was shot?"

"Quartering shot, heart and lungs. But not by a rifle. By an arrow, ma'am."

"You could tell?"

"A bullet cuts one kind of hole into an animal. An arrow cuts another kind. Bigger 'n' wider. Not so deep."

"Did you bring the arrow back with you?"

"It wasn't there."

Queenie thought that over. "What kind of dog is it?"

"Big. A male. Not a kind I ever seen. No ID tag and no collar."

"If I show you a map, do you think you can point out about where you found this dead dog you think was shot by an arrow and was cosied up in a down sleeping bag?"

In her mind's eye, after she had dealt with the tunneling four-tiered wound that a modern steel arrow would make through a canine heart and lungs, she pictured the topography of the Elk Mountain Range. The area described by the Clark brothers struck her as being on the border of Pitkin County and Gunnison County. If it was on the Gunnison County side, she would call her counterparts at the Gunnison County Courthouse and let them deal with the problem.

Queenie led the brothers to a large topographic wall map in the next room. Fred studied it for a while, then pointed with a blackened fingernail. " 'Bout cheer—'cause we could look over at the Maroon Bells to the south. And Pearl Pass was a few miles that way, to the north."

" 'Bout cheer" was in Pitkin County. An arrow to kill a dog. Queenie wondered why. "Can you give me a more detailed description of the animal?"

With his other hand, from the pocket of his hunting jacket Fred Clark took out a little yellow-and-black box. Queenie realized it was a throwaway fixed-focus Kodak camera, the kind that sold at Wal-Mart for $9.95.

"Harold took pitchers of the bucks we shot. Took a couple pitchers of that dog too."

He had moved a little closer to her, bearing the gift of the camera, and Queenie inhaled the three-day-old aroma coming from the depths of his thick woolen lumberjack shirt. She backed off a step.

"Mr. Clark, if y'all see your way clear to leaving that camera with me, I'll get the roll of film developed. You give me your address in El Jebel, I'll put the prints and negatives in tomorrow's mail. The county will pay for the processing. "

Queenie thumbed through the file on missing dogs, but all she could come up with was a Labrador in heat that had run away from a famous actor's home on Smuggler Street in the West End. She was wondering if the dead dog had been killed legally, while molesting human beings or wildlife, or illegally, for the hell of it, in which case whoever did it would be liable for prosecution under the state cruelty-to-animals statute. Or maybe it was an old dog or a sick dog and the owner had taken it up there to put it out of its misery. It wasn't illegal to bury a dog on public land in the high country.

But then Queenie decided that if *she* were going to put her sick or suffering old dog out of its misery, she'd have a vet inject it. And if she were a hunter and had hiked up to Pearl Pass with poor old Fido on his last legs, she might shoot him in the head with a pistol, but she didn't think she'd take what amounted to target practice with a bow and arrow.

Back in her office after a visit to the one-hour photo shop, Queenie stood in front of a large poster distributed free by the Gaines dog food company. It showed colored drawings of 150 recognized breeds of dogs, complete with characteristics, average weight, and known colorings.

The two photographs taken by the Clark brothers revealed a large body swathed in shadow and laying in a hole that presumably was intended to be its grave. But Queenie had never seen a head like that. She didn't know the breed. She scanned the Gaines chart for a few minutes, then buzzed through to the Sheriff's Office. Doug Larsen answered. He was patrol director of the day.

"Doug, I need your keen eye and razor-sharp powers of deduction."

When Larsen arrived, Queenie showed him the Clark brothers' photographs. "Pick out the breed on the chart."

"What's the prize?"

"The warm feeling of having helped a fellow law-enforcement officer. Just do it, buddy."

Doug studied the chart for a few minutes. "Scottish deerhound?"

"That's what I think too," Queenie said triumphantly.

The last of the Roaring Fork Valley veterinarians whom she called said yes, he had given a rabies booster to a male deerhound maybe three or four years ago. No, he didn't know any other deerhounds in the valley—he seemed to remember discussing that very fact with the owner, whom the file card listed as Mr. Henry Lovell Sr. of Springhill, over in Gunnison County. The dog's name was Geronimo. If still alive, he'd be nine years old.

Queenie had been to Springhill only once, about ten years ago, on a summer hike with friends. They didn't encourage visitors up there on the back range, and there was little reason to go unless you had business with the marble quarry. Only a few families lived up there, with a fair amount of inbreeding over the generations, or so it was assumed. There were rumors of idiots.

Queenie got the number from Information and tapped it out. A woman answered. The connection seemed a little blurred, as if it were an overseas call. Queenie identified herself and explained that she was trying to locate a Mr. Henry Lovell Sr.

The woman said, "Mr. Lovell is deceased."

"I'm sorry. With whom am I speaking?"

"Jane Lovell. Henry was my father-in-law. His son, Henry Lovell Jr.—Hank—is my husband."

"Mrs. Lovell, did your late father-in-law have a Scottish deerhound named Geronimo?"

With just a slight hesitation, Jane said, "Yes, he did."

"And did that dog disappear recently?" When Jane didn't reply, Queenie asked, "Were you taking care of it? After your father-in-law passed away?"

"No, I wasn't taking care of it," Jane said, and paused again for a long time. Weird woman, Queenie thought. Then Jane resumed: "I just came home for lunch, and I need to get back to the office. I'm a dental assistant and we've got an emergency today. Perhaps you'd better talk to my husband about this."

"I'm sorry to tell you the dog's been found dead," Queenie said. "I'm trying to locate whoever was taking care of it."

"I'm not sure who that was."

Jane Lovell didn't sound at all upset about the dog's death. Maybe dental emergencies did that to you, Queenie decided.

"Mrs. Lovell, when was it that your father-in-law passed away?"

"In August."

"And he was a widower?"

"Well, not for long. My mother-in-law passed away too. Shortly before he did."

"Gosh, I'm sorry," Queenie said, "but that's common, isn't it? That's what happened with my uncle and aunt down in Sarasota, Florida, last year. She was so dependent on him." She sighed. "And you don't know who cared for the dog after your mother-in-law died?"

"My husband will be home for supper. Could you call back then?"

"Can I reach him now at work?"

Jane gave her the number. Queenie thanked her and hung up. Without waiting even a second so that Jane Lovell could get through before she did, she punched out the number.

"Quarry. Hank Lovell here."

Queenie identified herself, then launched into her speech about the finding of Geronimo.

"Yes, we were concerned," Hank Lovell said quietly. "We didn't know what had happened."

"You mean *you* were caring for the dog?"

"That's right. We have two other dogs. Two Akitas."

"Your wife . . . well, never mind. Did Geronimo run away, Mr. Lovell?"

"Disappeared. Around September. But don't hold me to that. I haven't got a good memory for dates." Hank Lovell laughed pleasantly.

"Did you report the animal missing, sir?"

"No, that seemed premature. We thought he'd come back."

"I'm sure sorry to give y'all the news this way," Queenie said.

"It clears up a mystery. I appreciate it. Darn shame."

He's not asking me how the dog died, Queenie realized. And he's definitely not grieving. Henry Jr. was not at all nervous or hesitant like his wife, who hadn't known who was caring for the dog. Queenie waited a beat or two, listening to the crackling silence on the line.

"Mr. Lovell, if there's anything at all you want to know, just call me here at Animal Control in Aspen."

Queenie sat at her desk for a long while, once again studying the photos of Geronimo. It was only then that she noticed, at the lower left-hand edge of one of the photos, something that glinted dully in the shadows. She'd missed it before because she'd been studying only the dog. Queenie opened the desk drawer and took out a magnifying glass.

A partially dirt-covered silver object lay there in the grave. A box, she thought. Maybe a pillbox.

3 *March–July 1993*

A Lawyer in Love

IN HIS MID-THIRTIES Dennis had met Alma Bennett, a model from a small town in Virginia, a beautiful young woman much courted and admired in the New York fast lane, and one who relied on the unceasing approval of men and the comfort of cocaine. Dennis was smitten, however, and focused only on her vulnerability and need for nurturing—the knight-errant who had ridden down from Watkins Glen would save her life and sanity. She seemed to respond, to accept his caring. They married, had two children, and then one summer afternoon a tired Dennis came home to Westport from court and found Brian, his two-year-old son, wandering toward the highway a block from the house. He carried the boy home and found Alma passed out on the living room couch with a straw and a mirror and some white powder spilled on the wood of the coffee table. With the aid of a middle-aged gemütlich German housekeeper and a married sister living nearby in Greenwich, Dennis began raising the children while Alma shuttled in and out of expensive drug programs and the beds of cocaine dealers. She's the mother of my kids, Dennis kept telling himself. I care for her, I have to help her. For two years he tried and failed. Later he wondered how he could have been so quixotic and so stupid.

After the divorce, Alma moved back to Virginia and married a man seven years younger than she. She wrote to Dennis: "Nobody here knows I had children and I want to keep it that way. I was never interested in being a mother, and they're better off with you anyway." It took Dennis a while to get over that, and telling the children was the hardest task of his life. A year later Alma's heart failed; the autopsy showed it to be almost double its normal size.

In his private life Dennis had brief affairs, but he balked at involvement. He had been brought up to believe that you persevered at commitments and didn't quit until they lowered you into the grave. You could forgive yourself for making a mistake once. In his moral scheme of things a second failure would be unacceptable.

The incorporated township of Springhill nestled at nine thousand feet amid dense forests of blue spruce. Creeks seemed to flow everywhere. Dennis visited there with Sophie on the last evening of his vacation, two days after their first dinner at a restaurant in Carbondale. During those two intervening days he fretted; he wandered about Aspen, wondering what change he was undergoing.

Years ago a wise person said to him, "Before you get involved with the daughter, know the mother. The daughter may grow to be like her." Alma's mother had been an alcoholic and a chain-smoker. Dennis in love had ignored the wise person's advice. Older, and bearing the scars of that failed marriage, at Sophie's parents' dinner table he paid close attention to her mother. Bibsy Henderson's calmness and slightly wry turn of speech were comparable to Sophie's. When the discussion veered to politics and Scott Henderson thumped the dinner table to punctuate his views on Bill Clinton and gun control, Bibsy said to Dennis, "My husband sometimes believes he can make a fact out of an opinion by raising his voice."

But even as she spoke, she was lightly stroking the back of Scott's hand, and Scott smiled apologetically in response.

Bibsy reminded Dennis of his own mother back in Watkins Glen. He couldn't think of a higher compliment. "Why 'Bibsy'?"

"It's Beatrice. When I was a kid I couldn't pronounce that."

Dennis liked Scott too. To a friend in New York he described Sophie's father as "a talky Gary Cooper. Arms like an oak tree. He can outhike you and outchop you and probably out-arm-wrestle you. For a man of sixty-five, which is what I guess he is, he's in amazing shape."

After that first February meeting on the bumps of Aspen Mountain, Dennis could not push Sophie from his thoughts, day or night. He had not made love to her but already he felt possessed. His fears were not realized; she had told him there was no other man in her life. He flew back to Colorado two weeks later, leaving his children with his sister in Greenwich. Sophie picked him up at Aspen airport. Dennis tossed his ski bag and suitcase in the back of her Blazer and she bore him up and away to the village of Springhill.

The drive wound through the icebound valley of the Crystal River, past herds of unmoving horses who looked to Dennis like black cutouts pasted on white cardboard. The evening was cold and the river glistened in the setting sun. Layers of snowy mountains fell away in all directions. Where avalanches had poured from the crests and smashed paths to the valley floor, rows of mature aspen trees were broken like matchsticks.

"I love the aspens," Sophie said. "See the black spots against that pure gray of the bark? When I was a girl I thought those spots were eyes, looking at me. Protecting me."

"From what?"

"From whatever might do harm."

Above the town of Marble the narrow road was freshly plowed. This was the only way into the town of Springhill, and the only way out. Sophie's home, on the far edge of town, was a high-beamed pine cabin built in the heyday of mining in the nineteenth century. The Roaring Fork Valley had prospered after silver was found in 1877, but a scant sixteen years later, to protect the nation's gold reserves, President Cleveland demonetized silver. Most western Colorado mines and business enterprises became bankrupt; coal mining and marble quarrying saved the valley from blending back into the wilderness. And then, during Christmas week in 1936, a group of skiers were carried in a four-horse sleigh to the top of Little Annie Basin above the little town of Aspen, to float down from there on wooden skis through the deepest, lightest powder they had ever known. The valley's economic and social revival began immediately. Not even World War II could stop it—the Tenth Mountain Division, the army's crack ski troops, trained and partied in the Roaring Fork Valley. Many came back after the war to make their home and their fortune.

Sophie and Dennis drove along the snowplowed main street of

Springhill, past the Volunteer Fire Department, the little gymnasium, the funeral parlor, and the violet-colored wooden bank that looked like part of a Western movie set. Above the bank, Sophie told him, Edward Brophy had his dental office. On the far edge of town, off Quarry Road on forty acres of woods and rolling meadow, they came to Sophie's log house. The house and land had been a gift from her parents. Sophie had rebuilt the old miner's cabin, adding a second story, a kitchen with Mexican tile, and a greenhouse. Spanned by a wooden footbridge, a creek wound through the property. Aspens and spruce grew in a glade. Deer drank from the creek and sometimes browsed on the edge of the glade.

Sophie lit lamps. The light was warm; the cabin had a hint of an enchanted place in a forest. A Swiss cuckoo clock ticked in the living room. An old dark brown violin case stood propped against the coffee table.

"You play it?"

"Since I was a child. My great-grandmother taught me. Shall I?"

"Later, yes. Not now." Dennis sank into the pillows of the living room sofa. Sitting next to him, Sophie touched his hands. He kissed her for what seemed half an hour: it was only five minutes. Her hands were so cool, and they seemed fragile. It made him want to protect her from whatever might do harm.

"Do you want to make love?" Sophie asked.

"Of course I do," Dennis said.

Taking his hand, she led him upstairs.

Moonlight shone into the bedroom. From afar Dennis heard water singing over rocks. When she took off her clothes he saw that she was more lovely than he had imagined.

In the morning she said, "It's been two years since I was with a man. And that was very brief. I was starting to think I'd be an old maid."

"How could that be? A woman as lovely as you?"

"I don't go out. And I'm not easy to please. Listen to what I have to say. The sex was wonderful. I'm sure it will get even better. But I don't want to be just a sweet diversion—your Colorado girlfriend. If that's what it is, or will become, be honest and tell me. We'll both get over it."

Dennis didn't want to make promises he wasn't sure he could keep.

He knew she was more than a diversion but he was afraid to admit, so quickly, how much more he already dreamed of. He was silent, but the way Sophie smiled at him and touched his cheek with cool fingers made him feel she had read his mind.

For a week they stayed cocooned in the rumpled bed. Sometimes it was two o'clock in the afternoon before they padded downstairs to throw open the door to the refrigerator. Other days they reached the ski slopes of nearby Snowmass Mountain at the crack of noon.

Together they skied the Hanging Glades. Dennis heard the quick rush of her breath when she dug her edges hard on the turns, the dry *swish* of both their pairs of skis schussing the last long steep glide to the bottom; and he heard the beating of his heart when he simply looked at her.

He flew back to New York on a Sunday and the next morning went straight to court. His caseload piled up. Briefs were unwritten, telephone calls unanswered. Court dates had to be adjusted. He began to work fourteen hours a day. But until July, with his sister and his devoted German housekeeper caring for his children and assuaging his guilt, he managed to jet to Colorado twice every month for a three-day weekend.

In April he and Sophie skied on cross-country trails that wound through the forests between Springhill and Aspen. Another time she borrowed a snowmobile from a friend. On the back of an eagle, as she had told him on the day they'd met, it was only fifteen miles between Aspen and their isolated hamlet. But the high peaks of the Elk Range—the Maroon Bells—interdicted the passage. The Bells were recipes for disaster, Sophie said. Not extreme technical climbs, but deceptive ones, for the rock was down-sloping, loose, and unstable. The snowpacks were treacherous. The gullies through which a cross-country skier had to trek were in the path of avalanches that began as early as October and ended as late as July. Expert climbers who did not know the proper routes had died on the Maroon Bells.

A network of a dozen good-sized cabins existed deep in the mountains between Aspen and Vail, for emergencies and rental by summer hikers or adventurous cross-country skiers. Run by the not-for-profit Tenth Mountain Division Hut Association, they were often stocked with food, cots, firewood, medical supplies, a two-way radio, and avalanche rescue equipment. Sophie knew these huts well. In June, between tourist seasons, she took Dennis to the hut at a place called Lead King Basin and they made love there in the wilderness. By July he believed that life without Sophie made no sense for him. He asked her to marry him.

But it was not quite that simple.

They were hiking along the bank of a high creek near Springhill. Mountain bluebirds streaked across the meadows, as if flecks of summer sky had been torn away. Dennis's eyes narrowed like a sea captain's peering into a haze of battle smoke.

"Sophie, listen. Criminal law is what I do. You should see me in trial. I shine. I take my work and the law seriously. It would be hard for me to leave New York. It has nothing to do with the city itself—I could give that up. But it's where my practice is."

"And it would be hard for me to leave Springhill," she replied calmly. "That's where my life is."

He had no ready answer. Could he compare his law practice to her life itself?

"Dennis, it may not be simple for you to grasp this—not yet, not now—but if I weren't here, if I couldn't remain here, I wouldn't be the person you think you love."

"I don't believe that," he said.

"You must."

"I would love you anywhere."

"I'm sure you would. You're not hearing me. If I were elsewhere, I would be different."

"How?"

Sophie didn't respond. He had already learned that she was capable of breaking off a conversation when she had said all she needed to say. In that she was stubborn to the point of intractable. He understood that she was begging him to reflect on her words, pursue no further. He was puzzled, but he cherished her and he would not try to command her to fit into his scheme of understanding.

The cold creek flowed over rocks and broken branches. They sat on a boulder by the edge of the water. In the Ice Age, such boulders had been carried southward by the glacier on its route from the polar cap. When the glacier retreated northward again, the boulders remained—"for us to sit on," Sophie said, "and occasionally, if we don't plan well, to tumble down on us."

A choice and a kind of sacrifice were necessary: either he or Sophie would have to bend. He knew there were always alternatives to the way one lives. Not always easy ones . . . but they were there. And he had been looking for them.

"Sophie—"

She placed a finger on his lips. She led him off into the forest, spread the flowered cotton picnic sheet, and made love to him in the cool shifting shadows of the trees as the afternoon breeze began to blow. She took off his shirt and bit him lightly on his shoulders and chest, then began to suck his nipples. In the act of love she had no inhibition. She straddled him so that he felt the soil and pebbles and twigs dig into his back. He heard an owl and the trill of a hummingbird far away. Sophie's catlike cries seemed to fill the forest. No bird or creature would dare intrude.

The next afternoon he walked up the carpeted stairs to the offices of Karp & Ballard on the Hyman Avenue Mall in Aspen, not far from the gondola.

"I'm going to marry a woman from Springhill," Dennis said to Mickey Karp, his old friend from the United States Attorney's Office in Manhattan. "Can you use a middle-aged trial lawyer to pick up paper clips and teach you guys about the real world?"

Mickey Karp was a trim man in his early forties, with black hair and twinkling dark eyes. "Yes, we can definitely use the man you describe. But, Dennis, this is Aspen. Famous for its peace and quiet—its basic dullness. A New York criminal defense attorney . . ."

Dennis waved away his past life with a flick of the hand. "I'm not in it for the money and the ego. This is for sanity. A new life."

Mickey and his partner, Bill Ballard, took a day to work out a simple partnership arrangement. Dennis would need some time to clean up his caseload in New York, put his Westport house on the market, sell out, pack up for him and the children, say goodbyes. Change his life. Change his world.

4 *Thanksgiving 1993*
Memories of Dylan Thomas

DENNIS'S EXODUS WAS delayed by a continuance in a drug case. He wouldn't leave the children yet again, so he persuaded Sophie to fly East and spend Thanksgiving with them all. Brian was eight, Lucy six.

At first she was quiet with the children, and they were shy. But within a day they were friends. She brought her violin and played for them. She fiddled Irish airs and Gypsy songs and danced around the carpet as she played, head bobbing, auburn hair flying. She laughed as she played. The children laughed too, and Lucy clapped her hands. Then Sophie played a movement from a Bach sonata. The children fell silent. After the Bach, Sophie stopped.

"Will you show me around your town?" she asked them. "If you do that, one day I'll show you around mine."

"Where do you live?" Brian asked.

"In the mountains, high up near the sky. There are wonderful places in the forest there. A wonderful warm spring—the town is named after it. A very special place. I'll take you. I promise."

The next day all four drove the two hundred miles from Connecticut through the Catskills to Dennis's parents' home in Watkins Glen on Seneca Lake. Dennis's two sisters, one from Greenwich and one from Rochester, joined them for the holiday dinner. His Aunt Jennie came down from Rochester as well; she was ninety-five years old and ailing.

"Can she make the trip?" Dennis asked his sister.

"It might be her last Thanksgiving. She wants to come."

The autumnal eruption of crimson and gold had faded more than a month ago. The trees were bare, and a raw wind blew across New York State. Dennis's father was a former history professor at Ithaca College. Now that he was retired he kept a pair of old saddle horses, goats, pigs, a yard full of chickens, and a cow, and was realizing a life-long ambition to write a book proving that Shakespeare's Hamlet was a decisive young prince much maligned and misunderstood by schol-ars, theatrical producers, and filmmakers.

In the living room, while Aunt Jennie napped and the others were off on a tour of the barns, Dennis's mother said to him, "I like your young woman. She's so even tempered. So warm and bright. The chil-dren like her too."

"She's what they need," he said. "This time it will work. I won't fail again."

"You didn't fail the first time, Denny darling. You chose the wrong woman."

"That's a failure of judgment, Mother."

At the Thanksgiving feast, after he had carved the turkey, Dennis's father said to Sophie, "Dennis told me you went to Cornell. I taught at Ithaca College. Did he mention that? It was about a hundred years ago. But if you spent four years far above Cayuga's waters, you can't be a stranger to Watkins Glen. All the students come to our waterfall when the weather warms up."

"I remember," Sophie said. "I came here to swim under it. You felt as if you were drowning, and it was thrilling, not frightening. It seems like a hundred years ago to me too."

"What did you major in?"

"Chemistry. But what I really liked was nineteenth-century English lit. Wordsworth, Keats, Coleridge."

"Then you must have studied with John Yates. The expert on the Romantics. John was a friend of mine."

"No, with David Daiches." Sophie began to cough, and reached for another helping of turkey and cranberry sauce.

"I knew Daiches too, but not well. More of an expert on Scotch whisky, he was. He went off to the Chair of Poetry at Cambridge, in England. And before him there was the illustrious Vladimir Nabokov. I go a long way back, you see. Were you a good student? Did you love the Hill?"

"I wasn't very industrious. I was homesick, and I was so cold there."

Across the table, Dennis's Rochester sister laughed. "Dennis says that in Colorado you live at nine thousand feet! Now that's what I call cold!"

"Cold," Aunt Jennie repeated, nodding, her hands shaking.

"But it's not so," Sophie said politely. "There's no humidity high up in the Rockies, and hardly any wind. People in the East talk all the time about the windchill factor. We don't have it. The snow is so soft and dry you can't make a snowball with it until April. They call it champagne powder. In winter the sun is strong enough for me to grow bougainvillea in my greenhouse. And gardenias, and orchids. Dennis will tell you . . ."

Sophie had spoken with all the quiet passion of a woman in love. But in this instance, in love with a place—her snowbound wilderness.

She went to bed early that night, and Dennis stayed up to drink a nightcap of scotch with his father.

"Daiches"—his father mused—"your bride-to-be's English professor, taught me the little I know about the making of single-malt whisky. 'You get the best brands,' he said, 'and cheap too, at Macy's in New York.' He drank a lot of it, so he should have known. Dylan Thomas came to visit him. Friendly fellow, but a serious boozer—gave a reading of his poetry up on the Hill. He and Daiches had a merry old time of it. I was introduced to Dylan. Tragic life." He frowned. "You know, Dennis, it doesn't make sense."

"What doesn't, Dad? That Dylan Thomas had a tragic life?"

"That Sophie could have studied under David Daiches. It was in the late forties and early fifties that he was in Ithaca. By the time she would have graduated, he was long gone to Cambridge."

Dennis knew his father forgot things and sometimes got dates confused. He had just turned seventy-five.

"I know exactly what you're thinking," his father said. "The old man's a bit gaga. First stage of Alzheimer's. But I'm telling you, Dylan came to visit Cornell in 1950. I went over to hear him read at Willard Straight Hall. Magnificent voice. I remember it like it was yesterday.

So how could she have been there? That would make her well over sixty years old."

"You're right," Dennis said, "she must have got him mixed up with someone else." He leaned over and gave his father a strong hug—the older man smelled comfortably of tweed and horses and old books. Dennis said, "I'm going to hit the hay. What do you think, Dad?"

"About what? Sophie?"

"Yes, about Sophie."

"Does it matter what I think?"

It was not the enthusiasm Dennis had hoped for. He waited, uncertain whether to go on. Finally his father said, "I think she's fine. Obviously she loves you if she'd come all the way up here to where it's *really* cold, just to visit your aged parents."

Dennis squeezed his father's shoulder. "That's it, eh? 'People in the East talk about windchill.' A slur on dear old Watkins Glen! That bothered you, did it?"

"Honestly, Denny, you can't tell me it's colder here at virtually sea level than it is at nine thousand feet, can you? Can you really?"

"It is, Dad. I've been there, and what she says is true."

"Go to bed. Your brains are addled by love. Keep your bride-to-be warm in our Siberia."

5 *November 10, 1994*

Crime Scene

"I CAN'T SEE the whole body," Sheriff Josh Gamble said, frowning, bending forward to study the photographs spread on Queenie's desk.

"Meaning what?" Queenie asked. "You don't think it's a Scottish deerhound?"

"Of course I do. You can tell by the head. I'm just saying that I can't see the whole body or the throat or the other eye."

"Why is that important, Josh?"

The sheriff handed Queenie a Xeroxed copy of a flyer faxed to his office the previous summer by the Colorado State Police. The flyer asked all law enforcement personnel in the state to be on the alert for any suspicious deaths of domestic animals.

"You remember?"

Queenie remembered, annoyed that it had slipped her mind. Last spring, for the second year in a row, what appeared to be an adolescent Satanic cult had cropped up in the suburbs of Denver and by summer had spread to rural parts of the state. Dogs and cats were found in out-of-the-way places, throats slit, eyes gouged out. Males were castrated. There was talk of a cult belief that domestic animals were polluting the planet with their excrement.

"But the theory was," Queenie said, "that the kids did this in summer, when school was out and they had nothing better to do."

"You don't know when the deerhound was killed, do you? You only know when this quarry guy up in Springhill claims it went missing."

Queenie thought it over for a minute. "I'd better go up to Pearl Pass and take a look."

That evening she called the Clark brothers at their trailer home downvalley in El Jebel. "Ever been in the service, Fred?"

Fred Clark said he had been a corporal in the army.

"Then you know what it means to volunteer."

"Yes, ma'am."

"Corporal Clark, I need you or your brother to volunteer for a trip by snowmobile to Pearl Pass."

In 4 A.M. winter darkness, Queenie drove her rattly Jeep Wagoneer up to the T Lazy 7 Ranch not far from the base of the Maroon Bells. Harold Clark and Deputy Doug Larsen awaited her, dressed in blaze orange jackets so no rampaging hunter would mistake them for a mule deer or elk, as happened now and then in the blood-soaked past of these peaceful mountains.

A small black-and-white dog bounded out of Queenie's Jeep and began running in circles in the snow, barking happily.

"What's that?" Larsen asked.

"*That*, which I think deserves to be called *who*, is my Jack Russell terrier. Her name is Bimbo."

"Cute. Where do you propose to leave her?"

"She's coming with us."

"Surely you jest."

"If Mr. Clark, with the best of intentions," Queenie said, "takes us to the general area up near Pearl Pass but doesn't know the exact spot where he and his brother found the dog—what do we do? Search every square foot of the Elk Range above twelve thousand feet?" Bimbo rolled on her back on a patch of earth. "You get *her* within fifty yards of that dead deerhound's body and she'll be all over it. She's a major-league sniffer."

A half-moon cast shadows as the three searchers and dog set out on two snowmobiles. The roar of the engines on the narrow trail shattered the silence. Harold Clark rode behind Doug Larsen in the lead snowmobile. Queenie brought up the rear, with Bimbo strapped to her ample chest and wrapped in a blanket.

East of the Maroon Bells broad expanses of snow stretched for miles on either side of the trail. The dawn sky filled with chalky light. The snowmobiles climbed noisily to 12,500 feet. Forests below appeared as distant ink splotches, and great rocks thrust up out of the tundra. Vegetation was ragged, some mountainsides so scoured by wind they looked sandblasted. Queenie pointed to the south, where the snowpack of the Elk Range was marred by a long, ugly avalanche scar down its middle.

"A big one!" Queenie yelled.

The wilderness was awe-inspiring but only at your peril could you convince yourself it was friendly. In the Roaring Fork Valley each year several people died in avalanches. When tumbling snow came to rest, it settled in chunks that had the consistency of concrete. Last March some of that lovely white powder, hurtling downhill at speeds reaching a hundred miles an hour, had flung one cross-country skier into a grove of trees with sufficient force to decapitate her.

Not friendly.

The searchers began the long upward traverse around the cirque leading to the Continental Divide. The wind flung whirling wisps of snow along the surface of the track.

Soon after 9 A.M., Harold Clark raised a mittened hand and pointed. "Down there!" Larsen and Queenie cut their engines and dismounted. Larsen's wrist altimeter read 12,840 feet. They strapped their boots into snowshoes and moved downhill, Bimbo yipping and jumping at Larsen's heels.

An hour later, when Queenie called a halt, Harold Clark shrugged helplessly. "Sure looked like it was round here. We could see the Bells over there." Clark glanced round in all directions. "Might be upvalley a ways."

Clouds gathered and shadows fled. In the high country such changes could happen in the space of a few minutes. A few thousand feet below them, the winter sun shone through the mist, but near timberline the wind and whirling snow scoured exposed flesh. Reaching into a drift where Bimbo had floundered, Queenie gathered the terrier into her arms. I shouldn't have brought you, she thought. I was a wiseass. As usual, I knew more than anybody else.

An outcropping blocked their path. A dangerous cornice along the east side prevented the searchers from taking the lee, so they had to tramp around the west side in the full sweep of the wind.

Bimbo began to bark, then squirm. At first Queenie thought the terrier was frightened. But she wasn't quivering or whining.

"Bimbo, baby . . ." Bimbo kept squirming. "Cool it!"

But Bimbo refused to cool it. And then Queenie smiled. "You smell a dead dog, sweet girl?"

She let go and was struck by a rush of fear as the dog catapulted from her arms. Crusts of ice had been blown clear of the week's heavy fall. If the terrier slipped on one of those crusts, she would slide and keep sliding until she crashed into a tree.

"Bim-bo!"

The dog was white and small: difficult to see against fresh powder. She vanished into the forest of spruce, swallowed by dark blue shadows. Queenie plunged down after her, snowshoes ripping into the soft surface, with Larsen following and Clark lagging behind. The air was full of blown snow.

A small flash of white finally split the shadows. Queenie followed it. She heard a shout from behind. When she turned, Larsen was down, half of his body out of sight. Queenie plodded back through the chopped-up path of her own snowshoes and grabbed Larsen's wet parka with her glove. His mouth and mustache had filled with snow. He was no longer wearing a hat.

Larsen gasped. "That fucking dog of yours could kill us all!" Using his poles, he wrenched himself to one knee.

Queenie set out downhill into the forest of shadows. High in the cloudy sky above her a pair of dark red eagles rode the thermals. They had been known to hunt mountain goats and deer. Eagles, like the snow, were not always friendly.

From off to the left, Bimbo barked. Queenie yelled, "I'm coming, girl! Stay, Bimbo! You hear me?"

She reached the dog at a clearing on the edge of a meadow where a mound of snow about eight feet in diameter rose above the angle of the slope. Much of the snow had been torn away.

Not by Bimbo, Queenie realized. As soon as she was close she smelled something sickly sweet. Bimbo wheeled, whining, and dug with her small claws into a patch of exposed brown dirt. The wind moaned through the clearing.

Queenie hauled her avalanche shovel from her backpack. She began to dig. In a few minutes a stronger smell befouled the cold forest air. A bit of dark cloth showed. Queenie kept digging.

By the time Larsen reached her, she had scraped away a pack of dirt from dark blue nylon cloth. Chewed-on flesh appeared. Teeth gaped in what had been a mouth.

Larsen gasped, "You found it. I apologize to your mutt."

"No, I didn't find it," Queenie said.

Larsen looked puzzled. "I can see it."

Queenie said, "You're not seeing an *it*. Not a dog. Two mouths. And the teeth in one of them have gold fillings."

Above them stretched a lifeless zone of rocks and cold silence. Light sleet began to fall. Queenie said, "I'm declaring this a crime scene. Nothing to be touched within a distance of fifty yards. Not even a tree trunk. Got it?"

She was operating under what was called the Federal Incident Command System. She knew only that there were two human bodies in a stage of decomposition. Until it was proved otherwise, under the guidelines of the Pitkin County Sheriff's Office all unattended and unclassified death was considered homicide. In a black leather holster on her belt, besides a Smith & Wesson .357, a speed loader, and a pair of handcuffs, Queenie carried a two-way radio with fourteen channels. Her first signal on the emergency channel bounced off a repeater site downvalley and from there to the day-shift dispatcher in the Sheriff's Office in the Aspen courthouse. "Josh there?" Queenie asked.

In less than twenty seconds she had the sheriff on the radiophone. "Where are you, boss?"

"Men's Club luncheon at the Little Nell. Between the burritos and the chocolate mousse, with fifty citizens of the Aspen business community hanging on my every golden word." She heard a ripple of laughter in the background. "What's up, Deputy?"

"I'm about three miles from Pearl Pass," Queenie said, "and I have what appears to be two dead human bodies buried at a depth of four feet. The grave seems to have been disturbed by animals, and the bodies look to have been chewed up. Hard to say how long ago."

The sheriff grunted. "How's the weather?"

"Getting colder by the minute. I don't recall any reports of missing people last summer, or even last winter."

"Neither do I. Anyone was missing, we found 'em. Who's with you?"

She told him.

"Queenie, I'm appointing you incident commander. I'll go set up a management page from the courthouse. What do you need up there?"

"Food, the coroner, and a couple of insulated tents."

"Can a chopper get in to you?"

"Negative. I think we'll need CBI. And the IAI people."

CBI was the Colorado Bureau of Investigation, headquartered in Denver. IAI was the International Association for Identification. A Rocky Mountain division had been formed in 1976 after the Big Thompson Flood.

"Any ID on the bodies?"

"None visible."

"In about ten minutes," the sheriff said, "I'm going to get hold of all the available snowmobiles in the county, and send the coroner, and a deputy coroner, and pretty damn near all the people in our office that I can haul out of their beds and comas. Six of 'em will spend the night with you. Can you handle that, O'Hare?"

"Sure," Queenie said. "We can have a good party if someone brings beer."

6 *January 1994*

The Bear

EXCITED, APPREHENSIVE, NOT listening to anyone's advice, Dennis felt his heart pound as he sold his house in Westport quickly and cheaply. His real estate broker said, "Mr. Conway, the market is soft. If you were willing to wait another six months or so . . ."

Dennis said, "Don't you understand that I don't really care?" He sold his furniture to the first person who answered his ad in the *Times* and made an offer. There would always be money. He had a recession-proof profession, and there was nothing wrong with his health except twinges in one knee from the Vietcong mortar grenade fragment. He sold his Mercedes because he had already bought a stick-shift red Jeep Cherokee at Berthod Motors in Glenwood Springs. He shipped everything else, including mahogany desk, paintings, books, CD collection, law library, and an entire container full of children's toys, to Springhill.

He was upset when at almost the last minute his German housekeeper declined to make the move with him. His children were six and eight years old when they all moved West to live with Sophie Henderson. He sensed it would not be the easiest of adjustments. But if I'm happy, he reasoned, so will they be.

"Kids, the winter's long, but there's lots to do. We'll ski and ice-skate. You'll like the school—Sophie's one of the teachers. I know you'll miss your friends here, but you can call them, and when we come East you'll see them. And there'll be new kids. New friends."

Lucy and Brian seemed a little glum about these prospects.

Sophie's house was large and old, with separate bedrooms for each of them. It was warm, dry, and comfortable, with fireplaces and wood stoves that could burn without polluting the Rocky Mountains, deep easy chairs, sofas, and an oak dining room table large enough to seat a dozen people. Sophie kept a freezer in the garage—after the hunting season, village friends or family would give her part of an elk to keep there. Reading glasses parked on the end of her nose, with the aid of French cookbooks she cooked venison stews.

Oil paintings and watercolors hung in the house among sporting prints and Hockney and Matisse calendars, and Dennis thought the oils were as good as anything he had seen lately in the better New York galleries. One of the oils—nude bathers on the edge of a river in a dreamlike fire-consumed summer landscape—hung in their bedroom. "There's a little combination-lock wall safe behind it," Sophie said, "where I keep a few bearer bonds. And my private papers."

"What's the combination?" Dennis whispered in her ear.

"It's in my will," she said.

But it was the painting that held Dennis's attention. "Who did it? And the others? There doesn't seem to be a signature except that funny little green bird in the corner of each one."

"My former father-in-law," Sophie explained, "is named Harry Parrot. He's the town painter and eccentric. That bird is his signature. He's not terribly social, but I like him."

The children had brought their cats with them, a neutered male named Donahue and a spayed female named Sleepy. As soon as they were freed from their traveling cages, Donahue and Sleepy began sniffing their way around their new domain. Sophie already had a cat door installed in the kitchen.

Before school opened Dennis took the children to ski at Snowmass, where there was easy terrain. Sometimes, with Sophie, they went cross-country skiing on a trail that led into wilderness.

"Don't worry about them," Sophie said. "They'll adjust. Once they make friends you'll wonder why they're never home."

They had hired a nineteen-year-old girl to clean and be there when the children came home from school. Her name was Claudia Parrot; she was the painter's granddaughter. She had just graduated from Carbondale High.

"I'll be working most days in Aspen," Dennis said to her, "and Sophie's still going to teach at the school. The kids will need a lot of tender loving care. Can you do that, Claudia?"

"I love kids," Claudia said. "You know, if I didn't have this job I'd be working at the quarry, or down in Glenwood Springs as a supermarket checker. I'm grateful to you."

"She's perfect," Dennis said to Sophie.

"I remember when you talked about bringing in an au pair from Switzerland. I told you: you can have everything you want in Springhill except the New York Giants."

Dennis was a man of great optimism. "I'll have them too," he said, "when it comes time for the NFL play-offs."

He asked about her husband, Ben Parrot, who had been killed in an avalanche while heli-skiing in Canada. "You hardly ever mention him."

"It's been six years," Sophie said, pulling her hair back. "I don't want to sound cold, but his death was a shock, and I grieved for two years, and then I got over it. He was my second cousin. At a certain age we became sexually aware, and the other one just happened to be at hand and available. Sex led to marriage, marriage led to continuity . . . but there was something missing. It wasn't a passionate marriage. Ben was a good man, but he was far from a great mind, and he could be a bore."

Sophie had told Dennis that she and Ben had tried to have a child and failed. "Do you want to try with me?" Dennis asked.

"I'm sure it would be great fun trying"—Sophie's broad mouth curved in the smile that always touched his heart—"but I'm not really up for it. I feel too old."

"You're only thirty-seven. These days women have children well into their forties."

"I know, but . . ." She loosened her hair, letting it cascade around her face. "Lucy and Brian are enough to satisfy my maternal instinct. I love them, Dennis."

He was disappointed but it was not an issue he could press. Let it be, he instructed himself. You love her. Don't try to change her.

Almost right away Brian and Lucy cleaved to her and seemed to benefit from the harmony that was at the heart of her nature. She read to them from Dr. Seuss books, hauled them with her when she went shopping in Carbondale, and sent them on errands to the little general store in Springhill. She thanked them for helping, and hugged them. One day after school she had a snowball fight with Brian, and they banged into the house through the kitchen door, red-faced and laughing. She began teaching Lucy to play the violin.

Scott and Bibsy Henderson fell immediately into the role of grandparents and spoilers. Dennis was delighted, realizing that the children had lacked all that in Westport. He had been both father and mother to them for too long. Bibsy said to him, "We never thought it would happen. Sophie was so standoffish with men. Thank you, dear Dennis."

In February of 1994, a month after Dennis moved to Springhill and a year after he had met her on Aspen Mountain, he and Sophie were married at the Interfaith Chapel in Pitkin County. No honeymoon until spring, they agreed—let's give the kids time to settle in. Then they would board an Air France jet in Los Angeles and spend two weeks on the island of Mooréa in the South Pacific. "I fell in love with the name when I was a child," Sophie said.

"I'm glad you weren't taken by the cadence of Timbuktu," Dennis said, though he would have gone there or anywhere with her.

He drove to Aspen four or five days a week to his wood-paneled office at Karp & Ballard. On the wall he hung his law degree from Yale and his framed certification of membership in the National Association of Criminal Defense Lawyers. All that winter in the early mornings he heard the distant boom of explosions as ski patrols set off avalanches to clear the mountain slopes. By early March he was in court defending the seventeen-year-old son of a visiting film star on a drug-sale charge, and then a local bar owner on a DUI. He plea-bargained both cases before Judge Florian, the local district judge. Both his clients received suspended sentences. Dennis was pleased, and so were the clients.

New clients began to call. He began to feel he could make a living here—not a fortune, but enough to live on. That was enough. His ambitions and his vision of the future had changed.

In Springhill Dennis spent so much time with Sophie—talking, making love, listening to Mozart and Verdi in front of the log fire on winter and spring evenings—that he had little time for anyone else besides the children. Occasionally some friends came to dinner: Hank and Jane Lovell or Edward Brophy. The mountain hamlet was small. Life was simple. He had never seen a Springhill man wearing a jacket or tie, and the women, including Sophie, wore jeans not only to work but at home and in the evening. Yet there was nothing tawdry or common about them. In New York and Connecticut he had been accustomed to a physical cross-section of Americans, from the slim, beautiful, and fashionable to the weird, plain, and frighteningly obese. The inhabitants of his new hometown, however, were almost uniformly attractive and well formed. There seemed to be a simplicity about them and their lives that he grew more and more to admire. Within a few weeks Dennis had met all of Sophie's friends, neighbors, and family. She told him she had at least a dozen first and second cousins who lived in the town. "In fact, Oliver Cone is one of them."

"What does the town do about inbreeding?"

"As much as it can. Oliver is the result of inbreeding—the positive side of it. He's got a master's in hydraulic engineering. He's smart as a whip, although you wouldn't know it unless he trusts you, and the only people he trusts are Edward and those pals of his he goes hunting with. He's a first-rate bow hunter, did you know that? He supplies me with most of the venison every fall. He only works at the quarry because . . . well, because the quarry is a town-owned enterprise, and everyone pitches in."

Sophie paused. "But of course you're right. When I was younger I remember a girl who had an epileptic fit and died, and then there was a twelve-year-old boy who we couldn't control, and he had to be sent away. That was all unfortunate. Since then, as far as I know, we don't have any feebleminded Snopeses locked away in padlocked barns. We keep a good check on the family trees. We try to keep the bloodlines separate."

"Who was ever able to deal with teenagers in rut?"

"In a community like this, if there's a genetic risk, we have no misgivings about encouraging abortion. Obviously the kids can say no, and then there's nothing we can do. But they usually listen to reason."

Something about the concept, and the way Sophie expressed it, troubled Dennis. At first he didn't grasp it. Then it came to him.

"Who is the *we* you talk about? The *we* who keeps a check on family trees? The *we* who can 'do nothing about it.' Don't tell me it's part of the mayor's job."

"Believe it or not," Sophie said, "the town Water Board does it."

"The Water Board? Are you serious?"

"It's a small town. Just three hundred and fifty of us—anywhere else, we'd be a wide spot in the road. We don't have committees or agencies for every little thing. The Town Council handles the finances, the legislation, and the school and the quarry. The Volunteer Fire Department deals with emergencies, organizes holidays, and does avalanche control in the town and even on the road down to Redstone. So everything else, like pollution control, and even genetics, got dumped on the Water Board. It just fell out that way. Kind of elegant, I think."

Dennis nodded, silent. What did it matter? What did it have to do with the new heart of his life?

Some evenings Sophie read poetry aloud. She read Wordsworth and Mallarmé to him. She had taught herself French with videos from the Pitkin County Library. He loved the sound of her voice; its clarity was like that of a lightly struck gong. And at least three or four times a week she played the lovely dark violin kept in the battered leather case. She caressed its gleaming wood and its taut strings. Her playing captivated Dennis. Whatever cares the world still inflicted on him vanished. He was borne away to a womblike place where he seemed to drift in warm, slow-moving water.

"Sometimes," he admitted, "when I shut my eyes, I could go to sleep while you play."

"Do," Sophie said, her eyes bright with pleasure. "I wouldn't mind. Music can take you to another world. And it can reach you while you sleep."

Dennis had sometimes watched television at night when he lived alone, and before, when he had been married to Alma, but he realized one day that here in the mountains he rarely turned on the TV except for a movie on PBS or a sporting event that he couldn't resist. His real world was sunny and celebratory—entertainment enough.

Before meeting Sophie he had considered himself a sexually sophisticated man. He had been a bachelor for many years before his marriage to Alma, had made love to many women. One of his long-term partners in New York had been a French art magazine editor, another a dark-skinned psychiatrist from Brazil. He had always been willing to experiment, and on several occasions had made love with two women together. But he was never arrogant about his sexuality. Like most men, he believed he was a good lover. Women had told him so—why doubt it? Even more, he had been fortunate in having experiences with women who were skilled in the arts of love. It *was* a skill, he'd begun to see. It was not always enough to follow your instincts. You could learn. You could experiment. You could go beyond the ordinary.

And now there was Sophie. Whatever he thought he knew before about womanliness and sex, with Sophie he was reeducated. There seemed to be nothing that she wouldn't do or didn't know how to do. The bedroom was her dominion. By candlelight, they romped. In the dark, she whispered in his ear and conjured images of all his fantasies. And yet despite her skills, everything was achieved with the delight of carnal freshness. He wondered where such knowledge came from.

After making love, if it was not too cold they would walk out on the deck together. "To let the starlight wash our eyes," Sophie said. At nine thousand feet the darkness was absolute. The stars were diamond hard in their brilliance and seemed to give off a faint hum. From the mountain fastness came the howl of coyotes, which occasionally woke the children. On starry nights a nesting owl hooted, and on warmer nights as spring moved toward summer they heard deer or elk moving through the brush.

"Are there grizzly bears around here?" Brian asked.

"Black bear," Sophie said. "In the winter, they hibernate. Now that it's spring you can see tracks and fresh droppings. And in summer you might spot one or two young ones on the other side of the creek. They won't come near the house unless they're really hungry."

One night in April Dennis was awakened by a series of thuds behind the kitchen. The heavy-duty green plastic garbage cans stood unprotected in the snow next to Sophie's Blazer and his Cherokee. A quarter moon hung clear and brilliant above the mountains. Dennis peered out from the upstairs window and saw a large animal nuzzling at one of the garbage cans. A neighbor kept cows and often forgot to close the barn.

He looked at his watch: not yet midnight. The remains of a log fire glowed in the living room fireplace, and the room was still warm. He put on his toweled bathrobe and padded downstairs. Shadows danced on the walls as he took a flashlight off the kitchen counter. Hearing a soft footfall above him, he turned. Brian stood on the staircase, wearing his red flannel pajamas with pictures of Mickey Mouse and Pluto.

"I heard something, Daddy."

"I think a cow's poking around in the garbage. We threw out all those delicious chicken teriyaki bones from supper, remember? Let's go look."

With Brian at his side, Dennis opened the kitchen door—the bitter cold night air struck them a solid blow. He stepped outside, flicked on the beam of the flashlight, and said, "Shoo!"

A black bear turned its great head toward him. It crouched on all fours by the laden garbage cans. Its eyes, crimson buttons in the yellow cone of the flashlight beam, suddenly and unaccountably blazed with what struck Dennis as malevolence. Dennis smelled the animal's meaty breath. It took a shuffling step toward them. Dennis shoved Brian behind him. The boy screamed and wet himself.

Dennis could never afterward recall where he had read or heard what to do, but some clear memory lay rooted in his mind. The white toweling bathrobe was only loosely knotted. Rising on tiptoes, he thrust his arms up and to the sides. *Look larger*, he remembered. At the same time he lowered his eyes to avoid challenging the animal.

The bear turned and shuffled off quickly into the darkness of the forest.

For a month, whenever Dennis spoke to friends and family in the East, he related the story, although he left out the part about Brian's wetting his Disney World pajama pants. He began to feel like some kind of modern-day mountain man—nearly naked under the moon and sharing the turf with Neighbor Bear. An adventurer, a former city boy happily out of his element: this image pleased him.

7 *May 1994*

Trust Me

BRIAN REMEMBERED HIS stepmother had told him the town of Springhill was named after a nearby warm-water spring.

"You said it was a special place, and you promised to show it to us. Why is it special?"

"When we go there, I'll show you."

Brian kept nagging, and early on a Sunday morning in May Sophie announced that she would escort him and his sister and his father through the woods to the spring.

"Grab your snowshoes, gang."

During the night it had snowed four inches of corn snow. The snowshoes had been Sophie's Christmas present to everybody. The family tramped through the property and across the creek and onto a path that led into the forest. There they halted and strapped on the snowshoes. A hundred yards deeper into the forest they came to a sturdy wire gate set into a four-foot-high barbed-wire fence that snaked between the trees as far as they could see. The gate was padlocked with a combination lock.

Sophie twirled the dials. With a snap, the lock sprang free.

"This isn't your land, is it?" Dennis asked.

"No, this is village land."

"How come you know the combination? Is that one of the mayor's privileges?"

"Every adult in Springhill knows it."

"If every adult knows it, why bother locking the gate? To keep out the children?"

"The path leads to the spring, and then beyond to Indian Lake. We don't want strangers poking around here."

"Sophie, in case you haven't noticed, strangers don't come to Springhill."

"Valley people go hiking in summer. Do you think they know which creeks contribute to a drinking water supply and which don't? They can contaminate without realizing it."

She plunged ahead in the snow, where drifting powder had piled up in some places as high as her head. The pines were hung with tufts of snow and the blue sky shone through branches like a winter postcard on a drugstore rack.

"There," Sophie said, pointing to a small hill, a thin waterfall that dropped perhaps a dozen feet from a rocky ledge, and a stream below. Only three feet wide, the stream coursed turbulently along its bed for fifty feet, widened briefly into a pool of five feet in diameter, and then disappeared in an abrupt dogleg into the hillside. Its surface carried moss and ferns, some rotting branches, and dark vegetation.

"That's the spring?" Dennis asked. "That skinny waterfall and rivulet? And the hill? That's what the town is named for?"

"The spring is hidden. The water you see is about eighty degrees Fahrenheit. In summer it goes up to eighty-five. That pool you see used to be quite a bit bigger, and people sometimes bathed there. Come. I'll show you something else."

There was no path, but she knew exactly where she was heading. Dennis and the children followed. A tumbledown cabin showed itself suddenly against a small mound of dirt.

Lucy said, "The wicked witch lives here!"

"No," Brian cried. "She lives in a castle! This is a poor woodcutter's cabin."

"No one lives here now," Sophie explained, smiling. "But many years ago, a miner did. William Lovell, an ancestor of Hank Lovell, our friend who manages the quarry. That man, Hank's ancestor, was one of the first settlers in this part of the range."

Brian's eyes grew wide. "Is there still some gold here?"

"Mr. Lovell mined copper, not gold, and his little mine, which used to be on the side of that hill, was called El Rico—Spanish for 'the rich one.' The copper gave out about twenty years ago. No one works the mine anymore. Now I'll show you some of the reasons it's special. Sometimes, odd things happen around here."

"Scary things?" Brian asked quickly.

"No." Sophie put one gloved hand on each of the children's shoulders. "Take off your snowshoes. Come into the cabin with me."

The children followed her. Dennis, lingering a few feet behind them, watched. The old cabin was dark. Its sod roof had been replenished several times during its more than century-old lifetime. The floorboards creaked.

"Which one of you is taller?" Sophie asked.

"You know I am," Brian said. "By two inches."

"One," Lucy said.

Sophie nodded. "Stand back-to-back."

The children stood inside the cabin in winter morning shadow on the old plank floor, which seemed perfectly level. Sophie pressed the backs of their heads together.

"Dennis, you be the judge. Which of them is taller?"

"Whatever they're standing on," he said, "makes them seem the same height."

"I'm two inches taller," Brian insisted. "Well, maybe one and a half."

"The floor must slope," Dennis said, puzzled.

"Why didn't I think of that?" Sophie asked. From the deepest pocket of her parka she took out an old tennis ball. Bending, she placed it on the floor just a few inches past Brian's feet. The ball rolled slowly toward Lucy and bounced against her heel.

"If the ground slopes the way that ball rolls," Sophie said, "then Brian should look a lot taller than Lucy. Even more than two inches."

"The whole cabin must be on a slant," Dennis said. But even as he said it, he knew that the words and the concept made no sense. He was baffled.

Sophie picked up the tennis ball. "Look at me."

Clasping her hands high in the air, she leaned far to the left. Her body canted at an angle that seemed impossible; it seemed that she should fall to the floor.

"Cool," Brian said.

"Wait a minute," Dennis said. "That's *weird*. How are you able to do that?"

Sophie straightened up again, offering no explanation of the impossible angle she had assumed. "Come outside."

There in the woods she said, "Strange things happen here. And strange things *don't* happen here. In summer, for example, there are no birds. They don't fly over these trees and they don't land in the branches. They make a detour around the whole area. And look at the trees. What do you see?"

Some of the aspens were twisted like gray corkscrews.

"In the summer," Sophie continued, "squirrels jump from one of those trees to another, and often they miss the branch they're jumping for."

"You've *seen* this?" Dennis asked.

"Yes, I have."

"Give me a rational explanation. What's the nature of this place?"

Sophie led them back through the snow toward the distant gate. "Some say the deep veins of copper cause all these odd things to happen. Others say that thousands of years ago a dense meteorite struck here. It's supposed to be embedded not too far below the surface. There's a magnetism we can't explain. The gravity is out of whack."

"Who told you that?" Dennis asked.

"A geologist from the University of Colorado came here. That was before my time, but I heard all about his conclusions. I imagine he's right, but who knows?"

"You're a teacher," Brian said. "You should know why this place is funny."

"You're right. I should know, but I don't." She touched Brian's cheek. "There are some things in life you can't explain. You can theorize, you can speculate, but you can't reach a scientific conclusion. Maybe it's all an optical illusion."

Brian turned to the supreme authority. "Dad, what do you think?"

"I don't know what to think," Dennis said. "I've lived in New York and I thought I'd seen it all. Obviously I haven't." He laughed, and so did Sophie, and it was infectious: the children began to jump around in the snow and fall down and say, "I'm a squirrel and I can't find my branch!"

But Dennis's laughter hid his puzzlement. It was more than puzzlement: he couldn't yet find a name for what he felt. Something about the place disturbed him deeply, and he was glad to go.

The huge snowpack on the back range melted so slowly that even in late May it was still piled to a height of four or five feet in the forest surrounding the Conways' home. Lucy came to Dennis at the breakfast table in the kitchen, where he was having a Saturday midmorning cup of coffee and doing the crossword puzzle in the national edition of the *New York Times*.

Lucy said mournfully, "Donahue is gone."

"Are you sure?" Dennis put his pen down and looked up. "He could be in one of the sweater drawers, like the last time you thought he was missing."

"No, Daddy, he's gone. He didn't sleep with me last night. I've looked everywhere."

"When did you last see him?"

"Last night after supper. I fed him and Sleepy."

"And where is Sleepy now?"

"On your big chair that you like to watch football in."

"If Donahue was really gone, do you suppose Sleepy would just go to sleep like that? Wouldn't she be out looking for him?"

Lucy began to cry. "Daddy, you're making fun of me, and I'm trying to tell you that Donahue is gone."

Dennis hugged his daughter, then got up and tested the cat door to make sure it hadn't jammed. It swung freely.

"Let's go look for him, sweetheart," he said.

Sophie was in town at a Town Council meeting. Dennis and Lucy, soon joined by Brian, searched the house. They looked everywhere, including a chest of drawers that contained T-shirts and long johns, and the tops of Sophie's closets where soft woolen sweaters were piled.

In the nearby meadow and forest Dennis showed the children how to conduct a logical search in ever-widening ovals. They tramped through snow and mud, searching for paw prints, calling Donahue's name and making hissing noises. They peered up trees and poked under bushes. They found nothing.

"He'll turn up by nightfall," Dennis said, "as soon as he gets hungry."

In the evening when Sophie returned home they all went round to their various neighbors to ask if anyone had seen a gray-and-white medium-sized cat without a collar. Sophie's parents, Scott and Bibsy, lived just to the north along the creek. They had seen nothing.

The neighbor with the cows was an older woman named Mary Crenshaw. Her husband had run the town's tiny funeral parlor and been part-time police chief. He had died several months ago and his son had inherited both jobs. Mary Crenshaw rarely came out except to shop for food and quantities of port wine that the general store carried on its back shelves. Dennis had noticed that few Springhillers drank to excess; this sobriety had impressed him.

"Better let me talk to her," Sophie said. "She's odd."

Dennis and the children waited outside on Mary Crenshaw's porch. They heard Sophie inside asking about the missing cat. Dennis thought he heard her say, a little louder, "The tweeds' yank tomker, Mary. Zacky and grease . . ." He could make even less sense out of Mrs. Crenshaw's reply.

Sophie came out of the house. "She hasn't seen Donahue, but she'll keep her eye peeled."

"What was it that you asked her?" Dennis asked. "I couldn't make head or tail out of it."

"She's an old woman," Sophie said. "She slurs her words."

"It was you I heard, Sophie. It was like gobbledygook."

The children had gone off to make hissing and clicking noises among the pines behind Mary Crenshaw's house, hoping the cat would respond.

"Dennis, darling, please. I've had a long day and I'm upset. I don't think we're going to find Donahue."

In the next few days Dennis scoured the woods in the search for a body, or remains, or even for a bit of fur. He found nothing.

Lucy came to him a week later, with Sleepy cradled in her arms. "Maybe," she said, "Donahue fell in love with another girl kitty and she lived somewhere else, like you did with Sophie. So he went there to be with her. Do you think so, Daddy?"

"That's a definite possibility."

"And he might come back one day to visit."

"Yes, he might."

"Or for good, if he stops liking the other girl kitty."

"Yes, darling, that could happen," Dennis said, "but don't count on it."

• • •

He had planned to take Sophie to the South Seas in June for their be-
lated honeymoon. They would do nothing except swim off the reef of
Mooréa and sail outrigger canoes and eat tropical fruit and make love.

The plan included leaving the children with Sophie's parents. Taking his cue from Sophie, Dennis said, "I don't think the kids will miss
us. By June they'll have friends."

But by May it hadn't happened. The children clung to him more
and more. They came home from school with or without Sophie and
did their homework, and played with each other and the cats, and
watched television when it was allowed. After Donahue's disappear-
ance, they played only with Sleepy.

"Why aren't they making friends?" Dennis asked Sophie.

"It takes time. The village kids are clubby."

"What can we do?"

"Let it work itself out."

"I don't like to just do *nothing*. It's not my nature."

"Dennis, you can't change your children's social lives. They'll do it
themselves, when they're ready, in their own way. Parents only stand
and wait, like civilians on the home front in a protracted war. It's difficult, it's frustrating, but that's the only way that makes sense in the
long run."

Sometimes he felt that Sophie had wisdom and knowledge beyond
her years.

"You love them," she said, "and they know that. Be supportive and
instructive, not interfering. Let them work out their own destiny."

"I hate to fly off to Tahiti if things are like this."

"Air France is a friendly airline—they'll let you change the reserva-
tions. Let's wait until winter."

"Life is short," he said. "Usually when you postpone things you
want to do, it's a mistake."

Sophie was silent for a long moment, as if she were struggling with
a concept or wanted to say something but wasn't sure it was the right
time to say it. Then she sighed and said, "When you genuinely believe that good things will happen, it works out to be that way. I know.
Trust me."

All right, he decided. I can do that. And I will.

8 *June 1994*

Under the Full Moon

WHEN DENNIS FIRST unpacked his luggage in Springhill the locals referred to him as the new lawyer. The new lawyer had skied cross-country to Owl Creek with Edward Brophy. Restless fellow, the new lawyer: did you see him walking through the village in the middle of the night?

As he settled in, his title changed to "Sophie's man." You heard?—Sophie's man helped June Loomis in an argument with a garage owner in Glenwood Springs. Didn't charge her a penny. Those kids of Sophie's man had been hunting for a lost cat.

Dennis smiled at the quaintness, but it faintly annoyed him that he lacked a name. He understood there was no malice intended. People held aloof from him in some ways, but he felt they liked him. He sensed he was being tested: the villagers were waiting to get to know him better before accepting him. He had to serve his apprenticeship.

Mountain life was wholly unlike the electric and frenetic world he had known in New York. People were calm, unhurried. He was fascinated by the village, had never dreamed he would—or could—live in such a quiet, remote place, no matter how beautiful. Sometimes he wondered if after a time he would grow tired of it and yearn for the dynamism of the city he had thrived on for so many years. He realized he had cast his lot with Sophie; had accepted, at least for a while, a dependency. But it had not been out of weakness. Love had not blinded him: he'd made a clear-cut choice to change his world. To change, to grow. To learn.

But there were peculiarities about his new mountain home, and he needed to come to grips with them.

He went to Sophie with his questions and soon grasped that Sophie was not quite as forthcoming as he might have liked—indeed, as he felt he deserved—when it came to talking about her past life in Springhill and the people of the village. When he probed too deeply in either of those areas, her common answer was, "One day soon, my sweet, I'll tell you. Not now."

Dennis thought his questions were innocent enough. "You know," he said one Sunday morning while he squeezed fresh orange juice, "I've noticed something about the people here. They seem to be in unusually good physical condition. Robust—active—cheerful."

Sophie smiled at him from the stove, where she was cooking pancakes. "Clean mountain air does it."

"And maybe clean living. I don't know a soul up here who smokes except Harry Parrot. And no one really carouses or whoops it up on the weekends, not even the teenagers. Remarkable. Reassuring, and delightful. But . . ."

Sophie looked up the stairs, where there were sounds of activity. "Dennis, you promised to take the kids biking today."

"And I will, I will . . . let me finish this first. Just about everyone in town is healthy and vigorous. No invalids. No one seems gloomy or depressed. Isn't that so?"

"I suppose it is," Sophie said.

"Are they all on Prozac?"

Sophie laughed and set out the maple syrup and applesauce. "You'd have to ask Grace Pendergast. But I don't think she'd breach medical ethics and tell you."

"Jack Pendergast told me that Grace complains all the time—says she's got hardly anything to do except give kids polio shots and treat broken bones at the quarry. And yet here's what's peculiar." He had thought about this often, but shunted it aside. "There are no very old people here. Everyone seems to die off more or less in their seventies. If everyone is so healthy, which seems to be the case, then that doesn't make sense."

"The investigative legal mind strikes again."

"Don't you see what I mean?"

"I never truly noticed it," Sophie said.

"Come on, darling. Every town always has a few ancient geezers. But here, where everyone is physically vigorous, there isn't one old fogy sitting on a porch in a creaky rocking chair. They get to be seventy or thereabouts, and *bang*"—Dennis snapped his fingers—"they just *go*. As if by appointment."

Sophie said nothing.

"When did your grandparents die?" he asked.

She considered for a while. "My maternal grandparents died in their mid-seventies, I guess. My paternal grandmother died young— cancer of the uterus. But my father's father—a wonderful man—lived to be eighty-five. Dennis, you're like a dog worrying a bone. As a matter of fact, a few months before you got here, a woman named Ellen Hapgood died at the age of ninety-one. Before that, she sat in her rocking chair talking to herself all day long and swatting imaginary bats with a broom. Scott and Bibsy, I'm sure, will live a long life. That's Brian upstairs, knocking into chairs. He's trying to get your attention."

Dennis took Sophie's arms in a firm grasp. He was not willing to be sidetracked this time.

"One more thing. What's this second language all about?"

He had heard it the first time outside Mary Crenshaw's house when he and the children hunted for the missing cat. Sophie had said, "She's an old woman. She slurs her words." But Dennis heard odd words spoken again. Oliver Cone, walking down the road from the town gym with one of his pals, had pointed to a large-breasted girl and sniggered something about her "socker muldunes." Dennis had also learned that in Springhill a car was often a "horker," an apple was a "babcock," and a deer rifle was a "boshe gun."

"I've begun to pick up on it," Dennis said. "I know that when something is good quality it's 'bahler.' I even know that 'mollies and ose' are tits and ass. So tell me, Sophie—what's that all about?"

"It's been around forever," Sophie said. "It's called Springling."

"And you speak it, of course."

"Since I was a child. It gets passed from one generation to another."

"Then why is everyone secretive about it? Why did you never mention it to me?"

"I was waiting for the right time, and I guess this is it." Sophie smiled. "It originated in California and was brought here around the turn of the century by some miners. At first it was a children's language, so their parents wouldn't know what they were talking about. But it caught on. We speak it . . . sometimes. Give me a barney," she said.

"What's a barney?"

"A kiss. It's your reward for being so einy and bilchy."

"Which means . . . ?"

"Smart and sexy."

"Will you teach the language to me?"

Sophie hesitated.

"Why not?" Dennis asked. "I live here, don't I? I'm your husband."

"Yes, I'll teach it to you," she said. "But don't let anyone know you understand it. People here are funny about some things. They like you to live here awhile before they let you in on their secrets. Will you agree to that?"

Dennis thought it was odd, but he agreed.

"Bahl. Now where's the barney you promised me?"

He kissed her and would have done more if the children had not thundered down the stairs.

A few weeks later, on a Saturday night in June, Dennis couldn't sleep. He was concerned about a real estate case in Aspen that had taken a wrong turn. He went down to the kitchen, microwaved a leftover cup of coffee, and settled into a big easy chair in the living room. He made notes on a legal pad for nearly a hour. By the time he had finished he was still wide awake, and since it was a bright night with a warm breeze coming from the south, he decided to go for a walk on the path by the creek.

Mountain people retired early. At nearly midnight, under a full moon, the world at Springhill seemed sound asleep. The path along the creek led to his in-laws' house and land. The moon cast strong shadows. Dennis strolled through the darkness, listening to water bounding over rocks—the spring meltdown reaching its zenith. A night breeze hummed overhead through the pines. He took deep breaths of the thin air.

The Hendersons' house was a huge A-frame, and the first thing Scott showed visitors was his party-sized redwood hot tub squatting on the deck outside. Fifty yards from the house itself, Dennis saw that lights were on upstairs and downstairs. Blurred light from the patio broke through the ponderosa pines. Then he heard voices.

The blue-gray shadows of a clump of firs cloaked his presence. The roar of the creek drowned out the sound of his footsteps. He could see the hot tub now, steam rising. It was ringed with candles. Naked people moved about in the tub, and he heard throaty laughter.

Somebody's broken into the property, he thought. Scott and Bibsy must have gone to Denver, and the kids from town decided to have a hell of a good time. But when his eyesight adjusted to the distance and the flickering light of the candles, he saw that the people in the tub were not kids from town. He heard warmer, softer, older voices.

The back door to the house opened. Rich strains of a Mozart flute concerto flowed from the living room. Bibsy stepped out of the house, a man's arm encircling her waist. She wore a white robe half open, trailing along the dark red hand-rubbed Mexican tiles of the terrace. Under the robe Dennis could see she was naked.

The man with his arm about her waist was also naked. He was short, well built, with a silvery gray beard. It was Edward Brophy, the dentist, Sophie's good friend whom Dennis had first met on Aspen Mountain. Dennis's gaze shot back to the tub, where he saw Scott in the steamy water with two men and two other women.

Realizations flowed into him so rapidly that he had trouble sorting them out. He recognized the women in the tub: one was Grace Pendergast, the town doctor—a handsome, dominating woman with black hair and cool blue eyes. The other was Rose Loomis, a plump and sexy widow who ran the Springhill general store with the help of her two children.

His father-in-law, Scott Henderson, was in the hot tub, kissing the breast of Rose Loomis while with his other arm he fondled Grace Pendergast. Grace's husband, Jack Pendergast, a retired building contractor, was behind Rose Loomis, sitting on the edge of the tub. He was grunting, rocking back and forth.

My God, Dennis realized. He's *fucking* her.

Jack Pendergast had to be even older than Scott. The other man who sat on the edge of the tub, naked, clutching a bottle of vodka, was Harry Parrot, the painter.

An orgy. Decorous, well-behaved, with Mozart for background music—an orgy on a warm summer night for a select group of Springhill's senior citizens.

Dennis chuckled, knowing he couldn't be heard. He was seeing it; he wasn't hallucinating. In moonlight the bodies, though far from young, had a sculpted beauty. The men were muscular. The women moved with light, quick steps. Rose Loomis looked like Botticelli's Venus rising from the sea.

Dennis retreated. He was not a voyeur: this knowledge had come to him by accident. He walked home along the creek, still shaking his head.

Back in his kitchen he brewed coffee, then sat on the porch, drinking and watching the serene light of the stars. The night air was soft, the color of the sky somewhere between royal blue and velvety black-violet.

He decided he would not tell Sophie—after all, Scott and Bibsy were her parents.

But when he finally went to bed he was still stimulated by what he had seen. He woke Sophie and made love to her in the darkness.

The next day he mulled over what he'd seen.

They were free, he decided, and certainly old enough to choose. If I'm lucky enough to reach that age, please let me be that open-minded and physically vigorous.

Bless them!

A few evenings later he was watching the NBA finals on television while his children played on the lawn by the creek. The June days were warm and dry. An occasional evening thunderstorm struck the back range and the nights following were always fresh. The mountains became greener every day, the grass turning from viridian toward emerald.

He heard the smooth rumble of Sophie's car approaching on the dirt road. She had gone to the village for a joint meeting of the Water Board with the Town Council, which she chaired. These meetings, which took place at least once a week, puzzled him. Sophie always attended them. Earlier that evening he'd said, "Sweetheart, tell me—how much business does a village of three hundred and fifty people have to discuss? I don't think the mayor of New York is as busy as you are, and he's got nine million disgruntled city dwellers to keep in line. What goes on here? Are you worried about being reelected?"

Sophie laughed warmly. Small communities, she explained, were the worst when it came to civic matters. There were endless debates about taxes, allocation of the budget, rezoning suggestions, equipment for the gym, school repairs and change of curriculum—the quarry business, road repair—the list went on.

"How long is your term as mayor?"

"We have a peculiar system. I wasn't elected, I was appointed by . . . well, I suppose you'd call it a council of elders. There's no set term. I stay mayor as long as I want to and as long as they like the job I do. It could last a long time."

"And you don't get paid for it."

"Of course not. It's an honor. And a community obligation. Does it bother you?" Her forehead knitted in a light frown. "When I met you, you told me you were impressed."

"I'm still impressed. I'm not suggesting you be a hausfrau. I'm just trying to figure out how things work in this village. It's not easy, you know. It's . . . different here."

He was still thinking about that when Sophie returned from the meeting. Dennis saw right away that something was wrong. He hit the mute button on the remote.

"What is it?"

"Jack Pendergast died of a heart attack."

"Jack? My God, I just saw him—"

He stopped. The nocturnal sighting of Jack and the others in the hot tub was something he had resolved to keep to himself.

"He was so damned healthy," he said.

"There was no warning."

Two days later they attended the funeral. Almost the whole adult population of the town was at the little cemetery on the edge of the forest. Jack Pendergast had been a popular man who had helped build many of the newer homes for younger couples. Grace Pendergast was doctor and friend to everyone.

Dennis thought of Jack as he had last seen him in the tub at the Hendersons', sharing his wife and Rose Loomis with Scott while Bibsy cavorted in an upstairs bedroom with the town dentist.

The sun shone from a blue sky surrounded by slow-moving cumulus. There was no church in Springhill. Grace, as the widow, conducted the ceremony. Hank Lovell, Oliver Cone, and two young men lowered the casket into the earth. On top of it Grace placed a stone, a handful of earth, and a small clear glass of water.

"We are here to affirm Jack's departure," she said. "We loved him, and we know he loved us. Jack left with full acceptance. The bond between us lives on."

A few people murmured; everyone nodded. Grace inclined her head toward the young men, and they shoveled earth on top of the casket. No more was said.

Dennis and Sophie walked home along a road bordered by wildflowers and unruly June grass. "What a peculiar little speech Grace made," Dennis observed.

"I thought it was fine," Sophie said.

" 'Jack left with full acceptance.' What's that mean? The poor guy died of a heart attack. Grace wasn't even around when it happened. Why does she think he accepted that kind of sudden end to his life? He might well have been in pain. How old was he? Early seventies? That's not old to go. Certainly, these days, too young to go with what she called 'full acceptance.' "

Sophie remained silent. After a few moments Dennis understood that she was not going to answer his question. He looked at her, and in that same instant, as they continued walking down the dirt road, her hand sought his and clasped it. Her head turned toward him. Her dark eyes, reflecting the sun, were exceptionally clear. Certainty beamed from them—beamed with such strength that Dennis felt reassured. She was answering his question; there was no doubt of it. Her smile and her whole being was saying to him: *You will see. You will soon understand.* Almost without realizing he was doing it, he nodded to her. He felt satisfied. He could not have explained why.

9
November 28, 1994

A Deputy Pays a Visit

THE WEEK FOLLOWING Thanksgiving, the official opening of the ski season, a snowstorm struck the Roaring Fork Valley like a beast thundering out of the wilderness. It began in the late afternoon and snowed heavily all night. Then it stopped, and the skies cleared. In the morning the slopes of Aspen Mountain were covered with ten inches of dry powder. The hardpack below those ten inches was already three feet deep. The temperature at the base of the mountain was fifteen degrees, and there was no wind. The blue sky was bright enough to hurt the eyes of anyone foolish enough not to wear goggles or good sunglasses. These were perfect skiing conditions.

Dennis finished the work on his desk by midmorning, grabbed skis, poles, boots, and ski suit from his locker at the law offices of Karp & Ballard, and prepared to tackle the mountain. He told Lila Hayes, his secretary, that he would be back at his desk by two in the afternoon.

"But, Dennis, if we want to reach you—"

"That will be difficult."

You had to draw the line somewhere, he believed. And when it came to carrying a cellular phone while he carved his way across the fall lines of Aspen Mountain, he drew it firmly.

At noon he boomed down the lower slope of Little Nell. In a blinding spray of white powder, he swung to a hockey stop. He was shouldering his skis and heading for the gondola when Lila Hayes appeared in his vision, bundled in a pale blue Norwegian sweater and wearing a Rockies baseball cap. She waved at him, but she wasn't smiling.

"What happened, Lila?"

"Your wife called." She saw his expression. "No, she's all right, and your children are fine. It's her mother."

He felt a flash of guilt following the vast relief. Stroke, he thought. Heart attack, broken hip. He had seen Bibsy at the senior citizens' orgy in the hot tub, a memory to cherish. And last New Year's Eve he had heard Scott Henderson refer to her as "that sexy blonde in the red dress, the one I've been married to forever and I'm still crazy about"— but even with all that, she was still vulnerable to the flaws of age.

Lila steered him down the steps toward the street and the law offices. "Sophie said that a couple of Pitkin County sheriff's deputies came up to Springhill to talk to her. To your mother-in-law, I mean. She didn't say what it was about."

Again he felt relief; Bibsy was all right. But he was puzzled. "Deputies? What for?"

"Can't be anything serious unless she's a secret drug lord of the western slope. But Sophie said to drop whatever you're doing and come up there. And call her right away."

Dennis didn't bother changing clothes except from ski boots into shoes so he could drive. On the highway, even before he reached the western outskirts of Aspen, he speed-dialed through on the car phone to his home. The answering machine came on after two rings, and he heard the beginning of Sophie's message. It was brief, without frills: no chanting children or music preceded it. He hung up and dialed his in-laws' number.

Sophie answered. "Yes?"

"It's me. What's going on?"

"Where are you?"

"In the car, just west of Aspen. Lila gave me your message at the gondola."

"I wish you would come here and deal with this."

"I am. I'm on the way. Is it true that two Pitkin County deputies were there?"

"Still are."

"To see your mother?"

"Exactly."

"Why?"

Sophie didn't answer. She wasn't alone, he deduced.

"They haven't accused her of doing anything illegal, have they?"

"Not yet."

"Where's your father?"

"Right here."

"Can't he handle it?"

"Dennis, just please get here as soon as you can. And be careful. The roads have been plowed but they could be icy."

She hung up.

Between the airport and the turnoff to Snowmass Mountain, Dennis battled his way through the Pitkin County switchboard and a secretarial deputy to Josh Gamble at the Sheriff's Office.

"Josh, I'm in my car heading downvalley. I've just had an off-the-wall conversation with Sophie. Two of your deputies are at her parents' home in Springhill, talking to her mother about I-don't-know-what. Did Beatrice Henderson get picked up in your bailiwick on any sort of charge? Like a DUI?"

He heard a crackling silence on the telephone.

"Josh . . . you there?"

"Yeah, I'm here."

"What's going on?"

The sheriff said, "I don't think I can discuss this with you on the phone, unless you're calling as Beatrice Henderson's lawyer."

Dennis let that steep for a few seconds. "Does she *need* a lawyer?"

"If you're calling as her lawyer, Dennis, I'll see you here in my office and I'll talk to you. If you're just fishing for what I know, then, like I said, I think I'd better put an end to this conversation."

Dennis felt a vestige of Irish temper rising in him. "Are you pulling my chain? I'm asking about my sixty-five-year-old mother-in-law! Is this some kind of practical joke?" He calmed down; it never paid to raise your voice to the law, even if the law was friendly. "I was up on Ajax on the best powder day of the year."

"It's not a joke," Josh said.

"Is she accused of something?"

"I can't talk about it. I have to go. Don't take it personally."

Dennis heard the buzz of a dead line. First his wife, and now his oldest friend had hung up on him. It was not a good day.

Outside the closed garage doors of the Hendersons' house were Sophie's gray Chevy Blazer, a Pitkin County Sheriff's Department black gold-trimmed Jeep, and a third car, a snow-covered pickup truck that Dennis didn't recognize.

No one in Springhill locked a front door. Dennis stepped into the warm hallway of the house, and Scott Henderson, bronzed from the winter sun, emerged from the living room to greet him. His handshake was hard as a chunk of wood. His mouth was drawn down now at the corners, but he spoke calmly, as if this were a normal occasion and his son-in-law had arrived for a dinner party. "Glad you could make it, Dennis."

Dennis put an arm around Scott's shoulder. "What's Bibsy done? Run a red light?"

"We'll talk about it," Scott said.

"Wait a second. Is she all right?"

"Come inside."

Dennis found his mother-in-law sitting next to Sophie on the living room sofa. Mother and daughter both wore jeans and winter sweaters, and despite the fact that Bibsy was blonde and Sophie dark haired, the resemblance between them was obvious. Bibsy must have been a beauty, Dennis thought. And still was, for her age. He had seen the remarkable firmness of her body by candlelight as she approached the hot tub.

He glanced at Sophie, suffered the usual blow to his heart at the presence of her beauty—the liquid amber of her hair, the softness of her eyes—and smiled: a smile that was meant to say, I'm here, and I'll do whatever has to be done, and all will be well.

On the matching love seat sat a plump blue-eyed young woman. She wore a dark green uniform shirt over a white turtleneck, jeans, and workaday black boots. Dennis glanced at the chrome name pin that gleamed in the light streaming through the living room windows. It proclaimed her to be Queenie O'Hare, Pitkin County deputy sheriff.

Deputy O'Hare was drinking a mug of steaming coffee and eating some of Bibsy's chunky chocolate chip cookies. The cookies were still warm, the dark chocolate dripping a little onto the plate. Cozy, Dennis thought. There's nothing serious about this. All *will* be well.

Another Pitkin County deputy, a mustachioed thirtyish man introduced to Dennis as Doug Larsen, sat in a chintz-covered easy chair under a hanging plant. Behind a marble backgammon board sat an amiable-looking man in his early fifties. Herb Crenshaw, the local part-time police chief, looked after parking violations, littering by teenagers, and the maintenance of the local jail: a two-bunk cell attached to his mother's cowshed. In his eleven-month residence in Springhill Dennis had never known anyone to spend a night in the jail. It would have been the topic of conversation for a week: there was no crime in Springhill.

Scott's voice was mellow, deep, and relaxed. He explained to Dennis that Herb Crenshaw was there at the request of Deputy O'Hare as a courtesy to the municipality of Springhill. But Deputy O'Hare was in charge of the investigation.

Dennis turned politely to Queenie O'Hare. "May I ask—*what* investigation?"

"Sir, please sit down."

Trying to hide his discomfort, Dennis sat.

Queenie said, "On November tenth, to be precise, the Sheriff's Office became aware of two bodies buried three miles northwest of Pearl Pass in Pitkin County. We haven't a positive ID yet, but we have reason to believe that they were residents of this town, and that their names were Henry Lovell and Susan Lovell, husband and wife. However, officially, they're still John Doe and Jane Doe."

"I see," Dennis said. But he didn't see. Not a bit. It was a dark and mysterious undergrowth into which he peered. He was waiting for more information that would shed light and part the tangle of leaves. He was skilled at that. A good hunter and a veteran, he knew when to keep quiet and wait.

"I called Mrs. Henderson this morning," Queenie resumed, "and asked her if she'd be willing to come down to the courthouse in Aspen and help us out by answering a few questions."

Queenie halted, and Dennis still waited. He realized Queenie O'Hare was no fool: she had some interrogation skills. He finally asked, "What made you think that Mrs. Henderson could help you out in this . . . investigation?"

Queenie blinked a few times. "She said she'd call me back—she thought she ought to discuss it with her husband. Okay, I asked her to call back within an hour. I waited two hours. She didn't call." Queenie shrugged, as if to say, What could I do?

She hasn't answered my question, Dennis realized.

"So," Queenie said, "I drove up here with Deputy Larsen. When we arrived Mrs. Henderson called her daughter, who I take it is your wife as well as the mayor of Springhill." She nodded in a friendly, woman-to-woman manner at Sophie. "And then Mrs. Henderson said to me she didn't feel she should talk to me until counsel was present. And she said you were her counsel."

This was news to Dennis. But he was not about to challenge his mother-in-law. He nodded a few times, and said to the deputy, "When you first called from Aspen, did you tell Mrs. Henderson what you wanted to see her about?"

"No, sir, I didn't."

Bibsy interrupted. In a normal voice, she asked, "Dennis, would you like some tea and fresh-baked chocolate chip cookies?"

"I'd love both, Bibsy."

The offer served to reenforce his disbelief in what was happening. He turned back to Queenie.

"Is Mrs. Henderson under suspicion of anything?"

Queenie smiled winningly, showing one of her physical assets: white, beautifully capped teeth. "Sir, do you remember those Inspector Clouseau movies? *The Pink Panther* and the rest of them? And Peter Sellers always says"—she frowned theatrically and broke into a pseudo-French accent—" 'M'sieur, I suspect . . . *everyone.*' "

Dennis allowed himself the faintest of smiles. Again, Queenie had not answered his question.

"Is Mrs. Henderson in custody?"

"Definitely not."

He turned to Sophie's mother on the sofa; she was busy pouring his tea. "Bibsy, is it true you'd like me to represent you as your lawyer in whatever this matter is about?"

"If you don't mind," Bibsy said, handing him the cup of hot fragrant tea.

Dennis raised a questioning eyebrow in his father-in-law's direction.

"I think it would be more appropriate," Scott said, "for you to be her counsel rather than me. I've explained that to Bibsy. She understands."

I'm glad she does, Dennis thought, because I don't. But now he wondered if this was more serious than he'd first assumed.

He turned back to Queenie O'Hare. "Deputy, what is it that you want to know?"

Queenie reached deep into her big cluttered handbag. "I have a battery-operated tape recorder with me, Mr. Conway. Do you mind if I turn it on?"

Dennis whistled through barely open lips. "Is that necessary?"

"I'm a lousy note taker," Queenie explained. "My boss has been known to be displeased with my notes."

"Yes, I know your boss well, and one should not take his displeasure lightly." He let that hang there; he was trying to tell her something. "Can't Deputy Larsen take notes while you ask the questions?"

Queenie closed the handbag. "I suppose he could. This is a friendly talk. Doug, okay with you?"

"I haven't got a notebook," Larsen said, reddening.

Scott Henderson rose to his feet; he was tall enough that his head didn't seem too far from the ceiling. "I'll get you one."

He returned with a yellow legal pad and handed it to Larsen. Queenie said immediately, "Mrs. Henderson, are you taking any medication?"

Dennis put his cup down hard enough to make a clacking noise and to spill some tea from the saucer onto the old maple table. Bibsy reached out with her napkin to mop it up. Old maple stained easily.

"Deputy," Dennis said, "is that one of the questions you've come to ask on behalf of the Sheriff's Office, or is that just an impertinent inquiry?"

Calmly, Queenie replied, "It's a question I've come here to ask on behalf of the Sheriff's Office."

Dennis had been told only that two Springhill residents, the parents of the same Hank Lovell whom he had met on the day he had first met Sophie, had been found buried in a mountain grave in the wilderness of Pitkin County. They were still officially being called Jane Doe and John Doe. The chubby woman deputy had given no indication as to how they had died. Whatever had happened, Dennis was sure of one thing: his mother-in-law had nothing to do with it.

"Bibsy," he said, "you can reply to any of the questions that this young woman asks you—unless I tell you not to. I'm sure you have nothing to hide, but still, pay heed if I tell you not to answer. Understood?"

Bibsy nodded with solemn slowness. "May I answer the question about medication?"

"Yes."

"I am taking medication," Bibsy said in a clear voice.

"What medication is it?" Queenie inquired.

"A number of vitamins and minerals, and some garlic tablets in oil, that kind that don't make your skin reek. And a product put out by Herbalife that contains valerian root and yerba maté. Also, something called Rejuvelax, where the active ingredient is senna extract. That's all for regularity and internal cleansing—my cardiologist in Aspen, Dr. Morris Green, has forbidden me to have high-colonic irrigations, which I used to prefer." Bibsy hesitated a moment, frowning. "I have what's been diagnosed as Prinzmetal's variant angina. It's a tendency of the coronary artery to go into spasm for no discernible cause."

Larsen was writing notes. Dennis wondered what on earth this had to do with anything that the Pitkin County Sheriff's Office might be interested in. But Queenie O'Hare kept nodding as though she were being made privy to fascinating news. She said, "Do you have a medical background, Mrs. Henderson?"

"Until I retired, I was a registered nurse and a board-certified midwife."

"With Valley View Hospital in Glenwood Springs?"

"Oh no. Goodness gracious, that was only part-time. I worked here in Springhill. And sometimes I delivered babies in Marble."

"For this angina condition, do you take any medication?"

"Something called Ismo," Bibsy said. "It's a goofy-sounding name, but that's it. It's a slow-acting nitroglycerin. To keep the artery open. And Cardizem, a calcium channel blocker that does the same thing in an entirely different chemical way. And one aspirin a day. That's against clotting. I know it sounds like a lot of medication, but actually I'm fit as a fiddle as long as I take my pills and carry my nitro in case of emergency."

"Your nitro? The Ismo?"

"Ismo is long-term. I'm talking about nitro pills to use sublingually if I should have a coronary spasm—a heart event, as the cardiologists dearly love to say. They're a vasodilator—they open up the coronary arteries. *Boom.* Like dynamite."

"What brand nitroglycerin is it?" Queenie asked.

"Nitrostat. I'm told it lasts twice as long as any of the others."

Bibsy had begun to look pale. Dennis interrupted. "Are you all right? You're not feeling bad now, are you?"

"I don't enjoy talking about an infirmity," his mother-in-law said. "It makes it that much more real. In variant angina the artery goes into radical closure without any warning, so no blood gets through to the heart muscle. You can go like *that.*" She snapped her fingers, surprisingly loud.

Queenie asked, with apparent sympathy, "Do you have to carry all those pills around with you when you leave the house?"

"You bet your boots I do," Bibsy replied. "In one of those little gray plastic cylinders that Kodak thirty-five-millimeter film comes in. That's not chic, but I promise you it's marvelously practical. I used to have a silver pillbox that I carried them in, but I lost it a few years ago." She turned to her husband. "You remember when that happened, honey?"

"Sure," Scott said. "You went off to Glenwood one day to shop. When you came back, you didn't have it. You were so upset."

"I bought that silver case in Paris," Bibsy explained. "A long time ago, when we were on a kind of second honeymoon."

"On the rue de Rennes," Scott said, "in a shop that sold bric-a-brac. We were staying in Saint-Germain-des-Prés at the Hôtel d'Angleterre, where Hemingway first stayed when he lived in Paris."

Queenie O'Hare was studying her. To Dennis's ears the detailed husband-and-wife dialogue about shopping in Glenwood and second-honeymooning in Paris sounded hollow.

Queenie mused. "You believe you lost the silver pillbox a few years ago, is that correct?"

Bibsy nodded: correct.

"Can you be more specific about the time, Mrs. Henderson?"

"Two and a half years?" Bibsy shrugged. "Maybe three?"

"What month?"

"Summer, I believe. That's the best I can do. Does it matter?"

"And where in Glenwood Springs do you think you might have lost it?"

Dennis interrupted. "What's the significance of this, Deputy?"

Queenie said, "Sir, a silver pillbox was found in a grave near the graves of John Doe and Jane Doe."

Dennis thought about that. "Did you say, 'In a grave *near* the graves'?"

"That's correct."

"So there was a third grave? A third body?"

"The corpse of a dog, sir, was found in a separate grave."

Dennis sighed as if this were too weighty for mortal man to fathom. "Deputy, please, what's it all about? What if the silver pillbox found in a dog's grave once belonged to Mrs. Henderson? You heard her say she lost it several years ago. What do you want further from my client?"

"Truthful answers, that's all."

That annoyed Dennis. He gave Queenie a cool look and said, "Do you have any reason to believe that these two people you refer to as John Doe and Jane Doe were homicide victims?"

"Yes sir, we do."

Dennis looked at Bibsy, and then at Scott, and then at Sophie. He learned nothing from their expressions. He wondered why Bibsy hadn't gone down to the Sheriff's Office in Aspen and why she hadn't called back within the promised hour, and why she felt she needed a lawyer in this matter. A stab of unease worked its way between his ribs.

"How did these two victims die?" he asked.

"I don't think I can answer you at this point," Queenie replied. "But if you don't mind, I have a few more questions for Mrs. Henderson."

"I do mind," Dennis replied firmly. "There's got to be a little give-and-take here, don't you think? You've found a couple of unidentified alleged homicide victims buried in a grave far from here. You've got a silver pillbox found in a different grave altogether—a dog's grave, you say. It may or may not have been Mrs. Henderson's property a long time ago. As I'm sure common sense will tell you, there's more than one silver pillbox in this world. Will you be kind enough to tell me when these two victims were supposed to have been murdered?"

"Four or five months ago," Queenie said.

"Long after Mrs. Henderson lost her silver pillbox, correct?"

"We're just conducting an investigation," Queenie said. "We're not accusing anybody of anything. No one's in custody. Mrs. Henderson is in her own home—free to stay or go." She glanced at Doug Larsen to make sure he was still taking notes.

An alarm bell clanged in Dennis's head. The friendly deputy had twice stated that no one was in custody and now she had made it a point that Bibsy's movements were in no way restricted. If you were in custody—and by legal definition that could happen even in your home if you were not permitted to leave it—you had to be Mirandized and explained the nature of your constitutional rights. You had to be told that anything you said might be used against you. In theory, you had to be accused of a crime and placed under arrest. From a thousand TV shows and movies, everyone in the U.S.A. and probably even in Bangladesh was familiar with the reading of the accused's rights, usually at gunpoint with the accused spread-eagled against a car. But few citizens understood that until those rights were read, if you were not in custody you were wholly accountable for what you said to law-enforcement personnel.

Dennis wondered why he had let things go even this far. Because this is my wife's mother, he realized, and I know beyond doubt that she hasn't done anything illegal. Well, amend that. Nothing *wrong*.

"I don't think I'm going to let Mrs. Henderson answer any more questions," he said. "She has a heart condition, which I confess I didn't know about until today. We've had enough stress for one session. Is there anything else we can do for you, Deputy O'Hare?"

Queenie thought that over for about seven or eight seconds: a long time in a room full of silent, waiting people. Then she nodded positively.

"I'd like to ask a question or two of Mr. Henderson. Do you represent him too, Mr. Conway?"

Dennis waited. It was not his question to answer.

Scott said, "Go ahead and ask, Deputy. I'm a lawyer, even if I'm a little out of practice—literally. I understand my rights. If it's a proper question, I'll be glad to answer it and do my best to enlighten you."

Queenie said, "Do you own a Remington thirty-thirty rifle?"

"No, I do not," Scott said.

"*Did* you own one within the past year?"

"I did not."

"And have you or your wife lost or misplaced a down sleeping bag, blue in color? Or had it stolen from you?"

"No, ma'am. Neither lost nor stolen."

"Did you know Henry Lovell Sr. and his wife, Susan Lovell?"

"Henry and Susie were dear and old friends of ours."

"Do you remember when it was that the Lovells passed away?"

"Last summer," Scott said.

Quite a bit more than just "a question or two," Dennis realized, but he held his tongue. His father-in-law could handle himself, although maybe he didn't think this pleasant, cherubic young woman deputy was dangerous. Dennis disagreed.

"The Lovells passed away here in Springhill?" Queenie asked.

"At home, under a doctor's care."

"Was there a funeral?"

"Two funerals. They didn't die at the same time."

"You attended the funerals, Mr. Henderson?"

"Of course."

Queenie turned to Sophie. "Mrs. Conway, you're the mayor of Springhill, so I'll ask you, if you don't mind—who issues death certificates here in town?"

"Dr. Pendergast," Sophie said.

"Do you think we'll find him at his office today?"

"You'll find Dr. Pendergast at *her* office," Sophie said, "unless Grace is out of town for some very important reason, like downhill skiing at Highlands or cross-country skiing at Owl Creek, which is her favorite trail. She's in a blue Victorian on Main Street, three houses down from the post office, right across the street from the general store. You'll see a shingle."

The Hendersons' telephone rang. Scott picked up the cordless extension, listened, and said, "It's for you, Deputy O'Hare."

Queenie listened for a minute, gave a few yes and no answers, then turned to Dennis. "The sheriff's on the line, Mr. Conway, and he'd like a word with you."

Dennis picked up and said curtly, "Josh."

Josh drawled, "I understand you're in this thing now as an attorney, not just an interested bystander. So I can talk to you. Sorry about before. Sometimes I play by the rules."

"That's all right. Nothing is predictable."

"Want to come down and have a powwow?"

"The sooner the better," Dennis said.

"I've got to round up a few of the other players. I'll call you early tomorrow morning and let you know when. Don't plan on bringing the client."

10 *November 29, 1994*

The Painter

THE SHERIFF'S CALL came at seven o'clock in the morning while Dennis was in bed making love with his wife. He was invited to attend a meeting at 9 A.M.—a powwow, Josh Gamble had called it, without the client present. What that meant, Dennis wasn't quite sure. But he understood it was not a meeting to be missed.

"Thanks, pal. I'll be there."

He hung up, returning his attention in a timely manner to Sophie. The morning was his favorite time with her, when her body was warm from sleep, her slender hands cool. He would pad off to the bathroom first to brush his teeth. If he had time he could hold her in his arms for an hour, just touching her, being touched, dozing off now and then into short bursts of intense sleep, listening to her murmurs of pleasure.

She said to him softly, "This is so precious." Her words thrilled him: that she felt that way, that it was enough to be in his arms. When he made love to her she quivered, twisted, groaned with passion. She shut her eyes. Sometimes, tears fell.

Now, as he rose to the surface of another reality, he heard the refrigerator door slam in the kitchen downstairs. The children were up and about.

"Do you think they listen to us sometimes?" he asked.

"It can't hurt them to hear the sounds of love."

"It *is* love, isn't it?" he said. "It's not just lust and chemical reaction."

"Well, it may be that too," Sophie said.

He laughed, bent to kiss her, then swung off and vaulted out of bed. "I have to go. The sheriff is going to give me the lowdown about this crazy business with your mother."

"Dennis . . ."

He was already on his way to the bathroom, but something in her voice stopped him. "Yes?"

"Is anything unpleasant going to happen to my mother?"

"Not if I can help it." He realized his answer was unsatisfactory. "No, nothing. Law enforcement can sometimes be overzealous. They make mistakes. Don't worry." Still he asked, "Do you know anything about this that you haven't told me, Sophie?"

"I know she didn't do anything wrong," Sophie said.

"But is there anything I should know that I don't know?"

"No."

"Good. I'll call you at school after I've seen the sheriff."

Dennis drove in his red Jeep Cherokee down toward Carbondale for Aspen. On the outskirts of Springhill he passed Harry Parrot's house, an old gray Victorian set off the road in a thick grove of evergreens. It was the last habitable dwelling before the twisting descent to the Crystal River. A curl of dark gray smoke, like that of a cigarette smoldering in an ashtray, rose from the chimney into the cold morning air. Harry Parrot was at home. Harry was at work.

"Go for it, Harry," Dennis said softly.

One sunny January afternoon, almost a year previously, Dennis had been passing by that gray Victorian. He had seen the painter outside in the yard, smoking a cigar and shoveling snow to clear a path for his pickup truck. Dennis pulled over, parked his car, and introduced himself.

White bearded, of indeterminate age but dry as a wood chip and nimble as a monkey, Harry Parrot liked his vodka straight out of the two-quart Smirnoff bottle he kept in the freezer. In the mornings when he started work he was sober. By late afternoon there was no guarantee. The day of their first meeting, after some persuasion, Harry took Dennis down into the huge concrete cellar of his studio behind the old Victorian and showed him his work. It took the better part of two hours to look at it properly. There were dozens of unframed canvases too deep in the piles to be extricated and seen. Some were immense: six-foot or ten-foot squares. There were marble sculptures under yards of dirty canvas. The work was passionate, intricate, as if Brueghel and Cézanne—this was the conjoined image that occurred to Dennis—had been reborn in one skin.

"Harry, these are extraordinary."

"Think so? My boy, you've got exceptionally good taste."

"How long have you been painting?"

"I didn't start till I was damn near forty. Worked in the quarry until then. Didn't know any better."

"How old are you?"

Harry hesitated.

"All right," Dennis said, "don't tell me. Everyone around here seems to be elusive about their age. But I want to say something. I don't pretend to be an expert, but I think the quality of these canvases and pieces of sculpture is first class. Who did you study with?"

"Picasso. Matisse. Claude Monet. Henry Moore. Only the best. I taught myself out of books. No art school horse shit for me."

"You're from here, right? Like everyone else?"

"Wrong." Parrot smiled. "A goddam immigrant, just like you. The only other one around at the moment. I came from a dirt-poor mining family. Thirty-three-year-old hobo on the lam for putting some cop in the hospital back in the West Virginia coalfields. I walked up here to Springhill one day, asked for a job up at the quarry. They said hell no, you filthy bum, git. But I knew they was shorthanded. It was summertime—I camped down by the lake, took a bath, started eating berries and trapping rabbits and chipping away at those bits of stray marble you find all over the place, making sculpture. Got talking to people. They liked me—couldn't help it, could they? Liked my sculpture too. Then I got talking to this pretty widow gal, Rosemary. Husband drowned in the big flood, and she had two kids. They never could get rid of me after that—that there Cupid is a blind gunner, and it just takes one shot. Married her, just like you did Sophie. Lost her nine years ago."

"You mind my asking you questions?"

"You didn't ask. I just ran off at the mouth." Harry Parrot laughed. "Anyway, you're a lawyer, aren't you? Isn't that what you people do? Butt in?"

Dennis smiled. "Do you have an agent for your paintings?"

"Had a couple. Didn't work out too good. One stole, and the other was an idiot. The one who stole made more money for me than the one who was an idiot."

"Any exhibitions?"

"A few. Didn't sell much. And never the big oils."

"Look, forgive me," Dennis said, "I do know a few gallery owners and art dealers, but I don't keep in touch that much with contemporary art. Have any of your shows been in New York or London or Paris? Does the art world pay homage? Are you a cult? Am I a dolt for not knowing your name?"

Harry took a swig from the vodka bottle. "No, no, and no. I do what I do because I need to. Braque said, 'A painter paints because he don't know how to do anything else.' And old Renoir said, 'No misery in the world can make a real painter quit painting.' So that's me."

"Tell me this, if it still doesn't strike you as cross-examination. How do you make enough to live on?"

"The town helps me out."

"In what way?"

"Well, you know that the marble quarry and the coal mines are a town-owned corporation. The stock and the profits belong to the whole goddam town. A while back they voted me a salary so's I could paint and have a swig of vodka now and then. Don't need anything else."

Maybe, Dennis thought, such patronage might happen in an Israeli kibbutz or in a nineteenth-century socialist utopian community. But Springhill was a tiny Colorado mountain town—a capitalist hamlet— where everyone seemed to work at ventures far more prosaic and utilitarian than giant-sized oils on canvas.

"Does the town have a poet and a modern jazz composer they also support?" he asked, not quite sure if he were serious or jesting. You never knew around here, it seemed.

Harry shook his shaggy gray head. "Nope. I'm it. What they do for me isn't a matter of principle or policy. It's just the way things fell out.

Someone suggested it way back when. Next thing you knew, in a weak moment, the folks said, 'Hell, why not?' "

Dennis looked around at the heavy canvases stacked against every wall. "If you keep going at this rate, Harry, you'll run out of storage space."

"I have a problem there," Parrot admitted.

"You won't live forever, Harry. You might think of showing and selling, if not for your sake, then—this may sound pompous, but I really mean it—for the sake of art. If I can help . . ."

Here I go again, Dennis thought. His father had instructed him as a boy: "Son, in the next life the only gifts you'll get are what you gave away in this one." Dennis had handled more than his share of *pro bono* law cases, but even beyond the ethical dictates of his profession it was his nature to help anyone he thought was deserving. His mind brimmed immediately with ideas, speculations, road maps. He backed up his advice with time and money if that was the way to get done what he believed had to be done.

"Kind of you," Parrot said. "Maybe. If there's enough time."

"There's never forever, Harry."

"No, there sure isn't forever. Nobody gets forever. We decided that a long time ago."

Dennis frowned, not quite understanding.

"Come on upstairs and have a drink," Parrot said. "I've always thought Sophie was a hell of a woman and that stepson of mine didn't deserve her. She's all heart, and if she says a pet chipmunk can pull a freight train, you can hitch that varmint up and clear the tracks. I'm starting to like you. You may be a busybody but you have good taste in art. That makes you special. I keep tonic and clean glasses for specials."

Harry Parrot and Dennis became friends. Dennis would often stop by for a drink or to see new work. Once they went cross-country skiing together, the older man spryer and with more stamina than Dennis could have imagined.

It was to Harry that Dennis began to confess his confusions about certain things he had noticed in the village of Springhill. The health and longevity aspect continued to puzzle him. Then there was the question of consanguine marriage. He brought the subject up with Harry rather than Sophie, in the hope of a more satisfying response.

"You're goddam one hundred percent right," Harry said. "Not many people marry outside of the community."

"Well, your late wife did," Dennis said. "And so did Sophie, to me. But obviously it rarely happens."

"Right. Takes a hell of a lot more than a majority to agree. Has to be damned near unanimous."

Dennis leaned forward, not sure he had heard correctly. "A majority of who? What are you talking about?"

Harry waved the vodka bottle at him. "Figuratively speaking. Hey, man, Sophie's our mayor, our leader—you think we'd just let her marry *anybody?* She said you were smart and you skied almost as good as she did, and if the council or the board said no she'd quit. Hard to turn her down. So you're here. And that's what matters, *n'est-ce pas?*"

"Harry, you're drunk."

"When I speak French," the painter said, "you can bet on it. English too, for that matter."

"One more thing," Dennis continued, picking up the thread of his concern—"what doesn't happen here is that anyone marries someone from the outside and goes away to live there. The mate who's not from Springhill comes to Springhill to live. Isn't that so?"

"Not always," Harry said. "I have a nephew, went to USC, met a gal out there, got her in the family way, and married her. Stayed there to become a rich land developer in Orange County. Dumb kid, and that sure proves it. And I knew one or two others like that."

"I suppose what I meant is . . ." Dennis hesitated. "Sophie wouldn't consider leaving."

"Not at her age," Harry said.

"She's only thirty-eight."

Harry was cleaning some sable brushes as he talked. "I only meant that the life here is pretty simple. Pure, even. It's hard to beat it. After a while, staying here is as easy as getting up after you sit down on a thumbtack. What's out there that any of us needs? I've been around longer'n dirt and I sure don't know. Why would anyone want to give away the store, so to speak, and go back on the bricks? You tell me. You'll see."

You'll see . . . Sophie's favorite words to him too. What was it that he would see?

As for purity and simplicity, Dennis was no longer so sure to what extent they existed here. It depended on how you defined things. He'd known since his June midnight ramble along the creek that there was a sexual sophistication among the older generation that didn't exist anywhere else he'd ever been. Harry had been in that hot tub too. So that when Harry said to him, "Life here is pretty simple . . . what's out there beyond old Springhill that any of us needs?" Dennis had reason to wonder how Harry defined his terms.

He had also learned, to his surprise, that along with Sophie, Grace Pendergast, a young coal miner named Amos McKee, and Oliver Cone, Harry was a member of the town's five-person Water Board. The board's principal function, aside from keeping tabs on the genetics of the town population, Dennis still did not understand. "What *is* this Water Board?" he asked Harry, smiling. "Are they the ones who approve of marriages to skibtails?"

Harry reached for the vodka bottle. "You got a good memory. No, I like to joke. Aside from all the other stuff they dump on us, the Water Board is just what it says it is. We monitor the supply, check for fecal chloroform, lead, stuff like that. Bacterial contamination. Groundwater here can kill you, man. Comes into contact with mine tailings, all kinds of shit. I don't give a bedbug's ass about any of it, but under Colorado law every community has to file an annual goddam report to the state about its water."

"And *you* take part in all that?"

"I help, that's all."

Dennis laughed. "Harry, you're not just an artist—you're a con artist too. I don't believe any of it."

"Believe, man. It's a fact. The town supports me—remember that. Gotta pay the piper. So I go to the meetings. Half the time I'm so soused I can't hardly remember what goes on or how I vote."

He was still thinking and dreaming about Harry when suddenly he realized he had reached the stoplight at Cemetery Lane in Aspen. To his left the broad expanse of Red Mountain and the garish palazzos of the rich rose under the blue morning sky. Traffic was backed up on the two-lane road entering Aspen; the workforce was arriving from downvalley.

The world is going about its business, Dennis thought, and so am I. My business is to find out why my mother-in-law is a suspect in a murder case.

11 *November 29, 1994*

The Second Injection

WITH A HUFF and a snort, Josh Gamble twisted his bulk around in his swivel chair and glanced up at the grandfather clock in the far corner of his office. The clock ticked with the utmost gravity, as though apportioning the hours of humankind. The sheriff waved his hand in the general southerly direction of Aspen Mountain, which he couldn't see, since his office in the basement of the Pitkin County Courthouse faced the rear. Its single window offered a view of a mound of frozen dirt.

"Seven inches overnight!" he boomed. "I *hate* working on a day like this!" He pointed a blunt finger at Dennis. "You were up there yesterday. I can see my mamma was right—I should have gone to law school. I've got to sit here and battle evildoers, but you can hit the mountain whenever you feel like it. That's undemocratic. You know what sperm and lawyers have in common?"

"Unfortunately, yes," Dennis said. "Only one in a million has a chance of making it as a human being. I heard that one my first year at Yale."

"Age don't diminish truth."

Dennis sat on the sofa next to plump Queenie O'Hare. The lower part of Coroner Jeff Waters's torso had all but vanished into a sagging easy chair under the head of a ten-point elk.

"And to answer your earlier question—yes, yesterday I was up on the mountain in the powder until I was rudely interrupted by events that still haven't been properly explained to me."

Ray Boyd, the county deputy district attorney in the Ninth Judicial District, was the only person standing—he lacked the patience to sit and be confined. A former football star from the University of Colorado, he was now a redheaded man in his late thirties and a bodybuilder, more muscular than sinewy. He still helped coach the perennially winless Aspen High School football team. He owned a powerful baritone voice that he exercised not only on the playing field but also pacing the Pitkin County courtroom asserting the rights of the county's citizens. He was a man on the move. He twitched and fidgeted, stretched and paced. He was known to rush at the jury and roar, "Ladies and gentlemen, the defense attorney represents the accused. I, on the other hand, represent the state of Colorado, but even more I represent the victims of this crime. I speak for them . . . and of course for the *people* . . ."

"I would have liked to ski too," he said to Dennis now—"but let's face it, we don't get a double murder every day."

Picking some breakfast pancake out of his teeth with a gold toothpick, Josh Gamble nodded. "Yes, Ray, maybe once every hundred years, if we're lucky."

He meant that there had not been a double murder in Pitkin County since the previous century, when a local banker had shot his wife and her Ute Indian lover and been sentenced to three years at hard labor, of which he served six months. So Ray Boyd was excited. He leaned forward from his standing position to listen to the sheriff's every word and to the words of all others in the room, which resembled more a book-lined hunter's den than a sheriff's office. There were complete sets of Shakespeare, Mark Twain, and Jane Austen, an ancient *Encyclopaedia Britannica*, and six volumes of Dunsterville and Garay's *Venezuelan Orchids*. Like Sophie, the sheriff had a greenhouse.

"Dennis," he said, "the others know this, but I need to enlighten you. We do things a little different here in backcountry Colorado than you might be used to in badassed New York. A little less formal.

Sometimes downright friendly. We—and by that I mean all the county officials—are going to tell you everything we know about this alleged crime. Of course you don't have to do the same, and you'd be a lousy lawyer if you did, because you've got a client to represent, and that client might be guilty of some heinous act that you're unaware of, and might need all the help he or she can get. Is all that clear?"

Dennis nodded, pleased. It was what he had expected of his friend and college chum.

The swivel chair creaked under Josh's bulk. "Right now we're only interested in figuring out what happened up there at Pearl Pass. I guess you are too."

"Absolutely," Dennis said.

"And maybe," Josh said, "since we hicks ain't quite as stupid as some people would like to think, the bunch of us here, if we don't play lawyer-and-lawman games, can figure it out together. Work as a team. You game to try?"

Dennis was more than game: he was enthused.

The sheriff turned to the young coroner. "Jeff, tell us everything you know. If I get bored I'll yawn visibly, and you can take that as a signal to go into third gear. Dennis, if you have any questions, don't be shy. But I guess you never were, were you?"

It was going to work out fine, Dennis decided, and turned toward the coroner.

On the morning after the bodies had been brought down on snowmobiles from Pearl Pass—Jeff Waters said—he and Otto Beckmann, the forensic pathologist and medical examiner for Garfield County, had conducted a six-hour autopsy. It took place in Valley View Hospital, in Glenwood Springs, forty miles downvalley from Aspen.

The victims' bodies had spent the night in cold storage at forty-two degrees Fahrenheit, but still, splayed out on the steel gurneys, they smelled. There had been several months of rot. At high altitudes in winter a certain amount of mummification occurs, but it was clear from the outset of the autopsy that the bodies had been placed in their common grave during warm weather. To offset the smell, Drs. Beckmann and Waters wore surgical masks smeared with Vicks VapoRub.

One of the victims was male, the other female, Waters related in the sheriff's office. "We could tell because the uterus and the prostate gland are remarkably resistant to decomposition. Both victims were over the age of sixty-five and under the age of seventy-five—we could tell that from bone deterioration, particularly in the spinal column. If you need to narrow it down, I'd say the male was about seventy and the female maybe a couple of years younger. Any questions?"

There were none.

The pathologist and coroner sliced away bits of liver, heart muscle, and spleen, which they would need for tissue studies. They collected dried blood and cardiac fluid and a small amount of vitreous humor from one eyeball of the female corpse. The male corpse had no eyes. "Coyotes go for the soft stuff first," Dr. Beckmann had explained to Waters. He had considerable experience at examining bodies recovered in summer following the previous winter's avalanches. "Ears, nose, lips, eyes . . . This bother you?"

"Yes," Waters admitted, wishing he hadn't had poached eggs and pork sausages for breakfast.

Waters said now, "They had no broken bones. There was no evidence of violence. They both suffered sudden cardiac death. Heart attacks."

Dennis said, "Does that mean it was a natural death?"

"Not at all. I'm just telling you the technical cause of death. Normally if we can't find an obvious reason for death and people are far along in years, we call it 'sudden cardiac death.' It's a catchall. In this case, however, because of the peculiar circumstances, we did preliminary tissue and blood studies, and we found evidence of Versed and Pentothal in both bodies."

"Tranquilizers," Ray Boyd explained, his face twitching.

"They're a bit more than that," Waters said patiently. "Call them control drugs. Versed is a quick-acting, strong sedative, a Valium derivative but more powerful than Valium. Hospitals use it before major operations. It's for conscious sedation. If you had a badly dislocated shoulder and the doctor wanted to work on it without you screaming so that the patients in the waiting room would freak out, he'd use Versed. It's also used in death-penalty states, like Texas. It precedes the lethal injection. Pentothal, on the other hand, is an anesthetic. Combined with Pentothal, Versed puts you to sleep, and for a couple of hours you don't feel a damn thing."

Dennis made some notes, then asked, "How available are Versed and Pentothal?"

"Hospitals, medical supply houses, and pharmacies all have them."

"Then they're not hard to find."

"Not if you have access to those places."

"Can either of those drugs cause a heart attack?"

"I personally don't know of any cases where that's happened. Neither did Otto Beckmann."

Dennis frowned. "So Versed and Pentothal did *not* kill the two people at Pearl Pass."

"That's correct. I told you they died of a heart attack. But the heart attacks were induced. There was a *second* set of injections administered after the Versed and Pentothal—in other words, after the Does had been sent off to sleep. You follow?"

Dennis nodded. "What was in the second set of injections?"

"Beckmann and I did a study of liver tissue in both bodies, and we found a trace of potassium chloride. You know what that is?"

"A lethal poison."

"Right. Quick-acting but not necessarily painless, unless the subject is premedicated with something."

"Like Versed and Pentothal," Dennis said.

"You see the sequence?"

He saw it: sedate them, then kill them. Theoretically a humane way to go, if the deaths were in any sense necessary.

"Potassium chloride goes into a vein with a hypodermic needle," Waters said. "It induces immediate coronary infarction. You quit breathing, although in some instances the heart may actually keep on beating weakly for twenty or thirty minutes. Then you die. Heart stops, brain quits functioning. Dead by any definition."

"How available is potassium chloride?" Dennis asked.

"Same deal. Hospitals, supply houses, pharmacies. Veterinarians too."

"If it's a lethal poison, how come it's so readily available?"

"For doctors to give to people who have a major potassium imbalance. But I'm talking about very small doses, like three cc's in a thousand-cc bag."

"How much of it would you use if you wanted to kill someone?"

"It comes in vials of twenty milliequivalents mixed in with ten cubic centimeters of fluid for injection. Altogether, about a teaspoon. Ten of those vials—maybe a tenth of a liter—would do the job easily."

"So you're saying these people were tranquilized first and then murdered."

Waters smiled thinly. "Murder is a legal term, isn't it? I'm just telling you how they died. It could just as well have been euthanasia."

"Wait." Josh Gamble raised a hand. "In this state," he said, for the benefit of both Dennis and the young coroner, "euthanasia is classified as murder."

Dennis digested that and didn't like the feel of it going down.

"Who would know how to mix up those injections?" Queenie O'Hare asked. "And how to administer them, and in what amounts? I sure as heck wouldn't know. Would you, Josh?"

The sheriff shook his head. "I have trouble mixing a margarita."

"And you, Mr. Conway?"

"Please call me Dennis. And the answer is no."

Queenie was making notes on her yellow legal pad even as she spoke. "You'd have to be a doctor or nurse, or a medical technician of some sort, wouldn't you?"

"Probably," Waters said.

The sheriff groaned. "So have we got another Dr. Kevorkian in business around here?"

"Kevorkian never used a bow and arrow to kill his patient's dog," Queenie said.

"Yes, the dog." Dennis leaned forward. "Would you mind backtracking a bit? I'd like to hear a little more about this dog."

Queenie told Dennis about the Clark brothers' discovery of the dead Scottish deerhound, the probability that the deerhound had been shot with an arrow, and how she tracked down its ownership to the late Henry Lovell Sr. of Springhill. She told him about her peculiar phone call to a less than candid Jane Lovell, and then to Hank Jr. at the Springhill marble quarry.

"There were no ID tags, so there's no proof that it was *that* Scottish deerhound," Dennis pointed out. "Granted, it's a rare breed. However, it could have been a different dog."

"Faintly possible," Queenie agreed. "But highly unlikely."

She was naive on that score, Dennis realized. She didn't understand that criminal defense attorneys made a handsome living pointing out to juries that *faintly possible* was the equivalent of reasonable doubt.

Josh Gamble, like a man conducting a small orchestra, waved back at the coroner.

"There's another reason you'd have trouble drawing an analogy to Dr. Kevorkian in this instance," Waters said.

"And what is that?" Dennis asked.

"I told you we found the cause of death," the coroner said. "But we also searched the corpses for evidence of disease. Degenerative tissue, a tumor, anything. There was none. These people weren't dying. These were remarkably healthy older people. Excellent muscle tone, all organs in good condition. Why would anyone need to commit a mercy killing?"

No one answered.

The sheriff said slowly, "Jeff, isn't it possible that you guys missed something? Some esoteric brain or bone disease?"

"Possible," Waters said. "Beckmann isn't perfect. But it's unlikely."

Another *unlikely* to remember.

"Anyway"—Jeff Waters continued—"the bodies were pretty much mummified and frozen after the cold weather set in this past October, although the animal population up there had had their share of the extremities. We think both people died about the second week of August, but we could be off by as much as two weeks either way. We got good fingerprints, because there's what we call skin slippage. The epidermis detaches, just like a glove."

Josh nodded at Queenie. She said to Dennis, "But those prints don't match up anywhere. Neither of the Does had a criminal record. Neither one was in the armed forces."

"What about teeth?" Dennis asked.

"Dr. Beckmann called in the forensic odontologist, who also happens to be my dentist." Queenie showed those near-perfect white crowns again, as well as some ingrained laugh wrinkles around the eyes. "His name is Howard Keating. I've got a little crush on him but he's married to an ex-model from L.A. and they've got three-year-old twins, so I've given up a long time ago. Anyway, Howard produced a full set of postmortem X-rays for Jane and John Doe. I took them up to Springhill. Before I went to see your mother-in-law, Dennis, I dropped in on the local dentist, the one that Jane Lovell works for. You know him?"

"Edward Brophy," Dennis said. "A good friend of my wife's. I've skied with him. Tends to skid his uphill ski on the turns, but otherwise he's a fine fellow."

Queenie smiled and said, "Dr. Brophy still had the Lovells' X-rays in a file cabinet in his storeroom, and we compared the ones from the postmortem on the Does. They didn't match."

"So the bodies in those graves at Pearl Pass are *not* Henry Lovell and Susan Lovell," Dennis said. He was pleased, although he couldn't work out precisely why.

"Doesn't look that way," Queenie said. "Also, before I left Springhill, I dropped in on Dr. Pendergast and had a quick look at the Lovells' death certificates. Cause of death was congestive heart failure for him, pneumonia for her."

"Then who are these people you found up there at Pearl Pass?" Dennis asked.

"The clothes are too rotten to trace them. We've given them over to a lab in Denver, but we don't have much hope. We're trying to track the rifle we found in the dog's grave, but of course we don't even have any proof that it belonged to either of the Does."

Dennis leaned back in the easy chair and folded his arms. "Then will you tell me why you think my client, Beatrice Henderson, mother of three, woman of advanced years, is involved? That silver pillbox you found is hardly proof. She told you she lost it three years ago. Silver boxes, as I've pointed out, are not rare."

Queenie glanced at the sheriff, and Josh Gamble said to Dennis, "It's what's in the box, my friend, that gives us pause for thought."

"And what is that?" Dennis asked, already unhappy in his anticipation of the answer.

"Pills," Queenie said. "We had them analyzed. They turned out to be Cardizem, Ismo, and nitroglycerin whose brand name the chemist couldn't determine with one hundred percent certainty, although he believes it's Nitrostat. I'm sure those names are familiar, Dennis, after what your mother-in-law told us."

"Yes," Dennis said, "they do ring a bell."

"We checked every pharmacy in the valley. There are only two other people besides Mrs. Henderson registered for all three prescriptions. One of them is a Glenwood man of eighty-six who's paralyzed and gets around in a motorized wheelchair. The other is Judge Florian."

Everyone smiled. Dennis said, "I see."

"But as far as we know," Queenie said, "neither the man in the wheelchair nor Judge Florian ever kept pills in a silver pillbox made in France."

"Hold it," Dennis said. "You're leaving something out. Bibsy Henderson told you she lost her pillbox three years ago in Glenwood Springs. Scott Henderson, an officer of the court, confirms that. Even if the box you found in the dog's grave could be proved to be my mother-in-law's previous property, it's probable that someone else had it in his or her possession or control the past few years. And that someone could have dropped it by accident, or even left it deliberately, up at Pearl Pass. Although I can't for the life of me figure out why."

"Yes, at first that's what I thought," Queenie said. "That would certainly be possible, except for one thing."

"And what is that one thing?" Dennis asked, feeling a little battered. As a lawyer he had been battered before, in trial and in judges' chambers and in deposition, but he never quite got used to it.

"Nitroglycerin pills start turning to powder after roughly twelve to eighteen months," Queenie explained, "depending for the most part on whether the bottle they originally came in has been opened or is still sealed. I spoke to the cardiologist who prescribed the pills. People who use nitro are supposed to renew their prescriptions every twelve to eighteen months. If Mrs. Henderson lost that pillbox three years ago, the way she told us she did, the nitro inside it would be just white dust by now. But the Nitrostat in the pillbox was fresh. Without doubt it was less than fifteen months old. To kind of corroborate that, it was only last June that Mrs. Henderson renewed her prescription." Queenie shrugged. "So you see, it makes no sense that she lost the box in Glenwood three years ago, and then someone found it and dumped the old nitro, and put in fresh nitro last August, and then planted it in the dog's grave up at Pearl Pass. That would be a little unreal, don't you think?"

"But not impossible," Dennis said.

"That might be for a jury to decide," Ray Boyd said.

Dennis wheeled on him, glad to have an opponent. "You can't be serious."

Josh Gamble had already snapped an unfriendly look in Ray Boyd's direction. He turned back quickly to Dennis.

"Look, friend and able counselor, I personally find it hard to believe that a woman in her sixties who's never done an illegal thing in her life, at least as far as we know, could be responsible for a wilderness murder and burial of two older people, whoever the hell they were. If she is, she sure as shit couldn't have done it alone."

Dennis said nothing in reply.

"What I *can* believe, however," Josh said, "and what the evidence suggests, is that she or her husband might be mixed up in a case of euthanasia. Depends a lot on what Beckmann says about evidence of disease he might have missed. I don't know the answer to that. And for the moment we won't discuss the ethics of euthanasia. A lot of people don't see mercy killing as murder, but the state of Colorado disagrees, and it's my responsibility to investigate, and Ray's to prosecute. Aside from the fact that it's your in-laws involved, you got any reason to tell me my thinking is cockeyed?"

"Yes, I do," Dennis said. "I think you don't commit a mercy killing on someone you don't know. You believed these people were the Lovells—old and dear friends of the Hendersons—because the dog you found answered the description of a dog the Lovells may have owned. But now you know from the dental X-rays that it wasn't the Lovells who died up there at Pearl Pass. So who did you find? Who was it that might have been euthanized? Logic suggests that they would have to be people who were terminally ill with something like cancer or AIDS. So far there's no sign of disease. If you still intend to link these deaths in some way with the Hendersons, you'd better identify the victims and their supposed source of suffering before you start seeking to name the perpetrators. Doesn't that make sense?"

Dennis waited until Josh nodded slightly, then went on: "Have you established any connection between Beatrice Henderson and the victims? No. Can you? No, because you don't know the identity of the victims." He turned on Ray Boyd. "And let me tell you this, Ray. Without that connection, you take this one step further—to a jury, or even a grand jury—and you're going to be involved in reckless prosecution. I don't think that's what you want. I'm sure it's not what the

Sheriff's Office wants. So let's just back off and stop pointing fingers and making empty threats. It would be unwise."

"Bravo," said the sheriff, rising from his creaky swivel chair and clapping Dennis on the shoulder. "I sure as hell would like you to be my lawyer if I ever get caught doing anything illegal. But until that day, let me ask you a tough question. How do we account for the presence of the Lovells' dog in a grave less than a hundred yards from the grave of the two victims? And don't give me that bullshit that it was *probably* the Lovells' dog. Coincidence don't count in the real world. It *was* the Lovells' dog."

"Try this scenario," Dennis said calmly. "The victims, the Does, found the dog. They took it camping with them. Or found it up there near the pass, after it ran away." He turned to Queenie. "Are there any people missing from the town of Springhill? Any people who might fit the description of the victims?"

"Not that we know of so far," Queenie said. "But we'll look into it."

"What's your theory," the sheriff inquired of Dennis, "as to how the silver pillbox walked up to the dog's grave and fell in there?"

"I have no theory yet," Dennis said.

"Maybe you'll find one. You're good at that. Meanwhile, we've pulled latents off the pillbox and off a Remington rifle we found up there. We can't track the rifle down to any owner—it's pretty old, and it's a common enough model. You mind if I ask your client and her husband to come in here and give us a set of their fingerprints?"

"What if I did mind?" Dennis said.

"It would piss me off because I'd have to go to the trouble of getting a court order. Which I'd sure as hell get."

The courts had determined that fingerprints and handwriting samples were not deemed private in nature or protected by the Fifth Amendment. For even the flimsiest of reasons, the sheriff had the right to ask for them. "My client," Dennis said, "will be thrilled to come in and help you out with a set of her fingerprints. I don't represent Scott Henderson, my father-in-law, but I can't imagine that he'd object either."

The sheriff beamed. "See? I told you that if we all cooperated, we'd get somewhere."

And where is that? Dennis wondered, but didn't ask the question.

"One more thing," Queenie O'Hare said. "I'd like to open up Susan and Henry Lovell's graves in Springhill. Ray, I need permission in writing to do that. You might have to call the DA in Gunnison County."

"Glad to do it," Ray Boyd said.

"What do you expect to find in their graves?" Dennis asked.

"I don't really know," Queenie admitted. "Want to come along with me and see?"

12 *November 29–30, 1994*

The Cemetery

IN ANY CRISIS, Bibsy Henderson cooked. For Queenie O'Hare's visit the previous day, she baked chocolate chip cookies. For dinner with her husband, daughter, and son-in-law she went straight to her shelves of cookbooks above the cast-iron stove and with no hesitation brought down *The Food Lover's Guide to France*. Three hours later she delivered to the table a lamb-and-black-olive stew in red wine, a potato gratin, and finally a multilayered lemon-and-chocolate tart with a recipe from La Bonne Etape, an inn in Alpes-Maritimes where she said she and Scott had once stayed.

"This is not for dieters or fat-free fanatics," she announced, ladling out large, un-French portions of stew and potatoes.

"Bless your cotton socks, woman," Scott said, "I'm glad you told us that. Otherwise, who could have guessed?"

Dennis waited a few minutes and said, "We have got to talk about this situation, Bibsy. I hope it won't spoil the dinner."

"Nothing could spoil my food," Bibsy said.

"Good. So tell me what happened at Pearl Pass." He added in his most affable, lawyerly manner: "If you know."

"Well, it's just plain silly that they think I have anything to do with something like that. Don't you agree?"

"I'd like to agree. But for the moment, consider me your lawyer, not your son-in-law. Convince me."

Bibsy's face suddenly looked dry and hot, and a small nervous pulse beat in the hollow of her throat. Before she could begin to speak, Scott held up a quieting hand and moved forward on his chair.

"Dennis," he said, "isn't it a fact that the authorities down in Aspen don't know beans about who the victims are? They could be from anywhere. Could be vagrants. How can they connect Bibsy with strangers found fifty miles from here in the back of beyond? Let's face it, that ox won't plow."

Keeping his promise, Dennis had called Sophie from Aspen and told her most of what he had learned from Josh Gamble and from Jeff Waters, the coroner: about the injections of Pentothal and Versed, followed by potassium chloride administered to the so-called male and female Does. He had also mentioned the longevity of the nitroglycerin pills. "You might pass all this along to your parents before dinner," he said.

He repeated these details to his in-laws.

Scott Henderson frowned; in the past day, Dennis realized, there seemed to be new lines scored into the brown oak of his cheeks. "I understand all that," Scott said. "But I think in court it'd be like throwing a saddle on a dead mule. Might look right, but where can you go with it? Don't they see that there's no *proof*?"

Dennis evaluated that response and didn't like it. It was accurate, but it had a taint of what some people called lawyerly evasion.

"Josh Gamble's theory," he said, "not to put too fine a point on it, is that Bibsy—probably with some help from you, Scott—committed euthanasia. Assisted suicide, if you care to stretch the language. As a former nurse she'd be able to procure the drugs, or she might even have had them on hand. And she'd be physically capable of administering them properly."

Scott stood up, amazed. "On people she didn't even know?"

Dennis looked at Bibsy. "Have you ever been up to Pearl Pass?"

"Many years ago," Bibsy said quietly.

This was a new experience for Dennis. He had never had a relative as a client and he had never discussed the details of a case in front of his in-laws and his wife. Not that his wife was involved in the discussion. Sophie maintained a rigid silence and looked pale, almost chalk white in the lamplight. She was not eating.

Dennis was hungry, and the lamb was perfectly cooked; nevertheless he only picked at his food. "How many years ago?" he asked Bibsy.

"Many," she said. "We were camping. Long, long ago. I don't remember exactly."

It was not the time or place to start an argument. Dennis turned back to Scott. "What's your theory as to what happened?"

This was a question that Dennis often asked his clients when he felt they might be guilty and when he didn't dare ask, *"Did you do it?"* Experienced lawyers rarely asked that last question of clients for fear of receiving a truthful answer. If they told you they had done it, whatever *it* was, you still had a right in court to force the prosecution to its proof. Putting your client on the witness stand, however, to elicit a false narrative of innocence violated the canons of legal ethics. For that a lawyer could be disbarred; in some instances, indicted—although half the criminal defense lawyers practicing in the United States, Dennis knew, would be out of work or behind bars if that canon were rigorously enforced. Therefore a lawyer, to save his skin as well as his soul, asked his accused client, "What's your theory?"

"My theory," Scott Henderson replied—after he had taken a swallow of St. Emilion—"is that if we don't let these law-enforcement galoots get their claws into us, things will quiet down. It will take time, that's all. One of these days the industrious and well-meaning Sheriff Gamble and the damnfool officious Mr. Boyd—there's a man who doesn't know 'Sic 'em' from 'Come here'—together will figure out that they don't have a legal brick to stand on. They're hollering down a rain barrel. In more proper language, so you don't think I'm just a hick from the backcountry, the evidence presented today fails to rise to the level required for an indictment. They don't have a case with the likes of a stolen or lost silver pillbox. No probable cause." He smiled at Sophie. *"Probable cause,* my dear, is a legal term, and all you really have to know about it is that the powers-that-be need to have it in order to arrest you. They need facts that point the finger. And they don't have them. No sir. Judge Florian is a smart old bird and he'll need a heck of a lot more convincing than these yokels can come up with."

Dennis regarded his father-in-law with dark-eyed displeasure. But Scott either didn't notice or didn't care. He was on a roll. "In a month or two, you'll see, it will be a matter of two unknown people, suffering from some incurable and painful disease, who came out here from Denver to the western slope in order to depart this world in a more majestic setting than their own once-beautiful but now frighteningly polluted metropolis could afford them. I take that act as a compliment to the purity of the Elk Range, where we have the extreme good fortune to live. 'We' includes you, Dennis. You're part of us, more than you yet realize. But you will realize it . . . I promise you. Meanwhile, let's enjoy this splendid dinner my wife has cooked for us. Just try this tart. Lemon and chocolate are my two favorite flavors. These tarts are so good they'd make you hit your grandmother to get another one.'

The patriarch had spoken in a firm voice larded with countrified certainty and a tone of finality. And that was the end of all nonculinary discussion. Dennis felt a deep distress, but he knew from experience that Bibsy and Sophie would not challenge Scott's words—at least not now, in public. So he set about to finish and somehow enjoy his meal.

The moon had set. Mist rose from the pines. Getting into bed, Dennis said, "Sophie, your mother is not being realistic about what's happened. And your father is being evasive. I need help."

Sophie was silent awhile, and then said quietly, "I don't think I should get involved in this. It's between you and my mother. Please, Dennis—that's the best way."

"They're your parents. You *are* involved."

"You heard my father. He says it won't come to an indictment or anything like that."

"He may be wrong."

"He knows the people up here better than you do, Dennis."

"The law is not quite as forgiving as he makes it out to be."

"Don't you think it's a good idea to wait and see?" There was the same finality in her voice that he had heard in her father's, but added to that was a pain whose cause he didn't understand: a sorrowing. "If you want to help me," she said even more softly, "keep me out of this. At least for now. Just do your best. I know you will. I have faith in you."

"Yes, I will," he said. "And I thank you for your faith. All right, let's see how it goes. Maybe you're right and your father knows more about things up here than I do. I hope so."

• • •

The following day the sun stayed behind cloud cover. A breeze in the high country smelled of coming snow. Dennis checked the weather report: it was raining heavily in California, which usually foretold snowstorms in the Rockies. The temperature fell to ten degrees. Bundled in parkas and wearing insulated gloves, Dennis and Sophie—Sophie pale and silent and distant in a way that he had never known her to be—met Queenie O'Hare and two Pitkin County male deputy sheriffs in front of the Springhill post office at the agreed hour of ten o'clock.

Sophie was there as the official representative of the incorporated township. "I'm sorry," she said to Queenie, "but on behalf of the Town Council I have to ask you if you have a court order."

"I have a fax from the circuit judge in Gunnison." Queenie waved a flimsy piece of paper in the cold mountain air.

Sophie looked at Dennis, asking a wordless question.

"It's not exactly proper," Dennis said, "but it's fair to say that if we objected we'd be delaying the proper course of justice. And bear in mind, all they have to do is drive over to the courthouse in Gunnison and get it."

Sophie turned back to Queenie. "You can open the graves."

The graves were side by side, with stone markers bearing the names of Henry Lovell and Susan Lovell, the dates of death, and two simple crosses.

There were three shovels. Queenie supervised, and the two male deputies dug. The third shovel had been jammed into a snowbank piled up at the edge of Henry Lovell's grave. To Dennis's eyes its lonely and upright presence seemed to grow more and more accusative as the deputies dug and sweated. But he restrained himself. It was not his job to make things easier for the opposition.

Fat snowflakes swirled from a heavy sky. The wind blew more strongly. The diggers began to stamp their feet as they worked.

Dennis's feet grew cold. More than cold, he was restless and unhappy. Murmuring some words of apology, he detached himself from Sophie and the diggers and began to walk toward the nearby woods, down the row of gravestones and small monuments and markers. It was a tasteful cemetery, a testimonial to modest lives and modest exits. Not many graves. Probably, Dennis decided, in the old days plenty of people were buried in their backyards in brief ceremonies, or maybe no ceremony at all. Maybe still. He came to a small mottled pink marble headstone with a smaller one beside it. A portrait of a dog had been carved into the smaller stone. Dennis read the words beneath the portrait: a faithful basset hound had died soon after its master had departed this earth.

The basset hound—DEVOTED FRIEND AND CHEERFUL COMPANION—bore the dignified name of Randall. Randall's master—upon closer examination, his mistress—had been named Ellen Hapgood. The name was familiar, but at first Dennis couldn't remember why. Then he remembered. Ellen Hapgood's passing, as Sophie had once told him, had taken place a few months prior to Dennis's arrival in Springhill. *"She sat in her rocking chair talking to herself all day long and swatting imaginary bats with a broom."* She had died at ninety-one, Sophie had said.

Dennis looked at the dates carved into the stone: *October 3, 1919— July 20, 1993.*

He made the calculation twice, but the laws of arithmetical subtraction did not change. She had been seventy-four. Dennis continued walking among the gravestones. Sophie could have made a mistake. Memory played tricks.

The wind gusted, making his eyes tear a little. The snow fell more thickly. His shoes crunched into the covering. Now there was purpose to his wandering. His back was to the gravediggers and he wondered if Sophie were watching him. But when he turned he saw he had moved to a point where a stand of pines stood between him and the diggers.

On the western fringe of the little cemetery he found what he was looking for. Bibsy's maiden name had been Whittaker. Here were the graves of the Whittakers, Sophie's grandparents. He checked the dates of birth and death. Nothing out of the ordinary. Both had died in their seventies. A few yards farther along he came to the graves of Scott's parents. Sophie had told him that her paternal grandmother, Janice Cone Henderson, had died at the age of forty, in 1956. Young. From cancer, he recalled. The inscription confirmed her date of death and age.

Next to her, Scott's father was buried. The carved inscription read: SCOTT HENDERSON. BELOVED FATHER TO PATRICIA AND SCOTT JR. And under that: *1894–1965.*

"My father's father," Sophie had said, *"lived to be eighty-five . . ."*

But the arithmetic of the gravestone said seventy-one. Dennis stared balefully for a minute or two. For Sophie to err about Ellen Hapgood's age was one thing; to make the same mistake about Scott's father was another. Why would Sophie lie about such a small thing like that? What sense did it make? Denial of mortality? Sophie was a sensible woman. He had never heard her express any fear of death or dying. She was as calm in facing the future as anyone he'd ever known.

He wanted the answers. But if he demanded to know why on earth she kept insisting that people in Springhill lived to a ripe old age, he would be digging a pit between them. Was it important enough to force a confrontation? He felt a chill in his blood. In its grayness and with its stealthy wind, the day was not a common one.

Still pondering, he returned to the Lovells' graves. The two men were digging. The gaze of Sophie's dark eyes rested on him with somber regard. Dennis felt the blood rush to his face. She knows where I've been. She couldn't see me behind the stand of pine, but still she knows.

He picked up the third shovel. He looked at Queenie O'Hare—she nodded at him: Yes, of course. Pitkin County thanks you, Counselor.

The bite of the blade into the soil jolted up his arms into his back. It felt appropriate. He needed to labor, to punish himself a little for his knowledge, his doubt, his effort at keeping all the negatives under control. Life was too good; he loved his wife too much to disrupt the harmony.

By the time the wood of the casket showed itself, a film of sweat beaded Dennis's forehead. A minute later Queenie said, "That will do it."

One of the deputies hunkered down and unscrewed the metal handles, snapped open the two metal clasps, then looked at Queenie for permission. She moved her head once. The deputy exerted a certain effort, cleared his throat, and raised the heavy wooden lid.

Dennis had been expecting the worst. In Vietnam during the Tet offensive, when Dennis's sapper platoon was blowing up Charlie's antipersonnel mines in the jungle, he had seen enough death and decay for a lifetime.

The casket—lined with dark blue silk that picked up highlights from the reflection of the sky—was empty. There was nothing inside but sawdust, wood chips, pebbles, and a single small clump of dry earth.

Dennis had no idea what to say. Queenie O'Hare grunted words to herself that he did not understand. She bent to sniff the silk lining. Her head moved slightly; her eyes shifted to Dennis.

"Put your nose down there."

He crouched, but already he understood the meaning of her quiet command. Issuing from the casket was a musty smell of disuse—but that was all. There was no evidence of decay. He grasped what Queenie had already realized: there was no smell of detergent or other cleaning materials. No body had decayed here and then been removed. No body had ever been here.

Queenie looked at Dennis and Sophie. "Are you surprised?"

Sophie blew out a frosty breath and turned her head away.

"Yes," Dennis said to Queenie. "Aren't you?"

"The God's honest truth?" Queenie jumped up, almost athletically. "Not at all. I would have bet the ranch and the mortgage that this grave would be empty as a church on New Year's Eve. So now let's open the other one. Any bets?"

A short time later they saw that the second casket was empty, and it too had no odor.

Walking back to town through the wind-driven snow, Queenie said, "You know as well as I do these graves weren't opened and robbed. Dennis, those bodies we found at Pearl Pass are what's left of Henry Lovell Sr. and Susan Lovell. Don't you grasp that now?"

When Dennis didn't reply, Queenie turned to Sophie, who had yet to say a word other than monosyllabic answers to questions of procedure. Her hands were deep in her pockets. She walked with her head slightly bowed. In her expression he felt a kind of stoicism: *I will get through this somehow if you are loyal to me.* It was as if the cold air carried the message straight from her body to his mind.

"I think your dentist up here was mistaken," Queenie said to her, "about the teeth identification. Maybe he made a mistake and pulled the wrong records. I'll talk to him again."

"Yes, of course," Sophie said.

"And Dr. Pendergast, the one who issued the death certificates, I want to see her too."

"I understand."

"I also need to know who put the bodies in the caskets, or claimed to have done it—not to mention whoever lowered these empty boxes into the ground and forgot to say, 'Jeez, folks, ain't they *light!*'"

Queenie laughed, but the mirth had a sour edge to it. "And I've got a job of fingerprinting to do today. That's the other reason we came up here. We prefer doing it at the courthouse in Aspen. I assume your client and her husband are available?"

"They're waiting for you at home," Dennis said. "Once you print them, how long will it take to get a matchup and a result?"

Queenie shrugged. "If it's a negative, we'll know by tomorrow. If it's a positive, it might take a couple of days. If we're not sure and the latents have to be faxed to Denver and the FBI in Washington, we could be talking about a week."

From the Hendersons' living room, Dennis drew Scott into the privacy of the indoor pool area. It was warm there, and Dennis mopped his forehead with a handkerchief.

"Scott, I have some important things to do here in Springhill, but I don't want to stall or play games with the Sheriff's Office. I'm going to call one of my partners and have him meet you at the courthouse—he'll fill in for me, he'll represent Bibsy. That means I won't be with you on the ride down to Aspen. Don't say anything to this deputy. Discuss the weather. Discuss the new four-lane highway. Discuss whatever you damn please, but don't discuss this case. Is that clear?"

"I'm a lawyer too, remember?" Scott offered him a warm smile—but then it faded. "What's so important you can't come down with us?"

Dennis said, "I have to talk to a few people up here about a pair of empty caskets."

13 *November 30, 1994*

A Lawyer at Work

A FAINT SMELL of antiseptic perfume hung in the air of Edward Brophy's dental office. Dennis had to wait until Edward finished adjusting the wire braces on Nancy Loomis, a local teenager. He tried reading one-year-old issues of *Time* and *Money* but his concentration wandered.

Ten minutes later Edward stood by a plastic-covered dental chair, writing treatment notes on the patient's chart. Dennis sat on the swivel chair that normally the dentist or his assistant occupied.

"First, Edward, spend a few bucks and get some new magazine subscriptions. Second, believe that I'm on your side in this matter. Bibsy is my client. You may not understand this concept, but that relationship counts just as much to me as the fact that she's Sophie's mother."

"You lawyers are peculiar fellows."

"That's often been said."

Edward sighed. "Dentists have ethics as well."

"I'm glad to hear it. I'd like you to dust off those ethics and check the Lovells' records again. The Aspen deputy sheriff thinks you might have made a mistake in identification. She's going to come ask you about it. At some point she may even require a statement under oath." Dennis hesitated, to give his next words a little stonier meaning. "I think, when she used the word *mistake*, she was giving you the benefit of the doubt."

Edward sighed and looked glum.

"Can you go through the records now?" Dennis asked.

"I have a patient due any minute. The Crenshaw boy. It's an emergency. I have to look through his charts."

"Do you want me to wait?"

"No. I'll do it later today."

"Edward, this is serious."

The dentist kept sighing like a man in pain. He took a turn around the small room, halted his pacing, and faced Dennis, who caught a quick blaze from his eyes like that of a wounded animal in a trap. But his voice was surprisingly soft. "Do you want some advice from me, Dennis?

"I'm always grateful for intelligent advice."

"Whatever you're trying to find, or prove—give it up."

Dennis felt his blood rising. "I'm trying to prove that Bibsy Henderson is not guilty of murder. Edward, what are you covering up? Were those people at Pearl Pass the Lovells? *Did* you switch their dental records? And if so—*why?*"

After a few moments, Edward sank down into the dental chair. So I'm right, Dennis realized. And if I figured it out, so will Queenie O'Hare and Josh Gamble.

"I need to know all about this," he said. "I'll wait until you've finished with your patient, with this emergency, whatever the hell it is."

"There's no emergency," Edward said. "There's no patient coming." His hands were shaking.

"Wrong, Edward. There *is* an emergency. And you're in the middle of it. Now take a shot of booze or Pentothal if you need one, and tell me why you switched those records."

Dennis arrived at the marble quarry after the end of the lunch break. It was at the end of Quarry Road, two miles past his and Sophie's house. Along the edges of the road were blocks and shards of marble that had tumbled from trucks and wagons and been left there. A couple of snowmobiles and a big orange Sno-Cat that was used for avalanche control were parked outside next to pickup trucks and heavy-duty, four-wheel-drive vehicles.

The quarry produced some of the purest white marble in the world; part of its product had gone into banks and monuments throughout the United States. Giant wool cloth curtains hung over the two large openings to maintain an inside temperature just above freezing. A dozen men were working, bundled in parkas and thick ski hats. Dennis watched while a twenty-ton marble block, cut that day from the side wall, was skidded by a front-end loader up a portable steel ramp to the bed of a truck for the trip down to the Denver & Rio Grande Western railroad yards at West Glenwood Springs.

A few minutes later he sat with Hank Lovell in the quarry director's office. It was sparsely decorated, with only a space heater to ward off the cold. Dennis kept his coat and gloves on. Hank was a well-built man with midnight black hair, a sensual mouth, and brown eyes with long lashes.

"What can I do for you, Dennis?"

"You can tell me the truth about your parents' death."

"My parents . . . " Hank barely articulated the words.

"Hank, this is not the time for evasion. If I'm going to give Bibsy the kind of legal help she needs, I have to know what's going on. Edward changed the dental records. I know that."

"He admitted that to you?"

"I can't answer that question. If he did, it would fall under confidentiality. Do you understand what I'm saying? These are not strangers we're talking about. Your parents were murdered, or they were helped to commit suicide, which under Colorado law is a form of murder. What were they doing up at Pearl Pass? And why did Bibsy and Scott go up there?"

Hank drummed his stubby fingers on the desktop.

Dennis sighed. "I'll try to make it easy for you. As far as you know, were either of your parents suffering from cancer?"

"I don't know," Hank said. "That's a fact."

"Anything degenerative? More esoteric, like bacillary dysentery or cerebral rheumatism?"

"I swear to you, I don't know."

"What about AIDS?"

"My God. They were a little too old for that, don't you think?"

"I wonder. In Springhill, anything's possible."

"Why don't you ask Grace Pendergast?"

"I already have," Dennis said, "after I talked to Edward Brophy."

"And what did she tell you?"

"Grace is a tough lady. Can't discuss her patients' illnesses with me, not even her patients who are dead and gone. She filled out their death certificates. Those had to be lies too. Hank"—Dennis reached across the desk and grasped the younger man's wrist—"I need to know the truth. Why weren't your parents buried in the Springhill cemetery?"

"I don't know," Hank said. But the vigor had fled from his voice.

"Why were they taken up to Pearl Pass to be buried?"

"I don't know," Hank said.

"My God, do you know *anything*? Did they die here in Springhill, or up there in Pitkin County? Did Scott and Bibsy go up there with them? To help them die?"

"What do they say?"

"They don't. They're sitting on it. You're *all* sitting on it. And under the circumstances, that's a terrible mistake." Dennis felt he was about to lose control.

"You'd better talk to Sophie," Hank said. "That would be the proper thing to do."

"Yes. Proper. Fuck you, and fuck this 'proper' business. But yes, I will." Dennis stood. He said, "There's one thing more. I asked Grace who the casket bearers were at the funerals here. I had to practically arm-wrestle her, but she gave me the names of the men. You were one of them, and the others work here in the quarry. They were the same men for both funerals." He glanced at his handwriting on a slip of paper. "Mark Hapgood, Oliver Cone, John Frazee. Cone is your foreman, right? I need to talk to them for a few minutes. To all four of you together, unless it means the marble business comes to a crashing halt and the town's whole economy is threatened."

Ten minutes later the four men stood waiting in the glare of a halogen lamp near one of the ten-foot-long diamond-particle chain saws used to cut the larger blocks of marble. None of the men smoked. All chewed gum. Hapgood was a sandy-haired, hard-looking, buck-toothed man in his middle twenties. Frazee seemed a few years older, swarthy as were all the numerous Frazee clan, with a dark mustache and a close-cropped bullet head. Oliver Cone, muscular arms and shoulders straining his parka, was their immediate boss.

All wore dark blue or khaki-colored parkas and frayed jeans. They were the town's younger element that Dennis hardly knew. They roared through the back range on their snowmobiles, and in season— and sometimes out of it—chugged deep into the Maroon Bells wilderness on the quarry-owned Sno-Cat to hunt elk with either rifle or metal bow. In the evenings they worked out at the gym on Main Street. Driving home from work in Aspen, if his car window was open, Dennis often heard their husky laughter over the clank of iron disks and the crash of barbells dropped to concrete. He had always found the young men a little menacing, strangely defensive and wary, as if his presence threatened them. He would have been friendlier if they gave him the opportunity, but they offered little more than a nod of the head when he ran into them at the general store or the local bank.

Sophie said, "They need time, that's all. They're not bad people. They don't know you. And I suppose Oliver had his eye on my bones for a while. He may have thought I encouraged him, but that wasn't so. It probably bothered him when you came along and swept me away. City slicker! Give them time, Dennis. . . . "

Whatever Hank Lovell had told them now had erased all cheer from their faces. They stood, jaws working, rocking on the heavy heels and steel toes of their boots, looking at Dennis even more suspiciously than usual. They looked at him as though he were a stranger in their world, not one of them. That was exactly how Dennis felt. He wondered if now he could ever be at home in Springhill. His life was hazed with layers of doubt like fog shutting off light from the land.

"You were the four men who carried the caskets of Susan and Henry Lovell. That was on two separate occasions, at the two funerals."

He waited for a response. Slack-jawed, they listened, like large mountain cats backed against a wall by a fiercer brute. But the cats had claws for slashing and teeth for mangling, and there were four of them.

"I'm not going to ask you any questions about those funerals and the work you did," Dennis said. "Not today."

He felt them relax slightly. Frazee scuffed his boots. Mark Hapgood shifted his wad of gum, his facial muscles working against his skin. Oliver Cone looked straight at Dennis—almost through him. His eyes conveyed no expression except indifference. Dennis had seen eyes like that in the faces of Mafia killers. He was a little shocked to see them here on the face of a Springhill man. But this man, he knew, disliked him for personal reasons.

"I want you, all of you," Dennis said, "now, in front of each other and in front of Hank Lovell, to ask me to represent you as your lawyer. I won't charge you a fee, but if any Pitkin County sheriff's deputies or investigators come round to ask you questions about those funerals, you can say to them—and it will be God's truth—'Dennis Conway is my lawyer. He told me not to discuss anything with anybody. You better talk to him first.' And don't say another word—just send them round to me. Clear?"

They all nodded sluggishly. One by one, in gruff tones, each asked Dennis to represent him as his lawyer. Each time Dennis said, "All right. I will." Like a marriage ceremony.

That evening Dennis confronted Sophie in the greenhouse, where she was pruning her bougainvillea. Brian and Lucy had finally made friends with one of the neighbor's children and had been driven down to Carbondale for a Christmas party.

"Sophie, when you were a kid, did you ever work on one of those connecting-the-dots puzzles?"

Sophie looked up and nodded, while Dennis, in ragg sweater and baggy corduroys, a vodka tonic in hand, paced the carpet bordering the soil.

"That's exactly what a criminal case is like," he said. "A puzzle where you connect the dots. The district attorney connects them to make it look like a predatory animal. The defense attorney connects them to make it look like a cow chewing its cud. The reality for the DA and the defense attorney is like two overlapping circles. There's an area of fact where they more or less agree, and an area of interpretation where they don't agree at all. Unless the defendant pleads out, the jury paints the final picture. And aside from that"—he laughed a little harshly—"well, let me put it this way. I used to know a homicide cop in Manhattan who said, 'Murder is so exacting. Only two people in the world know what really went down. One ain't talkin' and the other can't.' "

"Murder . . . ?" Sophie murmured.

"Yes. An ugly word. But the proper one for what happened at Pearl Pass."

"I thought there was a probability that it was euthanasia," she said.

"There is that possibility. Unfortunately, in Colorado, euthanasia is considered a form of murder."

"That's a foolish law."

"In most circumstances I'd agree with you. But that's not the point. It's still the law. You can't wish it away."

"My mother didn't do it," Sophie said. "She couldn't have."

"I believe that. And your father?"

"Not my father either."

"All right, let's assume that's true—"

"Assume?" Snapping shut her pruning shears, Sophie straightened up. "Is that the best you can do, Dennis? *Assume?*"

"It's the most important thing I can do," he said. "If I assume innocence I can build a case based on a solid theory of defense. If I have blind faith in innocence I wouldn't bother to do that, I'd simply let events take their course. And that might be dangerous—particularly because there are so many things in this case I don't understand."

"Such as?"

"The empty graves. The victims *were* Hank's parents. Edward admitted that to me. He changed the dental records."

Sophie's face seemed to crumple a little. "Did he say why?"

"He felt that if the Pitkin County authorities knew those were the Lovells' bodies at Pearl Pass, it would make a stronger case against Scott and Bibsy. Somehow the DA's office would tie the two together. Whereas if they were unknown people, there was no connection."

"It makes sense," Sophie said.

"To Edward, yes. But to the law, Sophie, it's conspiracy. Do you understand? Obstruction of justice. A crime, a felony. If Ray Boyd found out, he'd certainly prosecute Edward."

"But he won't find out, will he? Edward's not going to tell him. And you're not either." It was part statement, part question, part plea.

"No, I'm not." He had already wrestled with the dilemma. Just as he had done with the men at the quarry, he had said to Edward, "Consider me your attorney. What you tell me—what you *told* me—falls under attorney-client privilege. I can't reveal it without your permission."

He walked with Sophie into the living room, where he tried to speak calmly. "That solves the problem for Edward, but not for me. If your parents are truly innocent, Sophie, why would Edward believe he had to cover for them like that? And why would Grace Pendergast refuse to help me by discussing the Lovells' medical history? It's as if this whole damned town is involved in some sort of conspiracy."

"To do what?"

"Sophie, are you being deliberately naive? To cover up the truth about a double murder!"

"Why would they do such a thing?"

"To protect their own. That's the only reason I can think of."

Sophie stood close and laid her cheek against his neck. She was warm, almost flushed. She spoke quietly but with passion.

"They didn't do it, Dennis. I swear to you. Help them. All these other things that are happening—these inconsistencies—don't matter. They're innocent. I know it. Please help them. Do whatever it takes."

"You know I will," Dennis said uncomfortably.

"Swear it to me."

He frowned. "Do I have to do that? Don't you believe me?"

"Where are my parents now?" Sophie asked. "I called them. There was no answer."

"I called too." Troubled, Dennis turned away. "I had to see Edward and Grace and the people up at the quarry, including your cousin Oliver—I couldn't be in two places at the same time, so I let your parents go down to Aspen with that woman deputy, for fingerprinting. I asked Mickey Karp to meet them at the courthouse. I figured until then your father knew what to say and what not to say." He shook his head. "But I shouldn't have let Bibsy go without me. She's my client. I should have gone with her. And I don't know where they are now."

14 *December 5, 1994*

Confession

SHERIFF JOSH GAMBLE jammed his bulk into the leather client's chair in front of Dennis's desk at Karp & Ballard. Behind him stood Deputy District Attorney Ray Boyd, one thumb hooked into his carved Mexican belt and the other tightly holding his cowhide briefcase. His eyes were hard and unfriendly.

The sheriff looked displeased. "What the hell's going on, Dennis?"

"What are you talking about?"

"Couple of my deputies been up to see a few of your clients at the Springhill Marble Company. Went there to ask some questions about a pair of empty caskets."

"And my clients told you to come talk to me. Nothing wrong with that."

From behind the sheriff, Ray Boyd said, "We're here to find out what that's all about."

"Let me do this, Ray," the sheriff said, without turning his head. "Mind telling me, Dennis, what you know about those empty caskets?"

"I don't know a damn thing."

"Those four guys who work at the quarry put those caskets into the graves, didn't they?"

"So I'm told."

"Then they knew goddam well they were empty."

"Hard to say."

"You're telling me they hefted those caskets and didn't realize there was something missing from each one of them?"

"I'm not telling you that," Dennis said carefully. "I'm not telling you anything at all."

The sheriff leaned forward. "Don't fuck with me."

"I'm not," Dennis said. "I'm protecting my clients. They haven't committed any crime and they haven't told you any lies. All they've done is ask you to talk to their lawyer, which you know is their legal right, and you're doing it. And I have no answer to your question because your question doesn't deal with the possible commission of a crime—it deals with a matter of judgment that's more proper to a weight guesser at a county fair. You want to charge those men with something, Josh?"

"I've been good to you on this case," the sheriff said. "I've shared discovery right down the line."

"And I appreciate that," Dennis said. "You also shared with me your opinion that I might be a damned fool to reciprocate."

"Shit," Josh said. He nodded to Ray Boyd, who drew a sheaf of papers from his briefcase and handed them to Dennis.

"Two copies," Boyd said. "Read either one of them."

"Now?" Dennis asked.

"You might want to be alone," the sheriff said. "Come to think of it, I don't know if I want to be around to watch you bleed. Let's mount up and ride, Ray."

The sheriff and the deputy district attorney left. Dennis picked up the stapled sheets of papers and settled back into his chair to read.

SUPPLEMENTARY INVESTIGATION REPORT

This report is predicated upon the continuing investigation into the homicide on or about August 15, 1994, of Jane Doe and John Doe, whose remains were discovered on November 10, 1994, approximately three miles southwest of Pearl Pass at an altitude of 12,500 feet, in Pitkin County, Colorado.

Queenie Anne O'Hare, deputy sheriff of Pitkin County, Colorado, states:

At or about 10:30 a.m. on Wednesday morning, November 30, 1994, in Pitkin County vehicle #7, I left from the town of Springhill in Gunnison County to the city of Aspen in Pitkin County, with Mr. Scott G. Henderson and Mrs. Beatrice R. Henderson as passengers in said vehicle. My purpose was to conduct Mr. and Mrs. Henderson to be fingerprinted in the Pitkin County Sheriff's Office.

I had been informed by Beatrice Henderson that she had retained the legal counsel of Dennis Conway, Esq., a member of the Colorado bar, but Mr. Conway had not chosen to accompany us in the county vehicle. I had also been informed by Scott Henderson that he was a member of the Colorado bar and did not require legal counsel other than his own.

Neither Mr. or Mrs. Henderson was under arrest, or in custody, or had been told that they were under suspicion of having committed a felony crime. The ensuing conversation, which took place in county vehicle #7, was therefore not in the form of a custodial interrogation.

The conversation was not mechanically recorded. I made handwritten notes of the conversation as soon as we reached the Pitkin County Sheriff's Office, at or about 11:30 a.m. My memory was therefore fresh.

Based on my notes:

In county vehicle #7, until we reached the turnoff from state Route 133 through Main Street in the town of Carbondale, and from there via Catherine Store Road to Route 82 heading eastward to Aspen, the conversation between myself, Beatrice Henderson, and Scott Henderson was of a general nature. We discussed matters such as the weather, the proposal to increase the acreage at Snowmass by enlarging the skiable terrain at Burnt Mountain, and then the matter of whether or not it was feasible to widen Route 82 into a four-lane highway leading into Aspen in order to accommodate the increasing traffic flow in the valley. Mr. Henderson told me he was against four-laning, that it ruined the environment, and he was in favor of the proposal to install a railroad line along the old bed of the Rio Grande Railroad.

When I asked Mrs. Henderson for her opinion on these matters, she told me she had not been listening to our conversation. She stated, "I'm feeling terrible today. Not well. I guess I have other things on my mind."

I asked her what it was she had on her mind.

(Note: Beatrice Henderson, at the time, occupied the front passenger's seat in county vehicle #7, and Scott Henderson occupied the back of the vehicle by himself. Before beginning the journey I had offered Mr. Henderson the front seat, because he is a very tall gentleman, but he stated to me at the time, "No, actually I prefer the backseat, because I can stretch out there more comfortably. You never can get these front seats to run back far enough for me to stretch out. In my own Jeep I have the seat track unbolted and moved back four inches so I can slide the seat way back and be really comfortable. That little operation turns my Jeep into a luxury car.")

In response to my question as to what she had on her mind, Beatrice Henderson stated, "I keep thinking of poor Susie and Henry. How they always wanted to go to that island near Hawaii, and they never got the chance."

I said, "Susie and Henry? Do you by any chance mean Susan and Henry *Lovell?*" (Note: These are considered the probable identities for the victims currently known as Jane Doe and John Doe.)

At the same time, in the backseat of the vehicle, Mr. Henderson loudly uttered his wife's name. (He said, "Bibsy!" which I am told is Beatrice Henderson's nickname.) He seemed to be cautioning his wife not to say any more of what she was saying to me.

But Mrs. Henderson nodded in an affirmative manner to my question and stated to me, "Maybe that's where they were going. We never found out. We never even asked them."

Mr. Henderson sat up and said loudly, "Bibsy, shut up!" I could see him clearly in the rearview mirror. His tone was forceful and his facial expression was one of anger.

I said, "Mrs. Henderson, if you want to talk to me about it, you certainly can. But I must explain to you that if you make any kind of admissions to me, they could be used against you."

She said, "Oh, I know I'm not supposed to talk about it. But what does it matter now? Susie and Henry are gone, and I don't have much time left either."

She turned to her husband in the backseat, who was still trying to quiet her down. She stated to him, "You don't either, Scott. I hate to lie. I just hate it. It's a sin. God may forgive all of us for what we did up there at Pearl Pass but I don't think he'll forgive us for lying about it now. I can't lie. I won't lie to the police. I didn't hurt anyone. I didn't kill anyone. Neither did you. We just have to have the courage of our convictions."

Mr. Henderson said, "Bibsy, you're not well. You're under a strain. You're ranting." He said to me, "Deputy O'Hare, you're taking advantage of my wife's physical condition. She suffers from an ailment that makes her hallucinate out loud. Please stop interrogating her. I insist on it. I also insist you disregard what she said to you."

I said, "I'm not interrogating her, sir. She made her recent remarks freely and without any coercion on my part, and this is not a custodial interrogation. You're a lawyer. You know I can't disregard anything."

Mr. Henderson began talking to his wife forcefully in a language other than English, but a few of the words, which I do not recall, were recognizable to me, and seemed like some sort of slang in the English language. I believe in Springhill, in Gunnison County, where the Hendersons are from, the local people call it Springling. But I did not understand the meaning of what he said to her.

After that Mrs. Henderson declined to talk to me further. She closed her eyes and either slept or pretended to sleep until we reached the Sheriff's Office on Main Street, Aspen, where I parked by the side entrance.

We entered the basement office in the courthouse building, wherein I placed Mr. and Mrs. Henderson in the custody of Deputies Hermine Fuld and Jerrod Pentz for the purpose of fingerprinting. I retired to an office down the hall and there at my desk made handwritten notes of the prior conversation with Mr. and Mrs. Henderson.

Later in the day, referring to these notes, I reported the conversation orally to Sheriff Gamble. He instructed me to transfer my notes verbatim to a file in the computer, plus anything else I could remember. I did so.

It is from those typed notes that I have completed this report.

Subscribed to and sworn on this 5th day of December 1994,

Queenie Anne O'Hare
Deputy Sheriff
Pitkin County, Colorado

15 *January 11, 1995*

Judge Florian's Domain

OUTSIDE THE PITKIN County Courthouse, under a cold gray sky like an immense dome of steel, Dennis said, "I never should have let her go without me."

"You couldn't foresee it," Sophie said.

"That's no excuse."

"It's done, Dennis."

He had returned home to Springhill and handed Queenie O'Hare's report to Bibsy. His mother-in-law had scanned it, sighed, and said, "It's true that I said those things. Perhaps not those exact words, but something like them. And it's true that Scott was a little harsh when he told me to be quiet—when I think about it now, I don't blame him. But I will tell you just one thing. I've thought a great deal about it, and I truly believe it's the only thing you need to know in order to act properly as my lawyer. And that thing is this: I did not murder those two people. I didn't assist them in suicide. I did not inject them with anything. I want you to believe me, Dennis. Do you?"

"Yes, I do," Dennis said uneasily.

But belief in innocence did not rise to the level of religious faith. You could have it one moment, and it could be gone the next. If Bibsy were innocent, how to account for what she had said to Queenie

O'Hare? And why had Edward Brophy lied? Dennis had difficulty accepting the dentist's simple explanation of wanting to help his old friends. The whole matter of the false burial was ugly. The empty graves in the cemetery were not proof that the victims at Pearl Pass were Henry and Susan Lovell. But proof was one thing, knowledge another.

If it was euthanasia, why carry it out thirty miles away and well above twelve thousand feet? Stricken with a fatal illness, the Lovells might have said, "We want to die in the wilderness we love." But there was plenty of wilderness only a few miles away from their home. And why the arrow through the heart of their dog? Had the killers wanted to approach silently? Or was the death of the dog a mischance unrelated to the deaths of Jane and John Doe?

Dennis wondered about all this.

"But do you believe my mother?" Sophie asked him, standing outside the courthouse.

"Her fingerprints were on the pillbox. Your father's fingerprints were on the Remington rifle found near the graves. There has to be a theory for a rational defense. I haven't come up with one."

"That's not an answer to my question."

He stamped his foot on the pavement. "Sophie, what do you expect me to believe? I *want* to believe her. It's not easy."

Sophie measured him carefully. "Nevertheless, you're going in that courtroom to win this case for her."

"There's no case yet to win or lose. There's just an accusation."

"You've got to believe in her!"

The force of Sophie's cry startled him. "Listen to me," he said. "I'll do all that's humanly possible to get her and your father out of this mess. Guilty or innocent makes no difference. I'm her lawyer. I let her down by abandoning her the day she came down here for fingerprinting. I had a lot on my mind. I had other things to do, but I made the wrong decision. I owe her. If there's a case to win, I'm prepared to go all the way to win it. For her, Sophie—and for you."

Judge Curtis Florian gazed down from his leather chair behind the high oak bench. On the wall over his head in Pitkin County's only courtroom was affixed the blue-and-gold seal of the state of Colorado. Next to the seal hung an electric wall fan that the judge's court clerk would switch on two or three times each summer. It never grew seriously hot in Aspen, and even when the temperature soared into the eighties there was barely any humidity. But it was January now. The temperature on Main Street was twenty-five degrees Fahrenheit.

The spaciousness of the high-ceilinged courtroom added to the atmosphere and presumption of authority. The judge's domed forehead shone brightly under the fluorescent lighting. Judge Florian was a man well into his sixties, with sagging ears and narrow cold eyes. His downturned mouth gave rise to the notion that justice might be bad-tempered. For a while he gazed down in silence at the three lawyers standing in the well of the courtroom. Ray Boyd, powerful arms akimbo, pink face seemingly about to burst like a party balloon, represented the state. He was the deputy district attorney in the Ninth Judicial District and the prosecutor. Dennis Conway, the new boy on the block, was one of the two defense lawyers. The other defense lawyer, Scott Henderson, had double billing: he was one of the two defendants. Sophie and Edward Brophy were squeezed together in a rear pew of the courthouse.

The judge's thin chest rattled audibly. He didn't like it when a defendant insisted on his right to defend himself *pro se*. It usually meant that the court had to bend over backwards to help the "lawyer" proceed with his case, for it was generally agreed that such a lawyer had a fool for a client. In this case, however, the accused himself was a real lawyer, a member of the Colorado bar, albeit retired. He should not need help. The judge still didn't like it. You never knew what might happen and how an appellate court would deal with the proceedings. Judge Florian's sternness and lack of facial ease covered up a chronic indecisiveness. When he had to make up his mind about something he believed to be vital, he broke out in hives. In civil cases he always encouraged the adversary lawyers to come to a pretrial settlement. In criminal matters he encouraged plea bargaining.

Beatrice Henderson, the second defendant, sat alone at the long rectangular defense table. She looked at ease—Grace Pendergast had put her on twenty milligrams of Valium a day. Every now and then in the past few weeks since Dennis had read the deputy's report and seen the results of the fingerprinting, he had said to her, "Are you all right, Bibsy?" And Bibsy had unvaryingly replied, "Yes, Dennis, I'm on Valium, you know." Dennis worried about it but decided to let it be. If she were to take the stand as a witness in her own defense, that would be another matter. But they were a long way off from that possibility.

Dennis had made no decision yet about Bibsy's testifying. He rarely did in a criminal trial until the prosecution presented its case. It was usually better not to have the defendant testify; the cross-examination could be crushing. But sometimes it was the only way to save a lost cause. Amend that, Dennis thought. To *try* to save a lost cause. He had seen too many defendants commit legal suicide on the witness stand.

Soon after he had begun practicing law in New York, Dennis had as a client a man named Lindeman, a city official accused of accepting bribes. Prior to trial, Dennis asked Lindeman, "What did you think when you were first approached with the proposition?" Lindeman said, "I was worried. I didn't like to break the law. I was hurting for money, but it didn't seem right."

Dennis told Lindeman to say it that way, and in court with his client on the stand, he asked the rehearsed question. Lindeman replied, "I thought, How do I know this guy's not an undercover cop? And then I said to myself, 'There just isn't enough money in it.' "

Dennis broke into a sweat and was afraid to ask any more questions. Later, Lindeman said, "I can't believe what I did. It just flew out of me."

What had flown out of him was the truth. The truth, struggling for air to breathe, for space, for supremacy and vindication. Lindeman had been found guilty and sentenced to five to ten years.

But Dennis believed he could win the Henderson case—unless something more were to happen that he didn't know about and couldn't predict. His attention drifted, as often happened when he was someplace he didn't want to be. He certainly would have preferred not to be in this courtroom as lawyer for the defense. His client hardly talked to him. She was not angry at him. She was just distant, at ease under the influence of Valium.

The judge said, "You had a motion to make, Mr. Conway? Is that what you started to say a minute ago?"

Dennis's mind snapped back into focus. "Yes, Your Honor."

"Proceed."

Dennis moved forward into the well of the courtroom and looked up into the face of the judge. "Your Honor, even before any hearing regarding bond, I would like to move to dismiss the charge, the information, against my client, Mrs. Beatrice Henderson. I believe that Mr. Henderson will move also to quash the information against himself as codefendant."

Scott nodded genially in agreement. Dennis waved some papers in the direction of the bench. "This information submitted to the court by the district attorney's office," he went on, slowly gathering momentum, "is compounded almost totally of circumstantial evidence, and flimsy circumstantial evidence at that. There are fingerprints found at the crime scene on a silver pillbox. We freely admit that a box answering this description once belonged to my client, but there is a glaring lack of evidence to indicate that this box was left at the scene at the time the crime was committed. Or for that matter, that it was left there—at any time—by Mrs. Henderson. There are fingerprints found on a rifle, and those prints are alleged to be those of Mr. Scott Henderson, the codefendant. But the rifle, Your Honor, had nothing to do with the crime. It was merely found at or near the crime scene. No one knows who owned that rifle. It did not belong to my client. It was never in her care or custody or in the codefendant's care or custody. The state will be unable to prove any such allegation, and I'm pleased to note that they haven't even attempted to make it. So the prints prove nothing. They are fluff and bluff."

Dennis paused. He didn't want to go too quickly. He wanted the judge to absorb the facts, sort them out, and hang on to them. He had heard that the judge had a thoughtful, somber demeanor, but for the most part it cloaked a slowness of perception.

Judge Florian nodded at Ray Boyd. "And what say you to that, Ray, on behalf of the People?"

Ray? Dennis felt a twinge of dismay. Aspen was a sophisticated and overpriced part of the world, but it was still a small town. The legal community had done business together for years, broken bread together at Men's Club luncheons, waved to one another on chairlifts, cheered in unison at high school hockey games. Dennis wondered if he was being put in his place—and being so informed—by virtue of his being a newcomer. As for the Hendersons, it also bore in on him that they too might be looked on as foreigners; indeed, the local good-humored expression was *downvalley dirtbags.* How much was jest and how much was evidence of that class structure which Americans so vigorously denied and so religiously practiced? Springhill—remote, insular, supposedly unfriendly—might even be in a worse category than merely *downvalley*.

Ray Boyd stepped forward, blue eyes aglow with pleasure—a man who loved his work. To complement his no-nonsense blue serge business suit, the deputy district attorney wore black elephant-hide boots with pointed toes. After Vietnam, Dennis had gone through a boot period, and he knew that those elephant-hide boots on Boyd's feet had cost the prosecutor in the neighborhood of $1,000.

The heels clicked like gunshots as Boyd strode across the courtroom's parquet floor. "If it please the court," Boyd said, "I'd like to explain to defense counsel the way I see the nature of what he calls 'flimsy circumstantial evidence.' "

The judge nodded his approval. Boyd swiveled his narrow hips and turned his attention to Dennis. "This is a true story, sir. I'm sitting in my living room one Sunday and I hear a crash outside in the street, where my green Ford Explorer is parked by the curb. My wife and I run out and there's a brand-new big dent in the fender of the Ford, with a red streak. And about fifty yards down the road, at the end of a trail of antifreeze, there's this old red Chevy pickup that's run up on someone's lawn at a cockeyed angle. We can hear that the guy behind the wheel is trying to get his engine started. And his front bumper has a big streak of green paint that matches the color of my Ford Explorer."

Ray Boyd faced Judge Florian. "Your Honor, I didn't see him sideswipe my car. And no one else in the neighborhood saw it. I have only circumstantial evidence to go on, plus common sense. What does common sense tell me? The only intelligent explanation—and I'll bet my paycheck that counsel for the defense, even though he probably never saw a Chevy pickup until he moved here from New York, will agree with me—is that the guy in the Chevy hit my Explorer. If I had to I could have made a case out of that and won it hands down. Just like I can make a case out of what we've got against Mr. and Mrs. Henderson. And if we can get an impartial jury of Colorado folk with a minimum of common sense, which shouldn't be difficult, I believe I can win."

Dennis had already guessed that this speech was one that Ray Boyd made time and time again to the judge and to various juries. Before this trial's over, he decided—if there's going to be a trial—this man's going to make me puke. I just hope that when I do it he's close enough so I don't miss his boots.

Dennis stood again. "Your Honor—"

Judge Florian raised a pale hand. "I heard you out, Mr. Conway, and I heard Mr. Boyd. Anyway, the evidence isn't all circumstantial. Isn't there the matter of the confession? You don't call that 'circumstantial,' do you?"

Dennis took a copy of Queenie O'Hare's report from his briefcase. He arched his back a little, so that the vertebrae crackled. As firmly as he could without risking judicial wrath, he said, "Your Honor, I've studied the document you refer to. I'm obliged to point out to the court that it is not a confession. That word has a specific meaning and this report does not qualify. It's a report of a conversation in a moving vehicle in which, allegedly, Mrs. Henderson makes several statements about—I quote—'what we did up there at Pearl Pass.' Judge"—Dennis raised the pages between two fingers, far from his face and equally far from the judge's bench, as if they were contaminated—"read carefully. Is there anything that Deputy O'Hare claims my client said about what she did, specifically, up at Pearl Pass? No, there is not. The deputy leaves that out, because Mrs. Henderson made no such admission or confession. What she said barely rises to the level of vague reminiscence."

Dennis waited, mustering as grave an expression on his face as he was capable of.

"Anything more?" the judge asked.

"No sir."

Judge Florian said, "I'll let a jury decide about that matter. I'm the judge of the law—the jury is the judge of the facts. I'm going to tell them that. Let them decide if it's a confession, or an admission, or a reminiscence, as you put it, or even a daydream of this charming deputy, Ms. O'Hare. Mr. Conway, I'm going to deny your motion to dismiss the charge. The information has merit. This court accepts it. So let's move along."

Dennis absorbed the blow. He looked at Bibsy, who seemed calm. Sophie, in the rear of the courtroom, had gone pale.

"Did you come here prepared to plead?" Judge Florian asked Dennis. "And if so, how does your client plead?"

"Not guilty," Dennis said.

"And you, sir?" The judge looked down at Scott Henderson, who stood tall in his old, well-cut, wide-lapeled gray flannel suit, looking like a contemporary Moses.

"Not guilty," Scott said.

"Then we'll try these two cases together. Anyone object to that? If so, I'll hear argument." The judge looked from one lawyer to another.

"The People don't object," Boyd said.

"I don't either," Scott said.

Dennis knew there was no hope to ask for a severance. Under other circumstances he might have battled to separate the two defendants, on the theory that he didn't want to be burdened by what Scott might have done at Pearl Pass or might say in court. But these were his wife's parents: it was nearly impossible to separate them in terms of his feelings, or to let one of them suffer a fate different from the other's. And it certainly would be more efficient and less painful to try them together.

"Mrs. Henderson does not object," he said.

"The defendants will stand trial together. We come to the matter of bond. Ray?"

The prosecutor said, "Judge, this is first-degree murder. The People don't believe that bail is proper in such cases. There's plenty of precedent and I won't insult your knowledge of the law by quoting it to you. We request no bail for either defendant."

"Mr. Dennis Conway?"

Progress, Dennis realized. First I was "Mr. Conway," and now I'm "Mr. Dennis Conway." After twenty years of practice here and fifty more lunches at the Ritz-Carlton, I might be just plain "Dennis."

"These defendants," he said, "are long-term citizens of the community. They have absolutely no criminal record. All their property is in nextdoor Gunnison County. Their family is here. They're taxpayers. They're not young. It's not their habit to travel. On behalf of Mrs. Henderson, a registered nurse who served her township for nearly forty years before retirement, I ask for bail on her own recognizance. And Mr. Henderson—a lawyer, an officer of this court—joins me in that request on behalf of himself."

The judge made an effort to convince the lawyers that he was considering the request. The truth was that he had made up his mind on all these matters days ago, in chambers, while munching an apple and drinking a Sprite for his afternoon snack, and nothing short of startling new evidence would have forced him to change his intentions.

"Mr. Ray Boyd," he said, "I have to tell you the presumption of guilt in this case is not great. It's there, but it's not overwhelming. And there is definitely a great deal of circumstantial evidence alongside that reported confession. Mr. Scott Henderson was arrested on what I'd call bare probable cause. Mr. Dennis Conway's comments about the nature of Mrs. Beatrice Henderson's alleged confession have some merit. So, no, I am not going to pen these people up until the day of trial."

He turned to Dennis. "But I can't let them just wander around under their own recognizance, sir. There's no precedent for that in a first-degree murder case. These folks will have to post bond of two hundred fifty thousand dollars each. They own property up in Springhill, and everything's sky high these days, so that should make no problem. You can work out the details with my clerk. Now, as to the matter of the trial date . . ."

Scott Henderson stood. "Your Honor," he said in his deep, lawyerly voice, "under the Colorado speedy trial statute, I'm allowed to request trial within ninety days. I so request. I'll be ready in ninety days, and I'm sure Mr. Conway will be ready on behalf of my wife."

Color drained from what could be seen of Dennis's cheeks under his beard. This matter of speedy trial had not been discussed.

The judge's voice was surprisingly soft. "Yes, Mr. Henderson, it's your right under the law. You're correct about that. But . . ." His voice trailed off. He muttered something under his breath. Then his brow furrowed.

"Ray, what do the People say?"

"It's not convenient, Your Honor," Ray Boyd blurted. "We're talking about a crime scene that's under ten feet of snow! No one can get up into that Pearl Pass quadrant to gather evidence until June at the earliest—maybe not even until July. And if there's a heavy spring snowfall, not until August. Your Honor, a speedy trial would not be fair!"

"But it's their right under the law, Ray," Judge Florian pointed out.

"It doesn't serve the interest of justice, Your Honor. It would contradict the purpose of the statute."

"The statute doesn't say anything about melting snow. You can look till the cows come home, but you still won't find that clause. It just says that a defendant has the right to trial within ninety days of indictment, if he or she requests it. You knew that, Ray. It would have been smarter to hold off on the indictment until May—but you didn't do that. So I have to grant the motion."

Clucking his tongue, the judge consulted a calendar, while Ray Boyd silently fumed.

"Trial date will be Monday, April tenth, upcoming. Nine A.M. in the morning to pick a jury. Suit you, Scott Henderson?"

"Yes, Your Honor," Scott said.

"Anyone can't make it?"

No one spoke.

"You think you all might come to some kind of understanding," the judge inquired in his most winning manner—he almost, but not quite, managed to smile—"before that date?"

He meant: will you cut a deal? Will you crank up a plea? Will you save me a lot of decision-making?

"It's a heinous and brutal crime," Ray Boyd said, "but the People are willing to negotiate."

"My client will not plea-bargain," Dennis shot back. He took Bibsy's hand. "She's not guilty of any wrongdoing."

It was the obligation of both prosecutor and defense attorney to attack and defend with full arsenals of weaponry. From these warring polarities a hoped-for vision of facts—even truth—might emerge. The outcome was not a pure ingredient, but a soup that resulted from the mixing of sour and sweet, black and white, thesis and antithesis, accusation and defense. Did it taste good? That was not necessarily the point. It had to be digestible.

"Mr. Henderson?"

Scott said, "My client also doesn't choose to negotiate."

The judge's thin cheeks crumpled like much-folded sheets of gray paper. "In that case, let's all be here on April tenth."

16 *January 1995*

Connecting the Dots

IN DENNIS'S OFFICE, the sheriff gazed up at the smooth ascent of the gondola toward the top of Aspen Mountain. "Nice view," he said.

"If you had this view," Dennis observed, "law enforcement in Pitkin County could grind to a total halt."

"I know how to delegate."

"Did you come to talk about the view?"

"Your client's in the clear with the potassium," Josh said. "Never put in any request for any lethal drugs in the last five years. Not the Versed either, or the Pentothal."

"I could have told you that."

"I don't doubt it. I always tell people you're a Dartmouth man—a little closemouthed, but not dumb. You know a doctor in your neck of the woods named Pendergast?"

"Sure."

"She the only doctor up there?"

"It's a town of three hundred and fifty people, Josh. Two doctors would starve. Two lawyers, on the other hand, might drum up a nice little trade."

"Your Dr. Pendergast gets her drugs through a medical supply house over in Grand Junction. Hang on, I want to make sure I've got these figures right." The sheriff consulted his notebook. "In the past five years, in Grand Junction, Dr. Pendergast ordered about a hundred and fifteen vials of twenty microequivalents of potassium chloride. You remember what Jeff told us? Takes ten vials to kill someone."

"It's used for lifesaving reasons too," Dennis reminded him. But he wondered who in Springhill was that ill. He knew of no one.

"That's what I like about you," Josh said. "You always look on the bright side of things. Think it over. If you have any brilliant conclusions to share with me, you know where I live."

Dennis called on Grace Pendergast early the next morning. She had a small office in a blue wood frame building next to the bank in Springhill. He relayed the sheriff's discovery.

"They already contacted me about that," Grace said. "I have a patient with a chronic and dangerous potassium imbalance. An older woman. A neighbor of yours who doesn't care to air her troubles in the usual circles of gossip. You can figure out who it is."

"Did you tell that to the sheriff?"

"To his deputy, a woman named O'Hare. But I didn't give her the name of the patient. I can't do that."

"You could have, but you chose not to."

Dennis had come about another matter too. "You have patients' records, Grace, including those of Henry and Susan Lovell. I realize that under ordinary circumstances they contain privileged information. Your patients are deceased—those records could be subpoenaed. Or you could give them up voluntarily. I'm Bibsy's attorney, not the law. If you showed the medical records to me, you wouldn't at all be infringing on the rights of two dead persons."

"I know all that," Grace said.

"Good. I'm driving down to Aspen in about an hour and I want to take the records with me. I need to determine if either Henry or Susan Lovell had an incurable disease. I may not use that fact, if it's a fact, but it's possible that it could save Bibsy and Scott from going to prison."

Grace said, "There was nothing on the Lovells' medical records that indicates an incurable disease. You can take my word for it."

"I do, but I'd like to see them anyway."

"I've destroyed them."

Dennis stared at her. "When did you do that?"

"Thirty days after I filed their death certificates with the state."

Dennis clenched a fist and tapped it against his thigh. It was hard to hide his anger. "Is that your common practice, Grace?"

"I am not under cross-examination," Dr. Pendergast said, and turned away from her desk.

He went from there to the Henderson house and found Scott soaking in the hot tub on the deck, his face tilted to the winter sun. "Aches and pains," he said. "Old age."

"We need to talk about a few things," Dennis said.

"Fire away."

"Why did you invoke the speedy trial statute?"

"You really want to know?" Scott sighed. "Just to get it over with. It's hard on Bibsy, more than on any of us. The sooner we get to the end of it, the better."

"Is there anything up there at Pearl Pass under the snow?" Dennis asked.

"Not that I'm aware of," Scott said carefully. "But you never know, do you?" He twisted in the tub so that the strongest jet beat into the lower part of his back. "Listen, Dennis. You'll conduct the trial and I know you'll do a hell of a job. I trust you. Maybe I did a dumb-ass thing by representing myself, but the plain fact is there's no one else around here I have faith in."

Dennis nodded. Doing it alone was not the problem. "Have you ever been in court against Ray Boyd?"

"I wasn't a criminal lawyer. Maybe a DUI now and then for some kid from town. Ray is Pitkin County's prosecutorial answer to the neutron bomb. All the buildings remain standing, but all the people succumb to his speeches."

Dennis managed a light laugh.

"He's not stupid," Scott said, "just long-winded. And he's got a temper."

"Can he lose it in court?"

"Been known to happen."

Dennis veered back to what troubled him most. "It would help if you would tell me your version of what happened up there at the pass."

"I don't think I'll do that. I'll let you imagine it . . . as long as what you imagine is in my and Bibsy's best interests."

Dennis, who had been sitting on the edge of the tub, got to his feet. "Are you all trying to drive me crazy?"

He left the house, slammed the Jeep into four-wheel drive, and drove toward Aspen. The plowed road twisted and turned toward Carbondale, and he could feel patches of ice under his tires. Shadows of wind-driven clouds raced across the forest.

Imagine what's in our best interests, Scott had said. Not so silly and cavalier as it sounded, Dennis reflected. Defense attorneys in trial routinely concocted—imagined—a reasonable theory of defense that a jury might believe. Toward that end they called friendly witnesses to bolster their theory and ruthlessly cross-examined the hostile ones. But imagination had to have some foundation in reality. A lawyer didn't simply shoot from the hip and blow away the state's evidence with the brute power of argument. You could do that if you *had* an argument, but you couldn't have much of an argument if you didn't have a theory. And you couldn't have a theory unless your client gave you a nail to hang it on. How, Dennis asked himself, do I account for what happened? For the pillbox? The fingerprints? The admissions to Queenie O'Hare? He knew that the Hendersons had been at Pearl Pass—the tale of the pillbox lost at Glenwood Springs three years ago was nonsense. If Bibsy had moaned, "I have no idea where I lost it," Dennis might have found heart to believe. But what came out so brightly had been too rehearsed.

He drove slowly, absorbed in thought. A black delivery van appeared in his rearview mirror—it tapped its horn twice. When Dennis slowed down and edged toward the shoulder, it passed him, picking up speed.

All these people in Springhill, he thought, are friends of the Hendersons. They think they're protecting them but in fact they're harming them. Why can't they see that?

He heard the familiar low boom of a distant explosion. Less than a minute later a guttural *whoosh* rumbled from far above him, followed by what seemed like a light clap of thunder. Dennis's heartbeat quickened. He eased immediately onto the brake, slowing the car, looking in all directions. But his view was blocked by the forest itself. He saw nothing except a sunstruck glare of orange glinting through the trees against the skyline. Then the world was instantly silent again.

Beyond the next curve, up above, a steep chute led down to the road from an open bowl. Dennis's heart pounded even more rapidly as he slowed to nearly a crawl. Coming up on the curve, he peered up at the immense sloping quilt of white snow. Something growled again—this time it was like a faraway pride of lions disturbed in their sleep—and a spiderweb of cracks shot silently across the slope.

The slope folded up and began to slide. Jamming his boot hard on the brake, Dennis skidded to a stop against a snowbank in the lee of a protecting grove of aspens. He leaned forward, staring, hardly believing what he saw. A giant cloud of powder rose into the air. A hundred yards ahead on the road, the brakelights of the black van that had passed him were flashing a violent red—and then a split-second later the van became a child's tumbling toy. It pitched, yawed, and plunged down the slope below the road. Boiling white snow swept over it, bearing it in a crazy roll between the aspen groves. Suddenly it was gone from sight—completely vanished.

The snow settled; the rumble slowly died. The silence took hold again. The road ahead, blocked by the avalanche, had risen five feet. Dennis could no longer see ahead of him.

Sweat burst from his forehead. When he reached for his cellular phone, he was shaking so hard that he had to grasp it with two hands.

When the snowplows and emergency management force arrived from Glenwood Springs, it took more than an hour to clear the road. Dennis sat in his Jeep, shivering.

He was told he could go. He drove slowly down the winding road to Carbondale, and then on the crowded Route 82 to Aspen, thinking about what had happened. My God, I could be dead. If the van hadn't passed me, and if I hadn't slowed down when it did, the avalanche would have hit *me*, not the van.

From his office he called Sophie at school. Word had reached Springhill and she knew some details.

"Are you all right, Dennis?"

"Just a little shaken up."

"Did they find the driver of the van?"

"They told me they found the van. I mean, they could *see* it. They couldn't get to it. The driver's door was ripped off the hinge. The driver was nowhere in sight."

"Did you know he'd just delivered a new Sears refrigerator to Shirlene Hubbard?"

Somehow that news made the death of the delivery man even more absurd, even less acceptable.

Mickey Karp, Dennis's law partner, reached the office late that afternoon. He was a volunteer with Mountain Rescue, a citizen organization that served in such crises.

"I was on call," Mickey said. "but they didn't need me today. Not next week either. They won't dig that body out until summer."

"Are you serious?" Dennis asked. "You mean they're not digging *now*?"

"Dennis, that was a slab fracture. You can send people into the scene to dig for an avalanche victim, but if the chute fractures a second time—and they do that too often—what then? You lose a dozen people trying to save one who's probably dead already. You know how long you'd last buried under that snow?"

"I don't think I'd like to guess."

"Twenty minutes if you're lucky—or maybe unlucky. Sometimes you can't breathe. You inhale the snow. You're in a vise—it's like wet concrete. Or you've got some room but you dig in the wrong direction. Your breath can freeze and form an ice mask. Two feet of snow on top of you is enough to kill you. This guy thrown from the van was probably under five or six feet. And where to dig? They were looking at four or five acres of unstable snowpack—every square foot of it can fall out from under you. Last winter we had cross-country skiers, real assholes from Denver, who went up to the Tenth Mountain Division huts with avalanche warnings out, and they vanished in a storm. How many lives were we supposed to risk to save them? Choppers get knocked down in those storms like they were made of paper. We tried—by snowmobile, on foot, in the air, every way—and couldn't find them. They were lucky and got out on their own."

"What do you think caused the slide this morning?"

Mickey shrugged. "That was an open chute with an angle of about thirty-eight degrees. A classic disaster recipe. High wind chips off a piece of a cornice, an iced overhang. A bighorn sheep or a mountain goat wanders in there at the top, cracks it wide open. Fresh snow or hoarfrost may not bond to the old snow beneath it. A lot of snow, then warm weather to melt it—the snow falls off trees, hits a sensitive spot, and the whole mountain rolls. But the avalanche control guys from Springhill were up there this morning on the crest above the road, checking the chutes. They saw most of the slide. They said the guy in the van leaned on his horn just before the slope fractured—probably when he passed you."

"Yes, he did that," Dennis said.

"That kind of noise vibration could set it off."

"Were the Springhill people up there in a Sno-Cat?"

"I suppose so."

That was what he had seen, Dennis realized—that blink of orange far above, through the trees. And he had heard the muffled explosion a minute before the driver of the van tapped his horn.

"How do the people on the Sno-Cat control the chutes?"

"They get above the parts that look unstable, and they throw a TNT or dynamite charge. That fractures it, or if it's solid, it stays put and theoretically you don't have to worry. But they do that only late at night or before dawn. No way they would've been doing it in the middle of the morning with traffic on the road."

"No, of course not," Dennis said.

The weather cleared. One warm sunny day followed another. Serious skiers complained there wasn't enough snow. The skies turned gray and it snowed again. Weekend skiers complained there wasn't enough sun.

Dennis made discreet inquiry in the village of Springhill to determine who might have been up above the road in a Sno-Cat on the day of the avalanche. The usual crew, he was told, was made up of volunteers from the quarry, led by Oliver Cone.

Had there been time, he wondered, between my visit to Grace Pendergast and my leaving for Aspen, for Grace to reach Cone at the quarry? Did I tell her when I was going down to Aspen? He couldn't quite remember. But why would she do that? And why would Cone and his gang want to bury me under fifty tons of snow? I want to help them. Don't they know that? Don't they care?

The trial date seemed to be approaching like an express train—or an avalanche. This time, Dennis wondered, who'll be buried under it?

One afternoon, as he drove his Jeep up the icy driveway, Lucy sprang out from behind a snowbank, startling him.

"Are you all right, honey?"

"Daddy, what's wrong with Sophie?"

He was alarmed. "What do you mean?"

"She's so sad."

He hugged his daughter, stroked her soft dark hair, which crackled with the electricity of the cold air. "Because Grandma is in trouble. I told you—that's why I'm working so hard. So Sophie's sad."

"Did Grandma do something wrong?" Lucy asked.

He was always brought back to that. Not: was she guilty? But: had she done anything wrong?

"No," he said.

He could lie to a child, but not to himself. The children had gone to bed. Winter starlight bled through the frosted windows of the living room. Sophie curled on the window seat, looking out at black night and falling snow. Dennis prowled the carpet. In a corner of the room he saw Sophie's violin case resting against a bookcase. He picked up the case. "Why don't you play anymore?" he asked.

"I can't," she said. He saw tears forming in her eyes.

Dennis bent and took her in his arms. He had never known her like this: beaten down and drab. She was like a wooden replica of the live Sophie. She drove off to school and to her meetings; she cooked but rarely ate. Her cheekbones had grown sharper. In the nights she went to bed early and turned her back to him. The blaze of her hair—so lustrous that sometimes in the dark, as she slept, he could see its dark red shine—had turned to a mouselike brown.

"It will be all right," he said. "It will end. It will work out. Trust me."

He remembered how many times and for how many things Sophie had said those last two words to him. Now it was his turn.

Just before noon on a bright blue March day, he walked down the beige-carpeted corridor of Karp & Ballard to Mickey Karp's corner office, which faced both the ski slopes and the downtown mall. Feet on his desk, halfglasses perched on the tip of his nose, Mickey was studying a real estate contract. He was involved in a typical Aspen civil law case, representing a member of the Saudi royal family who had bought a $10 million estate on a property zoned for no further development other than barns for farm animals. The Saudi prince had built two such barns. Each contained three bathrooms with Jacuzzis and saunas and triple-jet showers, as well as six designated horse stalls with Berber carpeting and king-sized beds. Neighbors who were being kept awake by the midnight traffic and distant hilarity had filed a complaint with the county zoning board. They wanted the "barns" torn down.

Mickey was mounting a defense based on the theory that what's done is done. He had tried to imply that a stiff fine, which the prince seemed willing to pay, would do Pitkin County more good than a high-profile demolition job.

"How busy are you?" Dennis asked.

"Anything in the world can seduce me from defending the rights of the rich and arrogant."

"If you feel that way, why are you doing it?"

"*Somebody* has to plead the prince's case," Mickey said. "Isn't that what our system of justice is all about?"

Dennis scratched at his beard, which he realized needed trimming yet again. "After practicing law for twenty years," he said, "I still don't know what the hell it's about. I know what it pretends to be about. But what it achieves might be something else."

Mickey sighed. "And what can I do for you this morning, oh great hairy one?"

"I need help," Dennis said. "Someone to sit second chair."

Back in New York, Dennis had begun his career as a neophyte assistant United States attorney in the Southern District of New York. He was one of more than two hundred criminal lawyers working in an office with virtually unlimited FBI and ATF investigators at their service. Later, in private practice, he declined to become a member of a law firm, but he shared with some like-minded mavericks a midtown suite of offices and, more important, the pooled services of legal secretaries, paralegals, and young law clerks. It was only on TV that lawyers worked as lone gunfighters. In the real world of trial, a lawyer needed help—needed not only additional brainpower and shoe leather, but ears to listen, minds to criticize, and sometimes arms to restrain.

"I'm not a criminal defense attorney," Mickey said.

"You've litigated plenty of civil cases. I need to talk to somebody, that's the real point. It takes common sense, Mickey, and you've got plenty of that. I'm beginning to think I've lost mine. Right now I need help to pick a jury."

"When exactly do you go to trial?"

"April tenth. Three weeks."

"I've never asked, and neither has our partner, Bill—but who's paying for all this?"

"My mother-in-law doesn't think in those terms. But when the trial's over, the family, and that includes me, will cough up for my billable hours. Yours too. I'm not asking you for a free ride."

"Well"—Mickey sighed—"family is family . . . and if you let them, they'll bleed you dry. I once defended Bill's kid on a DUI and the kid didn't even offer me a drink. This thing you're hooked into is a little more complicated. But we'll work something out. I won't charge you more than double the usual fee. Meanwhile, let's go to lunch and you can tell me what I don't know about the case."

"More to the point," Dennis said, "I'll tell you what *I* don't know about the case. And it will be a long lunch."

He had never been to trial in Judge Florian's court. In all his Pitkin County misdemeanor cases so far, he had pled them out, made some sort of deal with the young assistant DAs who were his opponents.

The morning after his meeting with Mickey, he stopped by the courthouse to inspect the court calendar for the month. He noted three cases slated for trial the following week: two for burglary, one for assault. Dennis asked the court clerk if Ray Boyd was coming up from Glenwood Springs to prosecute in any of the cases.

"He'll probably do the assault case. He likes those."

On the appointed day, Dennis entered the courtroom at a few minutes past 10 A.M. He took a seat to the rear.

The courtroom was empty but for a few dark-skinned relatives and friends of the defendant, a Salvadoran road worker named Hernandez who was accused of using a five-inch blade to slash the arm of the bartender of the Heavy Metal Café on the Cooper Street Mall. The bartender was his brother-in-law.

Dennis sat through what remained of jury selection. He listened and made notes. Ray Boyd raced through a five-minute opening statement and then presented witnesses. He led them to say precisely what he wanted them to say.

"Are you trying to tell us, sir, that you saw the defendant grow suddenly angry at something the victim said? Is that what happened?"

A double-barreled leading question, but no one seemed to care. The young defense counsel from Carbondale raised only one meek objection all morning, and that was summarily overruled.

Dennis got the point. In Judge Florian's courtroom, if you represented the state of Colorado, you could do just about as you pleased. It would be bad form for the defense to object, and certainly impolitic. A local defense attorney had to live with the judge and prosecutor in the months and years to follow. Times might come when it would be important to cut a deal on behalf of a client. Why make enemies of neighbors and coworkers? Justice would even itself out in the long haul.

Ray Boyd moved forward like an engineer at the wheel of a train: it was on track, it would not veer; it might rattle, but it would hardly sway. At about eleven-thirty the defense attorney leaned over to whisper words of reality in his client's ear. Hernandez's shoulders sagged under his thin shirt. Slowly, he nodded.

The defense attorney asked to approach the bench. Within minutes a bargain had been struck, a plea of guilty entered, and the jury dismissed. Sentencing was scheduled for a month down the road.

Dennis left the courtroom, drove out Cemetery Lane, parked his car, and began to walk down the bed of the old Rio Grande Railroad line along the Roaring Fork River. Trudging through the fresh snow, he listened to the murmur of the river. Bright sun glittered off the whitecaps. After a while he sat on a boulder by the river's edge.

He was trying to connect the dots.

My client is guilty, and she's lied to me. She and Scott murdered Henry and Susan Lovell.

But I still have to fight to prove they're innocent.

17 *January 25, 1995*

Dental Amalgam

A SCRAWLED MESSAGE from Lila awaited him when he got back to the office. It said: *"Dennis, sheriff asks: Can you be at his office a few minutes after five o'clock?"*

He called and was patched through to Josh Gamble on a cellular telephone in Redstone, the farthest outpost of Pitkin County. The sheriff was there to let people know he was vigilant and thinking of their good and welfare.

"What's up, Josh?"

"Some discovery we're going to share," the sheriff said.

Dennis was silent a moment. "Give me a hint. Am I going to discover something that will make me happy or something that will make me weep?"

"Something that's given me a headache that would kill lesser men. What I'm saying is we don't know what the hell to do about this bit of information. Maybe you'll be able to tell us. Be there after five, okay?"

Dennis looked out the window later and saw bloated gray clouds overhanging the town. In just a few minutes they turned a gauzy white. You could no longer see Aspen Mountain. Skiers up there would be caught in a whiteout. You could ski out of it and hope that a tree didn't get in your way, or you could sit still and hope that you weren't in the way of someone trying to ski out of it.

At ten past five, with the wind whipping and the snow biting his cheeks, Dennis walked into the courthouse. He shook the white mantle from his shoulders and stomped down the steps to the sheriff's basement office.

Ray Boyd was there, kicking the snow off his boots. "Big one coming in," he said.

Dennis nodded politely. Josh Gamble waved him to a chair.

Jeff Waters sat on the couch next to Otto Beckmann, the balding, middle-aged pathologist from Glenwood Springs. Queenie O'Hare bounded through the door a moment later, cheeks red and wet.

"Just go ahead and soak my carpet," the sheriff barked. "It's only county property. And never mind that this is your boss's office. Your heartthrob called. His last patient canceled out because of the storm—he's on his way here. Prepare yourself, O'Hare. Don't just leap at him and wrassle him to the floor and rip off his clothes and take down his long johns. Well, all right, do it. But let him tell his story first."

"Oh, shut up," Queenie said to the sheriff.

Less than a minute later Howard Keating, D.D.S., bulked through the door, looking like an L.L. Bean–clothed version of the abominable snowman. He was a larger man than Josh Gamble, as cheerful and ebullient. In his youth he had played offensive tackle for the USC Trojans, failed to make the first cut with the Dallas Cowboys, and become a lifeguard in Santa Monica, where he partied nonstop until the age of thirty; and then, brilliantly, managed admission to UCLA dental school. "I'm a prime example," he liked to say to his patients, "of why you don't have to worry about your children who you think are lost souls. I came off the beach and got to be the most expensive dentist in the most expensive ski resort in America."

He was the county's forensic odontologist. When the legal system needed an opinion furnished by dental science, Howard Keating was called upon. Dennis didn't know him. Like everyone else in Springhill, if he needed a filling or a cleaning he went to Edward Brophy.

The sheriff reminded everybody that, the previous November, Howard had been called in by Dr. Beckmann to do a set of postmortem X-rays on the bodies unearthed at Pearl Pass. "The so-called Does—John and Jane." The sheriff raised the corners of his mouth, mimicking a smile. The postmortem X-rays had been escorted by Queenie O'Hare to Dr. Brophy in Springhill, to be compared to the X-rays of Henry Lovell and Susan Lovell.

"And they didn't match," Josh Gamble said. "But that's not what we're here about, except maybe in a roundabout way." He waved a large hand at the odontologist. "Howard, tell them."

Keating, a handsome man, shifted his bulk in the easy chair in an effort to get comfortable. Queenie's eyes never left his face.

"I have to go back to the day," he said, "that I first took those X-rays, at Otto's request. Those people were a long time dead and it was a little grisly. I took two semesters of gross anatomy at med school, so I'm used to the sight and the smells. What I do is flip a switch and tune out. Get the job done, go home to Jack Daniel's."

Everyone nodded.

"So when I was at the hospital," Keating continued, "I didn't really get my face down there and *study* the teeth in those corpses. But I thought about them later. I kind of conjured them up in my mind from to time, especially when I had older patients in the chair. Because something was odd. I knew it, but I couldn't figure out what it was."

Keating's eyes shifted to Otto Beckmann. "I called Otto about ten days ago and asked him if he still had the corpses."

Beckmann said, "We kept the bodies in the morgue down in Glenwood." His basso voice had a strong Austrian accent; he had been born in the Tyrol and worked there as a ski instructor to finance his studies. "Embalmed, and of course still at forty-two degrees."

For Dennis's sake, the sheriff said, "They stay there until we sign a form saying they have no more forensic value. And that moment has not yet come."

"I went down there to have a look," Keating resumed. "I brought a couple of textbooks. I had previously told the medical examiner that I thought the male was in his late sixties, and the female a bit younger— and he agreed. You can tell age from the periodontal bone loss. I can also examine the restorations—fillings and crowns—and figure out approximately how old they are. I didn't do that this past November. Didn't want to get up close and personal for too long."

He seemed to wait a moment for approval, and Josh Gamble gave it with a nod.

"This time I took a good long look at the restorations. If the male was sixty-eight, or even seventy, he'd have been born about 1925, right? And the woman would have been born around 1927. You usually get your first inlays in your teens. So when was that, for these victims?"

Dennis said, "The mid-to-late 1930s."

"Right. Any inlays done in that time frame," Keating said, "would be gold or amalgam. Modern dental amalgam is a mixture of mercury with some other combination of metals." He cleared his throat. "Am I boring you?"

"Not yet," Dennis said.

"Hold tight. All these inlays are what we call cast inlays. They're made by using the lost-wax process. The cast inlay was invented by a Chicago dentist in 1907—I looked up the date—and it's been used ever since. Before that time, the best thing you could do with an accessible cavity was gold foil restoration. You rolled some gold leaf into cylinders and passed it over a spirit flame to weld it cold, and then, basically, you stuffed it into the tooth. It usually meant a few hours in the chair with a rubber dam over the mouth. Not fun."

The sheriff grumbled, "You think it's fun *now*?"

Keating said, "Okay, here it comes. Both of these corpses had quite a few amalgam inlays in their mouths. But they also had gold foil restorations. Three in the male. Two in the female."

Dennis made some calculations in his head. "That doesn't seem possible. You told us that gold foil restoration wasn't used after 1907, when cast inlays came in."

"No," Keating said, "the fact that the cast inlay was invented in 1907 didn't mean that its use was immediately widespread. It took ten or fifteen years before it was standard practice."

"That still brings us up to 1922 latest," Dennis calculated. "At which time Mr. Doe and Mrs. Doe weren't born yet."

"Bingo," Keating said.

Dennis spread his hands in a gesture of puzzlement. He was thinking about the gravestones in the village cemetery, trying to make a connection. None came readily.

"So you're either wrong about their ages at the time of death," he said, "or they went to a hillbilly dentist who never heard of cast inlays and the lost-wax process."

Dr. Beckmann spoke emphatically. "We are not wrong about their ages. They were in their late sixties. The tongue may lie, but the prostate and the uterus, never."

"Then we're left with the hillbilly dentist," Dennis said.

Keating shook his head. "Gold foil restorations were sophisticated work. They were not the work of hillbilly dentists. In the old mining camps of Colorado, they yanked the tooth. Or stuffed the hole with soft wood."

Dennis frowned. "What else have you got?"

"With Otto's approval, I pulled the amalgam inlays from the corpses' mouths. I had them analyzed in my lab."

Modern dental amalgam, Keating explained, was a mixture of mercury with other metals in an alloy—a mixture that had remained essentially unchanged since about 1910. It was 68 percent silver, with specific amounts of copper, tin, and zinc. Using this mixture, expansion and contraction could be precisely controlled.

"Prior to the modern mixture, dentists couldn't do that. Before 1910 the amalgam had completely different proportions of silver and mercury. It had a lot more tin to reduce shrinkage. And it had cadmium. Well, the point is, two of the amalgams from Mr. Doe's mouth, and one from Mrs. Doe, were of that old kind. Cadmium and a lot of tin. It's amazing that they've lasted. Both the Does had very good teeth. So we have to conclude that the amalgams were probably made before 1910. Without doubt, before 1920."

Dennis turned to Josh Gamble and Ray Boyd. "What do you think is the significance of all this?"

"I thought maybe *you* would know," the sheriff said. "Or have a vision that you'd share with us hillbillies."

Dennis said, "If the victims had the fillings put in prior to 1920, it would mean they were born no later than 1910. Or probably before then, as Dr. Keating says. That would make them each a minimum of eighty-five years old . . ."

"That is not possible," Dr. Beckmann said stonily.

Dennis spread his hands. "Well, Doctor, how do you explain the amalgam? Older heads sewn onto younger bodies?"

"I do not know," Dr. Beckmann said. "Howard and I do not agree on this matter."

Dennis turned toward Keating. "Could you be wrong on the dates?"

"I looked it up. Got the books from the dental library at the university in Boulder."

"Historians make mistakes," Dennis said. "Writers are fallible. There are misprints."

Keating sighed.

Dennis looked back at the sheriff. "Dr. Beckmann puts these victims in their late sixties. Back in November Dr. Keating examined the peridontal bone loss, and he agreed. But now he says the fillings show that the people had to be at least eighty-five years old. Probably older—maybe even ninety or ninety-five. What does all that mean? Let's assume, for argument's sake, that the fillings tell the truth. The victims were in their late eighties or early nineties. First question: how the hell could they hike up to twelve thousand five hundred feet at Pearl Pass?"

"Slowly," Ray Boyd said.

The sheriff ignored him. "That's one of the points we're considering," he replied to Dennis. "It might mean the lethal injections were administered somewhere else. Then the corpses were carried up there to the burial site."

"Carried," Dennis repeated. "In summer. How wide was the track that led up there to the grave?"

"Narrow up to about eleven thousand feet. After that, nonexistent."

"Could a Sno-Cat or four-wheel-drive vehicle do it?"

"No way. A motorbike, part way. The rest is forest."

"Could a motorbike haul two bodies?"

"Shit, I don't know. You could rig something, I suppose. A sled, or a travois, like the Pawnee did. Wouldn't be easy."

"And it would certainly be noticeable if you met someone else on the trail."

"Hey, I agree. I can chew on it, but I can't swallow it."

"And why bother to haul bodies all the way up to Pearl Pass? Where does all this dental stuff lead? Is it good for the prosecution, or is it good for the good guys? What's it prove?" He turned to Ray Boyd, who had been uncharacteristically quiet and thoughtful. "Which of us makes a horse's ass of himself and puts Dr. Keating on the stand to testify? And why?"

Josh Gamble put a paw on Dennis Conway's shoulder. "Let's you and me go stagger through the storm and have a drink at the Little

Nell. Several drinks. You couldn't drive home in this storm anyway. Maybe something will occur to us. And maybe not. In that more likely case, we can talk about important things, like where are you going to spend the night, and where we can get a Cat to haul us up the back of Ajax later this week so that we can do some good powder skiing. Ray, you can come too. I'd like you two to get friendly, if that's possible. You game?"

"I'm game," Dennis said.

"Queenie," the sheriff said, straight-faced, "you escort Dr. Keating into your office, just the two of you, and rip—I mean, take down his—take down his statement."

18 *April 10, 1995*

A Russian Novel

THE ROARING FORK Valley was on its way toward one of the record winter snowfalls of the century. It had snowed every day for two weeks, and more was on the way from California. On the flats the snow would melt quickly, but in the cold mountain air it piled higher and higher. Avalanche warnings were posted. Cornices above cross-country trails were blasted by explosives three times a week. The entire Elk Range was designated as dangerous, off-limits to recreational skiers. The slopes of Aspen were meant to close for the season on the day after Easter Sunday, but SkiCo was already talking of weekend skiing through Memorial Day.

Sophie had fed the children; now they were upstairs watching television. Once again she was curled on the window seat.

"Henry and Susan Lovell were friends of your parents," Dennis said. "You knew them pretty well, didn't you?"

Sophie stared at the ceaseless, silent snow. Even if you stood outside it made no sound as it bonded to the earth.

"How old were they?"

Startled, Sophie swung up smoothly to a sitting position and looked him in the eye.

"Why?"

"Because there's a mystery about it. And it may have bearing on the case."

He told her Howard Keating's story, and the theories based on the gold foil and the dental amalgam. Sophie's eyes moved away once again, toward the drifting whiteness.

"It may not have been the Lovells' bodies that were found up there," she said.

"Come on, Sophie, we know it was them. I'll ask you again. Do you know how old they were?"

"A few years older than my parents."

"How many is a few?"

"Four or five. Six at the most."

"Are you telling me the truth?"

"Yes."

He remembered his father's questioning how Sophie could have studied under the English professor who had later gone off to Cambridge. He remembered how she had lied to him about the ages of her grandfather and the woman named Ellen Hapgood. They had seemed innocent lies or even mistakes. Now, in the light of what Keating had told them, he wondered if that were so. And what did it mean? How old were the two dead people in the communal grave at Pearl Pass? Did it matter at all whether they were in their nineties, eighties, or sixties?

Yes, Dennis thought, it matters, and it matters a lot. But I can't figure out why.

In the Pitkin County Courthouse, at 9:30 A.M. on April 10, Judge Florian struck his gavel and said, "This court will be in order."

Spectators shuffled their feet and adjusted their buttocks on the wooden benches to find a position of the least discomfort. Veteran trial watchers, sitting on cushions they had brought from home, placed their water bottles on the floor.

Judge Florian intoned: "The People versus Scott Henderson and Beatrice Henderson. Mr. Raymond Boyd for the People, Mr. Dennis Conway and Mr. Scott Henderson for the defense. Are the People ready?"

"We are, Your Honor." Ray Boyd's nostrils quivered like a racehorse being led into the starting gate.

The defense was ready too, affirmed Dennis and Scott, in that order. To the world they both projected confidence. But so did Ray Boyd.

Dennis wore his best navy blue pinstripe suit. He was superstitious; he had never lost a case when he wore it on opening day of trial. He had never told this to anyone, not even Sophie. There were some things you had to keep to yourself.

"Any witnesses in the courtroom?" the judge asked. "If so, please rise and leave."

No one did.

"We'll begin the voir dire."

Half of the wooden spectators' pews of Judge Florian's courtroom had been cleared for a panel of forty prospective jurors—they were called veniremen, after the Latin *venire facias*, or "make come." One of the judge's bailiffs, costumed in a skintight taupe uniform, .357 Magnum stuffed in a shiny brown cowhide holster at his hip, shepherded the panel into the courtroom. For a trial of this magnitude the resources of Pitkin County were not sufficient—additional staff had been brought in from Glenwood Springs. Network media had driven up from Denver. If anything developed, coverage would blast off and go national. Euthanasia was hot. The *National Enquirer* had already bannered a headline across its front page: CHIC SKI RESORT CENTER OF ASSISTED SUICIDE CULT. The *New York Times Magazine* had approached Dennis about a less lurid article, should euthanasia become the trial's major issue. Dennis had no intention of letting that happen. "Talk to me after trial," he said.

Trial by jury. The results sometimes defied logic and could make lawyers weep. On the other hand, in civilized Europe five hundred years ago, charges were often resolved by making a man walk barefoot and blindfolded over nine redhot plowshares laid lengthwise at unequal distances. If the accused were burned, he was declared guilty. It could almost make you believe in progress, Dennis decided.

The veniremen were led by the squeaky voice of the deputy district clerk in the taking of the oath of voir dire: to speak the whole truth and nothing but the truth. As if any one of us is really capable of that, Dennis thought, under oath or not.

Judge Curtis Florian introduced the court reporter, the clerk, and the bailiffs. Each stood and made a little bow in the direction of the jury, and then to the spectators. The judge said, "Folks, this case is based upon what we call an information, and it reads as follows: 'Mr. Raymond Boyd, deputy district attorney in the Ninth Judicial District, informs the court that against the peace and dignity of the people of the state of Colorado, in or about August 1994, in the county of Pitkin, Beatrice Henderson and Scott Henderson Jr. did unlawfully, feloniously, and deliberately cause the death of two persons known to us at present only as Jane Doe and John Doe . . .' "

When the judge had finished, the court clerk picked thirteen names at random from a bowl of number plaques. Thirteen live bodies soon filed into the jury box and sat in the old wooden chairs that looked as if they had been there since the days of silver mining. The rest of the veniremen were ushered out.

The judge asked each of the chosen thirteen to recite a brief autobiography.

The first thirteen candidates were a woman accountant, an out-of-work advertising man with a master's degree, a real estate broker, an airline pilot, a woman who did Bible education for the Latino community downvalley, a young hotel desk clerk, two ski instructors, a cowboy from Redstone, a retired dermatologist who Dennis knew was a leader of the Jewish community in Snowmass Village, a masseuse, a baker with a B.A. in philosophy from Princeton, and a taxi driver who informed the court that she had published two romance novels and that you could buy them on the rack at Carl's Pharmacy. None had been born in Pitkin County. Most were single or divorced. None were black. Not your average down-home Western jury, Dennis realized.

The clerk read the list of possible witnesses. "Do you know any of these people?" Judge Florian asked the jurors.

Aspen was a community of only eight thousand people year-round. One of the ski instructors explained that a few years ago she'd given Ray Boyd a group lesson in a weekend locals' clinic. The real estate broker said he was the father-in-law of the court reporter. Everyone knew one or two of the potential witnesses.

Ray Boyd had two assistants for the trial: Don Stone, a clean-cut deputy district attorney from Glenwood Springs, and his counterpart from Aspen, a blonde woman named Sarah Westervelt, who wore horn-rimmed glasses and seemed to have red Delicious apples stuffed in her cheeks. Ray Boyd led the attack. He told the jury, "You're going to hear a lot of what we call circumstantial evidence. So let's talk about what that is. I was sitting in my living room down in Glenwood, and I heard a crash outside in the street . . ."

Once more Dennis sat through the tale of the green Ford Explorer and the red Chevy pickup.

Boyd finished, then said, "You've heard the charge. That contains what we call the elements of the crime. I have to prove all that to you, and I will. But bear in mind—I don't have to prove anything beyond the elements."

Dennis saw the cowboy nod. Ray Boyd and the cowboy had already established a rapport; the cowboy was nodding at the DA's every word. Each side was allowed six peremptory dismissals of jurors—six strikes, so-called—and Dennis, although he was as fond of cowboys as anyone who had been brought up in New York could be, decided that this particular cowboy had to be sent home on the range for the course of the trial.

When Dennis's turn came, he tried to look every juror in the eye at least once. He had talked to many a past juror who had admitted leaning toward one side or the other because of his like or dislike of the attorneys in the case. "We're not going to contest the elements of the crime," Dennis said—"only Mr. and Mrs. Henderson's involvement in it. The prosecution is going to show you gruesome photographs of the victims in this case. They might fill you with such disgust that you'll have prejudicial reactions against the defendants, even though it hasn't been proved they had anything to do with these deaths. Are there any of you who can't deal with photographs of this nature?"

No one raised a hand. These were Americans, the spiritual descendants of Billy the Kid or Gary Cooper in *High Noon*. Violence filled the pages of their newspapers and their TV screens. Most of them who had watched parts of the O. J. Simpson trial were annoyed that the grisly portraits of the victims had been barred from view. If trial testimony was public, wasn't the evidence public too? Bring on the photographs.

"Mrs. Henderson may not testify," Dennis said. "But I'd like to remind you that Pilate said to Jesus, 'You're not responding to my accusations—you must be guilty.' In our system of law there's no obligation for the defendant to respond to any accusation, however farfetched. Does anyone here have a problem with that?"

The frizzy-haired masseuse in the first row of the jury box raised her hand. "I always think that if a person's innocent, he or she would want to testify. *I* would."

For the benefit of the other jurors—he already knew he would use one of his peremptory strikes for the masseuse—Dennis parried: "An innocent person can still be nervous. This courtroom is a pretty somber-looking place. I'd hate to stand here and be accused of something, especially if I hadn't done it."

From Mickey Karp he had a fair idea of Ray Boyd's standards for jurors. Although they denied it, the Colorado district attorney's office had profiles of what law enforcement considered prosecution-oriented jurors. If you were over forty, a Republican, and a blue-collar worker, you could be counted on to vote for a life sentence for any crime the far side of jaywalking. Retirees, civil servants, religious fundamentalists, young white males, and older black women were favored by the state. Anyone with a master's degree or better was generally excluded as too intelligent. But most defense attorneys mistrusted them for the same reason.

Pitkin County had its own peculiarities. Rural Coloradans had elbow room and therefore a more easygoing view of life. Many people had settled in the Roaring Fork Valley on impulse. It was not easy to get a clear read on the prejudices of impulsive people—by definition, they were apt to change their minds. Dennis had long ago come to the conclusion that the science of jury selection, like medicine, was no science. He liked people on his juries with whom he had good eye contact. It had to *feel* right.

In the late afternoon the voir dire ended. Dennis and Mickey Karp conferred in the corridor outside the courtroom. "If I were you," Mickey said, "I'd strike the Jewish dermatologist."

"Why?"

"He's retired. Came originally from Detroit, he told us. That's a violent city. He'll have a built-in bias against a defendant in a murder case."

"You can't equate Bibsy Henderson with some ghetto crackhead who holds up a liquor store and blows away the owner."

"But maybe, unconsciously, that guy from Detroit can."

"Did you see his feet?" Dennis asked.

"The dermatologist's feet? No, Dennis, I don't usually look at jurors' feet."

"He's wearing running shoes without socks. I'll bet his wife told him to wear socks to court, and he said, 'Hell no, this is how I always dress at home and that's the way I'm gonna dress today.' He's an independent thinker. I want him."

"You're in charge," Mickey said.

Dennis used three of his strikes on the cowboy, the taxi driver, and the masseuse. Ray Boyd struck the baker who had majored in philosophy, and the man with the master's degree.

An hour later, at 4:55 in the afternoon, the jury was picked. Things were moving along on schedule and the judge looked pleased. No TV cameras were immortalizing his errors, and no book publishers were soliciting his memoirs. He had only to do his job as he usually did it, and the devil with what people thought. He was in command. He struck his gavel on the broad bench; it rang with an authoritative *crack*.

"Court is in recess until tomorrow morning, nine A.M. sharp, at which time we'll have opening statements."

A criminal trial, it has been said often, is like a nineteenth-century Russian novel: it starts with exasperating slowness as the characters are introduced to the jury and the spectators—then come complications in the form of minor witnesses; the protagonist finally appears, whereupon contradictions arise to produce drama; and finally, as both jury and spectators grow weary and confused, the pace quickens, reaching its climax in passionate final argument.

A lot of interesting things, Dennis knew, could happen along the way, if the defense attorney was willing to take some risks. Dennis was willing. His client was guilty, his case was weak, but there was a weakness in the prosecution's case as well—no live witnesses would come forward to say, "I saw what happened." But that could be overcome—and had been overcome, time and time again—by a clever prosecutor.

No, in this case the weakness was there in the prosecutor himself. If I can get the jury to hate Ray Boyd, Dennis decided, I may be able to win.

19 *April 11, 1995*

Float Like a Butterfly

THE DAY BEGAN with the reading of the indictment. In her peach-colored fluffy cotton sweater and plain brown skirt—looking like everybody's grandmother who baked chocolate chip cookies, never forgot anyone's birthday and baby-sat the children so that you could go camping for a long weekend—Bibsy Henderson stood and spoke a clear, fervent "Not guilty."

White haired and gangling, Scott uncoiled from his chair and also said, "Not guilty."

Dennis's eye roved among the spectators. Sophie had found a substitute teacher from Marble and sat at the rear of the courtroom among more than a dozen people who had come down from Springhill. She was flanked by Harry Parrot and Grace Pendergast. Behind them were Rose Loomis, Hank and Jane Lovell, Edward Brophy, several members of the Frazee clan, and half a dozen other citizens of Springhill.

Dennis was struck by their appearance; somehow they were set apart from the rest of the spectators. They were dressed as always like country people, their clothes clean but old, slightly out-of-date, definitely out-of-fashion. They were an attractive, healthy-looking group. Except for Sophie, pale and drawn, they looked as if that very moment they had stepped in from the invigorating winter morning.

Judge Florian ordered three cans of soda pop to be taken out of the courtroom. "Mr. Boyd? Ready to make your opening statement?"

Ray Boyd's face had a flush that seemed permanent. He had a reputation for theatrical intensity and for sometimes approaching so close to the jury box with his appeals for common sense that he seemed to menace the jurors. Rocking back and forth on the balls of his booted feet but never moving from behind the prosecutorial table, he laid out the case for the state. Repeatedly using the phrase "The evidence will show," he outlined the tale of cold-blooded murder of two elderly people at 12,500 feet on a fine August day.

"Who were these people? We think we know, but we can't prove it, and so the law must identify them as Jane and John Doe. But we'd like you to remember, folks, that they were human beings. They probably have children, and even grandchildren. They certainly have names. We're just not legally sure of them."

He paused to let that register.

"Why did the two defendants murder these other two human beings? We don't have the answer to that. We can speculate, and I'm sure you'll speculate too, but the truth is: we don't know. The People don't have to prove motive. We only have to prove that a murder took place and that the defendants committed that murder. When it comes time, Judge Florian will tell you that what we call euthanasia, or mercy killing, or assisted suicide, is considered by Colorado law to be murder if it's premeditated. We're going to prove to you, ladies and gentlemen, that these murders *were* premeditated. The evidence will show that the defendants brought the murder weapons from their home to the scene of the crime. That's certainly premeditation. And these weapons have no purpose other than to kill. They weren't hunting knives or deer rifles that you might just happen to be carrying up with you in the backcountry. No! They were syringes filled with poison! I don't think that any of you, if you go hunting or hiking, carry syringes filled with poison."

Dennis rose to object. "Your Honor, that's argument. There's no predicate, and it's inflammatory. Mr. Boyd should know better."

The judge frowned down at him. "He did say, 'The evidence will show.' I don't think it's inflammatory. Let the jury decide. You'll get your turn, Mr. Conway."

"Thank you, Your Honor."

Dennis always said "Thank you" when he was overruled. He was not being sarcastic; he believed that jurors liked lawyers to be polite to juridical authority.

When Boyd had finished, Dennis rose to face the jury.

"Beatrice Henderson and her husband have lived in this valley all their lives. Until today they've never been accused of breaking any law. They should not be in this courtroom except as spectators or, like yourselves, members of a jury in another case. Beatrice Henderson and her husband didn't commit murder. They didn't commit euthanasia. They are being railroaded by a prosecutor who needs a conviction and a scapegoat in order to get it, and before this ordeal is over their innocence will be clear to you beyond any doubt."

The veins on Ray Boyd's neck swelled as he sprang to his feet, shouting, "Your Honor! That's unacceptable!"

The judge pounded his gavel until Boyd quieted down. "Normally," he said, in his most stern voice, "I would now call both attorneys to my chambers, where I would instruct you, Mr. Conway, to behave in a decent manner. But instead I am reprimanding you in open court. That accusation against Mr. Boyd was inexcusable. Do you hear me, sir?"

"Yes, Your Honor," Dennis said quietly.

"I order you to apologize."

Dennis hesitated for as long as he could without incurring further wrath. Then he turned to Ray Boyd, whose face had calmed now to a lobsterlike red. Dennis said calmly, "I apologize, Mr. Boyd."

"Do you have anything more to say, sir?" Judge Florian demanded of Dennis.

"Your Honor, I've concluded my opening statement."

"Mr. Henderson?"

"Nothing further, Your Honor," Scott said. "I'm going to leave most of this to Mr. Conway. We're eating out of the same lunch pail. If I want to chip in something I'll wave my hand in the air, like I did when I was a schoolboy."

The jurors smiled. The tension had been eased.

"Call your first witness," the judge said to Ray Boyd.

Dennis understood that the prosecution's approach to proof of guilt would be a simple, straightforward one. Boyd would progress chronologically toward the shining moment that made all else come together and work: the moment of Bibsy Henderson's confession. Queenie O'Hare's testimony about that confession was the key to a guilty verdict.

Harold Clark, the first witness, was a simple man who strained to tell the truth. His presence gave the jury the sense that good people were on the side of the prosecution. Young Sarah Westervelt conducted the direct examination. She moved along with a slow, student-like precision, but her cheeks were flushed with excitement. When Harold had finished his tale of the dead dog and his visit to the Animal Control Office right there in the Pitkin County Courthouse, Ms. Westervelt looked at Ray Boyd, received his nod of approval, and said, "Pass the witness."

Dennis stood. "Your Honor, at times during this trial, I will be speaking both as attorney for my client, Mrs. Beatrice Henderson, and also for Mr. Scott Henderson, who's representing himself. This is one of those times."

There was an old legal adage: If you have nothing to gain by cross-examining, don't. Most lawyers, however, couldn't resist. Just a *few* questions, to air their lungs, to make the jury aware of them. Some felt it a sign of weakness if they didn't do any sniping; it might lend additional credence to the witness. And defendants sometimes grew upset if their knight-errants didn't level their lances at anyone who dared to get up there in the quest to put them behind bars.

Dennis said cordially, "We have no questions of Mr. Clark, and we thank him for taking the time to appear."

Ray Boyd promptly called Queenie O'Hare to the witness stand in order to continue the chronological thread of his narrative.

Queenie told of her trip to Pearl Pass on the snowmobile and of the way that Bimbo, her little Jack Russell terrier, had discovered the bodies. She was a credible witness: sympathetic, well spoken, intelligent, and sincere. The jurors smiled. They liked Queenie. Many of them had dogs. They loved the story of brave Bimbo skipping through the steep icy glades at 12,500 feet.

After Queenie told of discovering the bodies, and the French-made silver pillbox and its contents, and the Remington rifle, Ray Boyd said, "The People will recall this witness later, Your Honor. We ask that she be on call. For the moment, we have no further questions."

"No questions either at this time," Dennis said.

• • •

The state called Deputy Sheriff Michael Lopez, the sheriff's photographer and video camera operator.

Dennis had been to many murder trials in which the defense attorney had argued against the display of photographs that showed the full extent of the victim's wounds and the amount of blood that could jet or flow from a human body. Such a display was "inflammatory, unnecessary, not probative," the defense attorney always argued. The judge seldom agreed, and most of the photographs were usually shown. After those trials, when Dennis had queried jurors, many said they felt the defense attorney's reluctance to have the photographs shown indicated that the defendant was responsible for the carnage.

You have to get inside their minds, Dennis believed. They don't think like lawyers. They're always wondering why you did this, why you didn't do that.

Ray Boyd said, "The People will offer into evidence this videotape of the crime scene and these six color photographs." He held high the color photographs of a rotting Jane Doe and John Doe in their hidden unmarked mountain grave.

Dennis said, "Mrs. Henderson has no objection." With the firmness of his tone and with his body language, he was telling the jury: *Look at them all you like. Beatrice Henderson had nothing to do with this horror.*

The videotape was shown. The lights went back on, and the photographs were passed round.

Although Bibsy's eyes had blurred with tears, Dennis felt he had no choice. Placing a hand on her shoulder, he said, "Your Honor, after the jury's seen them, Mrs. Henderson would like to see the photographs too—if the prosecutor has no objection."

After lunch came the parade of medical witnesses. Their authoritative presence usually weighed against any defendant. Doctors were godlike and hospitals were temples, even if some of both on occasion killed you. The public tended to assume there were no incompetent or even second-rate doctors. But Dennis always remembered the riddle: "What do you call the man who graduates last in his class at medical school?"—and its answer: "Doctor."

Otto Beckmann, the gray-faced pathologist and medical examiner, came first. He testified as to the cause of death: Versed and Pentothal injections followed by potassium chloride. Dennis asked only a few questions. He decided to sidestep the issue of whether or not the two victims had any incurable diseases that might have led to an assisted suicide. If the prosecution had brought it up, Dennis would have counterpunched. It was no longer necessary. The jury might wonder just as Dennis had wondered, just as Josh Gamble and Ray Boyd had wondered. The answer had died with the man and woman at Pearl Pass.

Boyd called Dr. Richard Shepard from Carbondale. He established Dr. Shepard's credentials as a man who had practiced general medicine in the valley for twenty years after first having been attached to a prestigious hospital in Denver. He had white hair and a loud voice.

"Do you know the female defendant in this case?" Boyd asked his witness.

"Objection," Dennis said lazily. "We're not on network television. This isn't Los Angeles, this is Colorado. We're all neighbors. Mr. Boyd knows Mrs. Henderson's name. He doesn't have to keep demeaning and depersonalizing her by continually dubbing her 'the defendant.' Worse, 'the female defendant.' "

Ray Boyd protested, "Your Honor, I have a perfect right to call her 'the defendant.' He *knows* that. And I called her 'the female defendant' to make it absolutely clear that I meant *her* and not the male defendant."

"You do indeed have that right," the judge said. "The defense's objection is overruled."

"Thank you, Your Honor," Dennis said pleasantly.

Boyd resumed: "Dr. Shepard, do you know a woman named Beatrice Henderson?"

"Yes, I do."

"Is she in this courtroom?"

"Yes, she is." Dr. Shepard pointed to Bibsy.

"For the record, the witness has identified the female defendant. And did the female defendant ever work with you, Dr. Shepard, in Valley View Hospital as a registered nurse?"

"Objection," Dennis said. "He's leading the witness."

The judge looked at Dennis with an expression of mild surprise. Leading the witness was the sine qua non of cross-examination, but it was forbidden on direct examination. In this instance no harm had been done: the question was leading but it was innocent, and it would certainly come out, one way or the other, that Bibsy had worked as a registered nurse with Dr. Shepard at Valley View Hospital. But the judge was forced to say, "Objection sustained. Rephrase your question, please, Mr. Boyd."

The muscles in Boyd's jaw worked. "Doctor, when you were working at Valley View Hospital—"

"Objection," Dennis said. "No predicate."

Jab, even if you don't connect. Muhammad Ali had said: *Float like a butterfly, sting like a bee.*

"What do you mean, sir?" the judge inquired, a bit testily.

"It's been established by the witness," Dennis said, "that he practiced medicine in Carbondale. It's not been established that Dr. Shepard ever worked at Valley View Hospital. So the prosecutor can't say, at least not yet, 'When you were working at Valley View Hospital.' "

"Sustained," Judge Florian muttered.

"*Did* you ever work at Valley View Hospital, Doctor?" Ray Boyd asked.

"Yes, of course," Shepard said, sighing. "On and off for ten years, in the seventies and eighties."

"And when you were at Valley View, did you work with the female defendant?"

"Yes, I did, from time to time."

"She was a nurse, a registered nurse?"

Dennis raised a finger. "Objection. Leading the witness again."

"Rephrase, Mr. Boyd."

Boyd's jaw muscles tightened. "Dr. Shepard, in what capacity did you know the defendant?"

"She was a registered nurse. She was also a state-registered midwife."

"Did she on occasion assist you?"

"She did everything a nurse is supposed to do. She took care of patients. Yes, she assisted me."

"When particularly, Doctor?"

"Particularly in a couple of years when we had flu epidemics. She was very helpful then. Worked very hard."

"Did she give flu injections to patients?"

"Objection," Dennis said. "Leading the witness again."

Ray Boyd ground his teeth. "Your Honor, may we approach the bench?"

The judge nodded, and both adversary lawyers as well as Scott Henderson stepped forward to the judge's bench, where, in theory, if they kept their voices low, they could not be heard by the jury.

"Judge," Boyd whispered, "this is ridiculous. My questions are completely inoffensive. He's trying to make me look bad in front of the jury."

The judge raised a querying eyebrow at Dennis.

"His questions are leading," Dennis said. "That's not allowed. You know it, he knows it, and unfortunately for him, I know it too."

"You remarked before," Judge Florian said to Dennis, "that this is Colorado. We follow the rules of evidence, of course, but we like to get things done effectively and quickly, and in a friendly manner. Don't you think you're being a little picky and obstructive?"

"No sir, I do not," Dennis said. "The charge of murder is not a casual one. If I let the prosecutor lead his witnesses in minor matters, it will establish a precedent. I can't allow that."

The judge's faced turned from its usual sallow color to slightly pink. "May I remind you that this is my courtroom? *I* do the allowing here."

"I'll rephrase," Dennis said. "The court can't allow it. Should not, and must not, allow it. Leading the witness is against the rules of evidence. I intend to hold the prosecutor and the court to the highest standards of ethics and procedure."

"And so you should," the judge snapped. "But there's a proper way. Mr. Henderson will tell you that. You may have done it the other way in New York, but that's not *our* way here."

"The court's way will have to change," Dennis said, "when I'm counsel for the defense."

Judge Florian bared his teeth—then became aware of what he had done. "We'll take a ten-minute break," he said harshly.

In a corner of the hallway Dennis wiped a little sweat from his forehead. He said to Mickey Karp, "What do you think?"

"You're making enemies."

"Do you think the jury will see that too?"

"The judge can pull the rug out from under you."

"At his peril."

"Ray's going to fight you as hard as he ever fought anybody in his life."

"I'm counting on it," Dennis said.

After the break, Dr. Shepard testified that Nurse Beatrice Henderson had given flu shots to hundreds of patients over a period of years, that on other occasions she had administered intravenous injections, and that she was highly skilled at her work.

"Do you know what Versed is, Doctor?"

"It's a sedative."

"Do you know what Pentothal is?"

"An anesthetic."

"And potassium chloride? What is that?"

"A chemical generally used to correct an imbalance of potassium in a patient."

"In what dosage is it generally administered?"

"Relatively small. Two or three cubic centimeters."

"Why is it not given in larger doses?"

"In large doses it becomes a deadly poison."

"Would the defendant, as a skilled nurse, be able to administer those three items—the sedative, the anesthetic, and that poison—to a person? Does she have the necessary skills to give those three injections?"

"She could easily do that," Dr. Shepard said.

"Pass the witness," Ray Boyd concluded.

Dennis stood but stayed where he was at the defense table, with Bibsy on one side and Scott and Mickey Karp on the other. Only in the movies and in TV courtroom scenes, for the benefit of camera angles and melodrama, did lawyers move close to the witness chair and invade that sacrosanct territory. In real trials it required permission from the judge, and the permission was given only for a valid reason, such as the examination of a document.

"Dr. Shepard," Dennis began, "have you personally ever given a patient an injection of potassium chloride?"

"Yes, but not recently."

"I didn't ask you when you gave it, Doctor. Please try to answer just what I ask you. Can you do that?"

"Yes, of course."

"Have you ever administered what you would call a large and deadly dose of potassium chloride to a patient?"

"Of course not," Dr. Shepard said, frowning.

"Why not?"

"Because I told you, it's a deadly poison. It kills you."

"Did you ever see Nurse Beatrice Henderson administer such a lethal dose of potassium chloride to a patient?"

"No."

"Have you ever seen such a lethal dose of potassium chloride administered to a human being by *anyone?*"

"No. Definitely not."

"But you know how it would be done, don't you?"

"Well, it's an intravenous injection—goes into a vein—and you just inject it the way you inject any large dose of anything intravenously."

"But you've never seen it done."

"No."

"So your knowledge of how it's done is only theoretical, isn't it, Doctor?"

"Objection," Ray Boyd snapped. "He's badgering this witness."

"Your Honor," Dennis said, "I'm trying to get at the truth and to find out what the witness means."

"Objection sustained," the judge said. "You don't have to answer the question, Doctor. Rephrase, Mr. Conway."

"That won't be necessary, Your Honor. Thank you." Dennis turned back to the doctor. "Sir, considering that you yourself have never administered a lethal dose of potassium chloride to a patient, and by your own admission you've never seen it done by anyone else—you cannot say, beyond doubt, that Beatrice Henderson is now capable of administering such an injection, can you?"

"Well . . ."

"I repeat, Doctor—beyond doubt."

"Well, not beyond *any* doubt. But she was a nurse. She knew how to give injections. It's not so difficult. It's not like an operation or anything."

"Do you have reason to believe that she knew how to give *lethal* injections?"

The doctor stared at him. "I don't know how to answer that question," he said.

"Try yes or no," Dennis said.

"Would you repeat it?"

"Do you know for a fact that Beatrice Henderson, a retired nurse and midwife, knew how to administer lethal injections?"

"Not exactly, the way you put it," the doctor said. "I just assume she would."

"Is that an answer," Dennis asked, "leaning toward yes, or is it an answer leaning toward no? Which, Dr. Shepard?"

"If you insist, it's leaning toward yes. She knew."

"But with a little push, a little tap perhaps, it could lean toward no?"

"Objection!"

"Sustained."

"No further questions." Dennis sat down.

20 *April 12, 1995*

Bubo Virginianus

MORRIS GREEN WAS a first-rate cardiologist who had moved with his family from Miami to Aspen. Under questioning by Ray Boyd he testified that Bibsy Henderson was his patient, and that for the sake of her blocked coronary arteries and history of variant angina he had prescribed a daily regimen of Ismo, Cardizem, enteric aspirin, and magnesium with vitamin B_6.

"And did you also recommend that she carry nitroglycerin with her at all times?"

"Yes, I did."

"Do you have the defendant's case file here with you in court?"

"I do."

"Referring to that file, Dr. Green, can you tell the jury when you last wrote a prescription for Mrs. Henderson for nitroglycerin?"

"On June 17, 1994. About ten months ago."

Boyd then elicited from Dr. Green a concise explanation of the tendency of nitroglycerin pills to disintegrate over a period of time, and thus the need for renewed prescriptions every twelve to eighteen months.

Dennis asked no questions.

Next came a registered pharmacist, Margaret Easter, from the City

Market pharmacy in Carbondale. She produced a computer-generated printout of her pharmacy's records and testified that Beatrice Henderson had filled her nitroglycerin prescriptions at City Market for more than five years, and the last such batch of pills had been given to her on June 17, 1994.

"That's ten months ago, more or less?"

"Yes sir."

Never one to neglect what he perceived as an opportunity to strike two blows where one would do, Ray Boyd queried Ms. Easter about the disintegration time of nitroglycerin pills—particularly the brand called Nitrostat. She repeated what Dr. Green had said.

This time Dennis took the opportunity to cross-examine.

"Ms. Easter, am I correct that Nitrostat is sold by Parke-Davis, a pharmaceutical supply division of the Warner-Lambert Company?"

Margaret Easter turned a little pink. "I think so, but I'm not a hundred percent sure."

"Would it refresh your memory if I showed you a bottle of the pills?"

Dennis held one up in his hand: a tiny bottle an inch and a half long and about half an inch in diameter.

"No, you don't have to do that," Easter said. "You're right."

"And the pills are manufactured in Morris Plains, New Jersey, isn't that correct?"

"I believe so."

"And sold in pharmacies throughout the United States?"

"Yes."

"In Florida, and New York, and California, and Texas, and Alaska, as well as in Colorado, wouldn't you say?"

"I'm sure that's true."

"And all those states have different climates, don't they?"

She thought a moment. "I think they do, yes."

"Well, does Colorado have the same climate as Texas?"

"No, certainly not."

"But Parke-Davis sells the same bottle of Nitrostat in Houston as it does in Carbondale, doesn't it?"

"Yes, it does. Yes, certainly."

"Have you ever been to Houston?"

"I was born and brought up there," Easter said, as Dennis knew she would.

"What's the climate like?"

"Generally hot and humid."

"Your Honor, I object," Ray Boyd said. "What's the relevancy of this? Are we here in this courtroom to discuss the weather, or are we here to discuss murder?"

"Get to the point, Mr. Conway," the judge instructed.

"I will, Your Honor, and thank you. Ms. Easter, when the manufacturer, and Dr. Green, and you, tell us that these nitroglycerin pills will disintegrate into powder in a year to eighteen months, are you all taking into account the different climates where the pill will be used and stored?"

"Objection," Ray Boyd snapped. "Calls for a conclusion on the part of the witness."

"Withdraw the question," Dennis said swiftly. "Ms. Easter, in your opinion as a registered, certified, experienced pharmacist, isn't it a fact that pills disintegrate considerably faster than normal in a hot, humid climate?"

"I'd say that's true."

"And more slowly than normal in a dry and generally cold climate?"

"Yes. Also true."

"How would you describe the climate in Carbondale, where you live?"

"Dry and pleasant in summer—dry cold in winter."

"And what's Springhill's climate compared to Carbondale's?"

"It's colder up there."

"And dryer?"

"I guess so."

"What's Carbondale's altitude?"

"About five and a half thousand feet."

"What's Springhill's?"

"Nine thousand?"

"It happens to be nine thousand two hundred, but we won't quibble. No further questions," Dennis said.

Late that afternoon Dennis and Sophie left the court together and drove downvalley toward Carbondale. "What do you think?" he asked.

"It's not like *Perry Mason*," she said, managing a smile. "It's not even like *L.A. Law.*"

"No. It's tedious. It's detailed. It's rarely melodramatic. It's every trial lawyer's dream to cross-examine a witness who suddenly turns pale and says, 'I can't stand it anymore. I confess, *I* did it!'—then pitches forward from the witness chair, dead of a heart attack. But it's never happened to me. How are you bearing up?"

"I just want it to be over," Sophie said wearily. "For my mother's sake."

"For everybody's sake," Dennis said, reaching out to touch her cheek.

At the City Market in Carbondale, while Sophie shopped for groceries, Dennis bought Colorado Rockies' baseball caps and a softball for the children. The long major-league baseball strike had just ended—time to celebrate, he decided, even in the midst of uncertainty. And he wanted to do something with the children. He saw little of them these days. He had tried to explain that to them, and they said they understood. But at some level he knew they felt set aside.

The day was sunny, the aspen trees were budding, and suddenly it seemed as if the winter snowpack was finally beginning to melt.

"Let's go down to the creek," Dennis said to Brian and Lucy, after giving them the softball and caps. "Let's have a catch, like we used to do in Westport." He turned to Sophie, who was unpacking plastic bags of food. "Come with us."

She started to protest, but he took her hand.

"No," he said, "that can wait. Come."

"All right," she said, and suddenly smiled.

They all walked down to the creek together in the early evening light, with Sleepy trailing along behind. She was a pale gray color with tigerish orange stripes. Her fur felt as soft as mink.

Near the creek they played a game of catch. "Now let's play running bases," Dennis said. He explained the game to Sophie and she surprised him by saying, "Okay, sounds like fun. I'll be the runner." They used their jackets for bases and Sophie ran back and forth between him and Brian, who tried to tag her with the ball. Lucy watched and cheered: "Run, Sophie!" Dennis deliberately dropped the ball that Brian had thrown to him. "Run!" Lucy cried. "She's safe! You're safe, Sophie!"

Through patches of snow the softball bounced a little too close to Sleepy for her comfort, and she quickly clawed her way up a spruce tree to a lower branch, where she stretched out in the slanting shadows, nearly invisible. A few small birds that had been twittering in the trees flew away.

It grew chilly. The April nights came quickly. "Okay, kids, I'm beat," Dennis said. "I think Brian's the winner. Let's go back to the house."

He heard a soft ruffling sound, looked up into the violet evening air, and saw an unfamiliar bird descending rapidly toward them from the sky above the forest. It seemed to have the tufted head of an owl and the broad wingspan of a hawk. Its flight was as soundless as the evening breeze. Brian drew closer to his father's protective grasp, and Lucy grasped Sophie's hand.

"Daddy, what's that?" Brian asked.

"A damned big bird, I can tell you. Where's Sleepy?"

"In the tree," Lucy said.

Brian turned quickly. "No, she's following us."

Sophie thrust Lucy to the ground, crouching over her in a fierce protective gesture.

The descending bird—a Rocky Mountain great horned owl, *Bubo virginianus*—rushed past their heads; they could feel the cold frenzy of the disturbed air.

Sleepy raced across the grass toward the safety of an aspen tree. She had clawed halfway up the trunk when the stooping owl dipped a few degrees in its trajectory. With hardly an effort, it plucked Sleepy off the gray bark with its outstretched thick talons. Its grip was sure. The cat screamed.

Dennis stared, disbelieving, as the owl flapped into the sky, clutching the wailing cat. Lucy screamed too, and Sophie covered her eyes with one hand. But she and Dennis and Brian still gazed up in amazement at the evening sky, where the owl's wings beat silently in the direction of the mountains and rose toward the first stars. The doomed cat wailed steadily, and then weakly, and then faintly, and then not at all; and then the bird and her prey were gone. Nothing remained to show what had happened. Not a feather, not a patch of fur. Dennis's heart pounded violently.

In the living room, Lucy shuddered in Sophie's arms for an hour.

Then she turned to Dennis and said, "Daddy, Donahue won't come back either. I know that now. The bad owl ate him."

Neither Dennis nor Sophie could reply.

Brian watched television. He would not talk. Lucy went early to bed, still weeping. Both Dennis and Sophie sat on her bed in the darkness for nearly an hour, until she was quiet and finally slept.

Early the next morning, while Sophie was upstairs on the telephone to her mother, Lucy came to Dennis, who was alone at the breakfast table.

"I don't like it here anymore," Lucy said. "I'm scared, Daddy. So is Brian. He thinks a bear's going to come one night and get him and eat him, just like the owl got Sleepy and ate her. We want to go home."

"Home?" Dennis reached out to enfold his daughter in his arms. He stroked her hair. "This is home, darling."

"No, Daddy." Lucy whispered into his neck. "Home is where we were before. In Connecticut. Where nothing could hurt you."

My God, Dennis thought, this is a savage place. This is the edge of the wilderness. Why have I not seen that before? What else can happen here?

21 *April 13, 1995*

The Doctrine of Optional Completeness

THE ABDUCTION OF the cat scraped like a ragged and rusted blade at the edges of Dennis's mind. He begged Sophie to stay home and be there when the children came back from school. "I'll explain to your mother. She'll understand."

"Yes, of course," Sophie said. "Of course I will. But I promised Harry I'd give him a lift to court in Aspen."

"I'll take him," Dennis said.

He pulled up to the painter's house a little before seven o'clock the next morning. Harry was standing on the porch in a navy pea jacket, stamping his feet to keep warm.

"Hop in, Harry."

The sun rose over the tall eastern rim of the mountain range, at first a blood orange arc against pale blue, then a lightening half disk, and half an hour later a blinding sphere heaving clear from the mountains entirely and spreading long shadows over the snow. The Crystal River glittered like a field of diamonds. The sky lacked a single cloud.

Dennis told Harry what had happened to the cat, and how the children had reacted.

"You got to tell them the facts of life," Harry said. "Horned owls and black bears are part of the scheme of things. The kid wants to go back to Connecticut? Back there you got rapists and cops."

Dennis was silent.

Suddenly Harry said, "Didn't you once tell me you knew some art dealers in New York City?"

"Yes. I do."

"And a while ago you told me I ought to get my work out there into the world. Get it seen before I died."

"I remember."

"I've been thinking about that. Especially lately. You're a friend. You want to help me?"

"Sure. How, Harry?"

"I thought I might go East. See people. Show them pictures or slides—even ship a crate full of my stuff and haul it round to the galleries. Try to get someone interested."

"In the land of rapists and cops?"

"I'm old. I'll take my chances."

"You should go," Dennis said firmly. "As soon as this trial's over, I'll talk to a couple of friends."

"It's not so simple. People won't like me leaving."

"I don't understand." Dennis frowned. "What people? Why will they care?"

Harry lapsed into silence again, and his chin sank down. "You don't need to know all this now," he said. "We'll talk about it later. I shouldn't be pestering you—you've got plenty on your plate already. Like you said, when the trial's over. How's it look?"

"What do you mean, I don't *need* to know? Need to know what?"

"I'm hung over," Harry said. "I babble. Tell me about the trial."

"Hard to predict," Dennis admitted. "Juries are human beings. You never know what they're really thinking, or what they'll do."

Harry nodded sympathetically.

"You've been watching it," Dennis said. "Imagine you were on the jury and you don't know the Hendersons at all. Would you get the feeling that they did it, or that they're not guilty?"

"Oh, you can't ask me that," Harry said.

"Why not?"

"I'm from Springhill."

A little chill touched the base of Dennis's spine and spread upward.

"What do you know," he asked carefully, "that I don't know? And that I should know?"

"Nothing."

"Yes, you do. You're not hung over. Damn it, tell me."

Harry stared out the window. The snow-dappled valley—houses, horse farms, trailer parks, the swollen river—rushed by the car windows. From the west they were approaching the midvalley town of Basalt. Rain clouds had begun to darken the mountaintops.

"It would look to me like they were guilty," Harry said, slowly.

"Based on the evidence?"

"It just seems likely."

"You're not answering me." Dennis suddenly realized that Harry was trying to tell him something. "You're bullshitting me." His tone sharpened. "You know something."

"Only what I hear in the courtroom."

"Why do you think they're guilty?"

Harry said nothing.

"You're lying," Dennis said angrily. "You call me a friend and you ask for my help, and then—goddamit!—you lie to me. Like everyone else around here does! What the hell is going on?"

"You better stop the car and let me out," Harry said.

"Tell me!"

"Talk to your wife."

"My wife? Harry—"

"Pull over. Let me out of here."

Harry was already fumbling with the car door. Dennis braked firmly and swerved the Jeep to the side of the road, near a gas station and a traffic light. "See you in court," Harry mumbled—and before Dennis could stop him, he leaped from the car and was gone.

"Are you all right?" Dennis asked Bibsy.

"I wish it would be over," she murmured, "no matter how it turns out."

"You're doing fine." He kissed her lightly on the cheek. No matter what she had done or not done, he felt nothing evil or destructive in this woman, or in his father-in-law. He wondered if he would ever understand what had happened and why.

Dennis settled into his chair at the defense table. His eyes swept the banks of spectators. The Springhill people were there: the Frazee and Hapgood clans, Grace Pendergast, the younger Lovells, Edward Brophy and others. Oliver Cone sat next to his uncle. Dennis wondered if the marble quarry had been closed for this occasion.

Harry Parrot had not yet arrived. Dennis was still trying to make sense out of what had happened in the car.

The clerk called the courtroom to order.

Ray Boyd called as a witness the Pitkin County deputy who had taken the fingerprints of the Hendersons. He then called a different deputy sheriff, who had received the Remington rifle and pillbox from Queenie at the crime scene near Pearl Pass, bagged them, sealed them and labeled them, and brought them by snowmobile down to Aspen. To complete the untainted chain, Boyd called the evidence custodian, and then the CBI agent from Denver—he had a mustache and looked like an old-time fireman—who had analyzed and matched all the prints.

"Once again, sir, is there any doubt that the prints on these two items belong to the two defendants?"

"No doubt at all," the agent said.

To complete the case for the People, Ray Boyd recalled Queenie O'Hare to the stand.

Again she was in uniform. Dennis saw some jurors smile at her. They felt they knew her already from the first day of her testimony. Her face was open and friendly, her expression one of unassuming and modest competence.

The prosecutor took Queenie back to her first meeting with the Hendersons in Springhill.

"And did the defendant, in her own home, say anything to you about a pillbox?"

"Yes, she said she'd once owned a silver pillbox. She bought it in Paris many years ago—she wasn't specific about the date. And she lost it. Lost the pillbox three years ago, she said, in Glenwood Springs."

"Did you ever show her the silver pillbox recovered from the dog's grave at Pearl Pass?"

"Yes, I did, here in Aspen."

"Did she have any comment?"

"She said, 'Oh, that's mine. That's the one I lost in Glenwood Springs.'"

Ray Boyd moved from there to Queenie's account of the attempt to exhume the bodies of Susan and Henry Lovell, whom she believed at the time—and still believed, she said—were Jane and John Doe, and how the caskets were found to be empty. And in her judgment had always been empty.

"Did you make further inquiry in Springhill about this matter of the empty caskets?"

"I did indeed."

"With what result?"

"I couldn't find out a thing."

"I don't understand," Boyd said.

"I couldn't get the local doctor or the local dentist to cooperate with me. The doctor, a Dr. Pendergast, said that as far as she knew—"

Dennis objected that it was hearsay. "Mr. Boyd is asking for a statement made out of court. The doctor isn't here to testify."

"Sustained."

Boyd smiled. "All right, Deputy. Let me put it to you another way. After you spoke to Dr. Pendergast up there in Springhill, were you satisfied that she was telling you the truth about the cause of death of Mr. and Mrs. Lovell?"

"No, I was not satisfied at all," Queenie said.

"Were you satisfied that the dentist, Dr. Brophy, was telling you the truth about the dental records?"

"No, I was not. I believed he was lying to me."

"What made you feel that?"

"Objection," Dennis said. "We're going into the realm of pure speculation here."

"Withdrawn," Ray Boyd said. As Dennis suspected, the prosecutor feared opening up the matter of the dental amalgam and out-of-date restorations: he had no idea where it would lead. And neither did Dennis.

"Did you talk to anyone else up there who might have shed light on this mystery of the empty caskets?"

"I talked to the men who dug the grave, and the men who carried the caskets—that was on the occasions of both funerals. These were all men who worked at the Springhill marble quarry, including the director, a Mr. Henry Lovell Jr."

"Did you learn anything of value from any of those men? Anything that shed light on the mystery of why and how the graves came to be empty?"

"Nothing."

"What was your impression after talking to the men, and to Dr. Pendergast, and to Dr. Brophy?"

"My impression was that they were all involved in some kind of cover-up."

"Objection," Dennis said sharply. "Pure speculation."

"It's offered not for the truth of the statement," Boyd said, "but to explain Deputy O'Hare's state of mind at the time. What she thought, what she believed."

"That's fine," the judge said. He looked at Dennis. "Objection overruled."

Boyd quickly said to his witness, "A cover-up regarding the true identity of the two people murdered near Pearl Pass?"

"Objection," Dennis called again. "He's leading the witness!"

"Overruled."

"Yes," Queenie answered.

"And you believe those two victims discovered in their lonely graves near Pearl Pass—those two human beings murdered by lethal potassium injection and half eaten by wild animals—you believe they were Henry Lovell and Susan Lovell, former residents of Springhill, is that correct?"

"Objection," Dennis said. "What she believes is irrelevant. She can testify as to what she believes are facts, but not to her speculative beliefs."

"Overruled."

"Yes, I'm sure they were the Lovells," Queenie said.

"Let's move to the late morning of November thirtieth of this past year, Ms. O'Hare. Did anything happen around that time that's relative to this case?"

Queenie related to the jury how she had driven from Springhill to Aspen in her Jeep, county vehicle #7, with Beatrice Henderson in the front seat beside her and Scott Henderson in the rear, for the sole purpose of fingerprinting her passengers.

"During that ride, did either of them say anything to you that surprised you?"

"Yes, Mrs. Henderson did."

"Before you tell us what she said, Deputy, let me ask you this. Did you make any notes about the conversation we're talking about?"

Queenie explained that when she reached the Sheriff's Office in Aspen she had made handwritten notes as to what had been said. And then, with the aid of her notes, she had reported the conversation to Sheriff Gamble. At the sheriff's request, a few days later she typed her notes into the office computer.

"When was the last time you consulted those typed notes, Deputy O'Hare?"

"Just an hour or two ago. They're in the form of what's called a supplementary report. It's printed out by the computer. I have a copy right here." From her lap, Queenie raised a sheaf of papers.

"You keep them," Boyd said. "Look at them only if you need to refresh your memory. And now tell us what, if anything, was said in your Jeep that surprised you."

"Mr. Henderson and I had a conversation about the transportation problem in the Roaring Fork Valley. I asked Mrs. Henderson what she thought about it, and she replied that she had other things on her mind. I asked her, 'Like what?' "

Queenie glanced down at her report, where Dennis and others could see that some passages had been brightened by a yellow highlighter. "She told me," Queenie said, "that she was thinking about poor Susie and Henry. She used those words: 'Poor Susie and Henry.' "

Boyd raised his head quickly. "Susie and Henry who?"

"I assumed Lovell."

"And what did Mr. Henderson say when his wife mentioned 'poor Susie and Henry'?"

"He tried to stop her from going on," Queenie said. "But he couldn't. He told her to shut up."

Boyd looked startled. "He said, 'Shut up!'? To his wife? He used those words?"

"Yes, he did."

"Go on."

"And then she, Mrs. Henderson—"

"Wait a moment, please, Deputy O'Hare. Before you tell us any more—was Mrs. Henderson under arrest at this point in time?"

"No, she was not."

"Was she in your custody?"

"Not at all."

"She was a passenger in your vehicle, on the way to getting her fingerprints taken, is that what you mean?"

"Objection," Dennis said. "He's leading her again."

"Rephrase, Mr. Boyd," the judge said mildly.

"Deputy O'Hare, what was the status of the female defendant at that point in time?"

"She was just a passenger in my vehicle."

"And after her husband told her to shut up, tell this jury what happened then."

Queenie read directly from her notes this time. "I said, 'Mrs. Henderson, if you want to talk to me about it, you certainly can. But I want to explain to you that if you make any kind of admissions to me, they could be used against you.' "

"Did the defendant respond?"

Queenie lifted her eyes from the papers. "She said she wasn't supposed to talk about it, but what did it matter? Susie and Henry were gone, and she didn't have much time left either. And then she turned to her husband—he was in the backseat—and she said, 'You don't either, Scott.' She said, 'I hate to lie.' She said, 'God may forgive all of us for what we did up there at Pearl Pass, but I don't think he'll forgive us for lying about it now.' "

Queenie halted. Ray Boyd waited too, to let the words reverberate in the jurors' minds and sink into their memories.

"After that," Queenie resumed, "Mr. Henderson succeeded in getting her to stop talking. He told me she was ranting. He told me she hallucinated out loud sometimes. He insisted that I disregard what she'd told me about God forgiving them for what they'd done up at Pearl Pass. Then he spoke to her rapidly and sharply in a slang I couldn't understand. I've heard it's a second language they have up there. After that she wouldn't talk to me anymore. She closed her eyes and didn't say another word until we reached the courthouse."

"Did Mrs. Henderson seem ill to you, Deputy?"

"No."

"When she spoke to you, was she incoherent?"

"No."

"Did you have any reason whatever to believe that Mrs. Henderson was ranting and hallucinating, as her husband contended?"

"Objection," Dennis said. "Requires the witness to draw a conclusion that she's not professionally qualified to make."

"Offered for state of mind, not truth," Boyd said.

The judge said, "You may answer, Deputy."

"I didn't think she was ranting or hallucinating," Queenie said. "Not at all. I thought she was penitent. I thought she was confessing to a double murder."

Dennis jumped to his feet. "Objection! I ask that the response be stricken and the jury so advised."

Judge Florian said, "We'll strike that from the record, and the jury will not take into account the witness's statement that she thought Mrs. Henderson was penitent and confessing to a double murder."

Or *try* not to, Dennis thought.

"Pass the witness," Ray Boyd said, triumphant.

It is always a problem for a lawyer to cross-examine a sympathetic witness who is also a hostile witness. If you cross-examine harshly, jurors are offended. You are a bully. But if you treat the witness gently, in the jurors' minds that translates into a sense that you trust her. Moreover, if you are gentle, you might never budge the witness from the rock of accusation to which she has anchored herself.

Dennis rose to his feet. "Good morning, Deputy O'Hare."

"Good morning," Queenie said cordially.

"You and I are acquainted with each other, isn't that so?"

"Yes."

"And outside of this court we're on a first-name basis, isn't that also true?"

"Yes, it is."

"But this is such a serious occasion that I'm forced to be formal—in the sense that I'm going to call you Deputy O'Hare. Will you be offended if I do that?"

"Not at all."

Some of the jurors smiled. Such a nice young woman. Such a pleasant man, even if he'd been rude to Mr. Boyd.

"And of course, out of fairness to my client, I'll have to treat you like any other witness."

"Yes, of course," Queenie said, before Ray Boyd could object.

Object he did, though, hard on the heels of Queenie's response. "Your Honor," he asked, "do we have to listen to this kind of banter?"

Judge Florian said, "Begin your cross-examination without any more prelude, Mr. Conway."

"I will, Your Honor. Thank you." Dennis said, "Deputy, do you have some papers there on your lap?"

Queenie glanced down. "Yes, I do."

"May I ask what they are?"

"That's a copy of my supplementary report. I mentioned it before."

"And what does that report deal with?"

"It's the report about the conversation between myself and Mrs. Henderson on the day I drove her and her husband down here to be fingerprinted."

"Ah. Yes, of course. May I look at it?"

Ray Boyd said, "He has a copy of it, Your Honor. He's always had a copy of it. I don't see why he has to see *that* copy."

"That's Deputy O'Hare's copy," Dennis said, facing the judge on the bench. "And I believe she's made some marks on it, and some possible additions. She's read from it during sworn testimony. Therefore, under the rules of evidence, it must be made available to opposing counsel."

"Go ahead," the judge said. "Look at it."

"May I approach the witness, Your Honor?"

The judge waved him forward. There was a document to be consulted.

Dennis took the necessary steps across the well of the courtroom into the territory of the witness. But he approached softly, almost as if he were reluctant to invade and violate. The jury could see that.

Queenie already had the report in her hand and was extending it toward him. He took it from her and began to study it.

"Would you like to take a short break to go over it more carefully, Mr. Conway?" the judge asked.

"No, Your Honor, but thank you for asking. It's all pretty clear. Deputy O'Hare . . ."

Queenie waited.

"This supplementary report is all your own work, isn't it? In the sense that no one helped you write it?"

"That's correct."

"You wrote it first in longhand and then discussed it with Sheriff Gamble, is that correct?"

"Correct."

"And then you typed it into the office computer?"

"Yes."

"Had you written down everything that was said during the car ride that you thought was of significance?"

"Yes, I had."

"And at some later point you discussed this supplementary report, of course, with the deputy district attorney, Mr. Raymond Boyd?"

"Yes."

"How many times did you discuss it with Mr. Boyd and go over it?"

"Two, maybe three times."

"Try to remember. Was it two or three?"

"I . . . I'd have to say three."

"And on each of those three occasions when you discussed the supplementary report with him, was the report, or a copy of it, physically present?"

"Oh yes. Definitely."

"So Mr. Boyd has read, or looked at, your report at least three times that you know of. I mean, you've *seen* him reading it?"

"Yes, I have."

"And did Mr. Boyd tell you that he would ask you questions about the contents of the report when you testified in court today?"

"Objection," Boyd said. "That's privileged."

"No, it's not," Dennis said. "It's full disclosure as to the preparation of a witness."

"Overruled," the judge said.

Dennis faced Queenie. "Did Mr. Boyd tell you he'd ask you to quote from this report?"

"Yes."

"Did he tell you *which* parts of this report he would ask you to quote?"

"Well . . ." Queenie hesitated. "Not in so many words."

Dennis raised Queenie's copy of the report before her eyes. "These yellow marks on your copy of the supplementary report—please tell the jury what they are."

"They're marks made by a yellow highlighting pen."

"Who made those marks, Deputy O'Hare?"

"I did."

"Why did you do that?"

"So that it would be easier to pick out certain sentences."

"Do you mean the sentences you quoted to us here today in court?"

"Exactly."

"Did Mr. Boyd tell you which sentences to mark, and which to quote?"

"Sometimes."

"You memorized some of them, didn't you?"

"Yes." Queenie raised her jaw a little. "I didn't think there was anything wrong in doing that."

Dennis nodded in apparent agreement. "Did Mr. Boyd tell you what questions he would ask you today, relative to this report?"

"He went over the parts of the report he felt were important. For example, there's a part in there about Mr. Henderson's having the seat track of his Jeep unbolted. Mr. Boyd didn't feel that was important. He told me he wouldn't ask me about that, and I needn't mention it."

"So you're telling us that you rehearsed with him not only what he would ask you, but also how you would respond—is that correct?"

"Objection," Boyd said, rising. "The implication is unfair, Your Honor. There's absolutely nothing wrong with preparing a witness."

"Your Honor," Dennis replied, "I didn't say it was wrong to prepare a witness. Every lawyer prepares a witness to some extent. The jury is entitled to know that. Nothing hidden, that's the rule. I just asked the question, 'Did they rehearse what he would ask and how she would respond?' Mr. Boyd can take his witness on redirect if he's unhappy with the way she answers."

"Yes, he can do that," Judge Florian said. "You may answer, Deputy."

"I'm not sure I remember the exact question."

"Did you rehearse?" Dennis asked.

"*Rehearse* in that context is a strong word," Queenie said.

"It certainly is. All right, strike the question as phrased. Try this one. Did you go over on more than one occasion those parts of your report that Mr. Boyd wanted you to quote here today?"

"Objection," Boyd said. "Asked and answered."

"Did I ask that question?" Dennis said, surprised. "What did she say?"

"She said yes," Boyd snapped. "Yes, we went over certain parts of the report."

"Did she say you went over certain phrases too?"

"*I'm* not on the witness stand!" Boyd's face reddened. "Judge, this is wrong! He's baiting me!"

"Mr. Conway, go on with your cross-examination of the witness." The judge lowered his head, trying to hide a rare smile.

"I'll withdraw the last question too," Dennis said. "I'll ask another one, Deputy O'Hare. Did Mr. Boyd tell you to exclude from your testimony before the jury those specific parts of the statement—I'm referring to certain remarks by Mrs. Henderson—that might tend to suggest she was innocent of the crime she's accused of?"

Boyd was on his feet again. "I object! I object!"

"On what grounds?" the judge inquired.

"It's insulting!"

The judge looked down at Queenie. "You may answer, madam."

Queenie glanced at Ray Boyd. It showed in her face that she felt sorry for him. "Not exactly," she said.

From behind him Dennis heard Bibsy sigh. He wanted to turn and say, "*Stay with me, we're almost there,*" but he could do nothing. He directed his attention to the witness chair. "Are you telling us, Deputy O'Hare, that *you* made the decision—on your own, and without Mr. Boyd's advice—to leave out the remarks of Mrs. Henderson that tend to suggest she is innocent of the crime she's accused of?"

Ray Boyd stamped his foot so sharply that the crack of leather on wood echoed throughout the courtroom. "Your Honor, may we approach the bench?"

The judge beckoned.

The prosecutor strode up there in a kind of charge, as if time were of the essence. Dennis walked slowly. Scott Henderson also lagged behind. On the way, Dennis turned to look at the jury. They were watching the prosecutor and the judge. Boyd was already whispering and gesticulating when Dennis arrived.

" . . . Your Honor, Mr. Conway is fully aware of the doctrine of optional completeness! He knows that we don't have to put into evidence exculpatory statements that are self-serving to his client. This happens all the time! I mean, we exclude exculpatory parts of confessions and statements—that's the way it's *done*. He's just trying to make it seem that we're loading the dice!"

"Which is exactly what you're doing," Dennis said quietly. "That's the nature of state prosecution. It's the job of the defense to restore the balance. Make the game honest, if you like. Which, obviously, you don't."

"Your Honor—"

Judge Florian raised his pale hand and spoke so quietly that both men had to lean farther forward to hear him. "I don't like the fact," he whispered, "that the jury sees you two arguing like this in public. They're not blind. Now listen carefully. Neither of you is in the wrong. Ray, you have every right to have your witness testify to some but not all of the defendant's statement. Mr. Conway, you have every right to poke around a little bit on that score, and I'll allow it." His eyes bored into Dennis's face. "The only thing is, you're doing it in a way that's too slick for my taste. Not the way we do things here. You've got to learn that. I'm giving you fair warning that if you keep it up, I may cut you off at any time."

"And that might cause a mistrial, Judge," Dennis whispered calmly.

"We'll see about that," Judge Florian muttered. "Now go back to work, both of you. And try to be a gentleman, Mr. Conway."

22 *April 13, 1995*

Sting Like a Bee

QUEENIE SEEMED TO have retreated into the depths of the witness chair. Dennis wanted to smile at her, even wanted to wink. It's not you I'm after. You're just a conduit. I'm trying to save my client's life. No more—but no less. And you're in the way, Queenie.

With a warning frown, he resumed cross-examination. "I asked you a few minutes ago, Deputy O'Hare, if you and Mr. Boyd had gone over this supplementary report together in preparation for your testimony. And you said yes, you had—isn't that correct?"

"That's correct."

"Then I asked you—but we were interrupted before you could answer—if you yourself, on your own, had made the decision to omit from testimony certain remarks that tended to suggest Mrs. Henderson's innocence. Will you please answer that question now?"

Queenie hesitated. She had been boxed in.

"It was . . . I'd say it was more of a mutual decision with Mr. Boyd. But not such a stated decision as—more of an assumption."

"An assumption of what?"

"That some things Mrs. Henderson said had no bearing on her guilt or innocence. And weren't worth quoting in front of a jury."

Dennis stayed silent for a minute. Then he raised Queenie's copy of the statement toward the bench. "Your Honor, I'd like to enter this report into evidence, as Defense Exhibit A."

Startled, Ray Boyd said, "No objection."

The court clerk stamped the report and marked it, then returned it to Dennis, who glanced at his own notes and said to Queenie, "You told us you asked Mrs. Henderson her opinion on some matter to do with the four-laning of Highway 82, and she told you she had other things on her mind. Is that about right?"

"Yes, that's right."

"Would you read from your own statement where she said she had other things on her mind?" He handed her copy of the report back to Queenie. "It's there," he said, "at the top of page three, highlighted in yellow by you."

Queenie read: *"She stated, 'I guess I have other things on my mind.' "*

"And now please read us the full statement made by Mrs. Henderson in that paragraph, as set down by you in your report."

More slowly, Queenie read: *"She stated, 'I'm feeling terrible today. Not well. I guess I have other things on my mind.' "*

"When you testified on direct examination, you left out that part of her saying that she didn't feel well, didn't you?"

"I didn't do that maliciously," Queenie said.

"It's the jury's job to figure out your motives, Deputy, or the pressures used upon you. I'm only here to ask you questions. And you're only here to answer them honestly, which I'm sure you will. Would you look at the bottom of page four of your sworn statement?"

Queenie bent her head.

"Please read that full statement of Mrs. Henderson's, the part you highlighted in yellow during your pretrial discussions with Mr. Boyd."

Queenie sighed. "I'd like to say—"

"Just read what you highlighted," Dennis said coolly.

Queenie read: *"She said, 'Susie and Henry are gone, and I don't have much time left, either.' She turned to her husband in the backseat, who was still trying to quiet her down. She stated to him, 'You don't either, Scott. I hate to lie. God may forgive all of us for what we did up there at Pearl Pass but I don't think he'll forgive us for lying about it now.' "*

"And now please read the next sentences, until the end of that quote. Up to the word *convictions.*"

Queenie drew a deep breath and read: *"I can't lie. I won't lie to the police. I didn't hurt anyone. I didn't kill anyone. Neither did you. We just have to have the courage of our convictions."*

"That was also what Mrs. Henderson said?"

"Yes."

"Do you know what the word *exculpatory* means?"

"It means tending to show that someone is innocent rather than guilty."

"And aren't those sentences—the ones you omitted, where Mrs. Henderson says, *'I didn't kill anyone. Neither did you'*—aren't they exculpatory statements?"

"I suppose they are," Queenie said.

"Those sentences are clear and unequivocal declarations of innocence, aren't they?"

"By themselves, yes, they are."

"You omitted the exculpatory statements, didn't you, when Mr. Boyd asked you what Mrs. Henderson said to you?"

"I shouldn't have done that," Queenie volunteered. Quickly she added, "But Mr. Boyd and I agreed that they were self-serving and therefore irrelevant."

"Who decided they were self-serving and irrelevant? You or Mr. Boyd?"

She hesitated.

"Please answer," Dennis said.

"It was Mr. Boyd," Queenie said quietly.

"Didn't Mr. Boyd say to you, flatly, 'Deputy O'Hare, when you take the stand, you've got to omit the exculpatory parts'?"

"No, he didn't."

Dennis took the gamble. "Didn't he say something like, 'Deputy, it would be *better*, when you testify, if you omitted these parts'?"

"Well . . ."

"The truth, Deputy. Didn't he?"

"In a sense, he did."

"Didn't he tell you that the parts he wanted you to omit were exculpatory?"

"He—"

"Did he?"

"It was understood," Queenie said sadly.

"We're almost done," Dennis said. "And we'll change the subject."

Queenie's sigh of relief was audible.

"We'll get back to your actual conversation in the vehicle on the way to the courthouse. I think you said that Mr. Henderson told you his wife was ranting—am I correct?"

"Yes, he did."

"And you testified, didn't you, that he spoke to her in another language?"

"Yes, that's right."

"A language you didn't understand."

"Correct."

"Was it French, or Portuguese? A dialect of Chinese? Something like that?"

"No, it was a local slang."

"Local?"

"It was like English, but it was different."

Dennis smiled. "Pig Latin?"

A few jurors laughed. Even Queenie O'Hare smiled.

"In your written report, Deputy, you even gave it a name, didn't you?"

"Yes. They call it Springling."

"I see." Dennis knitted his brow. "It's a known fact that it's called Springling?"

"Well, that's what I've heard. They speak it up in that part of Gunnison County."

Dennis repeated, "In Gunnison County they speak a slang called Springling. And that's a known fact. Interesting. Deputy, who in this case is the 'they' who speak this so-called local dialect or slang."

"People from the town of Springhill."

"I see. People from Springhill speak Springling. You're sure it's not called Springlish?"

This time a few more of the jurors laughed.

"I object to this line of questioning," Ray Boyd said. "It's irrelevant."

"Make your point, Mr. Conway," the judge said, "and move along."

"I'll drop it, Your Honor," Dennis said. "I'm confused enough already."

He turned back to Queenie. "You generated this computerized supplementary report from your handwritten notes, Deputy O'Hare—isn't that what you told us before?"

"Yes."

"And those notes were notes you wrote down in the Jeep, driving down from Springhill?"

"Oh, no, of course not." Queenie looked alarmed. "I was driving—I couldn't possibly take notes."

"Well, did you use a recording device in the car to take down Mrs. Henderson's exact words? In English and in—what did you call it?—Springling."

"No, I didn't. Not in either language."

"When did you write up your notes as to what she said, in English?"

"I wrote them in my office, at my desk, after we got here and I'd delivered the Hendersons to Deputy Pentz, who was going to fingerprint them."

"How much time had elapsed between the time the statements were made in the moving car—let's say, by the time they were completed—and the time you sat down at your desk to reduce them to writing?"

"Twenty to thirty minutes, I'd guess."

"Have you got a good memory?"

"I believe I do."

"Please answer this next question with a yes or no. It's not tricky. It's very simple. My question is: Are you an expert at taking notes on conversations?"

"I've taken a five-day course in Denver, at the Reid School of Interviewing & Interrogation."

"Just yes or no," Dennis repeated.

"Not an expert, no. I would not say I was an expert. But I told you, I've had training—"

Dennis raised his hand.

"Cast your mind back, Deputy, to the afternoon of November 28, 1994, just five months ago. Does that date mean anything to you?"

"Not offhand."

"I'll refresh your memory. Wasn't that the date when you first met the Hendersons? The day you drove up to Springhill to question them about this case?"

"It may well have been."

"But you do remember the day when you first drove up there to the Henderson home?"

"Yes, I remember that day."

"Where did you question the Hendersons?"

"In their living room."

"Who was present?"

"The Hendersons. You were there. And your wife—she's the daughter of the defendants and also the mayor of Springhill. Deputy Sheriff Doug Larsen of my office was there. And the police chief of Springhill."

"You questioned Mrs. Henderson first? Before you questioned her husband?"

"Yes."

"Did you record the conversation on a tape recorder?"

"No, I wanted to. And I'd brought one with me. But as I recall, you objected."

"I objected?"

"Yes sir, you certainly did," Queenie said firmly.

"Do you remember what I said by way of objection?"

"Not exactly. I think you just objected. You said—I think you asked, 'Do you really have to use a tape recorder?' Words to that effect."

"Close," Dennis said. "Didn't I ask you, 'Is that necessary?'"

"That may be it," Queenie replied. "I'm not a hundred percent sure. It was five months ago."

"But I did object. You're sure of that."

"Absolutely certain."

"And after I objected, didn't you then say, Deputy—in front of Deputy Sheriff Doug Larsen of your own office, and in front of Springhill police chief Herb Crenshaw—didn't you then say to me, in an effort to talk me into accepting your use of a tape recorder—*I'm a lousy note-taker. My boss has often been displeased with my notes'?*" Dennis waited a few moments. "Didn't you say that to me, Deputy?"

Queenie was not an actress, not a professional expert witness who had testified at a dozen trials. She groaned softly. But everyone heard it.

"Yes, I may have, but—"

"No buts or may haves, Deputy. You know better."

"I was only trying—"

"Did you say those words, or didn't you say them?"

"I said it," she replied quietly.

After Ray Boyd had tried to rehabilitate his witness and then rested his case on behalf of the People, Judge Florian gazed coolly at the defense table.

"The defense may call its first witness."

There were only three witnesses on Dennis's list. The first was a medical examiner from Grand Junction who would testify to the slim possibility that the victims had died from other than injections of potassium chloride. The second was an Aspen pharmacist who would further discuss the possibility of Nitrostat retaining its form—not crumbling to powder—at extremely high altitudes.

I don't need them, he thought. I've made my point.

The third potential witness was Bibsy Henderson. Valium or no, he believed she would make a good witness under direct examination. He was less positive that she would stand up to the thundering dose of cross-examination likely from Ray Boyd, even if Dennis was there with a barrage of objections to keep the prosecutor reined in.

In his office, with Scott present, he had coached his mother-in-law. Don't do this, he had said, and don't do that. Boyd will try to show such-and-such by asking you this question. Be careful not to answer in this fashion. *This* is your answer, Bibsy. He had done exactly what Ray Boyd had done with Queenie O'Hare.

Once again, he remembered what had happened in New York with his client Lindeman.

At the defense table he cupped his hand and whispered to Scott Henderson, "I want to rest my case. I don't think I can improve Bibsy's position. Do you agree?"

"It's your show," Scott whispered back.

"You're representing yourself. *You* can call Bibsy if it'll help you."

Scott said, "I don't mind people thinking I'm stupid, but I sure don't want to give them any proof. Let it be, Dennis."

Resting his hand firmly on Bibsy's shoulder, Dennis rose to face the jury. "Neither Mr. Henderson nor I feel the need to put on any witnesses." He turned to the judge. "Your Honor, Mrs. Henderson rests."

Scott rose. "I rest on the evidence, Your Honor."

• • •

In Colorado the judge delivers his charge to the jury before final argument. Judge Florian explained that by their oath they had sworn to uphold the law of the state. That law, if they found the defendants had committed an act of assisted suicide with any premeditation, required a verdict of guilty to the charge of murder in the first degree.

Ray Boyd spoke first for the People. He would have one further chance to rebut the defense's final argument. As compensation for bearing the burden of proof, the state was always granted the last word.

Dennis counted on that.

Keeping his anger in check, Boyd focused on the evidence that proved the defendants had been at the crime scene. He spoke of the fingerprints, the silver pillbox, and of Beatrice Henderson's skills as a registered nurse. He came to Bibsy's statements to Deputy Sheriff O'Hare on the drive from Springhill to Aspen.

"Despite the clever manipulation of the witness by the defense attorney," Boyd said, "there is no doubt that the defendant, Mrs. Henderson, was confessing to a heinous crime—a double murder by injection. I beg you, ladies and gentlemen of the jury, to use your common sense. What did Beatrice Henderson mean by the phrase 'what we did up there at Pearl Pass?' Did she want God to forgive her for littering in a wilderness area? Does she mean that perhaps she and her husband had shot and wounded an endangered species? No, she meant that she had committed the gravest sin of all. She needed God's forgiveness because she had murdered two elderly people—for reasons we may never know—by administering a deadly injection of potassium chloride. And she said *we*. Common sense, ladies and gentlemen, leads you to the one correct conclusion. The law of Colorado that you are sworn to uphold tells you unequivocally that Beatrice and Scott Henderson did not have the right to play at being God and snuff out two human lives, as surely they did." He pointed a rigid finger at Bibsy. "She was there! We know that! She was a nurse, and she had access to the drugs. Doctors have testified that she knew how to inject them. *And—she—confessed!*"

Ray Boyd pounded the table with each of the last three words. "I'll bet she'd like to bite off her tongue for saying what she said to Deputy O'Hare—but it's too late! You *must* find her and her husband guilty."

• • •

"Ladies and gentlemen," Dennis said, "the defense did not present witnesses. We didn't have to. Because the prosecution's case is not merely flawed. It's not merely incomplete. It is tainted."

He reminded the jury that Dr. Shepard, the state's witness, had not been certain that Beatrice Henderson would have been capable of administering the lethal injection. He reminded the jury that the pharmacist Margaret Easter had explained that nitroglycerin pills have a longer intact life at a high, dry, cold altitude than at sea level. "Mrs. Henderson lives above nine thousand feet. Even if those were her pills in the pillbox, logic tells us that they could have been the pills of an old prescription—indeed, could have been the pills that were in the box when she lost it three years ago in Glenwood Springs, as she described to Deputy O'Hare."

Dennis glanced over toward the prosecutorial table, and then looked back at the jurors with a steady gaze.

"And now we come to that part of Mr. Boyd's case that's embarrassing. I can't think of a more polite word than that. On last November thirtieth, in a Jeep driving from Springhill to Aspen, Deputy O'Hare talked to Mrs. Henderson. In English, and in a language we're told is called Springling and is rumored to be spoken only up there in the boondocks of Gunnison County." Dennis shrugged. "Never mind that, by her own admission in my presence, Ms. O'Hare is 'a lousy note-taker' and that Sheriff Gamble, her boss, has often been displeased with her notes. Put that aside for a moment—if you can.

"Deputy O'Hare typed that statement from her notes. Mr. Boyd referred to it as a 'confession.' Deputy O'Hare's copy of it is in evidence—you can have it right in front of you in the jury room, if you wish. You can see the yellow markings on it that she was told to make *by Mr. Boyd*. You can see which parts of it *Mr. Boyd* instructed her to repeat when she was his witness yesterday. But do they include any of the exculpatory parts? No, they don't. Because the exculpatory parts don't fit into Mr. Boyd's scheme of things. I wonder, when Deputy O'Hare put that statement into computer memory, if she knew that one day she would be told *by Mr. Boyd* to repeat only certain parts of it under oath before a jury. And I wonder why he did that. Or am I being naive? Is it so simple that we don't have to wonder?"

Again Dennis turned and looked directly at Ray Boyd. And the jurors' heads turned with him. Boyd's lips were compressed, his face swollen with anger.

Dennis said, "The words 'the People' have a proud ring to them. But this case against two innocent, elderly, lifelong residents of the western slope does not. You, who represent the real People, deserve better. There is no evidence the Hendersons committed this crime, let alone that the prosecutor has proved guilt beyond the standard of reasonable doubt. The people of Colorado should not be associated with such a prosecution."

He sat down.

The judge peered down at Scott Henderson. "Sir, do you have anything to add?"

"Your Honor, I believe Mr. Conway has said it all. Except I should add that I did not confess or ever imply that my dear wife confessed to what she didn't do. We are not guilty."

With a pleasant air and in his most polite tone, Dennis said, "Your Honor, I think Mr. Boyd may want to rebut. To have the last word."

For a moment the judge looked annoyed at such impertinence masquerading as kindness. But there was nothing he could do without seeming churlish. He said, "Mr. Boyd?"

Ray Boyd flew to his feet. Like a maddened rhino he charged straight for the jury box, instantly invading that precious territory so that two of the women jurors in the front row leaned back into their chairs as if seeking shelter. Ray Boyd saw none of that. He saw only that he had been insulted and demeaned in a courtroom where he had always ruled.

He stopped short, his muscular chest heaving, and he waved a bundle of papers in the air.

"This is a copy of Deputy O'Hare's statement!" he shouted. "The original is in evidence, and she testified under oath to its truth! I don't need this statement to win this case, and you don't need it to see that these people are guilty! I'm sick and tired of having this statement attacked by the defense attorney's low tactics! I don't *care* about her statement! I'll show you just how much I need it to win this case! . . ."

Ray Boyd tore the papers in half—and tore them yet again—and then crumpled the torn pages and flung them to the floor at his feet, and stomped on them with his elephant-hide boots.

• • •

The waiting period was always agonizing. Dennis and the Hendersons and their coterie stayed in the courtroom.

"Is a quick verdict usually good?" Bibsy asked nervously.

"Usually," Dennis said, more to relax her than out of conviction.

But quick it was: in just under two hours the bailiff presented a note to the judge that said the jury was ready to speak. The judge swiftly convened the trial. The jury was guided to their seats.

"Mr. Foreman, has the jury reached a verdict?"

The courtroom went suddenly silent as the sockless retired dermatologist, the jury foreman, cleared his throat and said, "We have, Your Honor."

"How do you find defendant Beatrice Henderson?"

"Not guilty."

A loud murmur of approval rose from the spectators' benches, and Judge Florian rapped his gavel.

"Defendant Scott Henderson?"

"Not guilty."

Dennis embraced his mother-in-law, who began to cry, and then Scott. A few of the jurors marched boldly up to the defense table, and the Bible educator from Basalt threw her arms around Bibsy Henderson and told her how terribly sorry they all were that she'd had to go through this ordeal.

Dennis found a few minutes time to pull the dermatologist foreman into a corner of the courtroom.

"I'd like to know what happened in the jury room. It's perfectly proper for you to tell me, but you don't have any obligation to do it."

"I don't mind telling you at all," the doctor said. "I'd *love* to tell you. We took a vote as soon as we went into the jury room—twelve to none in favor of acquittal. That was that. That's all there was to it. That prosecutor is an idiot! Did he really believe that tearing up that statement was going to make us forgive him for what he did? What an ass! You showed that to us, and I personally want to thank you."

"Why did you take so long to come out of the jury room?"

"We didn't want the judge to think we were being frivolous. And we didn't want to be *too* insulting to the prosecutor and that poor deputy who admitted taking lousy notes and claimed these people spoke to each other in a local language. You know, I've lived in this valley for fifteen years, and I've heard that rumor about Springhill and that language, and so had some of the other jurors, but we all realize that's pure snobbism on the part of so-called privileged people in Pitkin County—it's like the Serbs and the Bosnians, or those New Guinea tribes who believe the people who live over the next hill speak gibberish and worship the devil and have tails. Incredible stuff, in this day and age. So we just talked, and chatted, and a couple of us played gin rummy. When a respectable time had passed, we came out."

Dennis took a deep breath. "Did you have any discussion about the case? What convinced you the Hendersons were innocent?"

"Are you kidding? That was never in doubt. Don't quote me on this—but some of us felt that even if it was euthanasia, no law passed by some gang of redneck politicians was going to make us convict these two decent people of first-degree murder. No way! We looked at them, at the Hendersons, and we *knew* they hadn't done anything illegal or criminal. You can see in their faces exactly who they are. They're good people. They aren't murderers. It was just ridiculous."

"Thank you," Dennis said. He could remember when he had felt that way too. He shook the doctor's hand.

Scott came up to him. "I'm going to call Sophie to tell her. Do you want to speak to her?"

"Not now," Dennis said. "Tell her I'll be home later. In a while."

He pulled away a little abruptly, noting the puzzled expression on Scott's face. He hadn't known he would do that, or say what he'd said; hadn't known that he would want to be alone.

He walked swiftly across town through the cold evening, taking deep welcome breaths of air, straight to the bar at the Little Nell. He straddled a fabric-covered bar stool and ordered from the barman a Wild Turkey on the rocks. My God, he thought, I haven't done anything like this in years. Not alone, anyway, and not on a bar stool. To hell with it. He downed the drink quickly and ordered another. The room was crowded and noisy; the après-ski crowd was there, talking about the day's runs and what they would do tomorrow and how fine the weather was and how lucky they were to be in Aspen. Dennis looked around and at first didn't see anyone he knew. That made *him* feel lucky.

Suddenly he noticed Oliver Cone and Mark Hapgood at the end of the bar, standing to one side, still wearing their jeans and worn parkas, and finishing what appeared to be straight shots of whisky.

They had come here, as Dennis had, straight from the courtroom.

The bourbon had made Dennis reckless. He walked over with slow, deliberate steps, but he was smiling.

"Gentlemen, can I buy you a drink? Shouldn't we celebrate together? A victory for one citizen of Springhill is a victory for all, right?"

Oliver Cone's face flushed. "We were just leaving," he muttered.

"Oh?" Dennis felt that his teeth were slightly numb. "Got to get up there above the road before I do? Got some dynamite handy?"

Cone glared at him. "Not funny, Conway."

"Let's go," Hapgood said quietly to his companion, taking his arm.

Cone shook him off. "You want what we've got," he said to Dennis, "but you'll never get it. Not if I have any say."

"I want what you've got? And what is that?" Dennis asked.

"Come on, Oliver," Hapgood said, with greater urgency this time, pulling Cone away.

Dennis did not object or interfere. An entirely new purpose had taken hold of him. He turned his back on Oliver Cone and Mark Hapgood and walked with the same slow, deliberate strides to the bar stool he had previously occupied. "You have a cordless phone?" he asked the barman.

When the instrument had been placed before him, Dennis punched out the number of his home.

"Yes?" Sophie said.

"It's me. I'm still in Aspen, but I'm coming home. And when I get there, I want you to tell me everything. I think I know part of it now, but I want to know it all."

"You don't know," Sophie said, "but I'll tell you now, Dennis. I swear to you. I'll tell you everything."

23 *April 13, 1995*

Sophie's Tale

SOPHIE THREW HER arms around him as she had not done in months. "Thank you," she said. He felt that all her heart went into those two simple words. But he was a little drunk, unable to stop his tongue from voicing what was on his mind.

"You're welcome. All in a day's work. I may have lost a friend or two and I had to pillory a deputy district attorney, but the son of a bitch probably deserved it. Never mind that he was in the right and I was in the wrong. I just keep wondering why I have this sour taste in my mouth. Is it the bourbon? Must be."

"Don't act like this, Dennis, please. Whatever you had to do, you did the right thing."

"Did I?" Dennis said. "Convince me. Tell me all."

The telephone rang. Sophie answered, and Dennis bounded up the stairs two at a time to hug his children. "Ouch, Daddy," Lucy said. "Too *hard*."

He flung off his suit, shirt, and tie, all his clothes, then plunged into the shower. In the frosted glass stall he shut his eyes and stood under the drumming beat of the hot water for ten minutes, as if soap and steam could wipe off the grime of the trial. When he finally came out to towel down, Sophie was waiting for him.

"That was my father who called. They wanted us to come over for dinner, to celebrate." It sounded so domestic, as if he had won a promotion or it was someone's birthday. "But I said no." Sophie wasn't smiling; she looked oddly flushed. "I need to talk to you, Dennis. I'm sorry about how you feel but I think after I've talked to you, you may feel differently. I want to explain Springhill. It can't wait. It has to be tonight. I have so much to tell you—all that I couldn't tell you before."

He was bewildered by her urgency, but not unhappy at the thought that he wouldn't have to spend the evening feasting with Scott and Bibsy. He had seen more than enough of them in the last week. He'd done what had to be done, but he wondered if he would ever feel the same warmth toward his in-laws as he had before he came to the conclusion they were guilty as charged. He had defended them with full vigor: that was his obligation as a lawyer, and he had won. It wasn't his obligation to forgive and forget.

The buzz of the alcohol began to wear off. "I want to spend some time now with the kids," he said.

"I understand. Do it, of course. I meant after dinner."

Sophie had barbecued two chickens and baked a peach pie. Later, at the computer, Dennis worked with Brian and Lucy on a new astronomy program. He showed them the planetal orbits. The moon whizzed around the earth; the earth flew around the sun. It was all orderly and yet it made no sense. Just like life, he thought. By the time the children were bored and ready for bed Dennis felt that life was beginning to move back to normalcy. The old fundamental truth struck home: whatever happens, life goes on. The planets move on their tracks and so do we.

Dennis kissed the children good night. Downstairs, Sophie ran toward him. "Oh, God, I'm happy," she cried. "Come out on the porch with me. Put on a coat." She couldn't sit still. She needed space, she said, to tell her tale. He wrapped himself in his ski parka. They stepped outside. "I need to tell you some of the history of this place," she said.

"History? Now? Sophie, what are you talking about?"

"We'll get where you want to go. You'll know what happened at Pearl Pass, and you'll know why it happened, and you'll see how good a thing you did."

That put a new spin on things. Dennis frowned.

A chill wind began to blow. He had to strain to catch her words. It was only because her face gleamed against the black background of the forest that he knew where she was, who she was.

"Will you listen? Will you believe what I tell you? Will you make an effort to understand? Do you promise?"

"Yes, I promise." A promise as to a child. But he sensed she was not about to speak of childish things.

Sophie said: "The first settlers came here after the Civil War. They were only three families and a few single men. When the people arrived they found abandoned miners' equipment over by the shores of Indian Lake. They also found a couple of mountain men who claimed they'd been trapping beaver here since 1860. The mountain men didn't like the settlers moving into what they considered their private territory, even though they'd never bothered to file any claims. I think there was some arguing . . . a man was killed, so the story goes . . . but it's an old story, gotten fuzzy over the years. The point is, the mountain men packed up and left Springhill.

"One of those first families was the Hendersons. Charles Henderson was my great-grandfather, from near Pittsburgh. James Brophy, our friend Edward's great-grandfather, was a muleskinner from Worcester, Massachusetts. And there was a William Lovell, a miner, and later a Frazee, who was a hunter, and a Cone, another hunter who opened a saloon some years later. Cone was supposed to have been the one who'd shot the trapper—bushwhacked him, they said, from behind a pine tree—and driven the mountain men off. A few Ute Indians lived here too, on the other side of the lake. But they were forced out of western Colorado after the Meeker massacre in 1881.

"Marble was the biggest of the settlements up here and later it became a good-sized town. Springhill was never more than a mining camp and no one paid much attention to it. The settlers were looking for gold. They found it in small quantities—small enough, fortunately, not to start a stampede. They also found silver and lead and zinc and copper, but again the holdings were barely worth working at. It wasn't called Springhill then. Charles Henderson and the first settlers called it Fortune City—you might call that the triumph of hope over reality. Naturally the name didn't stick, and then people remembered that the Ute name for the place was Wacha-na-hanka, which they'd been told meant 'the hill where the warm spring is.' That was a mouthful for white men, so it became Springhill. Prosaic, but appropriate. More than anyone knew.

"People hung on, scratched a living from the mines. Winters were hard but no one froze—there was plenty of wood to burn. No one went hungry—there was plenty of game. No one was ever thirsty—the drinking water was pure and virtually unlimited, depending on the accumulation of snow and the summer runoffs. People either took their water from the nearest stream or from Indian Lake.

"Up near the El Rico mine—a little copper deposit on a north-facing slope—there was a warm spring and a tiny waterfall. You remember the place I took you and the children to that day? Where the water gushes out of the hillside? That was the El Rico claim. They say that in the 1860s the creek ran more forcefully, and the bed was a foot or two wider. William Lovell owned the claim. That was his old mining cabin we went into, where the gravity seemed out of whack and where I told you no birds fly over.

"Bathing was not an everyday event in the nineteenth century, but miners get pretty dirty. William Lovell used to bathe in the warm spring the whole year round, just to get clean after a day's work. So did a couple of men who worked the mine with him.

"When you bathe in water, your body absorbs some of it. You may try not to take it in, like when you're swimming in a chlorinated pool, or in the ocean and you haven't got a particular taste for salt water, but the water gets on your lips and goes up your nose. So you imbibe minuscule amounts of it whether you realize it or not.

"It was around 1868 that the miners first started washing in the spring near the copper mine. There were three men. William Lovell was thirty-three years old. Francis Hubbard, who worked for him, was a widower of about forty, a laborer. Otis McKee, the third, was close to fifty—he was Mr. Lovell's junior partner. All three imbibed the water from the spring.

"William Lovell's wife, Rebecca, didn't bathe in the spring. She bathed at home two or three evenings a week in a big iron tub with creek water she heated on the wood stove. That was also true at the time for the Lovells' three children—Caleb, Naomi, and John.

"Pay attention. Otis McKee's first wife died from influenza back in Ohio. He had recently remarried, to a young Ohio girl named Larissa

Orlov, born in this country but Russian in origin. They say that Otis McKee was crazy about her. She was over thirty years younger than he was—a clever, bold, imaginative girl. Larissa was a cripple. She'd been thrown from a buggy as a child and smashed her foot on a boulder, so that one leg was shorter than the other. She limped badly, but otherwise she was very well formed in her body, with dark eyes and long reddish brown hair. Not a beauty, but pretty. She'd learned to play the violin—taught by her Russian grandfather. Her father was a railroad switchman but he'd bought her a quality Italian-made violin, probably as some sort of compensation for the fact that he couldn't repair her broken body.

"Larissa loved Otis too, first for saving her from the fate of a spinster, and then because he was kind to her. By all reports he was a fun-loving, warmhearted man."

Dennis nodded. The snow had stopped falling and the sky began to clear. Starlight glowed on Sophie's face.

"That brings me back to El Rico," she said, "and the miners who washed off the copper dust every evening in the warm water of the creek that flowed out of the hillside. In 1900, William Lovell celebrated his sixty-fifth birthday. I want to show you something."

She drew Dennis back into the warmth of the house and then upstairs to the bedroom, where she removed Harry Parrot's big oil painting from the wall and twirled the dials on the safe. Dennis saw that her fingers were trembling. The safe didn't spring open. Sophie murmured, "Damn." She worked through the numbers more slowly a second time, trying to calm herself. The safe clicked open.

"Look." She plucked out and held in her hand a worn sepia-tinted photograph. It showed a gathering of people. They stood and sat erect, straightspined, facing the camera. The picture had the solemnity and stiffness of all old photographs; no one dared smile. A date had been written in ink on the bottom white border: April 16, 1900.

"This is a photograph taken at William Lovell's birthday party," Sophie said. "Look at that man"—her fingernail tapped the face of a handsome man just to the left of center in the middle row. "How old does he look to you?"

"Hard to say exactly." Dennis bent closer. "In his forties?"

"That's William Lovell. He was sixty-five. He still worked the El Rico mine nine or ten hours a day. You've seen pictures of miners from Appalachia—how holloweyed and worn they are. I'm sure you can imagine what their lungs are like. Look at Lovell . . ."

Dennis looked again. There was not a strand of gray in William Lovell's hair. He was not smiling but there was a glint of humor in his eyes.

"He looks vital, doesn't he?" Sophie said. "A remarkable specimen. His wife, Rebecca Lovell, was a year younger—sixty-four years old. That's her, next to him." Sophie tapped; Dennis saw an old woman— wrinkled, white-haired, starting to stoop. She looked more like William's mother than his wife.

"The Lovell children are in that photograph too," Sophie said. "Caleb was forty-two—at sixteen he'd gone off to work with his father as a miner at El Rico. Naomi was a married woman of forty. John, the youngest, was thirty-seven—he'd become a wagon driver on the route to Carbondale. See? That's John. He looks his age. That's thin-lipped Naomi. Ground down by life, a typical middle-aged working house-wife of her era."

True, Dennis thought. If you didn't know who everyone was, you'd believe that Naomi and John, William's children, were actually his sickly brother and sister.

"And there's Caleb," Sophie said. "The forty-two-year-old oldest son, the one who went to work in the copper mine at the age of six-teen." She pointed to a good-looking young man who looked to be about twenty-five.

"I don't understand this," Dennis said.

"You're not alone. Few people did. Let's go down." Sophie took the photograph and a brown manila envelope from the safe, twirled the dial, and slammed shut the gray metal door. Eagerly she led Dennis downstairs into the living room.

He stirred the fire, added two logs, and blew on the coals until they crackled, glowing cherry red.

"No doubt," Sophie said, "if all this stuff had happened a thousand years ago in Europe, or in Massachusetts in the seventeenth century, William and Caleb would have been burned at the stake. But this was a more scientific era. You could twist a few suppositions around, work out a thesis to account for the phenomenon—in the end no one would be able to challenge the logic of it. Except for one thing. Fran-cis Hubbard and Otis McKee and Larissa McKee had to be factored into the equation. Francis Hubbard was about forty when he went to work at El Rico for William Lovell. He quit working in the mine when he was eighty."

Dennis raised an eyebrow. "*Eighty?*"

"Eighty, still swinging a pickax. They say he had the physical strength of a forty-year-old lumberjack."

"Sophie, what's this all about? What's the point of it? You're confusing me."

"Wait," Sophie said. "Let me tell you about Larissa. Then you'll see. You'll start to understand."

Her cheeks were glowing; he had rarely seen her so excited, except in bed. "Go on," he said.

"Larissa and Otis McKee are a legend in Springhill. In 1868, when the settlers arrived over the pass, Otis was forty-nine. When he went to work at El Rico for William Lovell, Larissa, his wife with the crippled foot, was nineteen. Every evening, when the men quit work at El Rico, they bathed and went home to hearth and family. But not Otis McKee. He'd make some excuse and wait around while the others packed their gear. Why did he do that? Because after the other men headed back, Larissa, his young and sexy wife, would show up through the forest. Their cabin wasn't far from the mine.

"In deep winter it wasn't easy to work your way along the trail or through the forest, especially if you were crippled like Larissa. But from May onward, until the snow began to pile up in October, she came. Larissa was a young woman of purpose, and her purpose was to bathe with her husband in the spring. She liked to roll around there, winter and summer, in that warm water, and sit under the waterfall. Like a hot tub today, only this was totally natural, out in the forest in a little pool. Under the winter stars with the snow all around—or in summer with the scent of pine in the air and the breeze in the aspen trees—or in fall with those golden leaves rustling all around. The place was beautiful. Mysterious. They made love there—wonderful, passionate love—most every evening that she showed up. They splashed around and thrashed around. Oh! they were naughty. Married—I told you they were married—but still you can see there was something naughty about it. . . .

"And there's something else in their sex life that wasn't quite comme il faut, not in the late nineteenth century. Back in Youngstown, Ohio, after Otis asked her to marry him and she said yes, Larissa did what I believe was a remarkable thing, considering the time and place. She found a copy of a sixteenth-century Arab sex manual called *The Perfumed Garden*. She bought it from a peddler. It's an extraordinary book. Not only a hundred and one positions for lovemaking, but all kinds of instructions as to the use of fingernails, biting and proper kissing, creams and unguents, alleged aphrodisiacs, the use of the voice in the act of love. She pored over the manual night and day, because it seemed to promise such delight. When she and Otis came West to the Rocky Mountains, she brought it with her in her trunk. Grew her fingernails even before they reached what became Springhill—bought the ingredients for the unguents on a summer trip down to Carbondale. And then, with time, in that bubbling spring by the mine, she achieved that promised delight. She was crippled only in the foot—the rest of her was perfectly fine. Often she would play the violin to Otis to get him in the mood. Then they practiced just about all the positions *The Perfumed Garden* described except the ones where the woman has to be suspended by cords and pulleys. She wasn't kinky, she was simply crazy about sex. She knew the eleven basic positions and plenty of the other more esoteric ones like the Ostrich's Tail and Drawing the Bow and the Blacksmith's Posture. And there are wonderful stories in the book which she read to him, like 'Concerning Praiseworthy Women' and 'The Story of Bahloul.' "

Here Sophie blushed, and she squeezed Dennis's hand. He understood why: he had heard those stories. He had asked once where they came from, and in the shadows of the bedroom she had whispered in his ear, "Past lives."

"At first Larissa didn't tell her middle-aged husband she was getting a good part of her inspiration from a book. She thought he'd be shocked. But later she admitted it—and by then he didn't care. This went on regularly for as long as Otis McKee worked the mine. But in 1897 he retired, although he still had a small share in El Rico's profits. He was seventy-seven years old.

"I don't mean that he and Larissa quit bathing in the spring. That was their secret pleasure, which, considering the moral strictures of the time, I suspect they thought of as their secret sin. They came once or twice a week at night, and on sunny Sunday afternoons in winter when they knew that Lovell and Hubbard and other workers wouldn't be there. They did that until the day that Otis McKee died, in 1915, in perfect health except for mild rheumatism. If you'd bumped into him in the street you'd have thought he was a vigorous man in his early sixties. He might have gone on like that forever, or close to forever, but that wasn't to be. He went down in Glenwood Springs to see the dentist about a bad toothache. He was crossing Grand Avenue when a car's brakes failed. He was run over—his skull got crushed. He was ninety-five.

"Larissa was born in 1851 and lived to be one hundred years old—she died in 1951. She was in good health, and her passing was a cheerful, festive occasion. A big party was given for her a few days before the event. She played her violin, and she made a speech about how lucky she'd been in life, especially through meeting Otis. She thought she'd had a wonderful life and even a favored life. She made mention of the fact that when she was born there wasn't yet electric light and radio, and when she died there was already television and jet airplanes. But those things, she pointed out, were only fluff—the superficial trappings of life that we inaccurately label progress. What really blessed your life was a community you were part of, friends who were loving and loyal, and family you could count on.

"I didn't mention it yet, but she and Otis had children. There they were not so lucky. A son Malcolm died of polio when he was twelve. A daughter Clara died in childbirth. But a second daughter, named Sophie, was born in 1874. That Sophie married a man named Samuel Whittaker. She died on the same day as he did—both in good health, both aged one hundred, although the tombstone, as you noticed that day you went poking around while those deputies were digging up the Lovells' empty graves, claims she was only seventy-six. Sophie was my maternal grandmother. I was named after her.

"Beatrice Whittaker Henderson, my mother—whom you just saved from a terrible injustice, although you don't yet understand why—is that Sophie's daughter. Bibsy was born in 1903. She's ninety-two years old. Larissa McKee—who is almost like the patron saint of this town, for reasons that I'll get to soon—was my great-grandmother. It was she who taught me to play the violin. She'd tried first to teach her daughter, and then my mother, but Grandma Sophie wasn't interested and Bibsy wasn't gifted. I was both, and before Larissa died she gave her old violin to me. Yes, I still have it—that's the one I've been neglecting lately because I've been so upset about what was going on with you and the trial of my mother. And Larissa gave me her tattered old copy of *The Perfumed Garden*, which I've just about committed to memory.

"I loved Larissa enormously. She was a remarkable woman, a passionate woman, a woman whose sensitivity and powers of logic grew steadily over a long lifetime, and everyone who knew her says I resemble her in more ways than one. Nothing on earth flatters me more than that statement. I was twenty-one when she died. I was born in 1930. Are you starting to understand now? Do you see what happened, and why?"

Dennis rose angrily from his chair. He faced his wife, clasping her shoulders. "Sophie, you're insulting my intelligence." You're trying to tell me you're sixty-five years old. I know your body. I'm looking into your face right now. You are *not* sixty-five!"

Sophie laughed; her white teeth gleamed in the firelight. "You're right. I was born on November 5, 1930. I'm only sixty-*four!* Here, right in this envelope, I have my birth certificate. Look at it! Do you think I had it falsified? Your father almost caught me out. Do you remember he wondered how I'd managed to take English courses under Professor Daiches at Cornell? I felt so foolish then, I had to slither out of it."

Dennis was shaking his head, dumbfounded.

Sophie touched his face gently with her hand. "Do you think I have any reason to make up even a part of this story? Dennis, if you love me, believe me. Belief is the only way, the only path to where we need to go. Proof will come later."

24 *April 13, 1995*

Departure

NOT POSSIBLE, HE thought. He knew this woman intimately: the resilience of her skin, every curve, every bone, even every faint line around her eyes. They were the curves and lines of a young woman. He knew her in bed. She was not sixty-four years old. She held the paper in her hand that would be the proof. He hadn't looked at it. Would not look at it.

"I'll fill in some historical holes for you," Sophie said. "That will help. Then we'll get to what you're looking for."

"Go ahead . . ."

"Not ahead. Back. To understand what was happening to these people. In 1893 Grover Cleveland demonetized silver, which caused the ruin of Aspen for fifty years. But it didn't seriously affect Springhill, because the country still needed coal. And they wanted marble too. Marble is crystalline limestone that can take a polish. The coal miners were aware that the marble was there, but in early times it was difficult to cut it in the big blocks that were required for most building purposes, and then transport them, so for a long time no one much cared about marble.

"The Colorado-Yule Marble Company was founded in 1906 over in Marble by an Iowa colonel whose claim to fame was that he'd bought the horse-drawn streetcar lines in Mexico City, electrified them, then sold them at a pretty profit. The colonel was the entrepreneurial adventurer—Springhill merely followed in his tracks. The Springhill Marble Company didn't get going until 1911. It was a public company, with shares of stock, and bonds, and debentures, but it was entirely financed by the people in town. The consortium of miners and businessmen had to borrow money from Denver banks, but that was all paid off by 1927. The marble company's been a hundred-percent-town-owned enterprise ever since then.

"Around 1904 two families of miners, the Crenshaws and the Rices, arrived from Boonville, California, where their teenaged kids had created a new kind of slang so their parents wouldn't know what they were saying. But the parents caught on, and they began to speak it too. They brought the lingo here to Springhill, and we developed it our own odd way. You know: *Pat shied ottoing and Macree sized while the tweeds charled the broady. They chiggreled, then piked in the horker to Ute for a regal.* That means, 'Dad quit working and Mother cooked while the children milked the cow. They ate, then drove to Aspen for a treat.' A secret language was a natural thing to be adopted, and then adapted, by the people up here. Already they had secrets to keep—and others to come.

"Let me tell you more," Sophie said, beginning to pace the Zapotec rug in front of the fireplace, "about the spring at the El Rico. . . .

"You saw in the photograph how William Lovell looked twenty years younger than his age. A billy goat to boot—some of the young men in town wouldn't let their wives dance with him at Saturday night shindigs. He visited the brothel down in Glenwood Springs once a week regularly until just a few years before his death, well into his nineties. Rebecca Lovell died in 1901, aged sixty-four, a withered old woman. Caleb, who worked at the mine, was in every respect his father's son—a young-looking satyr. Naomi and John, the two other children, were normal. But what kind of fate had tapped this man on the shoulder and ignored the other? No one knew. Everyone speculated. People finally asked, 'What do Francis Hubbard and the McKees and William Lovell and his son Caleb have in common?' You didn't have to be a genius to come up with the answer, but it did take some boldness of logic, a willingness to be called an idiot. The common solution to the question of the age disparity was that it was a sexual freakishness, a disgusting randiness that kept a few men looking and acting younger than their years. But then why did Larissa McKee—a woman!—also look so amazingly young? Where did the vitality come from—the vitality that in her early fifties made her the physical equal of any Springhill woman of thirty? It drove those younger women crazy.

"The popular answer to that was also simpleminded. She was a slut! Danced naked under the full moon, brewed potions and drank them with Otis, a slave to her bidding. God would have his revenge! One night, lying in bed, that goatish husband panting at her side, lightning would strike straight through the roof and fry her crippled bones!

"And then Larissa McKee changed the history of Springhill.

"She heard these stories about herself. She knew they weren't true—so she wondered, what *was* true? She began to reason. She knew what no one else other than Otis knew—that she bathed in the spring in exactly the same way that the youthful-looking and long-lived men did.

"And she came forward. Not to defend herself against the scandal-mongers, but to clear the brush away and blaze a path toward the truth—because she'd seen how enormous that truth was, how it could change everyone's lives in a way they never even dared dream.

" *'The water,'* she said. *'There's something in the water at the spring.'*

"At first everyone slapped their knees and howled. The goshdarned fountain of youth! What was the name of that crazy Spaniard who'd hunted all over the place for it? Ponce de León! Where was it supposed to be? Florida, right? Hell, no! It's here in Gunnison County, Colorado!

"Larissa backed off from confrontation. She wasn't out to be canonized or make converts. But of course she kept going to the spring with Otis. And pretty soon, she and Otis weren't always alone there. The townspeople showed up on summer evenings, sometimes in pairs, sometimes alone. They may not have been convinced, but plenty of them said to themselves, 'Say, what if we're wrong? What if she's *not* crazy and there's something to it? What have we got to lose? And look what we might gain! Let's go there once a week.' They came out to El Rico and asked, 'Is that all right with you, William?'

" 'Be my guest,' said Mr. William Lovell graciously.

"Still it took another eight or ten years before it fully dawned on anyone with half a brain that there was no other rational explanation. Larissa's reasoning was ultimately seen to be simple, elegant, and inspired. William Lovell was the major convert. His three children were the proof, he proclaimed. One of them bathed in the spring and maintained his youth and vitality—two didn't, and they aged. 'Isn't that a fact? And look what's happening to the rest of you, the ones who are going there now and bathing. By God, look at yourselves! *You're barely changing.*'

"So in June of 1908 a town meeting was called, chaired by the mayor, my grandfather, Scott's father. By then everyone had a barrel or jug of water from the spring in their home, but a committee was formed to investigate properly. It was called—with a touch of humor, I believe—the Water Board. 'Let's get to the bottom of this,' folks said—'but let's not tell anyone else yet. They'd laugh at us. Or worse.'

"Funds were appropriated. A bottled sample from the spring was taken by hand to Denver and analyzed there in the best hydrological laboratory. The report came back: the water was drinkable. Unremarkable. Nothing in it that shouldn't be there.

"Since then, in the past eighty-eight years, that procedure has been repeated some two dozen times. Every time the Water Board hears of a new high-tech water analysis company that's been formed, or any new microbiological instrumentation, we send off a sample of spring water for chemical analysis. In my time samples have gone to the Colorado Department of Health in Denver, to labs in Los Angeles, Los Alamos, U.T.-Austin, Washington, D.C. Of course we never tell the true reason for what we want done—we just ask for a chemical workup. Nothing ever turns up that shouldn't be there. Maybe a tiny bit more n-butylbenzene and bromochloromethane than normal. Mild contaminants. Not significant. They're found in the water supply of Carbondale and throughout the Ozark Mountains.

"I'm a chemist. You're aware of that, but you never knew why, or how I got to be one. My education was paid for by the town. In the late forties Cornell had one of the best chemistry departments in the country. We always need a chemist here, to keep up with new technology. I'll have a backup soon—Jed Loomis is getting his Ph.D. in organic chemistry at the University of Washington. One of the Pendergast girls is studying gerontology at Florida State. I told you that Oliver, whatever else he is, is a trained hydrobiologist—and Shirlene

Hubbard has an M.A. in geology from the University of Colorado. We sent Oliver to seminars all over the country to study hydropathy, which is the curing of disease with water. A lot of it was crackpot stuff, but we have to know. We keep investigating. But we know no more now than we did ninety years ago. We may *never* know. If we did, if we could isolate the factor, everything would be different.

"That leads me to a vital decision made at the meeting in June 1908, and reconfirmed ever since. The decision of absolute secrecy.

"Back then, with the limited scientific resources available to them, the townspeople studied the spring. They brought in a big-time geologist from San Francisco. He was asked to determine the source of the water and approximately how much of it there was. Would it flow forever? The town told him they were considering starting a resort spa.

"This expert dug, and poked, and did a flow check, and consulted his charts and maybe even his crystal ball, and he said, 'The source of this flow is separate from the aquifer—it's an underground thermal spring. Might be mixed with snowmelt, or might not. It's more shallow than deep. It could gush forever, or one fine day it could dry up. Its flow is not strong.'

" 'But do you think there's enough water for a spa, a big public pool, like the one down in Glenwood Springs?'

"The geologist looked down his nose at these country bumpkins, and he said, 'This is quite a long way for people to come in order to bathe.'

" 'Never mind that. If we open a spa to the public, if the water is used lavishly, under those circumstances would it last fifty years?'

" 'Good people, I doubt it,' the geologist said.

"Then in 1909 the townspeople held another meeting. This kind of meeting has taken place every two, three, or four years since then. It's almost always the same. Someone said, or says now, 'I'm troubled. We have something that the whole world desperately wants. Do we have the right to be so selfish, to keep the secret to ourselves?'

"And someone else, probably a lot smarter and older and wise to the ways of mankind, always answers like this:

" 'Do you know what would happen if we told the world? First off, they'd call us crazy. But curiosity would get the better of them and they'd come and take a gander. Eventually they'd realize it's true. After exhaustive tests they'd conclude, just as we did, that the chemical content of the water doesn't yield to analysis—meaning that this is the only such finite pool known in the world. It can't be analyzed chemically and then patented and duplicated elsewhere, and bottled, and sold in supermarkets in Boston and Bakersfield, Berlin and Beijing.

" 'But word will get out. This is not a secret that can be kept by more than a handful of closely knit people. And when the knowledge of what's up here gets out into the world, whether by word of mouth, or newspaper articles, or radio, or on the *Today Show*, here's what will happen, sure as God made eggs. Human beings will flock to Springhill not by the thousands, not by the hundreds of thousands, but by the millions. They'll come by chartered jet, by bus, by helicopter, and on foot if they have to. They'll come by the family and by the battalion, in such numbers that even these mountains that have been here nearly forever won't be able to accommodate them. They'll be camping in the forest, drilling in the rock and dynamiting in the snow, beating each other to death over every drop of moisture that falls from an aspen leaf. *Chaos* will be a pale word to describe what will happen to this part of the world. Government will have to take over in order to prevent anarchy. And that will be the end of everything, as it always is when government takes over.

" 'None of us here in Springhill will survive these events. Even if we're not trampled to death by the hordes who crave life everlasting, our good life here will have been destroyed. And in time, since the aquifer is limited and the source shallow, the spring will run dry. Gurgle, gurgle, splat . . . *gone!* Despite their howls of anguish, everything the invading masses dreamed of will vanish before their eyes.

" 'By then the Elk Range will be a wasteland. Do we dare let that happen? Why?—so we can become rich? We don't need to be rich. We want to live quietly and happily in our little Shangri-la, in our minuscule corner of paradise, as we've lived now for more than a hundred years, harming no one. We have what no one else in the world has, and we've cherished and protected it all these years. The fountain of youth! We're unique. We're *blessed.* We want to give our children what we have: not the patently impossible gift of eternal life, but the realizable gift of healthful longevity. And we'll beg them to preserve and protect that gift. Pass it on as a legacy to future generations—at least, for whatever future the madness of this violent planet allows. Maybe for another century, maybe for eternity. Who knows?'

"So," Sophie said, "the townspeople decided not to tell the world. They took an oath of secrecy. Each succeeding generation as it came of age has been sworn to that same oath. Springhill began to cut itself off from the other towns. 'We'll get big enough just by normal breeding,' we said. 'We don't want new families. If the town gets too big, we'll lose control of the secret.

"Back in the late twenties some union people from Denver arrived to organize the marble quarry and the coal mines. That was an ugly chapter in the town's history. Folks told the union organizers to leave, and when they refused and tried to preach the gospel of the working class, *our* working class jumped on them one night over on Quarry Road—beat them up badly and sent them packing. The union gave up. 'Let 'em rot up in Springhill,' the union organizers said.

"There's never been a church here. That helped discourage people from moving in. The town developed a reputation—not undeserved—for being unfriendly to skibtails. I remember a sign on the road to Marble back in the fifties, which they said had been there since 1927. It read:

SPRINGHILL

INCORPORATED TOWNSHIP. POP: 282.

SPEED LIMIT, 5 MILES PER HOUR, STRICTLY ENFORCED

NO SALOON OR BAR

NO CHURCH

NO HOTEL

NO SOLICITING

NO CAMP MEETINGS ALLOWED

WATCH OUT FOR BEAR AND BOBCAT

NEAREST AVAILABLE DOCTOR, 35 MILES

"Those were mostly lies. Someone had a sense of humor. Later they toned it down a bit—but not much.

"Meanwhile our marble sold well. It was used for banks, courthouses, monuments, mausoleums, city halls, schools, post offices, hotels. The Great Depression came along, and then World War II. Those were successive blows that a one-industry economy just couldn't deal with. They didn't need marble for submarines or atom bombs. In 1941 the Colorado-Yule over in Marble sold their facilities for scrap. The Springhill quarry had to close too, but we didn't sell the facilities. We had our coal mines to live on—factories and homes still had to be heated in wartime. El Rico produced good-grade copper that was needed for rifle bullets. We tightened our belts a little. No one was rich, but no one was poor. We shared what we had. That became a tradition. People became one family—still are. Bound by their oath of the spring."

Sophie stopped talking. She looked at him, took his hand, squeezed it, held the grip. "And there was a second oath," she said.

He sensed the effort she was making to meet his eyes, not to waver.

"The water had to be kept a secret, that was clear, but even as far back as 1915 the people realized that it wouldn't be a secret for very long if everyone in Springhill lived nearly forever. You told me once, when you were trying to explain to me some concept of the law: 'Justice must not only be done, it must be *seen* to be done.' This was the reverse of that. Our people couldn't *let* it be seen.

"Not that they believed that drinking the water of the spring would allow them to live to be Methuselahs. Some people wanted to believe that, but common sense soon told them it wasn't true. The spring water retarded the aging process dramatically. But it didn't do away with it. And in 1920 the coal mine blew up from methane gas. A few miners were killed. You could bathe in the spring all you liked, but you couldn't avoid sudden death.

"William Lovell grew old. Never sick, though. He died with a smile on his face. So did Otis McKee, in the accident I told you about, and Francis Hubbard. Caleb Lovell, William's son, began drinking the spring water at sixteen. He lived to be ninety-four, though he always looked thirty years younger. On a scuba-diving trip to Jamaica in 1953, Caleb's tank ran out of air at a depth of a hundred feet. He had a stroke. He was buried down there at Montego Bay.

"Larissa McKee, who started ingesting the water at a younger age than anyone else, also grew very old, but by the time she died at the age of one hundred she looked and felt like an exceptionally healthy woman of, let's say, sixty-five. An autopsy was done on her by our local doctor. It showed that her arteries were beginning to close up, and she also had some minor liver damage." Sophie smiled. "I guess I forgot to tell you, she and Otis drank a lot of beer, and they both smoked

Camels and a pipe. She might have lived another ten or twenty years before a fatal coronary or something else claimed her."

Dennis interrupted: "Might have lived another ten or twenty years? What do you mean, 'might have'? How did Larissa die?"

Sophie was silent for a minute.

"Voluntarily," she said. "Larissa went voluntarily—as we all do. Or will do. Because we have to, and because we decide to. If we don't have a stroke or major heart attack or cancer, or get hit by an avalanche like my first husband, or like Otis McKee by a car whose brakes fail, we live to the age of one hundred. A century. Enough, don't you think? That was Larissa's idea, and it became the key idea to the safe existence of the secret of Springhill. She started her mature life as a devoted sensualist. When she'd had her fill, she began to change: it was her wisdom and foresight which allowed this community to survive. First, she convinced everyone that the water would allow them to live nearly forever. And then she convinced everyone that 'nearly forever' was far too long—that 'nearly forever' would lead to disaster. She was the one who said, at one of those town meetings back around 1910: 'If we live nearly forever, or even if we just live an unnaturally long time, the world will find out. We have to protect ourselves and our children from that catastrophe. We have to keep the secret, and guard against the invasion that would come if we didn't.' " Sophie paused. "Dennis, we can't be greedy."

He looked at her; at last he was beginning to understand.

"It took awhile," she said, "and there was a lot of protest. Some people wept and beat their breasts . . . but they finally saw that she was right, and in the end they gave in. You can't live a hundred and fifty years or more without the world finding out. Scientists and journalists demand to know the why and how of such things. They want to interview you and put you up there on the twenty-inch screen, or get you to endorse their brand of whole-grain bread and shake the hand of the president on the White House lawn and receive a plaque honoring the achievement. Centenarians aren't as rare as they used to be, and getting to one hundred is becoming more common. But imagine if they found out you were a hundred and twenty! Or a hundred and *sixty!* And you looked seventy-five! And you could still ski the Dumps and ride a mountain bike uphill, and hike to twelve thousand feet, and you had a full sex life—my God, you'd have a hell of a lot more than fifteen minutes of being famous! They'd hound you to your grave.

"And also we realized that even if you keep quiet about it, there are birth certificates, death certificates, IRS forms, passports, driver's licenses that need to be renewed, Social Security benefits, Medicare—records galore. Everything we do has documentation. Our lives are exactly the opposite of private. Government doesn't let you be. In Springhill we've learned over decades of study how to control all that. How not to be found out. That's why the dates aren't correct in the cemetery. It's why we have home rule and deal with our own local taxes and records. That's why so many of the men have the same names as their fathers. We make sure there's always at least one doctor like Grace to write out death certificates and file them with the state, and one dentist like Edward, who, if he has to, in an emergency, will get the records mixed up. One funeral home, and one registered nurse, as well as a few others trained by her, who are capable of administering the injection that people get—if they need it—on a day of their choice within a month of their hundredth birthday. It used to be cyanide. Now it's potassium chloride.

"That's what we do and how we do it. In each case we can manage the deception, we figured out, for a hundred years. Longer than that is too chancy. You might say, 'Well, why not a hundred and five?'—and there's no overwhelmingly correct answer. We simply decided on one hundred as a round number. A *good* number. A degree of deception to the outside world that we could deal with, that we could carry off with reasonable certainty."

"Wait," Dennis said, and raised his hand. "Look at my Aunt Jennie. There are plenty of people who live into their nineties now. Jennie might make it to a hundred. Or more. It's not that rare in our time."

"Jennie might make it to a hundred," Sophie said, "but in what condition? In Watkins Glen that Thanksgiving your sister told me Jennie wore diapers, that she left pots of water boiling on the stove, that during the night her arthritis made her cry out from pain. Dennis, what good is living to a hundred and twenty, or even ninety-five like your Aunt Jennie, if the quality of your life fades and erodes—if you're a burden to those you love—if you *suffer*? Do you understand that here in Springhill the man or woman who lives to be a hundred *is in the prime of life*? If we extended the departure to a hundred and ten or more, we would be found out, because at a hundred and ten we'd be easily as vigorous as a normal man or woman of sixty! Don't you see? I tell you: we are *blessed*.

"So that's the second oath we swear in that ceremony when each of us turns twenty-one. It's an oath that we'll depart voluntarily, and without fuss, at the mellow age of one full century. There'll be a going-away party a little before that time, to wish us well. We call it the departure ceremony. *Departure* is the formal word we use for what's essentially a voluntary death. A lot of songs and warmth and touching. Lots of laughs and reminiscences. And then we go. With dignity, surrounded by friends and family, and without pain. Can you realize how wonderful that is? What a fitting end to a long and decent life? How perfect?

"The amazing thing is, after that ceremony and before any injection is necessary, the person who's reached the age of one hundred often goes very quickly. They realize that their time has come, it's been a good life, and they depart. Did you ever hear of boning? It's something that happens in Australia among the aborigines. A witch doctor points a bone at a man—usually someone very old or with a supposedly incurable disease. The man who's been boned falls to the ground and crawls off to his hut. His spirit sinks. Within days, sometimes within hours, he dies.

"*Boning* is another word we use here for what happens. It started as a kind of joke. Then it became part of the lore. We often talk of the departure ceremony as the boning. But here our spirits don't sink, even though we know there's little time left. Do you remember when Jack Pendergast died?"

"Yes, I certainly do." Dennis was remembering what he had seen from the shadows by the creek on that June night: Jack Pendergast making his final bow to the world, embedded in Rose Loomis.

"He'd turned one hundred a few days before his departure. There was a little boning party for him given by my parents. Only close friends came. And three days later he lay down to take a nap and never woke up. It wasn't a heart attack at all, and he didn't need any Versed or potassium chloride. That's how it will happen for most of us. We'll go without remorse, with hardly anything undone, and without anger. With a full acceptance of death as a voluntary rounding off of a completed life. Because we know we've had more luck than any other group of people in the world. Where else on this planet is that true?

Larissa, my great-grandmother, was the first. The rest of us—well, almost all of the rest of us—have followed in her footsteps gratefully."

"Almost all, yes." Dennis nodded slowly. "But not all."

"That's right. There have been occasions when someone said, 'No, I've got things to do, places to see—I don't want to die yet. I don't care what I swore to when I was a kid. I want to keep on living!' "

"And then what happens, Sophie?"

"Usually we talk them out of it. We make a concerted communal effort, because we believe it's vital. And they come round. They realize how their death fits into the scheme of things—most particularly, how it benefits their children and grandchildren. How it makes it possible for all of the rest of us to go on living. They're boned, so to speak, and they depart quietly.

"But not all, as you said. I know of two such instances. About twenty years ago there was a man named Julian Rice. He had no children and so he didn't feel a great sense of continuity. Two of his brothers had died in a mine disaster that he believed could have been prevented—he blamed the community. Also, he was in love. Imagine, he was coming up on a hundred years of age, and he fell in love with Betsy Prescott, a woman of eighty-two who'd been widowed in that same mining accident. Julian and Betsy were having an affair. If you're full of good cholesterol and you don't smoke and you drink the water from the spring, it can happen.

"The bottom line was that they didn't want to die. He and the widow left town one night. They took a supply of the spring water with them, although that was unnecessary. One thing we've learned is that after a certain age the water becomes redundant. If you drink regular quantities from your twenties up to about sixty, you've ingested as much into your system as you'll ever need. It sets in motion a biological cycle that appears to be irreversible. You can quit imbibing—you still age slowly and gently, and you still keep your vitality. Do you remember *Lost Horizon*, the James Hilton novel?—it was a movie later, with Ronald Colman. His plane crashes deep in the Himalayas, near this monk-ruled paradise of Shangri-la, where the people live forever. Ronald Colman eventually leaves with a beautiful young Tibetan girl, but by the time they go through a snowstorm and reach the outside valley she's shriveled into a hundred-year-old hag.

"It's not like that here. Not so romantic, not so drastic. But Julian

Rice didn't believe it and he took water with him. We had to stop them—him and Betsy Prescott. They might have lived far too long and the secret would have come out that way, or Rice might have talked about it, because he was a boastful, hot-tempered man. We couldn't risk it. We did some detective work and found out they'd gone to the Pacific coast of Mexico. We sent people after them. What happened was horrible, and violent. Julian Rice was killed. So was one of our young men, Sam Hubbard. Rice shot him. Betsy was unharmed, although she was in shock. They brought her back here. She recovered, bit by bit, and died at the age of ninety, well before her time. It was sad, and I've often wondered if we did the right thing. But I think on balance we had to."

Sophie fell silent, waiting for his response.

"And of course," Dennis said, "the second time that anyone tried to break the pact was last summer. The Lovells tried. Susan and Henry Lovell."

"Yes. And I'm going to tell you about that. I'll tell you everything. But come with me now." She stood quickly. "Come outside. Dress warmly. Come."

"Where are we going?"

Sophie took his arm. "Don't you know?"

25 *April 13, 1995*

The Murderer

SOMETIMES HER GLOVED hand touched his. Sometimes she was a step ahead. They reached the gate in the forest. A few stars gleamed between tufts of snow hung from the trees.

"It's hard to believe, Sophie."

"I understand that."

She twirled the combination lock on the gate, and it clicked open. They stepped through. She led him along the path, the same path he and the children had trod nearly a year ago when she had shown them the old mining cabin and the odd way the tennis ball rolled and the seemingly impossible tilt of her body.

They reached the spring and the little oval pool. In the darkness a light mist of steam rose off the water. Dappled moonlight gleamed off the snow. Sophie took off her clothes. Her skin seemed the color of ivory. Her nipples stiffened in the cold. She was smiling at him.

"Now you, Dennis."

He undressed, dropping his clothes in a pile on the earth. There was no wind and he was not cold at all. She took his hand and led him into the water, carefully, because there were rocks and not all were eroded smooth. He lowered himself into the pool next to her. It was deep enough for him to sit and allow the warm current to flow around his hips and splash as high as his shoulders. He smelled no sulphur, no chemicals. The water soothed and calmed him.

"This is where they came," Sophie said. "My great-grandparents—Larissa and Otis. Do you feel their spirit in the air?"

"I'm not sure."

"I do. Do you want to make love?"

He remembered she had asked him that in her house on the first night they had been alone, when he had flown back from New York to be with her because he had known already that he didn't want to live without her. Then he had said, "Of course I do." This time he had no need for words. Already aroused, he took her in his arms and drew her toward him in the water of the spring. Even as she settled on his lap and he entered her greater warmth and began to rock gently back and forth, he felt water surge up and touch his lips. It was the water of the spring on his face. The sweet, warm water of the spring. He touched his lips with his tongue and took his first sip.

An hour later they were back at the house. Sophie brought feta cheese, crackers, and red wine from the kitchen. He stirred the log fire again, added more oak. He felt wonderfully tired, cleansed. The red-orange blaze sprang up in the fireplace.

"Are you worn out?" Sophie asked. "Do you want to go to bed?"

"No. I want to know the rest." In as calm a voice as he could recruit, considering all he had been told and all that had happened, he asked, "What was the Lovells' reason for refusing to honor the pact?"

Sophie said, "Henry and Susie told us they'd been thinking about it for years. Thinking, debating, and planning. They saw no necessity to die. Modern medicine, nutrition, and biological science had made enormous strides. Except for pneumonia and AIDS, we'd virtually conquered infectious diseases. One hundred years of life was no longer so remarkable. The age of departure should be changed to a hundred and ten, the Lovells believed. Or at least a hundred and five.

"They came to me and my parents with that suggestion, and the Water Board met, with other elders invited as well, to get some more input and a quorum. We discussed it, and we decided in the negative. It could have brought discovery and further requests for more and more extensions of life.

"My father, because he was an old friend of the Lovells, brought the decision to them. They were disappointed, to put it mildly. But they had a second line of persuasion. With the town's blessing they wanted to leave Springhill. Never come back. They said they understood the risks but they had a well-thought-out plan to obviate them. They were going to travel to a city in another state and start life there as a couple in their late sixties. After about twenty years they'd move to another city in another part of the country and there they'd tell people they were in their seventies. And then, later, move again. And so on. Each time they moved they'd lie about their starting age, so no one would ever realize how old they really were. They'd go on a long time that way.

"Their idea was plausible but not acceptable. Too much could happen along the way. They could become attached to the first community they moved to, not want to leave. How would they deal with Medicare, driver's licenses? Out of the protective aura of Springhill, they'd be vulnerable. And they might have the urge to confess the secret to someone. Maybe it would feel wonderful, one evening around the barbecue pit, to say to friends, 'Do you realize Susie and I are one hundred and twenty and one hundred eighteen years old? You don't believe us? We can prove it.'

"Aside from all those frightening and likely eventualities, there was the precedent they'd be setting for the whole community of Springhill. One exception could open the floodgate. All the years of discipline would go down the drain.

"They'd sworn to the pact. We all saw it as a nonbreakable agreement. 'No,' my father said—he spoke to them as a friend, not as an official of any sort—'it just wouldn't work.' The Lovells came to me as mayor and chairperson of the Water Board. I said, 'Please understand, we can't allow it.' I didn't say, 'Please forgive me,' because that would have been hypocrisy. I didn't believe I was making any sort of decision that required forgiveness.

"Henry had passed his hundredth birthday by then. A date had been set for the boning party and the departure ceremony. Susan was two years younger, but quite a while ago she'd told the Board she wanted to depart at the same time as Henry. This is common with couples who've been married sixty or seventy years or more, and where the younger one is close to the age of one hundred. The request has always been honored.

"Then one night Henry and Susan went for a walk with their son, Hank, and their daughter, Carol, and confessed what they planned to do. In effect, they said goodbye to their children. At first Hank and Carol didn't know what to do. In the end they came to us and told us. They feared their parents were endangering the lives of the community—and that meant their lives and the lives of their children and their children's children.

"But by then Henry and Susan were gone. Gone up toward Pearl Pass, where they'd intended to camp until the first snowfall while we went haring off on a bunch of wild-goose chases—because in the earlier discussions with my parents and with the Water Board, they'd hinted that they were thinking of starting out in the San Diego area, and then maybe heading for Hawaii.

"Hank remembered, when his father was younger, he'd always talked about spending some time in British Columbia, north of Lake Louise. Henry came from mountain stock—he loved the high country. He'd said, 'Up there in British Columbia is the last livable frontier.' And Susie couldn't stand extreme heat. What kind of a life would they lead in a coastal area like San Diego? Hank and Carol and I played detective. We looked through the Lovell house, through every stitch of their belongings, and between us we figured out what clothes they'd taken. They'd left a good part of their summer stuff behind. Some camping gear and a military knife were also gone, and in a garbage can we found a receipt for a new nylon tent. We also dug out of the attic an old set of Department of the Interior geological surveys of the White River National Forest. One of them was missing—the one that covered the area near Pearl Pass in Pitkin County. Dad and Henry and a couple of other elders had hunted for elk up there about ten years ago. Henry was familiar with the terrain and he was an excellent woodsman. So we made an intelligent guess and sent up three teams of people to find them."

"In this case," Dennis asked, "who exactly is 'we'?"

"The Water Board, whose emergency committee I chair. We were in charge, although we conferred with as many people in town as we could.

"One team went straight up to Pearl Pass and camped in the eastern bottleneck. That was the only way out of the area in the direction of Independence Pass and Leadville and Denver, unless you intend to head back down to Aspen by way of Difficult Campground. Peter Frazee was leader of that group. I went with a second team—with my cousin Amos McKee and Dan Crenshaw, who runs the gym, and Louise Hubbard, Grace's daughter by her first marriage. Nominally I was the leader, although Amos is a real mountain man and Dan was the oldest among us. But I'm the mayor—as you've begun to realize, that's quite a bit more than just a pencil-pushing sinecure.

"My parents, with Oliver Cone and Shirlene Hubbard, made up the third team. Dad's a great tracker, Oliver is a bowman, Shirlene's a geologist, and they were the ones who found the Lovells' camp. They found it in the evening but didn't go in until dawn. They had to kill the dog. That was unfortunate, but when it was discussed at the meeting before we left for Pearl Pass we all agreed that if the dog alerted the Lovells, Henry might do something foolish. Everyone remembered the debacle in Mexico with Julian Rice and poor Sam Hubbard. Henry Lovell had a rifle—that Remington which they foolishly left up there and was found with my father's fingerprints on it. We didn't think Henry would use it in anger, but we didn't dare take the risk."

Dennis bent to stir the fire again. He placed a thick oak log atop the others.

"My parents and the Lovells sat down and talked. Harped, as we say in Springling. It's a way of reasoning through a problem that tries to put the good of the community above all else—in a humanist and communal way, if you'll accept the use of those two words linked together. Because for us, *community* isn't a glorious abstraction, like *the state* in Marxism, or *all freedom-loving peoples* in that government claptrap we've heard for decades. This community is a specific group of people who have names and faces. Three hundred and seventy linked human beings, and their unborn descendants.

"They harped for a couple of hours. Henry began to come round, to see it, to be willing. And to be gracious, not angry. But not Susan. The funny thing is, what really got her back up was not so much my father's gentle insistence that she and Henry had to depart now, that day, for the general good, but that Oliver had put an arrow through the heart of their old dog, Geronimo. Susan kept saying, 'How can you be so all-fired high-and-mighty about the good of the community when you've just killed an innocent dog that wouldn't even harm a cat? You did that on behalf of the community? What kind of community that's of any lasting value does such a brutal thing?' It was remarkable—she carried on about that dog for the better part of an hour, and it was one of the last few hours of her life."

"How do you know those details?" Dennis asked.

"I was there by then, with my team. At the harping I didn't talk much. I listened. And my parents had no decent answer for that question of Susan's. It was just one of those many things that 'had to be.' After a while the discussion petered out, because it was clear from the beginning that there could be only one outcome. If the Lovells said no, some sort of force, however mild, would have to be used. That was a hateful idea. That's what we were trying to avoid at almost any cost."

"You were trying," Dennis said, "to get them to ratify their own murder."

"Their *murder?*" Sophie looked pale for a moment, but then recovered. "No, Dennis, not their murder. Their death, yes. Their departure. That universal act to which all of us without exception are doomed. It's ordained as part of life. It can't be escaped. It's just a question of *when.* So, no, my darling, my dear lawyer husband, not their murder. Their voluntary acceptance of the end of their life at the age of one hundred. Don't you see the difference? It's vast. Forget that they'd sworn to it seventy-nine years ago—forget even that, because I'm sure the law would not regard that oath as a binding contract. Just remember everything I've told you. Balance their deaths against the life of the community they and we both loved and wanted to perpetuate."

"I'm trying," Dennis said, "but I'm not quite succeeding. You're right that the law wouldn't see this assisted suicide pact as a binding contract. And the law wouldn't see their deaths under these circumstances as anything but murder. It's not even euthanasia. For God's sake, they weren't suffering—they were *healthy.* So it's the willful and deliberate taking of two fit lives. How can you call that anything but murder?"

"Because this act, which you call assisted suicide," Sophie said, a little heatedly, "goes beyond the narrow world of law. It goes beyond any prudent or useful definition of justice, which is what you lawyers are always trying to define and make happen—with results that all sane people agree are ridiculous bordering on disgusting. Yes! It goes to the heart of human life. It goes to what we all dream of when we dare to dream."

"No. I don't see it."

"Because you *daren't*, Dennis. Not yet. Listen to me carefully. Think before you answer. Can you do that?"

Dennis nodded. He could try.

"If you"—Sophie leaned forward—"*you*, Dennis Conway—today, at your present age of forty-nine, were given the opportunity—barring accident or foul play, or any nasty disease that your body might already be harboring—to live to the age of one hundred, in a harmonious environment among your loved ones—to live with physical vitality and sexual power and a ripening intelligence, right through to the very end of your days on your hundredth birthday—provided that you would vow to submit to a humane, peaceful death at that end—would you say yes or no? Would you make that bargain? Or would you rather take your chances like your Aunt Jennie?"

Dennis stared at her.

"Your look speaks volumes," Sophie said. "It's not the devil asking Faust to give up his soul for eternal life. You're getting a hundred-year guarantee of health. It costs you nothing."

Still Dennis did not reply, and Sophie went on: "Another codicil to the bargain is this. You'd be ensuring that your children would have the same opportunity to live that way, and that long. Barring the unforeseen accidents that make this an imperfect and often cruel world, you'd be guaranteeing them a hundred years of healthy life. What they make of it, of course, no one can guarantee. Think about it! Is there any evil in that bargain? Where is the wrong? The injustice? You tell me. I don't see any. Except perhaps for this one thing: that when your time came to depart, your friends and family would have to help you on the journey, because you can't really do it alone. Yes, in the eyes of the law of the state of Colorado and the other forty-nine states and the federal government and all those other wonderful governments the world over, the loyal people who helped you to keep your promise to depart at the age of one hundred would be committing the crime of murder under section such-and-such of the penal code. How sinful. How inhumane. But is it, Dennis? Is it murder most foul? Or is it life most fortunate and death most enlightened? And if it were offered to you—you personally—would you say yes or no?"

"I'm not sure," Dennis said. "It's hard to answer something like that in theory."

"*In theory?*" Sophie laughed with great gusto; he loved her laugh, even now, at a moment like this. "What makes you think it's a theoretical question? We don't take strangers into the community often. There have only been three in my lifetime. One died relatively young, of leukemia, which we found out he'd had before he began drinking the water from the spring. The second one is Harry Parrot, your friend and my former father-in-law, who's just about at the end of his hundred years now—in fact, we're going to talk to him and plan the departure ceremony this week. And the third one, my darling, is *you*. We decided a long time ago that we wouldn't accept immigrants. Couldn't control them. But if anyone came into our midst through marriage, that was a different story: we would welcome them. We would have a kind of probation period of a year, and if we saw by then that they measured up to our pretty moderate view of what a civilized human being should be, we'd offer them the same opportunity as if they'd been born and bred in Springhill. They would be offered the water. They'd be offered the same pact we were offered when we were younger. One hundred years.

"So it's not theoretical, Dennis. It's *real*. Your year has already passed. The offer wasn't made to you on time because it didn't seem wise to bludgeon your mind with all those facts while you were getting ready to defend my parents for a murder they didn't commit but would certainly have committed if they'd had to. 'Wait,' everyone said, 'until after the trial.' I had to abide by that. I had to be silent, even though I hated every moment of it.

"Not theoretical. Real! You can choose. Go back into the world and take your chances with biology, or stay with me in Springhill, in *our* world, and live to be a hundred. And then die voluntarily. You'd be starting late on the water, so you might only make it into your mid-nineties. No guarantee on that. Is it a hard choice? I doubt it. You just haven't confronted it yet as reality—you're still viewing all this as a kind of fantasy. But it's not. Soon, when you've spoken to more people among us and asked more questions, it will become real for you. And when you're ready to choose, you'll tell me."

"Wait," Dennis said, "before we get to that—if I'm able to get to it, because I'm reeling—I need to ask you something. You said a minute ago that the offer wasn't made to me before because it didn't seem the right time to do it, while I was getting ready to defend your parents for a murder they didn't commit. A murder they didn't commit? Sophie, I know they committed it. I fought for your mother in court, and I won, but I knew she did it. She told me she didn't, but I knew she was lying. She was guilty under the law I've sworn to uphold. And you've admitted to me today, right here, that they did it. They harped, you said, but everyone knew there could be only one outcome. Your mother gave a lethal injection to the Lovells. The trial's over, there's no double jeopardy. Why bother to deny it now?"

"Shirlene Hubbard hadn't really wanted to go along in the first place," Sophie said, "and my mother finally decided she didn't want to do it, even though by that stage of the proceedings both Henry and Susan were willing—although not what I'd call thrilled at the idea. I'm sorry, I don't mean to be facetious. It was an extraordinary discussion that took place in that tent at Pearl Pass. It clarified all the ideas we'd ever had. But Bibsy went through a kind of crisis. She'd known Susie Lovell too long."

"Nevertheless," Dennis said, his glance shifting away to probe the shadows cast by the fire, "she overcame her reluctance. She hastened their departure, to use your euphemism." He looked back at Sophie then—at his thirty-eight-year-old wife who was claiming to be sixty-four.

"No." Leaning forward, Sophie clasped her hands over her knees, like a child. "My mother didn't have to. There was someone else there who could do it, and was willing to do it and save that wound to my mother's conscience. I was there. I had the training from her, years ago. I injected both of them. First with the sedatives, then with the potassium. By your law, I murdered them."

26 *April 16, 1995*

Choice

DENNIS ATE FOOD and hardly tasted it; he played hearts and chess with Lucy and Brian and tutored them in American history and studied the solar system with them; he drove back and forth between home and his office in Aspen. He found time one morning, after they had agreed not to discuss the trial or the case, to ski the back of Aspen Mountain with Josh Gamble. ("It's not my job to be pissed off at lawyers for doing their job," the sheriff said. "It's my job to do my job.") He began work on two new run-of-the-mill cases—but all the time he felt that he was elsewhere: he was with Sophie, the snow silently falling, listening to her tale and watching the pale oval of her face against the blackness of the forest. Or framed against the crackling of the fire. Or in the spring, where he had taken his first sip of the water that could keep him alive for another fifty years. Was it possible? Was it a dream?

Whenever he was alone he talked to himself aloud. He asked questions and struggled to answer them. He had studied her Colorado birth certificate. The date was November 5, 1930. She snapped off the rubber band and unrolled her A.B. degree from Cornell University— the graduation date was June 1952. She handed him a magnifying glass and he bent in the brilliant halogen glare of her desk lamp to once again inspect the sepia-tinted photograph of William Lovell's sixty-fifth birthday party. Unless she was identifying the faces falsely, they were exactly as she had described them. A yellowed, brittle, and well-thumbed copy of the Tunisian Sheikh Nefzawi's *The Perfumed Garden* nested in the back of the safe. It had been published in London in 1846, its translator unnamed. In the flyleaf Dennis traced a scrawl in turquoise-colored ink: *This marvelous book is the property of Larissa Orlov McKee.*

He thought again about the Lovells' teeth—the gold fillings and the old-style amalgam that the forensic odontologist swore had to have been put in before 1910, at a time when Susan Lovell, born Susan Crenshaw, and Henry Lovell Sr., were in their teens. Henry Lovell Sr.—Caleb's son, and William's grandson . . .

If Dennis decided not to believe, then he was married to a charlatan, a woman with a twisted mind and the resolve to accomplish her ends at any cost. A fantasist and a murderer. If he elected to believe that his wife, the woman he loved, was sixty-four years old, then a door swung open into an amazing future. A new world beckoned. He could reject it, slam shut the door, and walk away to a normal life with its risks and possibilities—or walk through the portal and be part of a hitherto undreamed-of destiny: live to be a hundred, then willingly die. And until that moment of departure, not only guard the secret of the town, but ensure that it remain a secret. He understood he would have to help, because that was part of the pact: everyone helped. In the matter of the Lovells' death, everyone had helped cover up the truth. None believed they had done wrong.

If he accepted everything that Sophie had told him, there had been no murder. Assisted suicide, yes—and in such a case, whose law prevailed? The law of the state or the law of the community? That answer was clear to him. The state was an abstraction; the community was made up of live human beings. She was not a murderer.

He sat with Sophie again in front of the fire and pulled the cork from a good bottle of red zinfandel. There was so much he had to know.

"What do you do," he asked, "if a young person doesn't agree to the pact? Doesn't choose longevity and an eventual departure at the age of one hundred?"

"A few have done that," Sophie said. "They left Springhill."

"You let them go?"

"This isn't a prison."

"You didn't worry they'd betray you?"

"They left because they didn't believe what we told them. We asked ourselves: What's the worst-case scenario? Wherever they went, they would tell people there were these crazy people in the Elk Mountains who believed they'd discovered the fountain of youth. We think that happened once. A dozen fresh-faced long-haired people from Oregon came about six or seven years ago and asked if there was such a place. They used those words: 'A fountain of youth.' We laughed at them. Oh, we had a good cackle! We made them feel like fools who'd been sold a bill of goods by kids who'd smoked some mighty powerful dope. The poor people camped over by Indian Lake for a week or so, ate their granola, tried to swim there but nearly froze to death, and then cleared out. They haven't bothered us since."

"No one else has ever come to investigate?"

"No one."

"What about the state of Colorado? The federal government? Haven't any of you in Springhill ever been caught out on discrepancies?"

"Now and then. The county commissioner can be nosy, and we've had a few inquiries from the state Department of Health. They treat us like hillbillies—not very bright people who don't know how to keep records like good Americans. But we usually come up with whatever documentation is needed. Driver's licenses have to be renewed in person every five years, and you need to bring a photograph—so if there's a problem, we send someone else who looks the correct age. And every year we register a few extra births so that we have a supply of backup birth certificates. Grace is the present custodian. The Water Board keeps track of the paperwork."

Dennis asked, "Has it ever occurred to you that you could be mistaken about the cause of the longevity? That there might be other factors?"

"Of course. We know other things contribute to healthful longevity. Orderliness of life, for one. Farmers live longer than people in any other occupation. Mountain people tend to live longer. There are an unusual amount of centenarians in Kazakhstan and Armenia. For a while it was ascribed to eating yogurt, which of course was nonsense.

The truth is the long-lived Kazakhs were physically active peasants—goatherds and shepherds who climbed mountains seven days a week. That's a natural form of aerobic exercise. They ate sparingly and they breathed unpolluted air. A few lived to be a hundred. But plenty of them died in their sixties and seventies and eighties too. There was no consistent longevity. What we've always had in Springhill is consistency. More than that. *Unanimity.*"

Dennis nodded; he grasped it.

"And remember," Sophie said, "just down the road in Marble we have a control group, although they're hardly aware of it. Same genetic stock, same occupations, same altitude and climate. The only difference is they don't drink from the spring. They're pretty healthy, but on the average they don't live more than a few years longer than people down in Carbondale."

"What about diet? Couldn't it be a factor?"

"You think my mother's French cooking is conducive to long life? And my father's love for château-bottled burgundy?"

Dennis frowned.

"You still have a hard time believing it."

"Yes."

"What bothers you most?"

"The how and why of it," he said. "If chemical analysis doesn't reveal the unique element in the water that produces the phenomenon—then what *does* produce it? And how can it possibly *be?* Don't you see? Why *here?* Why nowhere else?"

"It might exist somewhere else," Sophie said, "and in that somewhere else they might have come to the same conclusions that we have—to keep it quiet. But you're right. We don't know the how or why of it. If we did, everything would be different. We would share the secret. I told you there's a theory that a meteorite struck here thousands of years ago and is buried near the spring, and that's what's supposed to account for the skewed gravity and the other weird goings-on. Maybe that's also what affects the water. Maybe not. We don't know. We've come to accept all of it as a kind of miracle, although I personally detest that word because I believe that if we had full knowledge we would see that everything has a logical, chemical cause. I prefer to think of it as a gift. A *blessing* is the word I always use.

From what or from whom, I don't dare speculate. What I do know is that gifts and blessings can be used wisely or foolishly. I believe—given the fact that we're human, and limited in our knowledge—we've used ours wisely."

That night, in bed, Dennis set all debate aside and made love with his beautiful sixty-four-year-old wife. Numbers were abstract, and Sophie was touchable, real. Her body glowed in the April moonlight as it had two years ago when for the first time they made love in this same bed. He heard her wild cry, felt her body tremble under his. Into her he poured the full measure of his passion.

In her arms, drifting toward sleep, he murmured, "It will be all right. *We* will be all right. No matter what."

He woke in the morning with a feeling that he had crossed a bridge. What he had said was true. Sophie's words came back to him. *You can choose. Go back into the world and take your chances with biology. Or stay with me in Springhill, in this world,* our *world, and live to be a hundred. And then die voluntarily.*

It's true, he thought. It's not a fantasy. I believe it. I'll stay, drink the water, swear whatever oaths have to be sworn. I'll live to be one hundred years old, and so will my children. How can that be wrong?

Later that day Dennis remembered his promise to Harry Parrot. After the trial was over, he'd said, they would talk. He would call friends in the East, prepare the way for Harry's trip. He also remembered what Sophie had told him: Harry was at the end of his hundred years. They were going to plan the departure ceremony this week. So much was working in Dennis's mind that the significance of this penetrated only slowly. Harry was slated to die—but Harry had told him that he wanted to go to New York to show his paintings.

Dennis left the office early and drove straight to Harry's house, the first house as the road entered Springhill. It had begun to snow again. Every day in the warm April sun the snow turned to mush, and every evening it iced. County snowplows were working overtime. Dennis had four-wheel drive and studded snow tires, but his big red Jeep skidded on the packed ice as he entered Harry's driveway.

There was no doorbell. When Dennis knocked loudly, Harry yelled from afar, "Come in!"

In the overheated living room Harry was sunk into an old leather chair near the fire, one paint-stained, big-knuckled hand maintaining a firm grip on a half-empty bottle of vodka.

"Knew it was you. You want a drink? Get yourself one. You been here before. You know where I keep the glasses."

Dennis brought a tumbler from the kitchen and sat down on the gnarled pine coffee table in front of Harry.

"I know everything," he said. "Sophie told me about the water. The pact. The whole story of Springhill. It's a little hard to believe."

"Well, it's true, my friend. All of it. She tell you about boning?"

"That too."

"That's what they're doing to me now. Go gracefully, your wife says. They all say it. They've got a right to say it. I agreed to it a long time ago. And they've been good to me. Couldn't have been better." Harry grunted; he even laughed. "The sons of bitches."

"You told me you were going to New York."

"To the big city. Never been there. Take my work. Slides. Meet the right people. You know them, don't you? Wha'd you say once? 'Pity if you blushed unseen the rest of your life.' I thought about that. Rest of my life's not a hell of a lot of time, though. I'm a good painter—I might damn well be a great painter. Hard to say. Not up to me. You know when it was I turned a hundred?"

"No, Harry, I actually don't."

"Yesterday. I came into this world April 14, 1895. You know I was in the First World War? Damn right I was. I couldn't tell you that before. Wanted to tell you, knew you'd been in Nam and you'd get a kick out of where *I'd* been. Corporal, Sixth Infantry—went to France, to Château-Thierry. Ten minutes in the trench first fucking day and I'm crapping in my pants, waiting to go over the top and get killed, and then I get hit in the shoulder by shrapnel from some goddam Kraut artillery shell. Luckiest thing ever happened to me. They sent me back to a hospital in Paris. Never saw action again. Got laid in Paris ten days in a row. Ginette, Marie . . . can't remember the others. *'Voulez-vous coucher avec mois, mam'selle?'* They always said, *'Oui, chéri.'* That was really something. You believe it?"

"I wouldn't have believed it a week ago," Dennis said, "but I do now."

"Sorry I had to shut up about it. Jumped out of your car the other day, felt like a goddam fool. I couldn't tell you."

"I understand."

"Wouldn't mind seeing Paris again after I get my fill of New York. Maybe they say *'Oui, chéri'* to an old goat of a hundred."

Dennis smiled. "You'll find out."

"I will? How will I? They won't let me go."

Dennis had thought about this all day. "They're not going to stop you with force, Harry. They want you to go through with the departure ceremony. But if you refuse, they certainly won't kill you. These are civilized people, not barbarians." As he said that, he remembered what had happened to him and the driver of the delivery van on the road from Springhill to Redstone, but with some effort he set that memory aside; it had nothing to do with what was happening now. "If you tell them you're going," he said to Harry, "that will be that. They'll have to accept it."

Harry tilted the vodka bottle to his lips. When he had swallowed, he shook his head. "You don't understand," he said.

"Sophie told me everything."

"About old Henry and Susie?"

"That too."

"Suppose Henry and Susie had said, 'No way. Fuck you, and fuck the horse you rode in on.' What do you think would have happened?"

He hadn't thought about that, Dennis realized. If the Lovells had balked, Sophie had said, "some sort of force, however mild, would have been used . . . that's what we were trying to avoid at almost any cost."

But he hadn't dwelled on that; he had blocked that too from his mind.

Harry said, "The needle would still have gone into their arm, my friend. Bet your paycheck on it. And they'd do that to me too. They got people who deal with just that kind of situation, and you know who they are. Don't look so innocent and so shocked. They'd throw me off a goddam mountain if they had to."

"I can't believe that," Dennis said.

"You don't *want* to believe it."

He couldn't afford to believe it. Because then Sophie was part of a system that would commit murder if it had to. The end justified the means.

"Harry, what if you just walked away? Got into your truck in the middle of the night and drove down to Carbondale and then up I-70 to Denver. Simply never came back?"

"Henry and Susie Lovell tried to do that," Harry said.

Dennis said slowly, "The people here knew where to look for the Lovells. What if they hadn't found them up at Pearl Pass?"

"They would have kept looking. Years ago there was a guy named Julian Rice. He got away. They hunted him down in Mexico. It took them two years, but they found him. They killed him."

In her recounting, Sophie had left out the time element, the dedication to the hunt.

"They went down to Mexico and harped with Rice to convince him," Dennis said. He was defending them now, he realized. Once a defense attorney, always a defense attorney.

"Julian Rice didn't want to harp," Harry said. "He wanted to drink margaritas in Puerto Vallarta and have fun with his sexy old girl-friend, and *live*."

"They won't find you," Dennis said.

"You don't know that. I'd have to be looking over my shoulder all the time. That's some fucking way to live."

"They won't know where you went."

"If I get a show in New York they'll sure as hell know. And if not, they'll know that you know, and you'll tell them."

"I would never do that," Dennis said sharply.

"You will if you're one of them."

"I wouldn't, Harry. I swear it to you."

"You'd have to do it."

Harry sounded so certain that Dennis hesitated. "Why?"

"They wouldn't let you live here if you didn't."

He paced the room. He saw the dilemma. The village made no exceptions. They couldn't. But unless Harry submitted meekly . . . they had to.

"What are you going to do?" Dennis asked.

"Don't know yet," Harry said. "I was kind of hoping you'd come round and drop some pearls of wisdom in my ear. If not wisdom, then some plain old good advice. I was using willpower, and I guess it worked, 'cause here you are. You're a lawyer. You been around the block a few times, and I get the feeling you don't take shit from too many people. And you're a friend. So what should I do? What would *you* do?"

Dennis sat down and faced the old painter. "Why do you want to live?"

"Does it matter?"

"It matters a lot."

"Then I'll tell you. I want to live a while longer to get my work out there where it's meant to be. I can't leave that job to anyone else because it takes all your energy full-time and no one else will do it right. I don't want to live to be two hundred, or a hundred and twenty, or even a goddam hundred and five. I don't care about the numbers so long as I can get some recognition for what I've done in there." He jerked a thumb in the direction of his studio. "For sixty-five years of sweat. Sixty-five years of pouring out my guts on canvas. That ain't the purest of motives, I know that. But it's the only motive I've got, and I'm stuck with it."

"It's decent enough," Dennis said. "Let me harp with them. I think they'll understand. I'm a good convincer. I proved that down in Aspen."

He talked to Sophie that evening in their bedroom. "He's not asking for forever," he said. "Not even a decade. Just some time in New York, then maybe Paris. Three years at most is my guess. He's got a body of work in that cabin which is marvelous. You people believe in him as an artist. You've supported him for more than forty years. This could be the payoff. For him, and for all of you."

"The town doesn't want any payoff," Sophie said. "They supported Harry out of the purest of motives. It was my mother's idea, did you know that? She and Henry Lovell were on the Water Board back then. They lobbied for a while, and finally there was a town referendum, which passed easily. People loved Harry back then. He didn't drink as much when he was younger. They felt proud to have an artist living and working here."

"And now?"

"I don't think that a lot of the young people understand it anymore. There's a faction thinks he's a parasite—got a free ride in the old days.

All they see is the Harry who knocks off a quart of vodka a day. The Harry who paints is a stranger to them."

"Why was he appointed to the Water Board?"

"Being on the board is not an easy job. There have been a lot of people who served for a few years and then resigned. A vacancy came up, and people felt that Harry could be more detached than a lot of other folks. He was the only one of us who didn't have dozens of relatives in the town."

"Did he want to be appointed?"

"He'd become one of us. And it was around the time when they told him they'd support him as a painter. It was hard for him to refuse."

"Let me plead his case before the board," Dennis said.

"The board isn't a court of law," Sophie said. "The rules are different."

"I can learn them."

"Dennis, listen to me. People are pleased you won the case for my parents. But in the process you stomped on some toes. Grace Pendergast's, for one. And Hank Lovell's, and those boys' who work up at the quarry. They see you as a kind of city slicker and they don't fully trust you. But they will—in time. Right now, if you were an advocate for Harry Parrot, you would be a liability. You would lose."

"Judge Florian thought I was a city slicker too. I need to do this. I want to do it. And I want you—I need you—to want me to do it."

27 *April 18, 1995*

The Boning

THE WATER BOARD met early the following Tuesday morning in the one-room Springhill schoolhouse on Main Street, before the children arrived to begin their school day. A simple rectangular red wooden building with a sloping shingled roof, the schoolhouse had been built in 1927 after the old schoolhouse had been destroyed by a March snowslide. Every two years it received a fresh coat of crimson paint, so that it resembled a schoolhouse from a children's storybook. It was not the sort of place, Dennis thought, where you should decide whether a man lived or died.

In late April the snow fell almost every day. No one could remember in recent decades a spring with so much snow. In the morning, though, the sun streamed at a sharp angle through the windows of the schoolhouse and fell in broad yellow bars across the blackboard, the teacher's desk, and the rows of pine tables and chairs. Motes of dust swirled in golden air.

Meetings of the Water Board were open to all Springhill residents. The schoolroom chairs were filled not only with the five members of the Water Board but with two dozen other interested townspeople. Bibsy and Scott were there. "It's not a trial," Sophie had told Dennis, when she told him the board was willing to listen to him. "It's a friendly hearing. You asked for a chance to explain Harry's point of view. They're giving it to you because they feel they owe you something for what you did for my parents. They may ask questions. That's all there is to it."

Harry Parrot hadn't been invited, which bothered Dennis. In human history there was plenty of precedent for trial in absentia, but none of it would give a defendant or his advocate much confidence in the outcome.

Sophie, in jeans and a white blouse, chaired the meeting. The others on the board were Amos McKee, Grace Pendergast, and Oliver Cone. Smiling, Sophie looked up from her desk and said, "Dennis? You wanted to say something."

Dennis stood and told them he was pleased to have this opportunity. He was a newcomer, he realized, and this was a rare privilege. He wasn't asking anything for himself; he was speaking on behalf of one of *them*, just as he had done in final argument in Judge Florian's courtroom. Then, for Bibsy Henderson; this time, for Harry Parrot, his friend. He repeated everything that Harry had said to him. He explained Harry's plans, Harry's needs, Harry's emotional life as an artist.

"I want to bring up the subject of immortality," he said.

There was a slight stir of unease among the listeners in the room. Dennis smiled gently.

"There are two kinds of immortality," he said. "One is physical—the idea of living forever. I'm sure that no one here believes that's possible, or even desirable. But there's another kind. The works of Shakespeare and Leonardo da Vinci and van Gogh and Picasso will be with us forever. And so will those artists, because of their work. That's a real kind of immortality. It's wonderful—it gives us a connection with the past and the future. It gives us a feeling of wholeness through time. And it's *achievable*." He paused. "But you never know which artist will achieve it and which won't, because contemporary judgment is never quite objective enough. That judgment has to mellow over decades. I think Harry Parrot has a chance to achieve immortality, and you people can choose whether or not to give him that chance. It would be a kind of sin to make the wrong choice. So I beg you: choose wisely."

He said, "If you have any questions, please ask them. I'll welcome them. There's nothing you can't ask."

From her seat on a student's chair behind a wooden table, Grace Pendergast looked in turn at each of the other members of the board. All of them except Sophie nodded slightly at her. Sophie sat motionless.

Grace turned back to Dennis. She smiled warmly and said, "We're grateful for the time you've taken and for all that you've told us. Harry can be happy to have such a loyal friend. We're going to think about it. And when we reach a decision, we'll tell Harry."

"You don't want to ask me any questions?" Dennis said.

"You've covered it all," Grace said. "We have to go now. The children will start coming in at any minute."

That evening, when Dennis arrived home from his office in Aspen, Claudia was in the living room with Brian and Lucy, helping them with their homework.

"Where's Sophie?" Dennis asked.

"Over at her parents'."

"Can you stay awhile, Claudia? I have to go out too."

After he had eaten a quick bite Dennis stepped out into the cold April evening. The clouds had been swept away over the mountains toward the north. The first stars glistened like the heads of vibrating white pins stabbed into black velvet.

He squeezed behind the wheel of the Jeep and drove to Harry Parrot's house. Springhill was quiet; except for a few lights there was hardly a sign of habitation. The violet-colored bank building gleamed ghostlike in the starlight.

Lights burned downstairs at Harry's. The worn wooden shutters were closed. Three four-wheel-drive vehicles were parked by heaped pyramids of snow that had been plowed into mounds along the road. One of the vehicles was a blue Bronco; the other a silver gray Toyota LandCruiser; the third a dark Ford pickup truck with a snowplow on its front end. By now Dennis knew many of the cars in town. The silver gray Toyota belonged to Grace Pendergast. The others he did not recognize.

It was rare that anyone came to visit Harry Parrot. Particularly rare of an evening. Harry invited no one. Dennis parked his Jeep farther down the road. He had wanted to talk to Harry alone, to tell him about the morning's meeting with the board. He walked slowly toward the house, then stopped, stripped off a glove, and placed his palm on the hood of the Toyota. The metal was ice cold to the touch. The visitors had been here for a while. Dennis hesitated—he hung back a moment in the purple shadows near the pines.

The front door of the house thrust open forcefully. Light rocketed out in a triangular beam over the beaten-down snow heaped on the path. Instinctively, Dennis took two steps back from the car into the pine grove.

Two men moved briskly from the house, with Grace Pendergast right behind them. Harry followed, then halted—a dark shape in plaid shirt and rumpled paint-stained jeans against the bright gleam of the living room, where an orange fire leapt in the hearth.

Grace said, "You know that we're trying to help you . . ."

"When I need your fucking help," Harry growled, "I'll ask for it."

The fire blazed up and a bold vermilion light flared across a man's face. Dennis recognized Oliver Cone. The other man's face, framed against the pyramid of snow, was that of Amos McKee.

The Water Board, minus Sophie.

Harry yelled, "You eesles—I'll outlive you all!"

For a moment Dennis thought that Amos McKee was going to hit Harry. Veins flexed in McKee's neck; his shoulders squared. Dennis tensed, ready to spring forward.

Grace stepped between the men. There were murmurings Dennis didn't hear clearly. Then the visitors moved toward the Toyota. The front door of Harry's house slammed shut behind them.

Dennis remained frozen in place, holding his breath. In the sudden darkness, Oliver Cone, Amos McKee, and Grace were only a few feet from him. They halted and faced one another, and Dennis could see the steam of their breath rising in the night air. Oliver's eyes gleamed in the starlight like the eyes of a mountain cat.

Dennis heard him say, "He could run. He's higher'n a billy and he's tuddish. We'll have to cane him."

McKee shuffled his feet. Oliver Cone looked at the doctor. "Grace?"

"I couldn't now," Grace said. "It would have to be Mandee."

The rest of Grace's words were blurred as Oliver moved toward his truck. She followed. McKee called something after them while heading toward his own car. The doctor's car door slammed. A minute later Oliver's headlights blazed a broken white path and gleamed across the red hood of Dennis's Jeep. Dennis crouched in the shelter of the pines. The lights veered off the Jeep. The engines roared in the night, a sudden burst of exhaust fumes fouling the air.

When the cars were gone, the smell remained for a minute, then faded. The pure night air took hold again.

Dennis rapped on the oak of Harry's front door. He waited, then pounded harder with his fist.

The door opened a crack. Harry swayed a little, and the gaze of his red-rimmed eyes flicked past Dennis into the darkness.

"Where the hell'd you come from?"

"I was outside," Dennis said. "They didn't see me."

"Come on in."

This time Dennis said no to the offered vodka. "What did they tell you?"

"Told me I was a stubborn hind end of a mule." Harry chuckled cruelly. "Pointed the bone at me."

"Wait a minute. What about my appeal?"

"Hell, I didn't thank you, did I? You're a pal, but it didn't do a goddam bit of good. Never thought it would—I just didn't have the heart to stop you. They knew I'd get back to Paris and never leave. Let Ginette and Marie's granddaughters screw me to death." Harry took a step toward the staircase, then stopped, uncertain. "Gotta get some sleep. Think about all this."

"Harry, I have to talk to you."

"You're talkin', aren't you? Or is it me doin' all the talkin'? I'm a little drunk, Denny."

Dennis seized him by the shoulders. "Sober up and listen to me. I heard them talking in the lingo. I don't think they're going to do anything quickly. Not until Monday, Grace said. *Mandee* is Monday, right? Then they're going to beat you up. But they didn't say why."

"Beat me up? What the hell are you talking about?" Harry laughed. "Why would they do an uncouth thing like that?"

"I don't know. Oliver Cone said you were tuddish. What's 'tuddish'?"

"Crazy."

"And he said they had to cane you. That's what I didn't understand. What's punishment got to do with this?"

Harry sat down again in the chair, squeezed the vodka bottle between both hands, and gazed for a long moment into the crackling fire. Then he turned back to Dennis. "Say all that again, will you? You mind?"

Dennis repeated what he had heard.

A harsh laugh flew from Harry's mouth. "Cane me? You thought they said 'cane' me? Like with a rattan cane, like they used to do to those poor little English schoolboys?" Harry tilted the bottle to his mouth, swallowed, then smacked his lips, and sighed. "That ain't it, amigo. Wish it was. What you heard was *c-a-i-n*—cain. Like from the Bible. It's the lingo for *kill*. Bastard will put an arrow through my heart if he has his way, like he did with that dog of the Lovells."

Dennis worked it through his mind for five minutes. He believed Harry. It was planned for Monday, by which time, he now understood, Grace would pick up the necessary vials from the medical supply house in Grand Junction.

"You know I've lived for a hundred years," Harry mused. "More'n most people even dream of. You'd think I'd be ready to go." He tilted the bottle of vodka, drained the last few drops, looked at it in disgust, and then pitched it into the fireplace. "But I'm not, Dennis. Can't help it. I'm just not fucking ready. And you know why."

"Yes, I know why. So let's get out of here."

"I can't go without my paintings," Harry said. "That's the whole point, ain't it? I guess they figured that out. They know I can't just cut and run."

Dennis thought about that for another long minute. "There's still a way. Pack what you need for a couple of nights. Come with me."

"Where to?"

"To my house. To talk to Sophie." Then he remembered Claudia had told him that Sophie had gone over to the Hendersons. "Harry, where's your phone?"

The painter pointed to an old black Bell handset on a table by a rocking chair in the corner of the room. Dennis picked it up, prepared to dial the Hendersons' number. But when he pressed the receiver to his ear he heard no dial tone, only silence.

"Harry, have you paid your phone bill?"

"Town does that for me."

"Then why isn't this damn thing working?"

"Sure as hell was working the last time I used it."

"When was that?"

"Day or so ago. Alarm clock stopped, so I called the operator to find out what the hell time it was."

"This line's been cut," Dennis said. He smiled thinly. "But I've got a cellular in the Jeep."

He squeezed behind the wheel, picked up the phone, and punched the on button. There was no dial tone. Attached to his ring of keys Dennis kept a penlight. He shone it on the telephone wiring and saw no evidence of tampering.

He remembered what he had learned long ago in a wiretapping case that involved the Mafia and the NYPD. In certain branches of the military you were taught to disable a telephone by inserting a pin through the wire leading to the battery. When the fuse blew, you clipped off the ends of the pin. If anyone replaced the faulty fuse, it blew again. No damage was visible to the naked untrained eye.

They had seen his car, he realized. They had disabled the cellular when he was inside talking to Harry. He wondered what kind of men he was up against, and he felt the first touch of fear.

28 *April 18, 1995*

Flight

Close to home Dennis saw lights in the kitchen. The mountains loomed beyond like walls of ivory, the night so quiet that from the road he could hear the roar of the creek coursing over its bed between slabs of ice. He turned off the car engine, and then he also heard the thump of his heartbeat.

"Come on in with me, Harry."

In the warmth of the kitchen Sophie pressed her cheek quickly against his. She had been back from the Hendersons' for half an hour. The children were in bed, probably asleep by now. Claudia had gone home. Sophie hugged Harry, who seemed suddenly sober.

"Dennis," she said, turning her head, "there's something wrong with our phone."

With no apparent hurry he picked up the kitchen telephone and placed it to his ear. He heard no dial tone. He moved a little more quickly than he intended into the little book-lined room he and Sophie called the library. A fax machine on a separate phone line stood on the leather-covered chess table. He picked up the receiver—that line was equally silent. In his mouth he felt a dry, sour taste he had last known twenty-five years ago in the jungle near Da Phong. But when he sat down again at the kitchen table with Sophie and Harry, he was calm. He tilted his chair back and accepted the glass of wine Sophie handed to him. He told her all that had happened at Harry's house.

"They didn't see me. Oliver Cone had my car in the headlights of his truck for maybe ten seconds. He didn't do anything about it, so I thought he didn't know whose Jeep it was. I was wrong. They cut Harry's phone line, then they cut the cellular phone in my car, then they came here and cut ours from the box on the road." The muscles round his eyes tightened. He took Sophie's hands in his. "They didn't tell you they were going to bone Harry tonight, did they?"

Sophie shook her head slowly, burdened with an enormous weight of dismay.

"They kept you out of it," Dennis said. "They could have found you if they wanted to. They don't trust me because I'm Harry's friend, and I'm still a skibtail. And they don't trust you now because you're my wife. The other day I told Harry they weren't going to stop him with force. These were civilized people, I said, not barbarians. Sophie, tell me. *What are they?*"

"Frightened," she murmured. "Trying to protect what they've got. If Harry leaves . . ." She didn't finish the sentence.

"If he leaves," Dennis said, "I understand there's a risk. But the alternative is worse. This community . . . no, I'll put it more kindly—an element in this community intends to stop him no matter what they have to do. This won't be assisted suicide, it will be outright murder. I heard them say they had to cain him. I can't let them do that. You understand that, don't you? Not for any reason. I'm not questioning anything you told me. But no civilized community has the right to execute except by law, and then only as punishment for a terrible crime. Sophie, what crime has Harry committed?"

A change came over Sophie, a collapsing of her lips inward against her teeth, the blood rising to her cheeks as if she had been slapped.

"They think he'll go to New York," she said, "and decide to live forever. They see that as a crime against our existence. And he drinks." She turned to Harry, placing a hand lightly on his cheek. "I'm sorry, Harry. They believe that if you leave here you'll drink—and talk."

"I wouldn't do that," Harry protested.

"You wouldn't mean to. But it could happen."

"And if it did," Dennis said, "and people came here and asked for the fountain of youth, you'd laugh at them and talk them out of it the same way you did with those people from Oregon. But even that wouldn't happen. If Harry told people, they'd think he was crazy."

"Not if he became famous," Sophie said. "And if he didn't grow old, then they would have to believe. They'd have evidence."

Dennis prowled the room, the glow from the fireplace passing across his face and making it seem almost savage. He picked up his glass of wine, drank it, then set it on the coffee table.

"Is it the whole town, Sophie, or just McKee and Cone and Grace Pendergast?"

"It's them, but they're doing what the town wants."

Dennis faced Harry Parrot. "You're sober now, aren't you?"

"I sure am," the painter said. "Might be better if I wasn't."

"When you came here sixty-five years ago and they took you in, you agreed to the pact, isn't that so?"

"You know I did," Harry said.

"You had a choice. You could have said no."

"Sure I could have."

Dennis realized he was cross-examining. Old habits died hard. "You understood what you were swearing to, didn't you?"

"Yep. I did."

"In the light of that, will you keep your word? Will you agree to go through with the departure ceremony?"

"No, I sure as hell won't," Harry said.

"You won't change your mind?"

"No way, amigo."

"What do you want to do?"

"Leave. Get the hell out."

Dennis spread his hands on the kitchen table, pressing hard enough for the knuckles to whiten. "I can't allow them to kill him," he repeated to Sophie.

"But they won't let him leave!" she cried.

"I'm going to drive him to Aspen right now. Mickey Karp will take him in." He turned to Harry. "Tomorrow we'll hire a truck. We'll come up here with a couple of deputy sheriffs. No one will be able to stop you from loading your paintings and anything else you want into that truck. Nobody will stop you from leaving this town and this valley for wherever you want to go. You'll be safe, Harry. You'll be free."

Softly, Sophie said, "If you do that, Dennis, they'll never let you back into Springhill. Not you, not your children. Not me."

"That may be so," he said. "I'll deal with that when Harry's in Aspen and doesn't have to worry about these fanatics pinning him down so Grace Pendergast can shove a needle into his vein."

He was quiet for a few seconds; he tried to read Sophie's mind, but her eyes told him nothing.

"Stay here with the children," he said.

Harry had brought extra socks and underwear in an old Adidas bag. He wore corduroys and fur-lined boots and a beat-up red parka that smelled of stale tobacco. He sat next to Dennis in the front seat of the Jeep, drumming his fingernails against the metal of the glove compartment. He reached inside his jacket and took out a cellophane-wrapped cigar.

"Do me a favor," Dennis said, "and don't light it."

"You sure are fussy at some funny times. How about back East? They let you smoke a good cigar when you feel like it?"

"I can't remember. Write me a postcard and tell me."

"You won't be here to get it. Didn't you hear what your woman said? They find out you did this for me, you'll be out of here."

Dennis tried to understand exactly what that meant. Sophie owned the house: they could not be dispossessed. The worst the town could do was shun him. Would they take it out in some way on the kids? He couldn't tolerate that.

It had already occurred to him that if he were forced to leave Springhill with his two children, Sophie might not come. If she renounced him, she would be able to stay. Her life was here. He was her husband and partner, but it might be more painful for her to give up her roots and home than give up a man she had known for so few years. I'm not sure what she'll do, he realized.

"You got a weapon with you?" Harry asked.

"Goddamit, of course not. Is this Dodge City? Am I supposed to be Wyatt Earp? They're not going to bushwhack us, Harry."

Chewing on the unlit cigar, Harry shrugged, which Dennis took as a form of agreement.

They passed through the town, turning north past the general store on the narrow forest-lined road that wound down with a dozen hairpin turns toward the flats of the Crystal River, the village of Redstone, and then the town of Carbondale. It was dark enough on Main Street for Dennis to be sure no one was following them.

They passed Harry's gray Victorian. The old Chevy truck was parked by the woodpile. The night had clouded over. The road took a sharp turn to the left.

Dennis slammed on the brakes. A massive dark load of snow blocked the road, plowed to bulk five feet above the level of the road for a distance of ten yards. The Jeep could not get through it.

"That's what I was worried about," Harry said. "You can't get out of Dodge if they don't want you to."

The two-lane road lacked shoulders. Beyond the tons of snow in the shadows of fir trees Dennis made out the black angular mass of the truck and attached snowplow. It sat there on the road like a silent prehistoric animal guarding a burial site.

"And my guess," Harry said, dropping his hoarse voice to nearly a whisper, "is that if you or me were dumb enough to try and walk through the woods and get around that bit of snow, either Mr. Cone or Mr. Frazee—or both, or some others—is sitting in the cab of that truck. And with a weapon. You think this ain't Dodge City?"

"These men are crazy," Dennis said.

"Maybe so, but you better get it through your skull that they're serious about being crazy. They ain't gonna let us leave."

Dennis jammed the gears of the Cherokee into reverse and began backing up along the road until he could swing into Harry's driveway, and then he headed home.

The fire still burned in the wood stove. A minute after Dennis and Harry arrived, two four-wheel-drive vehicles pulled up on the road outside the house, switched off their lights, and simply sat there. Boxing us in, Dennis realized.

With Sophie's long hair piled atop her bowed head he could see the slender white nape of her neck. She suddenly seemed fragile to him— this vividly beautiful woman, his wife who would probably live to be one hundred. He told her what had happened on the road.

"You can't get past the men in those trucks," she said.

"What about your parents' house . . . ?"

He meant: one of us can get there by way of the creek, use their phone to call for help. But Sophie shook her head.

"Why not? You think they've cut—"

He stopped, realizing that wasn't what she meant: the Hendersons' phone line had not been cut.

He felt the blood rush to his face. "They owe me," he said sharply.

"They would be loyal to the village," Sophie said. "They owe the village for ninety years of life."

And who do you owe, my love? To whom is your deeper allegiance? You haven't said anything about that. You haven't made *your* commitment.

He peered outside where no stars shone through the cloud cover and the mountains were barely visible. Now he understood there would be more men gathered outside than just Cone and McKee. Harry was right: they were determined men, protecting what they held dear, knowing that whatever happened, the town would in turn protect them. Dangerous men, armed and skilled in the use of their arms.

He tried to put himself inside their minds. It would be too reckless for them to come marauding in darkness: he could be armed too. But he had no weapon, not even a deer rifle. He had always refused, had seen no need.

They would wait until dawn. Light was on their side, darkness on his.

Tomorrow morning, he remembered, he had two appointments at his office and a lunch date with one of Mickey Karp's clients to discuss a federal tax evasion probe. He was not going to make those dates.

"Sophie, I've got to take Harry out."

"How can you do that?"

"The back door leads to nowhere except the forest. They'd never expect us to go that way—and from the road they can't see it. Do you remember the Tenth Mountain hut we once stayed in?" They had made love there, but Dennis was not so blinded by the event that he had failed to survey his surroundings. "Harry and I can get there on snowshoes. There's emergency equipment—a two-way radio and generator, remember? Josh told me those radios have a channel that gets through by way of Carbondale to the Sheriff's Office in Aspen."

Sophie took his hand in both of hers. "It's pitch black out there. Do you know where that hut is? In Lead King Basin, in the Maroon Bells. The Bells are a death trap."

"I know the way."

"We were there in warm weather. And in daylight."

"We'll go before dawn, when it's still dark—stay just the other side of the creek until it grows light. In daylight it won't be too difficult. Josh will send people to bring us out."

Sophie seemed to coil back into the shadows. "Dennis, you'll never find that hut. The only way into Lead King Basin is a pack trail at ten thousand feet. Otherwise it's just gorges, couloirs, gullies on the sides of fourteen-thousand-foot peaks. Do you understand what it's like this time of year? The leaves may be budding in Connecticut, but here it's still deep winter."

A pain pressed inside his eyeballs. "If we stay here, they'll come for Harry. And they'll murder him. Murder, Sophie. This time: *murder*."

She covered her eyes for a moment as if the world were too offensive to contemplate. When she lowered her hands she said, "I'll take you. I know the way."

He shook his head. "You have to stay here with the children."

"If I let Harry go without letting the board know," Sophie said, "my life in this village is ended. They'll never forgive me. And I could live with that, because I want to be with you. You're my life now, Dennis. But if you go alone out there, you and Harry, you'll die. You don't know the mountains. I'll take you. Lucy and Brian will come with us too. It's not far to the hut we were at. We'll get there and we'll be all right." A deep gasp broke from her throat, and she closed against him so that he took her full weight in his arms. "And I'll never come back."

Tucking Lucy and Brian into bed, he kissed them good night. "I'm going to wake you just before it gets light," he said. "We're going on a big adventure, a hike, to a cabin we know. Not far. You'll be quiet like mice."

At eleven o'clock he and Sophie turned out all the lights in the house. His stomach churned at the thought of taking Lucy and Brian, but Sophie was right: only dumb luck would allow him to find the hut on his own. All or none had to go—unless they were willing to surrender Harry. Was he risking the lives of his children to save the life of one old man? He dared not do that.

"Sophie, are you sure we'll make it?"

"If the weather holds—yes."

"How long will it take?"

"A couple of hours. Maybe three with the kids along."

"Are those snow clouds?"

"I don't think so. Just clouds."

"This whole idea is crazy," Harry said. "I know those huts. They're real popular. You have to reserve them weeks in advance." When no one laughed, he said more soberly, "The kids won't be able to do it."

"The kids are tougher than you." Dennis watched the clouds, looking for any threat of snow. "If the weather holds, we'll go. If not . . ."

No one slept. In their bedroom Dennis held his wife in his arms. She was crying softly. He understood what she was giving up to be with him, and he had never loved her more than now.

At four A.M. the night was still calm. The clouds were motionless above the mountain peaks. Dennis saw a handful of blurred stars.

"I'll wake Brian and Lucy," he said quietly.

Dennis and Sophie, with Harry and the two children, stood in the kitchen by the back door of the house looking like a quintet of moon walkers. All wore layers of polypropylene underwear, layers of Thinsulate sweaters, Gore-Tex parkas and hoods, pile-lined gauntlet gloves and liners, balaclavas, and ski goggles. Sophie had dug out every bit of winter equipment in the house; it was enough for a platoon. They had thick boots with Gore-Tex shell gaiters, snowshoes and poles, and each of the three adults carried a mountaineering backpack with food, flashlight, mummy bag, bivouac tent, and blanket. In his backpack Dennis had also stuffed a topographic map, compass, ice axe, snow shovel, Swiss Army knife, first-aid kit, and Primus stove. He reckoned they would be out in the mountains and in the hut for under twelve hours, but with the children along he wanted to take as few chances as possible.

Sophie gave the children apples and bananas and granola bars to eat. In the darkness, until they dressed, they were silent. Lucy clutched Dennis's arm as he lashed the little snowshoes onto her boots.

"Daddy, why do we have to whisper?"

"We don't want anyone to know we're going, darling. There are people on the road watching us, but they can't see us go out the kitchen door."

"Where are we going?" Brian asked.

"To a cabin that Sophie knows."

"The miner's cabin? The one where Lucy's as tall as I am?"

"No, Brian, not that one. A bigger one. Bigger and much better."

The outside kitchen door, where he and Brian had faced the bear, opened up toward the mountains. The house itself blocked any view from the road and the vehicles parked there. Dennis had worked for nearly an hour fashioning a wide flowing roll made up of folded woolen blankets, weighted down with books laid flat in the bottom of the roll. He cut a hole in the narrow end of the roll, inserted a length of cord, and tied the two loose ends to the glove hooks on either side of his parka.

"What the hell is that for?" Harry asked.

"You'll see."

"This is no time for Boy Scout stuff, amigo."

"We only have to get out there and hang on until it's light enough to see. When you're a hundred and fifty you can tell the story to your French grandchildren. They may not believe you, but at least you'll be alive to tell it."

Outside it was black and still, that moment before dawn when night borders on day. Sky, earth, and mountains waited in an expectant hush. Dennis eased the kitchen door open bit by bit. Don't squeak, he begged. He stepped clumsily down the back steps, boots firmly strapped into snowshoes, the blanket roll bumping lightly and trailing behind him. Harry followed after him, then Lucy, Brian, and Sophie. Dennis whispered, "You lead, Harry, but not quickly. We can't let the kids fall behind." He pushed the painter forward, pointing toward the creek. "Go. Now, kids, you and Sophie."

"Daddy—"

"Brian, do it, *please*. Go with Sophie, and be quiet as a mouse. I'll be right behind you."

On the flat field leading to the creek, their legs slid easily through the corn snow. With Harry leading they walked slowly, Dennis at the rear, the weighted blanket roll rolling across his wake and sweeping away most of the imprints left by their snowshoes.

In two minutes they reached the creek and were shielded by the swarthy shadows of the forest. There was no sound except their breathing, the purling water, the rustle of boughs in the wind. The cold wind stung Dennis's cheeks, but he could see more stars now.

"We did it," Sophie said. "They don't know we're gone."

Dennis bent to one knee in the snow. "Kids, are you all right? Are you cold?"

"No, Daddy," Lucy said. "But it's dark. I can't see anything."

"You hang on to Sophie. Brian, walk ahead of me." He turned to Harry. "Are you ready? Are you okay?"

"Sure." The old man grinned. "I haven't had this much fun since pussy was a cat. Which way?"

"Follow Sophie."

Twenty minutes later they came to the gate in the barbed-wire fence and the padlock that led to the spring. Dennis moved his flashlight to within a few inches of the lock and flicked the switch. Once again Sophie twirled the dials and the lock sprang open.

Five minutes later they reached the narrow stream that flowed forth from the snowy hillside—the stream whose source had changed the lives of all in Springhill. Here was the chance for the realization of mankind's oldest dream: the power to achieve immortality: the power for which some would pay fortunes; the power that others would kill to protect. Here, Dennis remembered, he and Sophie had made love. Here he had taken his first sip of immortality.

Dennis played the beam of his flashlight over the water. Sophie, looking down, hesitated for a moment. So did Harry.

"Let's get moving," Dennis said.

They trudged northeast toward the frozen shores of Indian Lake. Dennis walked slowly at the rear, planting his snowshoes to feel the laced leather sink and then grip the snowpack. Now and then he glanced behind to make sure the blanket roll was doing its job of erasing the evidence of their journey.

Brian was lagging. "How are you doing, son?" Dennis asked.

"I'm cold."

"We all are. Otherwise you're okay?"

"Yes, Dad."

"It'll warm up later. And when we reach the cabin we'll make a big fire. Eat another granola bar. Eating keeps you warm."

The terrain ahead sloped gently downward into the couloirs. The early morning was gray and shadowless. Wind blew wisps of snow along the surface of the earth. They began to angle off in a downhill traverse, snowshoes breaking through heavier crust. For the children's sake they stopped to rest. Spruce trees were black in the gloom. Above them the twin white peaks of the Maroon Bells towered like unscalable pyramids.

They headed for Lead King Basin, avoiding as best they could the gullies under the steeper slopes that might avalanche. Dennis knew from the map that they would pass the frozen North Fork of the Crystal River, then Geneva Lake and Hagerman Peak. If they bore east over Trail Rider Pass they would be heading toward Aspen, but if they continued straight on they would reach Lead King Basin and the hut. Sophie halted, beckoning to him, and he plodded forward until he reached her side. She touched his face with her glove, raising his woolen balaclava with one thumb so that his ear was freed.

"Do you hear something?"

He had heard the distant sound for a while, but it had barely penetrated his thinking. He listened more carefully now to the low throb. Not a distant avalanche—he knew all too well what kind of noise an avalanche made. This was more persistent, more varied in pitch, and with what seemed to be an echo.

Harry had joined them. "Snowmobile," he said.

Sophie shook her head firmly, so that snow cascaded on her shoulders. "A snowmobile couldn't get through in this terrain. It has to be a Sno-Cat. They have that big one up at the quarry."

Dennis shone his flashlight behind them on the slope they had traversed. Their tracks were not completely erased. A good tracker would find them. A Sno-Cat had heavy-duty tank treads and could access almost any terrain, although it had trouble climbing steeply on snow or ice. It could carry a dozen men.

"How did they figure it out?"

"Maybe they've split up into two or three search parties and this is just one of them. They may think we're back here, but they don't know where. We might just as well be trekking toward Aspen, not Lead King Basin."

Harry looked at them glumly. "What the hell do we do?"

As if in answer, snowflakes began to drift down. The wind swirled up icy grits that stung their faces. Visibility was suddenly so poor they could make out nothing but the towering ridges on each side of the gully. The narrow band of early morning sky overhead took on a harder, darker sheen. Lucy clung to her father's leg, while Brian put his mittens over his face to ward off the invisible violence of the wind.

Dennis brought his watch up to his face. It was a few minutes before eight A.M. The hut meant safety and security; the radio in it meant rescue. "How close are we?" he asked Sophie.

"An hour, if the weather doesn't sock us in."

As she spoke the falling snow cut off all sight of the sword-shaped couloir that lay ahead, and Dennis looked into an impenetrable white mist.

29 *April 20, 1995*

The Maroon Bells

DARK ELEPHANTLIKE CLOUDS rumbled in swiftly from the north, blotting out first this mountain peak and then the next, reaching down almost to the level of Lead King Basin and hurling showers of wind-driven snow to pile against the Bells in massive drifts. The temperature dropped with alarming speed.

Dennis staggered through the drifts, planting his snowshoes, fighting for air to fill his lungs. Wet snow worked its way between his gaiters and boots, clamping an icy hold on his ankles. The tips of his toes ached from the cold. He held Brian in his arms. He made no more effort to blot out their tracks—the falling snow would cover them in minutes. Now and then from above he heard the telltale *crump* when fresh powder high on the peaks collapsed part of the fragile snowpack. Ahead of him he could barely make out the gray shape of Lucy's little legs pumping and plunging forward between Sophie and Harry. She held tightly to both their arms.

"How are you, Brian?"

The boy said quietly, "I could walk if you let me, Dad."

"I know you could, son. But I think we'll go faster this way. We have to go fast. Fast as we can."

Before Dennis had picked him up Brian had been stumbling and falling. Each time Dennis had been forced to stop, haul him out of the soft trap of the snow, and wipe it carefully from any part of the boy's exposed face.

Now he saw Harry begin to slow his pace, then detach himself from Sophie and Lucy. He halted there in the gully, his head bowed.

Dennis reached him. "Harry, can you make it?"

Harry's breathing was ragged, and he was shivering. "My hands and feet are goddam cold. This ain't much fun anymore."

"It's the road to Paris, Harry. Never easy." He tried to laugh, but when he opened his mouth wide the cold air and snow struck his back teeth, and it hurt.

When they set out again Dennis kept his face to leeward in his parka hood, only now and then taking a quick glance to windward toward Lead King Basin. The pack trail was obliterated by the snowfall. But Sophie moved doggedly forward, bearing left whenever she could, tugging Lucy with her.

Alone, Dennis thought, we would have been lost. Harry and I would have vanished into the wilderness. We would have died.

"That hut nearby?" Harry gasped.

"It should be," Dennis said. "I'm telling you—trust Sophie."

The clouds lifted for a moment, and he heard Sophie's shout. He raised his head to see her pointing off to the left. Dennis peered between wisps of swirling white fog, and down a steep incline in a ravine among stands of snow-spattered spruce was the Tenth Mountain hut. If the cloud cover had not broken for that moment they might have passed it by. A sturdy pine log cabin, it had been cloaked with immense piles of snow heaped like whipped cream nearly to window level. Above it towered a slender radio antenna.

"We're there, Brian. We're safe. Sophie saved us." With his son still in his arms, Dennis lurched down the incline after his wife and daughter.

The hut was for travelers and for the lost and the desperate. In winter the door was never locked. Sophie thrust it open and stepped inside, bent to unlash her snowshoes, then began stamping her boots on the floorboards. It was almost as frigid indoors as outside in the storm, but the double-paned windows blocked the wind. The five of them were coated with snow. Like snowmen on Connecticut lawns, Dennis thought. He enfolded Sophie in his arms.

There were beds and canned food and plates, a 110-volt generator, a propane stove activated by a photovoltaic system, utensils in open cupboards, a toboggan, spare skis in a rack, a padlocked closet labeled AVALANCHE CONTROL EQUIPMENT, DO NOT OPEN OR USE UNLESS AUTHORIZED, and a slabbed stone fireplace with a wicker basket full of pine logs. There was no water supply but in summer a stream flowed nearby and in winter the snow could be melted.

On the shelf next to the canned Campbell soups was the treasure they had come here for: a black leather-covered transceiver.

"You all warm up while I do this," Dennis said. "And eat. We can't light a fire—the smoke will carry in this wind, and they'll spot it—but if you turn on the stove and pump up the Primus, Harry, we can warm our hands. Get some coffee brewing."

"My hands," Harry said. He was still shivering.

Sophie was busy rubbing her palms on Brian's face to warm him. Lucy sat in a worn heap in the center of the floor, head between her knees. Dennis pumped the Primus, then set the coffee to brew on the stove.

He turned to the radio, a ten-channel cellular-phone-sized Motorola transceiver. He flipped the on-off switch to on, and when the light flickered red, he smiled. It blinked, grew pink, then red again.

"Weak, but it's working."

But which of the ten channels was the emergency channel? He knew only that the signal would go from the cabin's antenna to a repeater site somewhere in Carbondale, and from there to the dispatch center of the Pitkin County Sheriff's Office. Dennis fiddled with the squelch knob to dampen the background noise, hit the PUSH TO TALK button, and began working his way through the channels.

"May Day! Is anyone out there? Anyone listening? This is an emergency! May Day . . ."

He heard only crackling sound: no human response. He tried another channel; then another. Still no response.

On the fifth try a woman's distant voice cut through the static. "Sheriff's Office . . . you . . . state your . . ."

Dennis heard nothing more.

"May Day!" he repeated. "This is Dennis Conway. I'm up in the Bells—"

The connection broke, the static returned, and he saw the red light on the transceiver fade to a pale pink, then go to black. He tried one channel after another. He heard only static.

"What's the problem?" Sophie asked.

"The battery's dead."

"But you spoke to them! Did they hear you?"

"I don't know. Even if they did, I didn't say where I was."

"Can't you recharge the radio with the generator?"

"Yes, thank God," Dennis said, "I can."

He hauled the gasoline-powered generator out of the corner, hooked up the transceiver, then yanked the cord that would fire up the engine. The cord came running out smoothly, and nothing happened. The generator made a faint *put-put* sound like that of an outboard motor or lawnmower reluctant to start.

He pulled the cord three times; three times the engine failed to start. Bending, Dennis lifted the machine off the floorboards of the cabin—he moved it from side to side, listening for the swish of liquid. He groaned. "It's out of gas."

"There's got to be gas here," Sophie said. Dennis was already examining the padlock of the closet.

"How are you going to break it?" Sophie asked.

"I'm not. I'm going to break down the door."

"Hang on there." Harry looked up from where he sat huddled in a corner of the cabin. "Read that sign inside the front door. Says, 'Please leave this hut as you would wish to find it. Thank you, Tenth Mountain Division Hut System.' "

In response, with his ice axe, Dennis pounded the door into splinters. In less than a minute he squeezed his way into the closet, and Sophie followed.

The closet smelled of pine resin. It contained twenty-five-pound ammonium nitrate bombs, a 75mm recoilless rifle and a 105mm howitzer. There were sticks of gelatin dynamite, blocks of TNT cast into cylindrical canisters, blasting caps and safety fuses and pull wire, pouches, and elasticized heavy-duty rubber straps. All of this was for avalanche control.

"My God," Harry said. He had risen and was peering over Sophie's shoulder. "Someone wants to start a war."

Dennis nodded his head gloomily. "But not a mechanized war. There's no gasoline."

"That's not possible," Sophie said, her voice trembling.

"They probably don't re-equip this place until winter's over and the hikers start coming. Why bother? Why would anyone be up in this part of the world now?" Dennis pressed his hands against his temples. His eyes blurred and he had trouble controlling his breathing. *I gambled,* he realized. *Fleeing Springhill to save Harry Parrot's life put my children's lives at risk, and I made the wrong decision. I gambled—and lost.*

Dennis heated thick vegetable soup and opened a tin of crackers. The three adults and two children sat on mattresses in a circle around the stove, huddled together for the body warmth they could generate. It was almost eleven A.M., still snowing, but the wind had slackened to an icy breeze.

Dennis said, "Sophie, . . ." and she raised her head slowly. She hadn't slept all night. "Who would be in that Sno-Cat following us?"

"Oliver Cone and the McKee brothers. Maybe a few more men from the quarry."

"Would they know about this hut?"

"Oliver hunts here all the time. They'll try the hut first before they do anything else."

They'll be close, Dennis thought. *And closing in.*

"What will they do when they find us?"

"You want to know?" Harry stretched out a gloved hand to tap Dennis's knee. "They ain't come up here to negotiate. You heard them say they were going to cain me—do what their daddies did to Julian Rice in Mexico. And since you're here with me, trying to keep me alive, they'll do it to you too."

Dennis looked at Sophie. Unhappily, she nodded in agreement.

Oliver Cone was a killer. He knew that.

"But not you," he said. "Not my kids."

"I'd be a witness," Sophie said. "So would Brian and Lucy."

"Sophie . . . they're just *kids.*"

She turned her head away, turned back to the children. They were leaning against her, eyes closed, deep in a merciful asleep.

He saw that the strength had ebbed from Sophie. She had acted against the needs of the people she had known all her life in favor of Harry and Dennis and his children. She had battled through the storm to lead them here to safety. She had done all she could do. The failure of the radio and generator had sapped her will to act. Dennis saw her head droop, her eyes flutter, then close. It struck him like a physical blow: she had given up. Surrendered to defeat and exhaustion and the cold.

Dennis clambered to his feet, took deep breaths for a minute. Then he crossed the room and squeezed into the closet through the smashed door. There he surveyed its contents of avalanche control and rescue equipment.

Harry had followed and peered in over Dennis's shoulder. "You know how to use this stuff?"

Nodding, Dennis laid a hand on the steel stock of the recoilless rifle. "Second World War. The howitzer is probably vintage 1925—a good year for howitzers. These charges are full of TNT. TNT is older than you, Harry. And it doesn't need batteries or gasoline."

Sophie and the children still slept. It had stopped snowing, and patches of pale blue sky were working their way down from the zenith toward the mountaintops.

Warming his hands over the stove, Dennis studied the topographical map. The men in the Sno-Cat knew these mountains well. They were hunters. There were only two routes they could use. One was straight down the North Fork of the Crystal from a southerly direction, but if they did that then above them would loom the wild monuments of the Bells with their unstable multiple layers of the long winter's snow. The safer way to the cabin would be the slower one along the route of the pack trail, the way Sophie had chosen.

Dennis picked a point on the map where the trail and the North Fork of the Crystal seemed to nearly converge, where the hunters would be forced to pick their final access route. It was at the southern entrance to Lead King Basin on the edge of a mountain called Devils Rockpile. Sophie and he had passed it without looking up; they had been battling wind and snow, keeping the children on the move.

"Harry, before you got blown out of that trench in Château-Thierry, did you fire a weapon?"

"Not at anything that moved," Harry said.

He showed Harry how to load and fire the recoilless rifle, which was meant to be fired from a pedestal mounted on a flatbed truck but could also be handheld over the shoulder or propped on a window ledge. It had no recoil, although its back blast was equal to the force that propelled the shell from the barrel.

"If it's loaded, Harry, and you stand behind it when you pull the lanyard, you never get to see that hundred-and-first candle on your birthday cake."

Dennis assembled the TNT canisters, crimped the caps and cut the safety fuses to one-minute lengths for a margin of retreat. He tried on some old cross-country boots left in the clothes chest by the ski patrol. One pair was too tight, another too big. With an extra layer of wool socks, the big pair would do. The boots were sized for one of the two pairs of cross-country skis standing in the rack.

Watching him carefully, Harry asked, "What are you going to do?"

"There's a mountain called Devils Rockpile. They have to go there, and I'll meet them." He spoke softly. "I'm not going to wake Sophie and the kids. If I'm not back yet when they get up, tell them where I went."

Harry hugged him fiercely. "None of this was supposed to happen, Denny. You didn't need to get involved. If they show up here, I'm not going to fire that goddam weapon. I'm going out to them. It's me they want, not Sophie and your kids. The world doesn't need another artist."

There was no time to debate it. Dennis looked once at Brian and Lucy, and then at his wife. He dared not bend to kiss them for fear they would wake.

He slipped out the door into the cold morning.

In snowshoes, the slender cross-country skis slung over his shoulder, binoculars snug against his chest, Dennis worked his way southward along a series of gullies and a feeder canyon. He had taken off his mittens and wore Thinsulate ski gloves with two pair of silk liners under them. In his backpack he carried two of the four-pound gelatin dynamite canisters. He had armed them in the hut; it might never be possible to do it on the icy peak he was bound for. He packed two safety flares. He had thought of taking a rescue beacon, but if an avalanche caught and covered him, whom would he signal? He would be alone in the Bells.

Devils Rockpile soared to eleven thousand feet. In the white heart of winter the rocks for which it was named were barely visible. Dennis plodded steadily and slowly up a bowl on the steep north face, trying to traverse and keep clumps of trees between himself and the peak in case somehow, above him, the snowpack fractured. His breath was ragged. The higher he climbed, the colder it grew.

The snow had eased but the wind swirled. Even in the gloves his fingers felt as if they were resting on a block of ice. His lungs ached from cold that could drain strength from muscles and will from the mind. The cold commanded you to obey. You could bend into the wind and by that fraction of angle shield your face from its force, but there was no way of evading the motionless cold that invaded from all directions, sucking out your warm core. You could give in to it, Dennis knew, could feel conquered by a power so strong there was no shame in defeat. He had heard that men, when they froze to death, in the last moments before sleep felt warm, peaceful, enwombed. Now he understood why. There was a moment when you felt you could not be any colder: you and the cold were one. Death, although not quite welcome, was no longer shunned. To surrender to the cold was purpose enough, and in that surrender was a form of glory.

The wind eased a little. He had to halt climbing to steady his breathing. For a few seconds he raised the flap of his ski hat so that one ear was free.

The faint deep chug of an engine broke the silence. It was coming from the other side of the tree line at the crest of the peak. He pulled the hat down again; he believed that in another few seconds his ear would have frozen.

But now he knew where the pursuers were—just where he had assumed: on the far side of Devils Rockpile, below him in the drainage canyon formed by the North Fork of the Crystal. He had been there in summer on a fine day with blue sky and green meadows; today it was unrecognizable.

He kept climbing, tramping through drifts below the tree line, staying away from the trunks where he knew the living warmth of the trees could create hidden pits into whose softness a man could sink up to his neck or vanish.

He emerged at the top of the Rockpile near a horizontal cornice of nearly frozen snow, and dropped quickly to a prone position.

Only a few hundred yards below him on the frozen riverbed he saw the hulk of the Thiokol Sno-Cat—six thousand pounds of bright-orange aluminum constructed like a giant tractor with an oversized plow in front. A heated cabin towered above the plow and on either side of it were huge black tractor treads to crush relentlessly through the snow. In the bed behind the cabin Dennis could see two men.

With one hand he unslung his binoculars from under the parka, and with the other hand he lifted his ski goggles from his forehead. The sudden brightness nearly blinded him. The binoculars clamped to his eyes felt like circles of ice. Made clumsy by the cold, his fingers spun the dials. The image shimmered, then cleared.

He focused on the faces of the men riding the Sno-Cat. He saw Oliver Cone and Peter Frazee. Frazee carried a hunting rifle with a scoped sight. Strapped to the back of Oliver Cone's parka were a steel bow and quiver of metal arrows.

These were the descendants of Larissa McKee and William Lovell. They don't hate me, Dennis knew, but they believe Harry and I stand in the way of their survival. And blood lust would also have taken hold. The hunt and the savagery of the mountains themselves would plunge these men back into a primitive world. Dennis saw that world in the machine chugging brutelike along the river toward the hut where their quarry—his friend, his wife, his children—waited. The Sno-Cat grunted like a beast in rut.

He remembered the night long ago when he chased away the bear and felt like an adventurer, a city boy happily out of his element. A year ago he had been sheltered with his family in a world where no harm could penetrate. A week ago in court he had played civilized games. That world had vanished. This was no game.

A cloud moved away from the peak and without warning the April sun blazed from a patch of hard blue sky. Before Dennis could drop the binoculars, light from the lenses flashed down into the bowl, sweeping across Oliver Cone on the Sno-Cat. Cone turned to gaze upward. He lifted a red-gloved hand.

The Sno-Cat halted. Its engine idled, the sound drifting up toward the peak. Awkwardly, like a cumbersome orange beast roused from torpor, the machine began to turn toward the upper reach of Devils Rockpile. Dennis calculated that between him and the Sno-Cat lay a distance of three hundred yards. The slope the machine would climb to reach him was an easy grade of twenty degrees.

He moved awkwardly. If he took off the gloves his hands would freeze within a minute. Twisting partly out of his backpack, he hauled out the first canister, armed the charge, set the blasting cap and fuse. He was tugging at the second charge when the air six inches from his head seemed to vibrate. He heard the crack of a rifle, then a plaintive whine echoing round the peaks.

He scrambled quickly behind a fir tree—a second later a steel-tipped arrow chunked into the tree, quivering there. Sophie had told him that Oliver Cone, using a telescope sight, could hit a bull's-eye at a hundred yards.

Dennis pulled the ignition wire on the first canister, raised himself up and slung the four-pound cylinder down the slope. When the rifle cracked again, a branch lopped off from the tree and fell silently into the thick snow at his feet, followed by the whining echo bouncing all over the Maroon Bells.

Quickly Dennis rose again, hurling the second charge over the cornice and to the right, trying to bracket the slope above the Sno-Cat.

He had the one-minute safety margin before the charges exploded. If the pack was unstable, it would slide. He feared only that the shock waves of the explosion would set off the slab on his steeper side of the peak as well. He crouched behind the fir, sucking icy air into his lungs. He was nearly at the crest. He reckoned the angle behind and below him to be forty degrees, swooping down for nearly a thousand feet to the aspen groves.

Waiting for the explosion, fists clenched, he stared at the second hand on his watch as it moved placidly on its journey to thirty seconds . . . forty seconds . . . and then a minute passed . . .

Whumpf! Whumpf! The canisters exploded, one after the other, the sound rising sharply in the bright midday air. Dennis waited for the following thunder of crumbling snowpack that would sweep down the slope and end his nightmare. He waited. And he heard nothing.

Then, louder than before, he heard the grumble of the Sno-Cat, ascending. The snowpack on the other side of the peak had held firm—it had not been steep enough to slide.

"Don't panic," Dennis told himself, aloud. "Just get the hell out of here."

He stripped the snowshoe lashes from his boots and unslung the cross-country skis he had carried on his back. Part of his plan had been not to go down the mountain in the awkward snowshoes, but to ski back to the hut. It had not been part of the plan that a tanklike vehicle manned by sharpshooters would be at his heels. As he clicked the first metal toe cap of a boot into the lock on one ski, from a corner of his eye he caught a flash of orange through the trees. Wrenching the second snowshoe loose, he jammed his foot into the second ski—then came a series of light crackling sounds with the familiar whining echo. Another arrow skidded across the snow a foot away, skipped like a stone, and vanished. He looked up to see the machine clear of the trees and topping the crest. The hunters had him in easy range.

In a sudden fury of strength he planted his poles, shoved off downhill, and in a few seconds he felt he was flying. He could outski a Sno-Cat but he could not outski steel-jacketed bullets. Bent low, ski tips dangerously deep into the powder, he headed at a sharp angle for the firs on the left flank of the slope. He peered around as the Sno-Cat tipped over the cornice and bounced hard down onto the snowpack.

A familiar low clap of thunder—a deep *whoosh*, the growl of disturbed lions—and the cornice on the crest of Devils Rockpile collapsed.

To his left Dennis saw zigzagging cracks, as of windowpanes breaking in soundless slow motion, while to his right the surface of the snow foamed like a caldron of boiling milk. Dennis shot left along the upper angle of a crack, toward the trees. He was thirty feet from them when the snow gave way under him. He let go of his poles, jerking an arm downward to snap the release of the binding on one ski. He was reaching for the other ski when he was lifted into the air and supported on what felt like an immense soft hand. He was floating, and then something slammed into his chest and deprived him of breath. A hard edge bit into his ankle, his knee twisted—pain rocketed through his body. He felt himself falling a second time. But there was no blow when he struck the surface of the mountain. He fell into white mist.

He began to swim. The snow was engulfing him, bearing him down the mountain at a speed he couldn't calculate. But he knew enough to swim through it, to try and stay on top of it. He needed only to breathe—to breathe was vital. *Breathe!* Hurtling, tumbling downward, he commanded himself to breathe. But something prevented him from obeying. He flailed arms and legs, tried to swim, and tried to work out what wouldn't let him breathe, until he realized that his mouth was full of snow, snow moving into his lungs, choking him, and that he was going to drown.

He tried to spit out the snow but it was a hard ball that had settled behind his teeth and bulged against his cheeks and refused to move. His nostrils were full of snow too. He heard a crunch, a convulsive settling. He had come to rest somewhere. He couldn't move, couldn't see. The world was completely white. Something was pressing into his chest and thighs. He felt comfortable but he knew it was death to be comfortable. He bit and crunched at the snow in his mouth. The cold assaulted his teeth and gums.

Breathe!

Chew!

Air moved minutely into his lungs. *Chew! Spit! Breathe!*

He flexed a hand and it touched nothing. He could move his fingers. He reasoned that the hand was up in the air. Close to the surface. I can get out, he decided, if I keep breathing and don't give up.

Breathe!

Inch by inch, he hauled himself out of the snow until out of the corner of one snowpacked eye he saw a blue blur of sky.

Ten minutes later he lay on an icy bed of hard slabbed snow, five hundred feet down the mountain from where the avalanche had first struck him. Every muscle in his body hurt; every bone felt bruised. He had fought a battle with the mountain and he hadn't lost—not yet. He sat up and began to drag himself painfully the remaining ten feet to the shelter of the aspen trees in case the snowpack of the Rockpile should fracture again.

He was alive, and that seemed miraculous. Not safe, but alive. He scanned the mountain for signs of the Sno-Cat, but at first saw nothing. Then his sight adjusted to the glare and he made out a spot of orange at the bottom of the bowl. Tumbled on its back like a giant bug, the machine had come to an ungainly rest against the border of the trees five hundred feet below him and a thousand feet below the crest. It was motionless and silent. No human being was near it.

Dennis sat huddled on the edge of the aspen grove. He had his backpack, but he had lost his ski goggles and the light was a dagger in his eyes. It was a sunny, beautiful day. His knee was blown, the pain violent enough so that when he tried to stand, he toppled over and for a few seconds lost consciousness. I won't try that again, he concluded.

His watch had been torn from his wrist but the sun told him it was early afternoon. By dark he would be asleep; by midnight, dead. But Sophie was safe now. After a while she would realize that somehow he had succeeded, that no one was coming to the hut. When she woke, she would have her confidence back. She would light a fire, leave Harry and the children in the hut, hitch a ride on a friendly eagle, and get through to Aspen. She'll do it. Somewhere, even if it's in Springhill, she'll mourn for me as long as she has to, and at the same time she'll raise my children. Raise them well.

Dennis nodded groggily; he had accepted his departure. He was not ashamed of anything he had done in the years of living, except perhaps the way he had won his last trial. But he had won it and there was a satisfaction in that. His mouth widened in a half-frozen smile.

He wondered who would find him, and when. It might take until summer. Maybe longer. Not many hiked here.

A strange thought worked its way into his fading consciousness. *Both my children will probably live to be one hundred years old.* That's the legacy I leave to them. He could depart with that knowledge fixed as a touchstone in his mind.

While he was pondering and speculating, drifting toward sleep and easy death, he heard a coarse grating sound he knew well. The grating noise changed gradually to a rhythmic pounding. It was a sound that years ago in Vietnam he had learned to love and hate. The pounding grew louder. He couldn't see its source. It was coming from south of Devils Rockpile. It was there; he was positive of it. How or why, he didn't know, but it was there.

Wearily he reached into his snow-clogged backpack and lifted out one of the signal flares. They were built to withstand any weather. He activated it and tossed it as high and far as he could. The flare landed in the middle of the slope, sputtered uncertainly . . . and then, with astonishing speed to the eyes of a man half dead, shot high into the mountain air in a dazzling pattern of red-white-and-blue light.

Fourth of July in the Maroon Bells! The snowpack glittered colorfully, reflecting the changing pattern, and didn't fracture.

An open-tailed Lama AS-315 helicopter, with a Plexiglas bubble and latticework boom, just like the rescue choppers Dennis had seen sweep the sky over Da Nang, hovered above him against the sun. Its rotor thudded and pounded and battered the air and he wondered for a few moments if the concussion would start another avalanche. He knew it couldn't land at an angle of more than six degrees. But it didn't need to land. From its belly there hung a fifty-foot static nylon rope, and in a cone-shaped net at the end of that wonderful rope which would neither stretch nor break crouched Mickey Karp and one other man from the Mountain Rescue team.

Ten minutes later the short-haul harness lifted Dennis into the Lama. The pilot was another stranger to Dennis. But the uniformed Pitkin County deputy sheriff working with the Mountain Rescue team to unhook and unstrap him was someone he knew well. She was Queenie O'Hare.

Dennis said, "Thank you," in a voice that seemed to him to be coming from some source other than his mouth, oddly far away. He told Queenie that his wife and two children and a very old man named Harry Parrot were in a Tenth Mountain hut not too far from Devils Rockpile. If they liked, Dennis said, he would be happy to guide them there.

Queenie asked if any of the people in the hut were hurt, and Dennis said he didn't believe so.

"In that case," Queenie said, "we'll get you to a vehicle at the staging area first, and they can take you down to the hospital. Then we'll go back for your family. Sounds like they'll be just fine."

That was all Dennis needed to know, and he passed out. But he woke again at the staging area, on Quarry Road in Springhill, when he was loaded into a rescue van by the Mountain Rescue team. Finally he focused his eyes on Mickey Karp. "I thought I was dead," he admitted.

"You probably would be," Mickey Karp said, "if you hadn't had appointments this morning. You didn't show, and none of your phones answered. I got worried. Lila drove up to Springhill. You weren't here, and that didn't seem right. So when the Sheriff's Office called me and said they'd had a message from you on the emergency channel from the Bells, it was pretty clear. Josh wouldn't send Mountain Rescue on land vehicles—the risk equation didn't balance. But he must have had some leftover cash in the treasury and he must like you, so he hired a high-altitude helicopter from Fort Collins. Don't worry, you'll get the bill. We took a ride with them, and you lit up the sky. Now there's only one thing we need to know, Dennis. *What the hell were you all doing up there?*"

"I need to sleep," Dennis said, and closed his eyes.

On the way down to the hospital in Glenwood Springs, Queenie patched through on her cellular to the Lama. They had been able to land near the Tenth Mountain hut. They were coming back with four passengers.

Dennis woke. "Everyone's all right?" he asked anxiously.

"Everyone except the old man."

"What happened to him?"

"Frostbite," Queenie reported. "He'll lose a few fingers off his hands."

"Both hands?" Dennis asked unhappily.

Queenie nodded. "But he's alive and cheerful. Tough old bird— they say he'll live to be a hundred."

30 *May 1995*

The Outer Limits

IN JOSH GAMBLE's office in the Aspen courthouse, Dennis sat on a stiff-backed chair, his knee clamped in a metal brace. Outside, the sun had begun to melt the snowpack.

The grandfather clock chimed the hour. Cracking his knuckles as he talked, the sheriff thumped back and forth on the worn, ash-stained carpet.

"Four avalanche victims, inside and around that Sno-Cat. Four! Count 'em. All of them armed. The month of April, in case you don't know, Dennis, is a hell of a long way before or after the hunting season. Sheriff over in Gunnison calls me every day—tells me no one in Springhill knows a damn thing. Bullshit is what I say. Someone knows. And I need to know too, because I don't sleep well when bullshit flows and things don't make sense. Those four men were hunting you. Tell me why."

"You wouldn't believe me," Dennis said.

"Try me."

"Give me time, Josh."

"You got Ray Boyd on your tail. He calls every day too, tells me he wants to charge you with *something*."

"What's he have in mind? Breaking and entering a closet? I paid the repair bill to the Tenth Mountain people. I paid for the helicopter. Those four men were killed by an avalanche. You know it and so does Ray Boyd."

"And two explosive charges are missing from that hut and you know *that*. You used them, goddam it. We can't find any evidence of it yet, but by fucking August, when the snow's melted, we sure as hell will."

Loosening his brace a little, Dennis flexed his knee; they had done arthroscopic surgery the day before at Aspen Valley Hospital.

"But do you think," he asked, "that in fucking August you'll find any evidence that the charges caused an avalanche back in fucking April?"

The sheriff sighed. "You intend to keep practicing law here in the valley?"

"I haven't made up my mind."

"Well, I hope you do, because I'm a man who believes in letting a hen lay her egg in her own time. But if you don't tell me the truth one day soon, and you stick around this valley—friend or no friend—I'll make your life miserable."

Four men were dead, and the village of Springhill was in mourning. It took a week to recover all the bodies. The funerals were held all at one time on a Saturday morning. Dennis did not go, but took the children to an ice hockey game at Aspen High School. Sophie drove up to Springhill early that morning and parked her Blazer among the other cars and trucks on the snow-covered road by the cemetery. When she approached the groups clustered by the open graves they moved to one side or turned their heads away from her. Edward Brophy showed her his back. His nephew Oliver's body had been the last one recovered from the chaotic snowpack at Devils Rockpile.

Sophie stayed for the ceremony, and then drove over to her parents' house off Quarry Road.

"It was strange," she said to Dennis later, when they were walking slowly from the Aspen post office along the trail by the side of the Roaring Fork River. "They were glad to see me but they were almost afraid to be seen talking to me. I felt that, and it was horrible. I didn't stay long. I told them we weren't coming back, and I was selling the house and I asked them if they wanted the money, because they had given the house and the land to me. They said no, they didn't want the money. I asked them, 'What *do* you want?' And then my mother began to cry. Because she doesn't know, Dennis. Neither does my father. Neither of them knows anymore. And no one in town knows either. They just know that a terrible thing happened and that some people went a little crazy. They don't know what was right and what was wrong about what happened. I guess they'd like to forget about it, to turn back the clock. But they can't do that. They could live nearly forever into the future if they wanted, but they can't erase any part of the past. My mother walked me out to the car and she said, 'We always thought the spring was our blessing. That's what Larissa taught us, and that's what you always say, Sophie dear. But now some of us have begun to wonder if it's become our curse.' "

Dennis was silent for a while as he limped through the mud and scattered snow. "And what are they going to do about it?" he asked.

"What can they do? The spring is there. The water is what it is. That hasn't changed, and the secret is still their secret. They asked me about that. My father wondered if you were going to tell the world, or anyone for that matter. I told him what you told me. I told him no."

"Did he believe you?"

"Yes, he did. And no one will come looking for us, he said. That's in the past."

"And they'll go on just as before."

"Of course. What else can they do? What else *should* they do? Their reasoning wasn't perverse or evil, it was just flawed. It bumped up against human nature. The only remarkable thing is that it hadn't happened before. I mean, it *had* happened, down in Mexico with Julian Rice, and up at Pearl Pass with the Lovells, but there was never any reckoning, never any terrible price for the village to pay. This time Springhill paid a price: four young men. That's a lot. It's a lot anywhere, but in a village of such small size it's worse than you can imagine—it's crushing. Everyone was related to at least one of those men. It took the heart out of everybody."

"Let's sit awhile," Dennis said.

"Your leg hurts?"

"Some. But I'm supposed to use it."

They sat on two large flat rocks near the river's edge. "What about Harry?" Dennis asked. "What do they have to say about him now?"

"That's odd too. They seem to have forgotten about Harry. It doesn't matter, now that those young men are gone. My father mentioned it to me. He said, 'We're not worried about Harry anymore. We're sorry about what happened to his hands, and we wish him well. We know he never meant to harm any of us by leaving.'"

Harry would not paint again. How long would he keep on living if he couldn't paint? Dennis wondered about that. Then he said, "How do you feel, Sophie, about never going back to Springhill?"

She held his arm more tightly. "Bad," she said quietly. "Like part of me is gone. Like Harry's fingers."

"Do you want to stay here in the valley? In Aspen?"

"I thought I did at first, but now I know I don't. It would be too close to Springhill. Let's go away, Dennis. Can we do that? Could we go back to Connecticut, where you lived? It was pretty there. The seasons are lovely—I remember in the fall the leaves turn all those wonderful colors. Could you practice law there, up in the country?"

"Yes," he said, "I could do that."

"Lucy and Brian would like it. We can go to the pound there and find new kittens for them." She smiled sadly. "Kittens that won't be taken away by horned owls."

"Yes, they'd like it." He touched her cheek with his hand; he loved its softness. "But when we met, you said if you didn't live in Springhill you would be a different person. You said your life was there. How has that changed?"

"Everything has changed," Sophie said.

"Except us. Isn't that so? You and I will live good lives now. If we're lucky, we'll grow old together."

She clasped his hand, and in that instant he saw the wise and calm Sophie he had always loved, the Sophie who had braved the storm and led them to safety in the hut: he saw her spirit emerge from the careworn woman of the last months.

She said, "You've forgotten something."

He frowned. "What have I forgotten?"

"Look ahead thirty or forty years. If you don't get hit by a bus, Dennis, or develop an incurable cancer, you'll be a truly old man. You'll need help and a lot of loving care. On the other hand, I'll be well over a hundred years old. And if I take care, I could be not very different from what I am today."

Dennis shook his head stubbornly, like a man emerging from a nightmare. "I know all that, Sophie. I believe it, and yet it still doesn't seem possible. All the business about the spring has become a myth in my mind. I wake up in the middle of the night—and I wonder if its powers really exist. Do they, Sophie? Or was it a hallucination with generations of an entire town as its victim?"

"They exist," Sophie said. "You might find it easier to deny and forget, but the myth is real, Dennis. The other reality is that human nature doesn't know how to handle the gifts the world offers. Are you worried about growing old?"

"No more than anyone is."

"And that's probably a great deal. But I'll take good care of you. Think about it, Dennis. I'll grow old—unless I have bad luck and the bus hits *me*, I'll grow *very* old. There's no one anymore to bone me or make me depart." She stayed silent for a minute, letting him absorb the idea. Then she said, "None of us knows the outer limits. No one's tried to go all the way. *I* could. Who knows? I could live to be older than anyone's ever dared dream. What will the world be like? Think of it. I may find out."

Rising in one supple motion, she looked down at him for a few moments with great tenderness. Then she gripped both his wrists in order to help him to his feet, the way she might have helped an unsteady old man.

"Oh, Dennis," she said wistfully—the sadness of all that had happened, all they had lost, welling up so that her eyes clouded, then blurred with tears—"what a shame you won't be there with me."

GLOSSARY

Springling Words Used in the Text

babcock	apple
bahl; bahler	good; high-quality
barney	kiss
bilchy	sexy
billy	billy-goat
borndy	birthday
boshe	deer
broady	cow
cain	to kill
charl	to milk [a cow]
chiggrel	to eat
codgy	time-honored
eesle	asshole [pejorative]
einy	smart; clever
grease	gray
haireem	dog [usually large breed]
harp	to discuss; philosophize
high	drunk

horker	car
horn	cup
jeekus	jackass; fool
Macree	mother
Mandee	Monday
mollies	breasts
ose	ass; buttocks
otto	to work
Pat	dad
pike	road; trail; to walk or drive
ree	really
regal	treat
shy	to stop; quit
size	to cook
skibtail	stranger
socker moldunes	big tits
tomker	tomcat
tuddish	crazy
tweed	child; kid
Ute	the town of Aspen
yank	young
zacky	white
zeese	coffee

ABOUT THE AUTHOR

Clifford Irving is the author of nineteen books. He was born in Manhattan a long time ago and now divides his time between Mexico, France, and the Rocky Mountains.